T. STYLES

ESSENCE MAGAZINE BEST SELLING AUTHOR OF
BLACK AND UGLY AND A HUSTLERS SON

THE *Face* THAT LAUNCHED A THOUSAND BULLETS

LOVE OF MONEY BROUGHT THEM TOGETHER, BUT THE
LOVE OF A WOMAN TORE THEM APART.

DEC 13

PUBLISHER'S NOTE:
This book is a work of fiction. Names, characters, businesses,
organizations, places, events and incidents are the product of the
author's imagination or are used fictionally. Any resemblance of
actual persons, living or dead, events, or locales is entirely coincidental.

Library of Congress Control Number: 2009907456
ISBN: 0-9823913-2-3
ISBN 13: 978-0-9823913-2-7

Cover Design: Davida Baldwin www.oddballdsgn.com
Editor: Right Way Editorial Services
Typsett: T. Styles
www.thecartelpublications.com
First Edition
Printed in the United States of America

What's Up Fam,

First and foremost we are overwhelmed with the continued support, well wishes and sometimes hugs we receive from our fans and followers. Ya'll have no idea how much we appreciate it. Believe me, all that we are and do is for you. Aight, enough of the mushy shit, let's get on wit' the reason for the letter. It is my Honor…My duty…My privilege to announce and introduce to you, "The Face That Launched 1000 Bullets". In my humble opinion, I believe this one is goin' be a CERTIFIED street classic. These boys are mean, but they didn't start out that way. Circumstances can make or break you or just form the person you become!! "T" put her heart into these youngins' and this story. Trust me, you will not be disappointed, I guarantee it!!

As always, in each book we pay homage to an urban street legend doin' his or her thing in the industry. This book is no exception, so without further delay, we show love and respect to,

"Deja King"

Deja is the authoress of the street classic, "Bitch" series. She has penned several other titles such as, "Stackin' Paper"; "Trife Life To Lavish"; "Stackin' Paper 2"; "Dirty Little Secrets"; "Hooker to Housewife" and "Superstar". She also co-authored wit' "T" along wit' Miasha & Daaimah Poole on, "Diamond Playgirls". Deja is the truth and The Cartel recognizes and congratulates her on all her success!

Ok Fam…I took up enough of your time. Get comfortable and get it in. I'll kick it wit' you again soon!

Charisse "C. Wash" Washington
VP, The Cartel Publications
www.thecartelpublications.com

Follow us on twitter @
www.twitter.com/cartelbooks

DEDICATION

This is dedicated to my customers at the Cartel Café & Books store.
Thanks for holding me down in everything I do.

ACKNOWLEDGEMENTS

I done put so many books out this year, I feel like I'm blogging when I write my acknowledgments. So I'm gonna keep it short and sweet.
I acknowledge all those who seek their dreams.
I acknowledge all those who fulfill their destinies despite naysayers.
I acknowledge all those who respect their fellow peers in the book game and beyond because they realize in order to legitimize this industry, we **must** form alliances.

I acknowledge all my babies behind bars who although you may get a little freaky in the letters you write me, support my work. I know it comes from a good place. LOL!! And just so you know, I don't read the freaky ones. *Sorry fellas*.

Well, I hope you enjoy this novel. The Face is the novel, which sparked the creation of The Cartel Publications. It was this very book, which gave me the inspiration to do it on my own. And now, a little over a year later, we're ten books in and getting stronger by the month. We don't intend on going anywhere but the top. I'm in it to win it. Thanks for staying by my side.

T. Styles
President & CEO, The Cartel Publications
www.twitter.com/authortstyles
www.thecartelpublications.com
www.myspace.com/toystyles

Visit our book store at:
Cartel Café & Books
5011 Indian Head Highway
Oxon Hill, MD 20745
240 724-7225

EVERY SAGA BEGINS SOMEWHERE

The Face That Launched A Thousand Bullets

The love of money brought them together.
The love of a woman tore them apart.

PROLOGUE
PRESENT DAY
TEN DAYS BEFORE CHRISTMAS

"You're askin' a lot from me right now, Daddy! I just don't love him!" The young woman paused momentarily to place her Gucci black purse on the counter and to plop down in the seat one over from him. She didn't mean for her voice to carry so loudly as she spoke into her Blackberry cell phone, but she was extremely upset." What about me not loving him? And what about what I want?"

Her eyes met a stranger's who was staring at her and she spoke a little lower. "I love you, too, Daddy." She sounded defeated. "I'll see you soon." She tossed her phone onto the counter.

Although her face was wet from the snow mixed with rain outdoors, the man sitting across from her at the restaurant counter could still tell she'd been crying.

"You okay? Can I get you somethin'?"

"If you can convince my father to let me marry who I want instead of some rich ass boy from my college, that'll be a start. I'm in love with a man he can't stand and it's killin' me!"

The wind outside whipped around Kristina's Diner, interrupting their conversation momentarily. When it settled down, the Temptations CD could be heard amongst the customer's cheerful chatter. It was truly a frosty winter day.

Moments later, the waitress came out and placed a slice of pie and a cup of hot chocolate in front of him before addressing her.

"Can I get you anything?" she asked, wiping the wetness from her leather coat off the counter.

"Yes…a cup of coffee, please." When the waitress left he addressed the distraught woman again.

"Why don't you put your foot down, shawty? You can't be layin' up with somebody you ain't feelin'. Tell him how it is and let him sort that shit out."

"You don't know my father. He's paying for grad school, my apartment and my car. If I don't marry him and leave Trent alone, he'll cut me off for good! I don't have the courage or the money to support myself."

"What about the man you love?"

"Who—Trent?" she asked dismissively. "He just got a job as a teacher. He can barely take care of himself, let alone me. I don't know what to do."

Her fawn eyes searched his for an answer and she reminded him of his woman.

"I feel you…but you can't worry about that. Naw mean? You got to do what's best for you. Straight up!"

"It's easier said than done." She rested her elbows on the counter and threw her face in her hands. "I'm confused."

"Let me tell you a story about my shawty. She went through something similar. Got time?"

She hunched her shoulders. "I guess so. I ain't doin' nothin' else."

"What's your name?" he asked.

"Tammy." She was hesitant.

"Well, Tammy, you're in for the story of your life."

Thinkin' of a master plan...
'Cause ain't nothin' but sweat inside my hand...
So I dig into my pocket, all my money spent...
So I dig deeper but still comin' up with lint...
So I start my mission-leave my residence...
Thinkin' how could I get some dead presidents...

-Eric B and Rakim

MAYOR CHRISTIAN GIBSON WASHINGTON D.C., AUGUST OF 1988
WHITE LIES

Mayor Christian Gibson of Washington D.C. stared at the large yellow envelope on his mahogany desk with a hopeful heart. Nestled inside were the long-awaited yearly crime statistics for the condition of his city. Perspiration dressed his ginger-colored face, and he attempted to soothe his dry mouth by swallowing his own saliva. To say he was apprehensive about its contents was an understatement.

Everything was on the line, his job, his rep and most of all his future. The mayor desired nothing more than to be re-elected. Still, he made huge promises and everyone wanted follow through for a safer city, and only those results could prove it.

"Sir...sir...do you want me to open it?" his beautiful white assistant, Janice Lindsay asked in her designer, two-piece black suit.

"What?" When he looked up, his bland expression revealed his emotional detachment.

"I said would you like me to open it?"

"Oh...no...I'll be fine, Janice. Just leave me alone please."

When she walked out and closed the door behind her, he grabbed the letter opener with the brass handle and unfastened the envelope slowly. Before even looking at the documents, he took a deep breath and looked around his office.

Awards of the accomplishments he had achieved adorned the walls. Mayor Gibson was sworn into office in 1979 and had achieved way more in Chocolate City than the mayor prior. He loved his career and the citizens more than he did his own life. But, even he fell victim to the woes of a prosperous city.

The report shook in his hands as he skimmed through it for what he wanted and needed to see. His eyes searched wildly until he found exactly what he was looking for. He was no fool. He knew that crime strong-armed the capital with a tight-fisted grip. But he hoped it wasn't as bad. In fact, he prayed it wasn't.

"Dear God", he said aloud. Based on what he was seeing, there had been a 30% spike in crime under his watch. He had failed. His opponents would eat him alive with those numbers and he knew it! His chest heaved a sigh of resignation and he fell into the soft leather chair.

Before crack ran as rampantly as a serial killer through D.C., the nation's capital was a place to be respected. And now it was nothing more than a jungle with human animals running around waiting to be extinct.

Opening his bottom drawer, he pulled out a locked grey box and flopped it on the desk in front of him. He needed to feel something outside of the colossal failure that loomed over his head. Lifting his keyboard, he removed a small silver key to unlock the box. Once open, he removed a black velvet bag and placed it down carefully before him.

The mayor's heart raced and he licked his lips as if he were looking at a sexy ass woman. Before indulging, he looked at the door once more to be sure it was closed. When he was certain it was, he cautiously untied the satchel, revealing what was inside. Carefully, he removed a small plastic bag filled with cocaine, a mirror and his business card.

He licked his lips once more, anticipating the high, as he poured the white powder on the mirror and divided it into lines. His reflection bothered him momentarily. What had he become? Once a soldier on the battlefield, now he had taken sides with the enemy. He knew firsthand the power the drug had on the body when the mind was weak and he chose to battle with it anyway.

How could he possibly fight the war on drugs when he was aiding in its future? But right now…for that second, nothing else mattered. Bending down slowly he inhaled the poison that theoretically fucked his city over and over again. He reveled in its power.

And as long as he remained in command, D.C…was doomed.

CRAYLAND BAILOR
WEST BALTIMORE, 1988
FOR THE LOVE OF POWER

Outside of the grungy snow on the ground, nothing in the air reminded people in Bmore that Christmas was right around the corner. It was just a characteristic gutter morning on Liberty Heights avenue. Cars whizzed up and down the busy city street while dealers moved their product with vigor. Behind the doors of a run-down apartment, which blended in well with the sense of despair in the neighborhood, sat a boy, who did his best to make sense of his life, or what was left of it.

Twelve-year-old Crayland, whom everyone called Cray, was a master at tuning out distractions. He'd learned this skill from the moment he discovered it could help him deal with the troubles in his home life. Sitting at the green tattered kitchen table, he poured the rest of the Captain Crunch cereal into his big yellow bowl. He pouted when he shook it twice and noticed he didn't have enough for a second helping. Raising the red and white carton of milk, he poured it carefully over his cereal. And when he lifted his spoon and prepared to eat his meal, he saw a red drop splatter into the milk within his bowl. The dot started out small, but eventually spread wider and wider.

On the verge of crying, Cray began breathing heavily. A few more crimson drops splashed on the table and Cray knew instantly it was blood. His eyes watered and he tried to fight back the tears. No longer able to block out the sounds around him, he heard his father's yells and his mother's pleas. They were directly behind him, the entire time fighting, but he'd been tuning them out.

"I shoulda let you die on the bathroom floor when I found you with ya wrists slit!" He yelled loudly, banging his fist against the wall for emphasis. "My father warned me about whores like you!"

Still hungry, he was preparing to eat the bloodied meal anyway, when his father shoved his mother's head against the table, knocking the cereal to the floor.

"I'ma wipe that smug look off ya fuckin' face!" His hand stayed firm against the back of her neck. From the waist down she wasn't clothed and the black hair on her vagina peeked out. He'd woken her up out of her sleep…again.

The milk drenched Cray's holey blue socks as he jumped up against the

6

green wall. He stood in silence as he watched his father punch his mother over and over with a closed fist in her face. Having seen this many times before, he was numb. Before the trouble came into their lives, the three of them went to Good Hope Baptist faithfully every Sunday. And all of a sudden, the visits stopped.

Cray had no knowledge that one Sunday morning when his parents stayed home from church, that Phillip Shackles, their longtime friend came over to celebrate his release from jail. And instead of bringing the cheap MD 20/20 he usually brought after he got out, he had heroin in his possession. Neither was strong enough to resist Phillip's persuasion because seeing Phillip meant good fun and happy times. Besides, he swore he'd been doing it for years and he appeared as right as rain. All three were wrong, and all three were strung out.

"You dirty bitch! I thought I told you to be in this house every night by seven! You givin' my pussy away—huh? Is that what you're doin'?!" His father punched his mother repeatedly in the mouth, not giving her a chance to answer.

"David, please!" She tried to shield her face. "The bus was late last night and I knew you'd be angry if I came in late! I swear I'd never cheat on you!" She was telling the truth. She worked as a housekeeper for a cheesy motel in Baltimore and the buses never ran on time.

"You ain't nothin' but a lyin' whore! My nigga told me he saw you on Liberty Ave, talkin' to some dude!"

"Suddenly her arms fell to her sides. She was tired, and no longer able to defend herself. "Please, I love you. Please don't hurt me anymore. You promised you'd stop."

"I'ma teach you a lesson, whore!" With one last blow, he pounded her so hard in the face she passed out, as she had many times before. He was surgical with knowing exactly how hard to hit her in order to knock her out.

He rubbed his knuckles and for the first time since the fight, looked at his son. Cray's body trembled and he prayed his father wouldn't hit him next. Although he never took his anger out on his only child, his father was growing more violent with each passing day and the boy couldn't be sure what his father was capable of.

David's arms were massive and he was tattooed from head to toe. Out of all of the tattoos, the one with a woman with a noose tied around her neck, as a man drug her on the ground spoke for the man he really was. David's skin was also dark chocolate and he had fine wavy hair. Wearing a white t-shirt and blue work pants that were one size to small for his muscular legs, he was entirely too big to be beating a man, let alone a woman.

"I know you think I'm wrong, son," he looked at him, rubbed his hands with the soiled towel he kept in his back pocket. He usually used it to wipe the oil off his hands from working on cars...now it was used to wipe blood. "When you become a man, you'll learn that you got to keep yo' house in order. And it starts by makin' sure yo' woman stay in line."

Cray zoned out and focused on his mother's half naked, limp, bloodied body spread out on the kitchen floor.

"Cray!" David yelled, breaking him from his trance.

He looked at his father, his eyes filled with deep-seated resentment.

"Remember...if you ever have to choose between *love* and *power*, choose *power*. Love fades." With that he kneeled down and lifted his wife's worn out body off the floor. "Now get ready for school."

In a daze, Cray looked on as his father carried his mother's pummeled body to their bedroom. When he was out of sight, his stomach growled and he swallowed his own saliva to feed his hunger, and trudged on to school.

Later That Night

Cray and his friends Jason Felts and Markise Johnson walked into an alley a few blocks from over Cray's place. They were watching neighborhood drug dealers Charm and Grimy Mike shoot craps with big time dealer Melody.

Grimy Mike was already into Melody for over a grand and he was heated. He was embarrassed and felt like taking his tension out on somebody. Glancing at the spectators, he saw Cray and his friends and then his victim.

"Yo, do you got anything without holes in em?" Grimy asked, referring to Cray's shoes.

Everybody laughed.

"I got stuff." Cray said embarrassed as his friends tugged at him to leave.

"Yeah but is any of your stuff, clean? You's a dusty ass lil nigga! Here take this and by yoself some gear." He threw him a fifty.

Cray looked at the money on the ground and shot him an evil glare.

"And get the fuck from around here." Grimy continued. "You giving me bad luck!" He told him, as everybody continued to laugh louder.

Cray was embarrassed as he looked at the dealers. He knew they had room to crack on him with their gold chains, fresh sneakers and five hundred dollar coats. And he vowed that one day Grimy would regret everything he said.

They resumed playing the game until they looked up and saw Cray and his friends still there.

"You ain't get the message?" Charm asked getting in on the fun. "Beat it!"

The friends walked away as well as a medium sized brown shabby stray dog named Frankie that followed them around in the neighborhood.

"Don't worry about them." Jason said taking his side.

"Yeah, they dumb anyway!" Markise added as they dipped through the alley on the way to Cray's house.

To get the attention off of Grimy and them, they talked about Cray's upcoming birthday. They made plans to come over because Cray's father said he'd buy a cake, rent movies and pop the boys some popcorn and he couldn't wait. The three of them were inseparable. And it was certain that if you saw one, you were bound to see the others.

"You see Ms. James today?" Jason struggled with his large blue coat. He was referring to their Math teacher. "Her titties were fat as shit!" He shook his head as he reflected on the low-cut, red top she wore in class. Jason was short and stubby but cute in the face. His beautiful flaxen-colored skin was ideal against his black kinky hair.

Jason's father and mother were hardly around, but spoiled him with materialistic things. Whatever he wanted he got. Despite everything, all he really wanted was their love. They worked two jobs, trying to buy a home and never spent time with him. Because of his parents' emotional neglect, he ran to the streets. And as always, the streets embraced him.

"I know! I was thinking the same thing. " Markise wore a thin red jacket built for the fall instead of the brutal winter. His mother was a hard-working woman and did all she could to clothe him but she simply wasn't making enough. Despite Markise not having a lot, the girls still loved him because of his smooth personality. He was taller than a lot of boys his age and looked older. His toasted skin and wavy hair were favorites with the fresh girls around his way. "I wanna suck them shits!"

"You ain't suckin' shit but my dick!" Cray retorted. He was dressed poorly for the winter weather with a thin grey jacket but Cray was a cute little boy. He had the same dark chocolate skin as his parents but his eyes were coal black and held a lot of mystery. And it appeared as if he had a permanent frown on his face. What Cray hated the most about himself was his curly hair believing it made him look soft.

They were still laughing at the idea of Markise sucking Cray's dick when they approached Cray's house and stopped. When Cray looked up at his crib, he noticed all of the lights were off, with the exception of the one in the living room and his parent's room. All he wanted was for things to be normal in his life.

"You wanna check first?" Markise asked as if he could hear his thoughts.

"You wanna give your mother her thin ass jacket back?" Cray didn't want anybody knowing his parents drug-use got to him.

"Whateva, man!" Markise responded, embarrassed by his comment.

"If ya'll comin' in come on!" Cray snapped angrily. "Otherwise you can stay out here 'cause either way I don't care."

"I'm comin' in," Jason responded. He wanted so much for Cray to like him that he hung onto his every word. Jason was the one person that thought everything about Cray was cool, including his insubordination.

"Me, too," Markise added.

The group of friends was just about to walk into the apartment building when dirty, *pressed ass* Kris loped up and asked if he could come in too. Frankie barked at him so viciously that Markise had to grab him to prevent him from biting him. Kris had dry inky skin and was tall and disheveled, not to mention his hair was knotted and matted to his scalp. He was dirtier than Cray and Cray often ragged on him to make himself feel better.

"Can I come over?" he asked, his hands in his tanned dirty coat pockets, eyeing the mutt.

"Naw, man," Cray said straight up. "You might piss on my floor or somethin'."

Kris put his head down.

"Please." Kris persisted, pressed to hang out with them.

"I said no!" Cray yelled, hitting him in the arm hard.

When he didn't move Markise said, "Bounce, Kris!" He was trying to protect him from whatever Cray was about to do next.

He held his head down and walked off. When he was gone, Cray jetted up the steps leading to his door with the missing screen. The dog knowing the routine ran down the block. Once inside the run down building, the wooden floor creaked as they walked up the stairwell. He could hear his friends close behind. As he opened the door, he prayed for one indication that things were okay.

Once inside there was a cloud of condensation in the air from Pam cooking all day. The apartment smelled of fried chicken, green beans and the rice brewing on the stove. The moment they came in, she greeted them at the door. The living room was to the left and an old yellow couch sat in the middle of the floor. In front of it, a large wooden older model TV sat as a platform for a smaller one, with a wire coat hanger sticking out of it as an antenna. Pam wore shades to conceal her bruised eyes and her busted lips still showed the evidence from this morning's session.

"Take your coats off, boys," Pam requested, trying to maintain *some* semblance of control over her household.

"Stop trippin', bitch! We'll do it when we get to my room." Cray put her in check quickly. He had no respect for her whatsoever. "Where's Dad?"

"In my room fixing Beverly's clock radio." She wiped her hands on her apron trying to rid herself of her only child's emotional abuse.

"Dinner ready?" Cray persisted as he watched his friends grabbing cups out of the kitchen cabinets and pouring Kool-Aid from the fridge all without asking, something he couldn't dare do at their houses.

"Soon," Pam said, realizing she was no match for her son's abrasiveness. She had been broken down so badly that she barely had enough strength to move around without being in pain, let alone defend herself. "I'll let you know when it's finished."

"Well hurry the fuck up, bitch! I'm hungry! And did dad get the stuff for my birthday?"

"No...but he will, son."

Cray sighed, pivoted on foot then headed toward his room with his friends right behind him, cups still in their hands.

When they got to his bedroom, Cray opened his door and flipped on the light switch. His heart dropped when he saw his father's pants down by his ankles, with his hands on the back of his mother's best friend, Beverly's head, while she blew him off.

Markise and Jason covered their mouths. Although *they* were excited to see his father getting his dick sucked, Cray was furious. The thing about Cray was this; all he had was *himself* and *his things*. So seeing his father's ass on his neatly made bed, with this woman in his room, upset him. He felt violated. If his father wanted to cheat on his mother, what the fuck was wrong with his own room?

"What ya'll lookin' at?" David yelled, as he pushed Beverly off his crotch and stood up to adjust his pants. "You ain't neva seen a dick before?" He glared at the boys.

The shocked boys remained planted where they stood.

"Don't talk to them like that." Beverly replied, standing up, wiping her mouth before fixing her loose blouse that exposed a titty. "They just kids."

"Woman, don't tell me how to treat my son!" He pointed at her.

Her eyes widened and afraid, she lowered her head.

A part of Cray wanted to reach under his bed and shoot her with the gun he stole from Grimy Mike, who ditched it awhile back while running from the cops. Nobody knew he had it, not even his friends. But the other part of Cray, the angrier part, felt that if his mother wanted to allow a whore into her home to mess around with her husband, then he could care less.

Now fully dressed, David and Beverly walked toward the doorway.

"You go ahead," he said to Beverly. "Let me talk to my boy."

Beverly walked off, smiling slightly at Markise and Jason who were having dirty thoughts of her in their minds.

When she was out of sight David placed his hand on his son's head and said, "Some day you'll understand this. And when you do, you'll become a man. I'll catch you boys later for Cray's birthday." With that he left them in the hallway.

It was quiet when they walked into his room, and they situated on the old blue quilt style rug on the floor. His eyes cold and filled with pain. Although he was focused in his friend's direction, his mind was elsewhere. He had so much going on in his young mind. So many questions with no one he trusted to answer him.

"You a'ight, man?" Markise asked, waiting for his response.

"Yeah...just thinkin' that's all."

What Cray didn't say or know was that everything he was experiencing was turning him into a menace. And the world would soon find out how.

NYZON PEATE
WASHINGTON, D.C., 1988
POPCORN LOVE

Twelve-year-old Nyzon was in the mirror singing, "Don't Be Cruel" by Bobby Brown, on WPGC 95.5, as he got ready for school. He had just gotten a shape up with a part on the side and was checking it to make sure it was perfect…it was. He'd brushed his hair so much that you could get seasick just looking at his waves. A fresh haircut was all his mother could afford to keep him in style. So Nyzon took full advantage.

After he was dressed, he ironed one of the three pair of jeans he owned. The crease was heavy in the middle of the pants. He didn't have much but what he did have he kept neat. After he got dressed he kissed his two fingers and pressed them against the boxing poster of Muhammad Ali. Nyzon was a natural when it came to boxing and looked up to him greatly.

Believing he was almost too fine for words, he remembered he couldn't leave without placing a gold chain he found a few months ago on. Nyzon felt it made him look smoother. Living in George Washington Carver apartments off of Benning Road in Southeast D.C., some fucked-up ass projects, made him appreciate the little he had.

Walking toward the kitchen, he hesitated for a second. Mustering up enough energy, he finally walked inside. Nyzon sat down at the kitchen table preparing to spend another uncomfortable moment with her.

"You hungry, baby?" Debra asked her son as she sat a plate full of pancakes on the table in front of him. Nyzon tucked his chain in his shirt so that it wouldn't dip into the extra syrup he was getting ready to douse his food with.

"Jive like," he said, a forkful of pancakes already in his mouth.

"Are we going to watch a movie tonight on Cablevision?" she asked with hopeful eyes as she adjusted her red, pink and orange flower housecoat before taking a seat in the chair across from him.

"I was gonna play Metal Gear on Nintendo with my friends." Nyzon never looked at his mother. All he could think about was how long it would take him to down his food and get out the door. Everything he enjoyed about life existed *outside* the confines of his home. And with them having no living relatives, outside of his friends, he felt alone.

Debra Peate was an average looking woman. She was mixed with black and white while Nyzon on the other hand had light brown skin with sexy, slanted eyes. Every time he looked in the mirror and than at her, he couldn't find one similarity. Often times, he wondered if she was really his mother. And every time he'd ask, she'd swear that she lied on the table for hours giving birth to him, and that his father abandoned them both when he was just six months old.

"Okay…maybe I'll bake you guys some cookies then," she said as she came behind him and rested her hands on his shoulders. "While you play the game. Would you like that?"

He shook his upper body causing her to remove her hands. Still chewing, he rose not facing her at first. Guilt rested on him and he slowly turned around and planted a kiss on her face.

"The cookies will be tight, Ma." He smiled. She smiled back. "My friends love your food. I'll see you when I get home." He grabbed his red Trapper Keeper off the box next to the door. It had been there ever since they moved in five months ago because Debra never unpacked. Nyzon and his mother moved twice a year so he never felt settled in. With his notebook in hand he barreled out the front door.

At School

Once at school Nyzon met up with his crew. He had two friends he rolled with no matter where he was going. They were Royala and Lazarick Quick, fraternal twins. Royala was a cute girl who dressed like a boy, and everything in her soul told her she was. People were so used to seeing her dressed boyishly, that they playfully referred to Royala as Lazarick's *identical* twin brother.

Nyzon was closer to Royala than he was to Lazarick because she was the only one who could spar with him and keep up in the boxing ring. She was almost as good as he was. The only thing about Royala that he couldn't handle sometimes was her temper. It was as if she had something to prove to the world. She'd been put out of school at least ten times since he first met her a year ago. As bad as she was, she only put it to people who fucked with her family or friends, so Nyzon could tolerate her fighter spirit.

Lazarick on the other hand looked like a young Al B. Sure with hazel brown eyes like his sister's. But Lazarick had a mouth and a tendency to run it. Lazarick hated on him a lot and for a while Nyzon thought he wanted to be him. But because he fucked with Royala, he dealt with him too.

"So you still messin' with that girl with the Jheri Curl?" Nyzon asked Lazarick as they walked to his locker.

"Naw…I already got that." He smiled, rubbing his hairless goatee. "She be on my dick hard now."

"Stop lyin'!" Royala frowned at her twin. "That girl stopped messin' with you to fuck with Jordan. So why you frontin'?"

"Hold up, she left you for pissy, no-neck Jordan?" Nyzon asked, all prepared to clown him if it was true.

"Man, shut up!" Lazarick said, unconsciously checking Nyzon's fresh haircut with the part down the middle. "I see you got that bush taken down."

"Yeah...you rides with this joint don't you?" he said, smoothing his hair with his hand. "Everybody can't be as fine as me."

"You always thinkin' somebody bitin' your style. I got my own flava!" Lazarick brushed his shirt with his hands.

"Damn! Who's the new girl?" Lazarick interrupted, looking in her direction, away from them. All jokes ceased. And she had their undivided attention. Her thick, phat ass filled her Guess jeans out fully, as she switched in their direction. To be twelve she had a body like a woman but a face like a baby. "Cause I'ma hit that if it's the last thing I do."

She walked past them and smiled.

"That looks like my flava," Royala added.

"Ain't nobody playin' the licky, licky parade wit your ass!" Lazarick joked.

"Yeah well both of ya'll don't waste your time. Cause I'm bout to find out! She look like my speed. So let me show ya'll how it's done." Nyzon said, running behind her. "I'll get up with yall later." He always had to be the first to put in dibs on a new girl.

He'd almost caught up with her until she suddenly turned around and stopped dead in her tracks. Instantly he collided head first into the pretty caramel-colored girl with a sandy-colored mushroom haircut.

"Ouch!" she yelled.

"Shit!" he responded.

They rubbed their heads, trying to wipe away the pain. When he looked down he noticed something on the floor. He'd knocked a piece of paper out of her hands.

"Sorry," he said, knowing it was his fault.

He was about to pick up her paper, but caught a look at her face. He couldn't move. She was beautiful...almost as pretty as Angel, his babysitter, the one girl he had a crush on forever.

"So you gonna stare at me or pick my paper up?" her breath smelled like the banana *Now and Later* candy.

He picked the paper off the floor and handed it to her.

"Thanks...now can you tell me where the office is? It's my first day." She looked around as if she hoped to find it herself.

"I will if you give me your name." Nyzon tried to gain his composure.

Instead of her telling him, she pointed to his head and started laughing.

"What?"

"It's…your…head." The girl held her stomach and bent over with laughter.

"What about it?" he asked, rubbing his head. The moment he did he felt a little knot forming next to the part in his scalp. "Shoot!"

It was impossible to be cute with a knot on his face.

"Don't worry. It'll be okay." She flashed a dimpled smile. "Just put a little ice on it when you get home." She reached up and touched it lightly.

He was stunned. It was the first time a girl touched him without him having to point to his penis and say, "Put your hand right here."

"And my name is Monesha. Monesha Heart. So *now* can you help me find the office?"

Nyzon stared at her again before he answered the question. He had to have her. She was the answer to his prayers. If he had a girl like *her* on his arm, everybody would *really* be jocking him. They walked down the hall together.

"Here it goes right here." He pushed the door open to the office for her to walk in. He was about to leave when one of the administrators saw him.

"Nyzon Peate…get in here!" Mrs. Tawney yelled.

"I'm goin' to class right now Mrs. Tawney. I was just walkin' the new girl to the office." Normally he and the twins would hang in the hallways a few minutes after the bell rung.

"You always walking the new girl somewhere. Nyzon get in here now!"

Slightly embarrassed he walked up to the corner of the desk and said, "What's up?" He focused on her chubby white face.

"I need you to take these documents to your mother. The board of education can't find a copy of your birth certificate on file or her driver's license anywhere in the system."

"What that mean?" He looked at the sealed envelope.

"Just tell her that every year the board does a random verification of a few students in the school to make sure everything's in order. And your information came back with a flag. So have her complete the documents and send them back to me ASAP."

"I'll bring them back tomorrow."

"Good…and Nyzon…get to class!"

He looked at Monesha and walked out the door nervous.

His heart raced. The last time there was a problem with the paperwork at school, his mother pulled him out claiming that the educational system was flawed. In fact anytime she was questioned about anything pertaining to Nyzon, they'd move. She took over protectiveness to the next level and Nyzon wanted it to stop. As far as he was concerned he had two options, hide the documents and never give them to her, or hand them over and risk being pulled out of school again. Thinking for a brief second he dumped them in a trashcan in the hallway and went to class.

After School

"Open your legs." Nyzon said to Starlette, the school's whore who let him finger her whenever he wanted.

His body pressed on top of hers in the backseat of an old yellow abandoned car.

"You not gonna say nothin' are you?" she asked as she spread her legs a little wider so Nyzon could get under her skirt, and move her panties to the side.

She had an older boyfriend and didn't want him finding out she was a freak. Royala was on guard outside of the car, as Nyzon got busy with the neighborhood freak.

"Naw I ain't gonna say nothin'." He lied as he stuck his fingers between her legs and inside her tight pussy. The only person he was going to tell was the twins. "I told you I wouldn't do that."

He wasn't getting anything out of it, just liked the idea of being able to do it. Nyzon peeped out of the fog stained window to be sure Royala was still watching his back. She was.

"Nyzon do you like me?" she asked as she moaned like she loved his fingers being jammed rythmlessly inside of her.

He didn't want to tell her he couldn't get down with sluts so he lied.

"You know I do."

"So why you neva talk to me at school?"

Right before he could answer, Nyzon looked out of the back window and saw a red Saab pull up. The gold BBS rims had his mouth open. The music was so loud coming from it, the windows in the car he was in rattled. Minutes later, Angel, his babysitter appeared from the car. She smiled brightly before waving goodbye to the driver and it was like she moved in slow motion. Nyzon felt jealousy consume him. He wanted to be with 18-year-old Angel. Instead he was finger-fucking freaky Starlette that everybody had a go with.

"You okay?" Starlette asked sensing his attention had been taken elsewhere.

"Uh...yeah. I'm cool." His eyes remained on Angel.

She tugged at her skirt and turned around to see what compelled him. She sucked her teeth when she saw cute big-tittie Angel.

"Ain't no need of you thinkin' bout her!" she continued with an attitude, pulling his fingers out of her vagina. "Girls like that only want one thing and you ain't got it! I don't care how deep your part on the side of your hair is. It's deep pockets that count."

With that she pushed him off and got out of the car.

Royala saw this and rushed to the door.

"You get it, man?" She asked.

"Yeah. I hit." He maintained his glance on Angel.

Careful not to put the finger he had inside of her in his face, he thought about what Starlette said. But he disagreed. He knew a day would come when he could get any girl he wanted, no matter how much it took. And he knew the day would come soon.

KAVON CARTIER
WASHINGTON, D.C., 1988
DON'T TRY ME

It was a brisk winter afternoon in Chocolate City, habitat to one of the most vicious narcotics games on the East Coast. Christmas was a little over a month away and the atmosphere was somewhat joyous if your pockets were as deep as Kavon Cartier's.

He was blasting a Rare Essence band Go-Go tape, when he pulled in front of Ben's Chili Bowl, a hangout spot in the city. His red Saab sparkled in the night despite the nasty weather. And the butter interior smelled of new leather and vanilla.

Leaned so far to the right, his face touched the glass lightly when he put his hazard lights on in front of the store and parked. Even though the thick brown ice made it difficult to find a parking space, he wasn't concerned. Rolling his tinted window down, he flagged the manager to come outside. It didn't take him long to get his attention because he was waiting on Kavon since he called an hour ago. He had to meet his partner Shy to discuss some serious business.

"What's up wit my parkin' space?" he asked the manager. The frigid air rushed inside and battled with the fury of the heat running in his car when he rolled down his window.

"I'm sorry, Kavon. Give me one minute." He threw up one finger. "It'll be taken care of." The old black man quickly hustled back inside the store.

Within the crowded restaurant, through the fogged window, he could see the manager yelling at a pretty black girl with golden hair. Next he grabbed her forcefully by her elbow and pointed outside. Kavon just knew a smack would follow, but it didn't. Seconds later she came bolting out the front door, irritated that she had to move her car. She even rolled her eyes at Kavon, the reason for her dismay. But just like that, a parking space had suddenly become available.

Once he parallel parked, he noticed Shy's new white Beemer with New York State plates a few spots in front of him. *This nigga got a new car every week*! Kavon shook his head, and hopped out of his ride like he owned the place.

As usual, Ben's Chili was loaded with people. The pungent fragrance of chili powder and garlic wafted throughout the restaurant. This was the place to be if you were looking for a baller or looking to get fucked. People were laughing and holding conversations. Sex, money and power were in the air and Kavon loved it!

When he saw the girl who moved her car so he could move in, he peeled off a fifty-dollar bill, threw it on her table and kept it moving. He winked when he saw a smile spread across her face, but to him it was nothing but a thing.

In the light, the girl could see how handsome he was and was mad she acted so immature earlier. His ebony colored skin, and thick eyebrows gave him a distinct, sexy look. And the small gash on his chin that he got as a child from falling on a glass table, gave him definition. Hands down, Kavon was fine as shit.

"I see you still givin' bitches your money," Shy joked.

"It ain't trickin' if you got it," Kavon responded.

"So, what up, B?!" Shy yelled as he approached Kavon and gave him some dap.

He was a big dude who ate all the fucking time. Despite his 6'2 inch frame and three hundred pound weight, he was extremely attractive and favored Heavy D in his younger years. His yellow-apricot skin was without flaws, except for the brown heart-shaped birthmark under his right eye.

"You know it's your world. I just live here!" Kavon responded, looking for Mr. Gilroy, the store manager who got him his parking place earlier. Whenever Kavon came to Ben's, he was given the VIP treatment that included a special section in the back of the restaurant, free from everyone else.

"Aye, Kavon!" the manager said, giving him a manly hug. "Your seats are over here and I'm sorry about the problem earlier. I told Sharice you were coming and to have your spot clear, but apparently she wasn't listening. You know how females are."

"Not a problem. Everything's cool now." Kavon wasn't the kind of dude to abuse his power although he could.

When they were seated Kavon noticed a few folks looking at him and Shy wondering who they were, especially considering the restaurant was so crowded they had to wait over an hour for a seat. But it was the 80's and cash ruled everything around.

"If you need anything just let me know." Kavon shook his hand and left a C-note.

After they claimed their seats, both of them ordered two chili bowls with extra cheddar cheese and the manager made sure a cute girl brought it over to them. When she was gone, Shy got right down to business.

"So what up?" he asked as he stuffed his face with four spoonfuls of chili in one breath.

"Everything and anything."

"No, what's *really* up, B? Cause I know you ain't got me out here to eat no fuckin' chili."

"True dat. I'ma be straight up wit you. You gotta come down on the prices of the brick." Kavon pushed the chili away.

"My prices are standard." Shy pointed his index finger at the table looking around to be sure no one was trying to listen in on their conversation. "You know dat."

"Shit's changed, Shy. And your prices got to too." Kavon peered at him. "So either you come down or I'ma be forced to conduct business with my new folks."

"I been hookin' yo ass up for six years."

"Hookin' me up? You can't be serious!" Kavon sat back in his seat and smirked.

"I'm dead serious!" Shy said as lines formed in his forehead. "So how the fuck you gonna come in here and try to pressure me? You and me both know that for the price I give you on them keys, I coulda charged anotha mothafucka double."

"Fuck you talkin' bout, Shy? Dat's some bullshit!" Kavon slammed his fist on the table, causing some of his chili to pop out and splatter. "I been payin' da same prices as everybody else you deal wit if not more. Don't forget you talk more than you can remember." He looked at him sternly. "Now I fucks wit you, but I'm not payin' more than I have to. And the truth of the matter is, if you not willin' to come down, I got somebody that'll charge me less. So what's it gonna be?"

Shy shot him an evil glare. Kavon's tone with him was out of the ordinary and he decided to try him.

"You funny as shit."

"What you mean I'm *funny as shit*?" Kavon mugged. He was sick of him. And although he'd known Shy for a minute, he was fully prepared to cease all business interactions with him today if he didn't meet his demands. Between Tara, his prize wife who had expensive tastes pressuring him every other day to get a legal hustle, and the cops bum rushing his house every other month, he was tired of living on the edge. He needed enough money to score big and get out, and Shy was making it difficult.

He had plans to ask Tara Pleasants, the love of his life, to be his wife. Just thinking about her naturally bronzed skin and sandy brown hair had his chest on swole and she was *all* his. Mixed with African American and Brazilian, she had an exotic appeal not common in the D.C. area.

Tara's beauty was unquestionable, but there were a few things he didn't understand about her. She depended on him too much to make decisions in her life. Kavon was a hustler, and a hustler needed a strong woman who could hold him down when times got rough and make decisions when the time was right. And with Tara, he couldn't say beyond a shadow of a doubt that she could. With that said, it was still obvious that she influenced his decisions.

"You think it's easy findin' niggas in this game who got your back?"

"Shy we ain't kids no more. I'm interested in gettin' my weight up. Nothin' more, nothin' less."

To some people it may have appeared as if Kavon was greedy challenging Shy on his prices considering Shy was the first dude to put him on. Before he met him, Kavon was a twenty-year-old, small time drug dealer with a couple of hundred dollars to spare. It was Shy who breathed the drug game in as if it were oxygen and brought Kavon along. Born and raised in Brooklyn, New York, Shy loved letting people know what city he claimed because with the reputation his city had for being violent, he felt it added to his credibility. And to most people it did.

Now Shy didn't come from a fucked-up home with both parents absent. It was quite the contrary. His mother, Karen, and father, Erick, were both New York City police officers. He had been raised in a home with law and order. But New York was New York, and despite the morals they bestowed upon him, whenever Shy left his house, all of that shit went out the window. There was nothing for him and his friends to do outside of hanging around drugs and violence. And Shy was a testimony to the old adage that an idle mind is the devil's workshop.

No matter what their past, Kavon knew Shy had been charging him extra for the keys a long time ago, but he let it slide. Besides, business was business and Kavon wasn't asking for handouts nor was he looking for any. But after being approached by a member of another crew, and seeing the offer they placed on the table, he believed a change was in order. Not to mention weed and coke wasn't moving as fast as crack, the new high of choice.

"Can't do it, man," Shy responded as he continued to eat his meal while talking with his mouth full of food. "I gotta treat you like everybody else. That's what you always said so I'ma hold you to it."

This nigga is lunchin'! Kavon thought. If that's the way he wanted it, he could suck his dick.

He jumped up, grabbed his hat and moved toward the exit. If he hurried, he'd still had time to beep Deuce on his pager and tell him he was prepared to accept his offer.

"A'ight!" Shy's voice trailed behind him before he reached the door. Although he spoke low, Shy's voice was loud enough to rise above the din of noises in the restaurant.

There was a lot of commotion so he stopped to be sure he heard him correctly. For a second he looked at the exit door and contemplated saying, *fuck this nigga.* But he took pleasure in finally being able to break his greedy ass down. Slowly he turned around and faced him.

"What?" he said, approaching him slowly, as if he didn't care either which way, although he did. He trusted Shy and knew he couldn't say the same for the new cats.

"I said a'ight, nigga! You got it!" He chewed the last of the food in his mouth. "I'll give you my *special* discount."

Kavon sat down. Although Shy accepted his offer, Kavon was irritated at his awful display of professionalism. All he wanted was to be able to stack chips so he could move his future wife from D.C. to Miami, where she always wanted to live. The plan was to buy a few beachfront properties, which would get Kavon out of the game for good.

As Kavon stared at Shy, something was eerie about the way he looked at him. They say the evil in a man jumps out for a second and presents itself, when there is so much hate inside that it consumes the body. Kavon couldn't help but wonder if resentment was what Shy felt for him now. He brushed it off when he remembered that they were bros above everything else, including money.

"Glad you came to your senses." Kavon grinned a little. For the first time *he* was in control. "Now let's get out of here so we can get some *real* food."

"Cool wit' me."

They left together, but when they got in their rides, they thought about how things ended, and knew in one way or another, things would forever be changed between them.

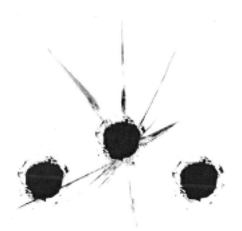

CAROLYN JAMISON
UPPER MARLBORO, MARYLAND
CHOOSE A SIDE

It was seven o'clock in the evening, the time where most people would be eating dinner at home. Not twenty-year-old Carolyn Jamison. She sat quietly in the front row of a secret "Klan of Young Conservatism" rally, which was nothing more than a modern-day Ku Klux Klan organization in Upper Marlboro, Maryland.

Behind the podium stood her father, wearing a chocolate suit, he controlled the audience's attention with the vigor and force only a leader could muster. If you placed his voice on mute, *still* his eyes would say exactly what he stood for...total dominance and control. And when Carolyn's eyes met her father's she smiled brightly doing her best to show her support for his cause.

"Blacks think they run our country because of the laws that are made today! And unless we do something about it now, drug dealers, basketball players, rappers and the rest of these niggers will continue to take the American tradition out of our homes and throw it into the streets! And I for one won't rest until we claim our country back! Are you with me?!"

"Yeah!" A thunderous cheer rippled through the hall.

"I said are you with me?!"

"YYYYYYYYYEAAAAHHHH!"

"What do we believe in?!" William yelled looking at his audience in a distorted evil glare.

"White POWER!" the crowd yelled.

"And what will we fight for?!"

"White POWER!"

"Now I'm not opposed to niggers getting with other niggers." The crowd settled down and laughed a little. "But now they want our women *and* our jobs! Are we gonna sit by and continue to let them push out everything we worked so hard to build?"

"Nooooooooooooooo!"

Raising his clutched fist into the air, he wanted it known that he would stop at nothing to ensure that whites regain control of their government and country. His coal black hair was as neat and perfect. In his late forties, at first sight William appeared as harmless as a catholic priest. But he was far from it.

"We must protect our white babies, our white women and white America! And as I look down at my God fearing beautiful white daughter, I'm reminded of the importance of our pure white heritage!

Anyone who was watching Carolyn could see that her beauty was riveting. And there was no denying that she looked like money in her royal blue Anne Klein suit and black pumps. Her red hair sat neatly on her shoulders and moved whenever she did. Out of habit and nervousness, she tucked it behind her ears several times that evening.

These meetings always had her on edge because she wondered if anyone would notice that she didn't believe in *everything* KYC stood for. It was difficult for her to digest that her father was nothing more than an extreme racist. He couldn't even be in the same room with someone black without commenting on their atrociousness. Day and night he preached of regaining the country through infiltrating public offices and big businesses. And he'd stop at nothing to see his plans followed through.

And right beside Carolyn sat her skinhead brother, eighteen-year old Todd Jamison. While everyone else was dressed in business attire, Todd wore a tight white t-shirt revealing his muscular body, and a pair of worn blue jeans. His steel toe boots were partially covered in dirt. He was the extreme of his father's beliefs and principles. Even William had to tell him several times that he'd gone too far. But it was his arms that revealed the inner battle he faced with being a racist. Because covered over his arms were both fresh and old scars, compliments of his indulging in self-mutilation.

Although she never spoke it aloud, she knew of the things Todd and his friends did to innocent people of other races. She recalled him coming in late one night to their large home in Georgetown, DC, covered in blood. She asked him over and over what happened, even though she didn't want to know. He never told her, but his glossy eyes showed that he was high on whatever he needed to follow through on his heinous crimes. That following day, when it was broadcasted on the news that someone had stabbed two black members of a Baptist church and pulled their bodies out on the steps for all to see, Todd smiled proudly.

His baldhead was skinned and a large black tattoo of the letters W and P could be seen from clear across the room. They symbolized, White Power. Through her brother's eyes, it was the first time she could honestly see how hate and love could co-exist. Because Todd loved to hate, and everyone in his presence for five seconds felt it.

"We have to regain control over our businesses and our government first. Because as long as we continue to allow them to make screwed up laws, we can't win! We have to unite in our purpose and do it now. Let's build strong fronts! We can do it!"

The crowd roared with excitement. A furor rose up, then settled.

"Now before I leave, I want to introduce to you *our* answer to the DC Government. He's young, he's intelligent and he understands what must be done to clean up the city. Please welcome Kirk Bowler, our future Mayor and the newly elected Chief of Police!"

The cheers continued to roar throughout the hall.

"Thank you Bill!" He shook his hand. "Before he leaves can we give this man a another round of applause?"

The cheers got louder and William stepped off of the stage after receiving a standing ovation. His chest swelled. Kirk remained as he gave his speech on how he would represent the KYC well, starting with increasing the white percentage in the police force. Kirk hated that over 50% of the officers were niggers and he had plans to change it. His speech went on for twenty minutes before it ended.

"Sir, I enjoyed your speech! And if there's anything I can do for you or your organization, please don't hesitate to let me know." Amanda Hertz owned six big banks and loved using her money to gain influence. "I mean that."

"Thank you, ma'am, but just having the support of good old fashion law abiding white women like yourself will be plenty." Williams said.

"You have that." She smiled hugging him lightly. "But I'll write another check too."

"That will be much appreciated." He winked.

When she dismissed herself, William walked over to his beautiful daughter and extended his hand. Todd was right beside her.

"How was I?"

"Wonderful, Daddy!" Carolyn hugged him. "They loved you."

"What do you think, son?" He turned and shook his son's hand.

"You ROCKED!"

William laughed.

"Why don't you go pull the car around front? I want to talk to your sister alone."

"No problem, Dad!" Todd often yelled like he was in the military and carried himself that way, too.

When Todd walked away, her father stared deeply into Carolyn's eyes. "You understand our purpose and why this is so important for our future don't you?" He knew of the rumors that surfaced about his own flesh in blood being nothing more than a *Wigger*, someone who enjoyed being in the presence of black people.

"Of course, father."

"I'm serious. They are poisonous, Carolyn. They'll rape you, take your money and leave you for dead."

He named his daughter after Carolyn Bryant, the woman that 14-year old Emett Till whistled at days before he was murdered.

"I know, Daddy." She shifted on her feet. "I would never do anything contrary to *your* beliefs. Heck, I agree with you. We need to do all we can to annihilate other races and win our country back." A light smile spread across her face.

"*Our* beliefs Carolyn. *Ours.*"

"Huh?"

"You said you'd never do anything contrary to *my* beliefs and I need you to understand our beliefs should be one in the same."

"I know, Daddy. It was a mistake."

"I understand."

"Honestly, father. It won't happen again."

"I know. Now have you given any thought to running your own chapter? I mean, you only have one year left at Catholic University. It's time you help us connect with some of these impressionable young women out there. And with that face," he rubbed her chin softly, "they'll never see us coming."

"I'm thinking about it but I don't want to let you down. It's a lot of work and I'm not sure if I'm ready."

"I have all the faith in you, Carolyn. I need you on board with me."

"Okay."

She was nervous, but poised because she wondered if he could read her mind or see her desires because Carolyn was quite the character. She had a fetish for the wild side of life and she managed to keep it under wraps, when she wasn't drinking.

Black men and their music and culture aroused her. Still, she knew her father was not a man to be trifled with. If one didn't go along with his philosophies, her father could become quite an adversary.

him a pound. Afterward, he handed Kavon the tiny remainder of the blunt. "I ain't gonna lie. You picked a winner."

"That's what I been tryin' to tell you, man." Kavon put the blunt out in the ashtray and left it there. "Now let's get some grub cause I'm hungry den a mothafucka." They exited the car, walked to the door and Kavon rubbed his stomach. "And Shy."

"What up, B?" Shy gazed at him with contrition in his heart. To the person looking outside in, they could see his agitation.

"Don't tell her about my proposal. It's a surprise."

"That's your woman not mine."

"Thanks, man."

The moment Kavon walked through his mahogany doors and saw his future wife busying herself with his meal, he smiled. But Shy sat on the sofa looking at the love in their eyes and it made his stomach rumble.

As always, everything was in order. And with his chest stuck out, Kavon felt proud for Shy to see what a beautiful home Tara and he had built together. Prior to Tara moving in, he had one couch, one bed and one toothbrush. But now, thanks to her exquisite taste, their home was filled with tasteful furniture imported from Italy.

Tara's long hair was pulled back into a ponytail. She wore a red, one-piece cotton Gucci dress and earrings with the word, *Kavon* engraved inside of them. As if she was moving in slow motion, she stopped the moment she saw the love of her life walk through the front door.

"Hola, Papi!" She ran up to him. She planted a juicy kiss on his lips. Instantly, she wrapped her arms around his neck as he ran his hands down the small of her back. For one minute they kissed without letting each other go.

"Damn, can I get some love, too?" Shy asked as he stood up from the sofa. The moment she acknowledged him, he opened his arms and tilted his head to the right.

"Shy!" Tara yelled, jumping up into his arms, as he lifted her up and lightly spun her around. It had been two months since she'd seen him and she missed him. Their friendship didn't threaten Kavon one bit.

"I didn't know you were comin' over. You told me you were in New York when you called earlier." Tara playfully hit him.

Shy placed her down. "You didn't know I was here cuz dis nigga had dem big ass soup coolers he got fo lips in yo face!" He laughed.

"Fire that shit up!" Kavon ignored Shy and pulled another blunt out of his pants pocket.

He was moving in to kiss her again when he heard Shy yell, "You mothafuckas not 'bout to be in my face fuckin'."

"What you jealous? I keep tellin' you, to find you a good woman and leave them busted ass bitches alone. Then you won't be worryin' bout what the fuck we do."

"What you think I been tryin' to do?" Shy fired up the blunt before pulling on it and releasing the smoke into the air. "I don't be knowin' they skeezas until *after* I fuck 'em." He passed the blunt to Tara but she refused. "All I'ma say is never have a kid cause these bitches out here ain't shit!"

"What's up with you and kids?" Kavon laughed.

"Yeah, Shy. You just got the wrong woman." Tara fanned the smoke in the air.

"My bad Tara, I wasn't talkin' bout yo fine ass. I shoulda got with you myself," he joked and his eyes searched Tara's. "Instead I played matchmaker."

"That's the story of your life. Always pickin' the wrong ones." Kavon smirked.

"You betta neva fuck up!"

Awkward silence filled the air.

"Even if I could you wouldn't have a chance. You got who you wanted right?" Kavon asked referring to his son's mother.

Another moment of uncomfortable silence hovered over the room as each tried to determine if the other was serious.

"You know I'm just fuckin' wit you." Shy laughed. "You gettin' all serious and shit."

"I'm just statin' the facts. Plus, Tara don't get down with big dudes. She got taste." Kavon pulled her toward him.

Shy and Kavon joked all the time with each other, but something about the mood tonight was different. Shy felt Kavon owed him his life. Six years ago, Kavon trusted this white cat called Paris Christal in Virginia with fifty thousand dollars of his hard earned cash in exchange for some weight. His supply was dangerously low and the demand was greater than ever. And Shy was in Vegas watching a fight thereby rendering him impossible to reach. If he waited, he risked losing his customers and soldiers to other *major* dealers.

Listening to a dude named Jodi, Kavon ran with from time to time, he reached out to Paris for some temporary weight until Shy came back and acted as if he had an operation to run. And because his source was *somewhat* reliable, he trusted Paris would not fuck him over. He was dead wrong.

Once a mule delivered the money, and Kavon hadn't received his product, he knew there was a problem. Two days went by and Kavon couldn't find Paris or Jodi. The old white man was missing in action. He knew without a doubt that he had been played.

Finally back in town, Shy discovered Kavon had been ganked for his money. It pissed him off that Kavon had been so lax with his cash and had he been in town, the dough would've been his. With the information Kavon supplied him with, he was eventually able to locate Paris's punk ass.

Having been familiar with Paris, Shy explained to Kavon that at one point, he was reliable. That was until he started gambling. Paris would bet on everything from whose dick hung the lowest to, which team would win the NBA playoffs. In other words, Shy was positive the money was unrecoverable.

After getting Paris's location confirmed, Shy loaded up his boys, Smokin' Tony, Dymond and Pauly, and went to his home to confront him. Although he didn't expect the money to be in Paris's possession, there was a point to be made.

When they pulled up on the red brick mansion, there was a black stone waterfall in the middle of the driveway in the shape of two women kissing. No cars were parked out front. But to Shy's surprise, the door was wide open. He and his boys hustled inside. *This honky's stupid.* Shy thought.

They ran all over the empty house but outside of a TV on a stand, it looked abandoned. It was apparent that either he had moved or was preparing to. Paris pawned everything he owned to fund his habit.

"That nigga got ghost," Smokin' Tony observed.

"Yeah. We missed his ass," Pauly added.

They were just about to leave when they saw the glass sliding door open leading to the deck. When they walked out, they saw him outside. His back faced them.

"I can't believe this shit," Shy laughed.

Paris was lying down butt ass naked on a lawn chair by the pool. A beautiful young girl was straddling him and giving him a serious blow job. She was wearing a red bikini bottom, no top. Shy and his crew stood for a minute and watched her wiggle her tight ass in the sunlight. When the show was over, they rushed him.

"Don't make a move," Shy demanded standing over top of him. "You know, Kavon? So where's his money?"

The life looked like it had been scared out of him. Paris's frightened white cheeks jiggled as he explained over and over that he didn't have a dime. Three barrels were aimed in his direction, ready to unload on Shy's command. The young girl shielded her naked body with a cream towel, as their eyes roamed from her back to the target.

"Stop, lyin'! Fuck is his money?!"

"Please don't hurt me!"

Frustrated with him, Shy grabbed Paris by the neck and pushed him inside of his home. He figured he'd have *something* in his bedroom even if it wasn't cash.

"What you got in here?" he asked when they reached his bedroom up stairs. Paris wasn't talking fast enough for him so he knocked him in his temple with the butt of the gun and he dropped to the bed.

"I don't have it. I promise," he cried, his pink limp balls resting against his thigh. His hands extended out in front of him. "Please stop."

"I'll find somethin' in this mothafucka!" Shy said. "Keep your burner on his ass," he ordered Dymond as he rummaged through his shit.

He pulled out dresser drawers and lifted up anything not nailed to the floor. He was sure he wouldn't find money, but if he was lucky maybe he'd get some jewelry instead. After all, he did live in a million dollar home. Shy made his way to his closet. It was empty but he looked for the slightest detail out of place. What he discovered was a discolored floorboard. When he lifted it up, he smiled when he discovered $100,000 in 100 dollar stacks in a shoebox. It was way more than what he expected. Hell, he found enough to pay Kavon back, plus interest.

"I see you've lied to me." Shy replied too happy to be angry over his deceit.

"That money isn't mine. Please don't' take it."

Shy laughed in his face and said, "Well fellas," he said throwing them a stack each. "Our work here is done."

They were backing out of the door with their newfound fortune when Paris said, "Kill me."

"Come again?" Shy questioned, stopping in his tracks. It's not often someone asked him to take his or her life.

"I'm asking you to kill me, because if *they* find me, and I don't have their money, they'll do far worst than put a bullet in my head." Paris was serious.

Shy looked at his boys and one of them shrugged their shoulders. "Kill the mothafucka and let's get the fuck out of here."

The way Shy looked at it was this, if he didn't kill Paris, who ever he owed the money to may come looking for him. Plus, if he'd rather die, Shy knew that whomever he was indebted to must be more dangerous than he felt like dealing with. Without another word, Shy unloaded three bullets in his head. *Pop. Pop. Pop.* The four of them hurried down the stairs and stopped when they saw the beautiful woman with her hair pulled back in a ponytail and wearing a pink sweat suit. At first Shy aimed at her fully prepared to put a bullet in her head too.

"Please don't!" she sobbed.

His thoughts immediately went back to the way she looked when he saw her sucking Paris's dick. Shy could tell by looking at her that although she may have been a whore, she was an expensive one. He imagined how pleasurable it would be to have her lips wrapped around his throbbing manhood. Had he been alone with her, he would've found out. She was crying her eyes out and in her vulnerability, she was provocative.

"You betta get outta here before I change my mind about letting you live."

He walked to the truck and she followed. Thinking she was up to something he drew his weapon and aimed at her.

"I don't have anything!" she said, her hands held in the air in surrender.

"Wanna kill her?" Pauly asked.

"Naw...let's roll." Shy told him.

Something in her eyes told him he didn't have anything to be concerned about. They'd just committed murder and there was no time to do anything but bail.

"Take me with you." The young woman grabbed Shy's upper arm.

"What?" Shy shook her off. "What you talkin' about?"

"Come on, man!" Pauly yelled from inside the stolen truck looking around them. "Lada for this shit! Let's bail!"

"Please...," she cried, gaining his attention again. "He paid for me to come here from Brazil. I don't know anybody here. I have nothing. If you leave me, I won't have anywhere else to go."

"I can't do it." He secretly thought of all the things he wanted to do to her.

Shy looked at her and was turning to leave again when she cried out, "I'm begging you...I'll do anything, but please don't leave me."

He decided not to leave her behind. But there was nothing charitable about Shy. He was always thinking about what was in it for him, and this situation was no different.

"Do you know what the fuck I just did to ya man upstairs? I'm not somebody you want to be rollin' wit."

"I do know, and I don't care."

"What's your name?" Shy opened the car door for her.

She wiped her tears. "Tara. Tara Pleasants."

"Well, Tara. Get inside."

They got away from the mansion. And after ditching the truck he and his boys went their separate ways. Tara stayed with Shy. He decided to put his plan into action by introducing her to Kavon. He figured he'd let him fuck her a few times, take his mind off the money and hook back up with her later. As fine as she was, he knew he could make some serious cash pimping her out.

But before doing anything, he told her to remain in the car. He needed to be sure it would work first. He knew Kavon was fucked up that Candy, his ex-girlfriend, left him two months earlier. So if things worked out the way he wanted them to, he'd be thanking him for the rest of his life and losing the $50 G's would never come up again.

Once inside Kavon's place in D.C., he told him he found Paris alive but when he didn't cough up the dough, he left him for dead. Kavon was disappointed that he wasn't getting his money back, but satisfied that he got what he deserved for ganking him for his cash.

"I couldn't get your money, but I got somethin' you'll like." Shy tried to conceal the fact that he took his money. Plus, he was sure Tara was worth more than fifty G's anyway.

"If you ain't got my dough I don't know what's better."

"Trust me. Stay right here," Shy said as Kavon stood in the living room, wondering what he could possibly have for him outside of his cash.

"Tara, this is Kavon."

The brightness of the light in his home stung her eyes after being kept in the dark so long. But when she opened her eyes, and saw his face, for some reason, she was at ease.

"My man's gonna take good care of you." Shy studied Kavon's reaction and hers.

Kavon's mouth dropped when he saw the stranger's beautiful but troubled face. Initially, he was upset about his money, but after seeing her, he knew what Shy was saying without words. He didn't ask why a woman so beautiful would be willing to be passed off as product. And he didn't know what he was planning to do with her himself. For now, Tara was his consolation prize, and for now, he'd accept her. The rest was history. *Their history.* Unfortunately for Shy, the silent plans to hook back up with her later failed, because the moment they laid eyes on one another, it was love at first sight.

Back to the Present

"You two do this all the time! Always fighting over me." Tara joked, playfully hitting Kavon and Shy. "I love both of you." She pranced to the kitchen to grab them two beers. "I have the best of both worlds."

"Yeah, okay. Don't be lyin' to this nigga," Kavon belted out a deep belly laugh. "You belong to me and only me, baby," he added half seriously, "Remember that."

Shy smirked, if somebody was looking at him, they would've sworn he had larceny in his heart.

"And there's nowhere else I'd like to be. Being with you feels like a fairy tale." Tara kissed him softly. "I put that on my life."

"You betta." He kissed her.

CRAYLAND BAILOR
WEST BALTIMORE
BROTHERS FOR LIFE

Cray and his boys sat on the steps of his house watching cars fly by. Cray was gobbling down a pack of grape Now and Laters, Markise had a box of Lemonheads, and Jason was begging for both of their shit. Someone played NWA's *"Dopeman"* song as they washed their car a few feet up and the boys recited the words until he finished and drove off. And just when they were getting into the lyrics, a black "Take Back The Streets" van passed by with Modell Muhammad driving. They hated when he came through the neighborhood telling them to stay away from drugs. They looked up to the Hustler's in the neighborhood and wanted to be just like them and Modell's presence clashed with their dreams. Frankie was barking uncontrollably until Cray stooped down and gave him a piece of his candy. His head tilted to the side as he tried hard to keep it inside his mouth.

"I'm glad his ass ain't stop here!" Cray yelled to be heard over the busy street noise, as he watched the van drive away.

"Me too, I don't feel like dealin' wit him." Jason said.

A brand new red Mercedes drove by and the driver nodded with gold medallions hanging around his neck.

"When I grow up I'm gonna be a kingpin." He looked into the sky. All he thought about was money and lots of it. "I'ma have more cars than Melody and them put together." Cray bragged. "I'm sick of havin' nothin'."

"Me too!" Jason added. "We gonna be rich."

"We?" Cray laughed. "You ain't gonna have more money than me."

"We gonna have money together. Watch! You gonna see."

The idea made Cray smile.

"Let's make a pact, when we grow up, we gonna run Bmore." Cray said looking at his friends extending his hand out in front of him. "We brothers for life."

"I'm wit you." Jason said quickly throwing his hand over his.

As they waited on Markise, Cray grew slightly angry. Instead of wanting fast money, all he talked about was being a teacher and having a legitimate job. Cray hated that about him.

"Are you wit us or not?" Cray asked impatiently.

Markise examined them as if he could see their future. He didn't take pacts lightly and didn't want to say he was down unless he really meant it. Thinking on it long enough he said, "Brothers for life." He placed his hand over theirs.

"For life!" Cray repeated.

The moment their hands dropped, they heard loud base and Big Daddy Kane's voice booming from a radio system. It was the song, "Ain't No Half-Steppin'" coming from Melody's silver Audi. He pulled up in the spot right in front of Cray's house, which nobody parked in. It was an unspoken rule that it belonged to him. Melody earned his nickname because he was always singing. It didn't matter if he was dealing dope or murder, if you were around him you'd hear him harmonizing. He owned the row house next to Cray's.

Jumping out of his ride with his Versace blue jeans and thick red Eddie Bauer coat, he sported a rope chain so big it put big Daddy Kane's to shame. Cray was in awe. He didn't want to be like him, he wanted to *be* him.

"Get my bags and my dug." He told a few of his friends who were with him.

The dug he was referring to was a black pit bull. Most Baltimore natives pronounced dog as 'dug' and Melody was no exception.

"And when you're done get the front door for me," Melody demanded as the two men rustled with the six shopping bags and his killer animal.

J-Swizz, one of the two, managed to get a free hand to open Melody's house door. He was handsome, tall and lanky. And where you saw Melody, you was bound to see eighteen -year old J-Swizz.

The thing that tripped Cray out was that the entire time, his hands were free. He was in charge, and although Cray didn't like him, he admired his use of power. He dreamed of having so much money he could buy who and what he wanted too. Already at a young age, Cray was learning that money ruled everything and everybody.

"Hey, Markise." Cray focused on the flunkies running in and out of the building and grabbing Melody's stuff.

"What up?" Markise asked, staring at some fat butt little girl across the street.

"Go get me some Kool-Aid," Cray ordered. He wanted to see how much power he had over them.

"Get it yo self!" Markise yelled.

Cray felt foolish for trying to get Markise to do what he wanted. You see, Markise was his own person. He was the only kid that didn't do what other people did just to fit in. That's part of the reason why *everybody* liked him so much.

"Jason, you get it." Cray said.

"A'ight!" Jason jumped up. "But I'm getting me some too." He disappeared into Cray's house.

Although he was able to control Jason, it wasn't enough. He wanted to be able to break down Markise, too. And if he had *real* control, he'd be able to do it. When Jason came back with the juice he handed Cray's his and gulped his own down with one breath. Afterward he placed the yellow cup down on the step.

"Ya'll little dusty ass niggas bet not think about comin' over here touchin' this car," J-Swizz said as he activated the alarm. "That's if you know what's good for you."

When he was gone Jason said, "Whateva! I'll touch whateva I want to." He boasted walking close enough to it to irritate him if he saw him, but not close enough to get his chest caved in if Melody caught his ass.

"Stop swellin'. You always fakin'." Markise tried to get the attention of three girls across the street walking to the store. He was doing two things at once. Trying to get at the cutie with the phat bootie and hear what his boys were up to. "Cuz if Melody came out here and saw you, you'd be pissin' your pants."

"I don't know why ya'll scared of him," Cray added, standing up from the steps and placing his blue cup full of juice down. He didn't even want it for real. "He a nigga just like me."

"Yeah, okay." Markise laughed and gave Jason dap. "Keep believin' that and see what happens."

"I'm serious. Just cause he older don't mean nothin'."

"If you so bad touch the car then." Markise edged him on. "Go 'head."

Cray had talked so much shit that a challenge was placed on the table. If he said the wrong thing, it could end in a dare. And if he was presented with a *dare*, and didn't follow through, he'd forever be a punk.

Cray looked at the shiny Audi. His heart raced just thinking about the beef he'd be in if he thought about touching the man's ride.

"I ain't doin' nothin' just cause you say do it," Cray retorted. "And I'm not scared either."

"Yeah, okay," Markise said.

"I *dare* you," Jason challenged.

The words resonated in Cray's head. It was official. He'd said the wrong thing and had to eat his own words. As the seconds went by, he hoped Melody would come back outside and pull off. Then he could get off easy. Because dare or no dare, everyone could agree that it would be suicidal to touch the man's ride with him present.

"Awwww...big bad Cray scared!" Jason pointed at him.

"Damn, dug! I thought you were tough," Markise added making matters worse.

Cray stood up straight and focused. There were positives and negatives to disrespecting Melody's request to leave his ride alone. The positive was that if he touched it, he could silence Markise and Jason's asses with the quickness, which would ultimately mean he could talk as much shit as he wanted to, and nobody could question him. The negative, and of course the most dangerous, was that if he touched his ride and got caught, he could see his grave before his drug addicted parents would.

He looked up at Melody's house door and saw it was closed shut. So he walked coolly over to the car, glancing back at his friends once. He smiled to let them know he wasn't scared. He was inches from his ride when he reached out and placed his left hand completely on the car. His mission was complete plus he proved his point. He wasn't a punk and he was still the kid that could be counted on to follow through on a dare. There was nothing else to be said.

And then he heard, "I knew you were scared!" Jason lifted his chubby arm and pointed in his direction.

What was the problem? He proved the exact opposite and yet Jason acted as if he'd done nothing. To silence him for once and for all, he moved back toward the car, leaned up against it and posed for thirty seconds. He was lifting his body preparing to move when Melody came out and saw him.

"What the fuck?!" He exclaimed as he jumped down three stairs at one time to get at him.

Cray leaped off his car and was about to take off running when Melody's flunkies caught him. Markise and Jason stood in shock.

"Aye…he was just playin', man," Markise offered.

"Yeah," Jason cosigned. "He wasn't tryin' to mess up yo ride."

"Did I ask you lil dirty mothafuckas to talk to me?" Melody questioned. They shook their heads no. "Den why you talkin'?"

Without waiting for their answer, he glared at Cray. His flunkies had Cray up in the air by the hood of his coat. His legs dangled inches from the ground.

"Put the lil nigga down," Melody instructed as he approached him. "You must got a problem puttin' yo dusty ass on my ride."

"Sorry, man." Cray said, shaking his head. He was so scared he could've peed on himself.

"Fuck sorry! What's ya problem? You think I want a dirty nigga like you leanin' on my ride?"

By this time Grimy Mike, Corey who was called Charms, Justin Doles and James had gathered around to see Melody punk Cray.

"Yo got high waters on!" Grimy yelled adding insult to injury. He wasn't nothing but an instigator. And because Melody had an audience now, he made things worse.

"I should pay one of these lil niggas out here to fuck you up! Which one of ya'll wanna to get paid?" he asked as he looked around and grabbed his stack of cash from his pocket. Grimy Mike and Charms raised their hands. Doles stood on the sidelines laughing.

"I said I was sorry." Cray kept his voice steady, trying not to show his terror. He heard of the things Melody did to people for less. He knew he had fucked up and fucked up royally. "What you want me to do? Damn!"

Jason and Markise's mouths dropped.

"Oh you tryin' to break bad?"

Cray didn't respond.

"Yeah you definitely tryin' to break." He cracked his knuckles. Whop! Whop!Whop!

Melody punched him three times in the chest. Cray felt the wind flow from his body when he fell to the ground. Markise ran over to Melody and swung missing him terribly. He wasn't even remotely close. Melody laughed the entire time as he bopped the hell out of his right ear. Jason didn't bother getting up after seeing his friends spread across the ground. But then again, no one expected him too.

Instead of Cray running home, he stood up, dusted the back of his pants off, and faced Melody again. Now instead of being scared, he looked at him dead in the eyes. More people started crowding around and Cray recognized the faces of Jinx who stayed in trouble and Vic who smoked cigarettes all the time and lived around the way. They pretty much stayed to themselves even though people said they were thieves.

"Oh shit! Let me find out this lil nigga got heart." *Whop! Whop! Whop!* Three more body blows.

This time Melody hit him a little harder. Although he wasn't putting all of the force he could have into Cray's body, he did hit him hard enough to do damage. Cray felt all sorts of pain ripple through his arms and chest. But the fighter in him wouldn't allow him to bow down.

Again Cray stood up and again Melody gave him two body blows each session. The final time Cray could barely stand up straight, yet he looked him in his eyes and stared him down. He was bruised but no longer afraid. His friends looked at him in utter amazement. This surpassed the clout he *ever* could've gained from a mere dare or double dare. He had gained the respect of his friends on a whole notha level.

"You's a tough little mothaphucka," Melody said as his flunkies agreed. "If your folks weren't linin' my pockets you coulda got hurt. Now get out my face befo' I hit you wit somethin' you won't be able to get up from."

Cray didn't know what *linin' his pockets* meant, and he didn't care. He just walked off slowly. His body was inflamed and hurt all over. But it didn't matter. He faced the beast and didn't back down and everybody on the street were his witnesses. No one knew it then, but what just happened formed the beginning of a monster. Right before the crowd dispersed Jinx walked up to Cray.

"I like how you handled that shit. He always fuckin' wit niggas." Jinx said.

Cray just nodded like he was extra tough.

"I'll get up with you lada."

"One." Cray responded.

Markise and Jason felt more powerful just by being around Cray. He was no longer the little dusty kid. Now he had clout.

"That was some crazy shit!" Markise said, holding his ear.

"I know!" Jason added.

"I told ya'll I wasn't scared." Cray tried not to limp. "He bleed just like me."

TARA PLEASANT
WASHINGTON, D.C.
TRUSTED FRIEND

After dinner, when Kavon remembered he left something in his car, Tara took the time to talk to Shy in private. She knew time was of the essence so she had to be quick. The moment Kavon shut the door, she said, "Come here, Shy!" She grabbed him by the hand and led him to the kitchen.

"What's up, baby?" he asked, noticing her excitement. "You a'ight?" He hovered over her. "Somebody fuckin' wit you?"

"Nobody's messing with me, Shy." She giggled at his over protectiveness.

"Well what's up?" He looked angered. Ready to unleash rage.

"I'm okay unless you consider being pregnant a problem." Tara grabbed his face, calming him down instantly. His shoulders relaxed and his face softened. Her touch soothed the most savage of beasts.

"What?" he whispered, looking into her eyes. "You what?"

"I said I'm pregnant, honey. Me and Kavon are having our first baby!" She jumped in place as if she was ready to explode.

"Word?"

"Word." She giggled.

He was silent for a moment until she said, "Are you gonna say somethin' or just stand there lookin' silly?"

For a second it looked as if he wasn't happy about it.

Eventually, he picked her up and hugged her lightly. She smelled the Irish Spring soap he always used on his skin.

Placing her down gently, he said, "I'm 'bout to be a godfather!" He beat his like King Kong.

"Yes. Are you happy for us?"

"You know I am."

He appeared enthused and she loved every bit of it. He was the first person Tara told because she didn't have family in the United States. They disowned her after learning she sold herself as an internet bride to Paris for money. And even though she didn't marry him, they never spoke to her again despite her constant letters. All she wanted was a better life in America, the place where dreams come true.

"He doesn't know so you can't say anything," Tara whispered. "I'm gonna tell him next week."

"Why you waitin'? I'm sure he'll want to know he's bout to have a seed. That's all that nigga talk about."

"Cause I know he's gonna ask me to marry him next week that's why." Tara threw her head back and laughed.

"And how do you know that?" He leaned on the counter.

The look on his face told her she'd gotten it right. But Shy had no intentions of confirming the proposal either which way and she didn't expect him to.

"Cause he's been running around here all week rubbing my ring finger for no reason, that's why. Come on now, you know men aren't good with hiding stuff from women."

"Some men aren't...but you'd be surprised in the stuff I can hide. I'm good at keeping secrets. You can trust me. Always." He gave her a look that said she could trust him with anything that went on between them. Tara noticed the difference in the way he looked at her and felt slightly uncomfortable.

"I know, Shy. And I love you for it."

"But forget all that." He stood up straight. "Let's talk about the fact that you let us smoke around you." He walked toward her and rubbed her shoulders. "You liable to give the baby a contact. You can't be around that shit, Tara!"

"I'll be fine. Don't start acting all funny on me, Shy." She looked serious. "Keep callin' me a knucklehead and all that other shit you say out your mouth. Besides, I'm only three months." She rubbed her slightly plump belly. As thin as she was, her stomach looked more like she was full than that she was pregnant.

"I'll treat you as if you never said a word to me." Shy smooched her head a little. "You can count on it."

"Good." She kissed him on the cheek. "Did I tell you I'm so grateful for everything you did for me? With bringing Kavon into my life and saving me?"

"Yes, but I keep tellin' you it's all good."

"I know, but I'm serious. If it wasn't for you, who knows where I might be right now."

"Somebody woulda scooped you up. If it wasn't Kavon, it would've been me."

"We would've gotten on each other's nerves."

"We'll never know now will we?"

"No. We'll never know." Tara touched his face. "Are you truly happy for me?"

"Yeah. I am. Kavon's a good dude. He loves you."

"What ya'll doin' in the kitchen?" Kavon questioned opening the front door closing it behind him. "Fixin' his big ass anotha plate?"

"Naw, man. I'm tryin' to get her to dump your ass and run away with me."

"You must be a glutton for punishment." He laughed.

"Naw. For real I'm tryin' to get her to let you roll with me to Curtbone's cabaret tonight."

"Well, what she say?" He smiled, marching into the kitchen.

"You can go," Tara said, pleased Shy had a lie available although it would mean not spending a night at home with her man. He walked up to her and wrapped his arms around her waist. "Just as long as you come back to me tonight." She gripped his dick before kissing him passionately. "That's all I care about."

"There's no place I'd rather be, girl. You know that shit."

"Well, have fun." Tara released her hold on him. She smiled, good-naturedly at Kavon.

"I guess I'm rollin' wit' you then." Kavon hugged Tara again but studied Shy quizzically. There was something in his eyes that he didn't like.

"Well get dressed, B!"

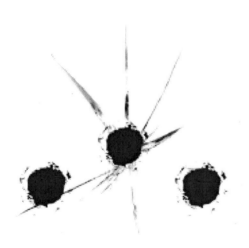

KAVON CARTIER
LARGO, MARYLAND
TASTE LIKE CANDY

The Largo Mansion in Mitchellville, Maryland was packed with all the heavy hitters of the industry for the All White Affair. Although it was a cold winter day in January, the air wasn't as brisk as it had been earlier.

Curtbone's cabarets always brought out the hottest females and the richest niggas on the scene. And the moment Kavon and Shy hit the doors, their shoulders dropped and they strolled in like players. They were among their element so for real, it was nothing but a thang. L.L. Cool J's "I'm Bad" roared through the speakers. They took a quick picture together to capture the moment and went on about their business.

"Would you like some champagne?" a beautiful white woman asked who was standing by the door with a bottle of Moet on ice in a gold bucket.

"Yeah," Shy said as he lifted two champagne glasses with 14k gold on the rim.

He handed one to Kavon who was too busy scoping the scene, that he didn't see him with the drink. It was so crowded inside the hall that you could barely move. But with all the thick asses rubbing up against them, who cared? But being majors meant that a special VIP section awaited them in the back of the cabaret.

"Nigga, take this shit." Shy said getting his attention.

"My bad. I zoned out."

Shy laughed. "It's a whole lot to give up ain't it?"

"There you go. Let's just enjoy the party."

Kavon finally accepted his drink as they moved through the crowd kicking it with a few dudes they knew.

With every pound or handshake he gave Kavon was beginning to wonder if getting out of the game for Tara was a good idea after all. He loved women, fast money and his freedom. But if he married Tara, all of that would change. *What the fuck I'm gonna do besides hustle?* He thought. Sure the real estate business was lucrative but it would mean learning the business from scratch and he didn't have anything outside of an eighth grade education.

I can't think about this shit right now. He thought as he sipped on his champagne and eyed a few women in their skimpy outfits.

He was still thinking about how much different his life would be when he saw Candy, his ex-girl. You see, Candy wasn't any ordinary girl. She was the one woman who captivated his heart, cracked it, and threw it away. Although she couldn't touch Tara in the looks department, her *Fuck Game* ran rings around Tara's.

She strutted toward Shy and Kavon, pushing a few people lightly to pass them. The moment Shy saw her, he almost choked on his champagne. Her hair was hard curled in a mean asymmetric and her gold earrings highlighted her chocolate brown skin.

When she finally came into view, Kavon saw the Le Coq Sportiff one-piece dress she rocked. Even though it was a little sportier than what everyone else was wearing, her large breasts, thick ass and flat stomach suddenly made it acceptable.

"Kavon, Kavon, Kavon," Candy sang, seductively, grabbing one of his arms and wrapping it around her waist. "I see you still lookin' good." She pushed her breasts against his muscular chest. Suddenly it was as if they were alone.

"Good gawd!" Shy gawked, eyeing her body. "Damn, Candy, is it sweet?" he said loud enough to be heard over the music. "'Cause it sho look good."

"I don't know why you worried about it," she informed him, glancing at him only briefly before returning her sights to Kavon's fine ass. "You never got a lick or taste of this pussy and you ain't gonna. Go sit your beastly ass down somewhere."

"And you mean!" Shy laughed, stealing one last look. "On that note, I'ma find me somethin' I can get into." He gave Kavon dap, then shook his head at how sexy Candy was again.

Kavon felt his heart beat increase slightly. Candy did something to him. And although he tried to hide it, not a lot had changed. He even caught a few niggas checking her as she played him close.

"How you been?" He inhaled her apple-smelling perfume.

"I'm good," he said as he wrapped both of his arms around her waist and looked into her eyes. He was doing this in an attempt to gain some control over the situation. "I see you still sexy as a mothafucka."

"Whateva, boy. If I'm so sexy, you wouldn't be with that Spanish bitch."

"Brazilian." He winked.

"Whatever." Her tone was sharp and he could tell she didn't like Tara being thrown up in her face. But if she hadn't fucked up, they would still be together. "You know I was trying to get back with you, K."

"I know you tryin' to play games that's about it."

"I'm serious, K!" Candy hit him lightly on the arm, never removing her body from his. "I tried how many times? You act like you don't even know me no more. What, you in love or somethin'? Just tell me and I'll stop callin' you."

Maybe this is a test. He thought. If he fucked Candy one last time and he still wanted to marry Tara, then he'd know his love for Tara was real.

"Stop fuckin' wit me, girl." Kavon pulled away to get the waitress to bring him two more glasses of champagne, one for him and the other for Candy. When he got them he placed his empty glass on her platter. "You like playin' games."

"Well, what I got to do to prove to you I'm not?" Candy licked suggestively on the edge of the glass with her pink wet tongue.

"You tell me." Kavon gazed right into her eyes. He wanted to fuck her on the dance floor. As they stared at each other, money started falling everywhere. A few ballers thought it would be a good idea to waste cash just because they could.

"I'm tryin' to be with you tonight." A fifty dollar bill fell on her breasts and he tucked it in her cleavage. "So what you tryin' to do?"

"You wanna bounce or what?" Kavon suggested no longer able to hold back.

When she caught the glimmer in his eyes, Candy said, "You ain't said nothin' but a word. Wait right here. I'll be back."

She sashayed away fast enough to get wherever she was going, but slowly enough for him to check her body out as she moved. She made sure her hips swiveled and swirled with each step. When she was completely out of Kavon's sight, he looked for Shy. He had to tell him he was gonna get up with him later and the way he ogled her juicy ass, he knew he'd understand. He spent five minutes looking for him but couldn't find his ass nowhere.

Where da fuck this nigga go so quick? He wondered.

He had given up his search when he saw the reason for his exit approaching him.

"You ready?" Candy smiled. She smelled more like apples than she did when she left and her lips were glossier. He figured she went into the bathroom moments earlier to freshen up.

"Yeah. Just let me make a phone call right quick," Kavon said as he spotted the waitress.

He asked to use the phone and she took him over to it. He paged Shy with the code that meant he got a ride. Although he hadn't used it in a while, he knew the moment Shy saw it he'd know the deal.

Candy led him out by his hand as all the dudes gave him the certified look of approval after seeing how thick she was. He had to hit that ass properly tonight because no matter what, he wanted her to know that she had a good thing and she lost it.

They were outside in front of her candy apple red Toyota Forerunner when she opened the car door for herself and threw him the keys.

"You drive now." She winked. "I'll ride later."

"No doubt." He said catching them.

They pulled up at the Holiday Inn off New York Avenue in D.C. With every turn he made, he started thinking about what he was doing to Tara. She loved him and he knew it was hard enough finding a trustworthy female, especially one as beautiful as Tara. And here he was risking it all. For a slut at that.

Kavon parked in front of the hotel, gave Candy the money for the room and she went to get it. His fingers tapped on the steering wheel and his mind raced.

"We're in room 614," Candy said, returning to the truck.

"A'ight," He said, shorter with her than he was earlier.

As he walked through the lobby and onto their floor with Candy still holding his hand, he wondered what Tara was doing. Glancing down at his watch he figured she was probably about to take a shower. If he dumped Candy's ass he'd be able to catch her in time to jump into the shower with her, something she loved.

When they made it to the room door she said, "Are you okay?"

Kavon reached down and kissed her. He loved to kiss.

"I can't do this."

"You can't be fuckin' serious?!" Candy yelled.

"No, shawty…I'm *dead* serious."

"Is this about that bitch?!" she demanded, her arms folded.

"Yeah. I can't do this to her, Candy. She don't deserve this."

"You sound like a weak ass nigga."

"Call it what you will. I ain't fuckin' wit' you."

"Ugggghhhh! I can't believe I even left with your ass! And yo' dick some trash." She angrily pointed at him.

"Is that right, bitch?" he scoffed.

"Yes, that's mothafuckin' right! Why you think I dumped you in the first place? I need a man who can handle this, and it's obvious you can't do it." Her tone was sassy.

Kavon knew she was mad that he was dropping her off without banging her back out, but the comment about his dick did bruise his ego a little.

"A'ight, Candy. I said what I had to say. Here are your car keys and I'll get up with you lada."

"Don't bother, you weak ass, bastard! You must be gay to turn down pussy this good!" she yelled as he walked down the hall.

"Fuck you, bitch! I'm out."

Candy screamed the entire time he was walking but he ignored her. He remembered seeing a few cab drivers circling outside of the hotel. If he hurried, he'd be home in time to lick the water off of Tara's body. And that was all he was thinking about.

In The Room

Candy paged somebody five times with 911 behind the number from the hotel room. She had to tell him that the plan was a bust. She knew that if she didn't get a hold of him, all hell was going to break loose and she'd be to blame.

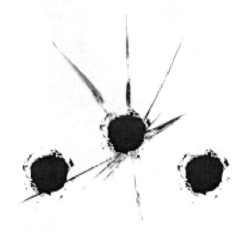

TARA PLEASANTS
OUT OF BODY EXPERIENCE

Tara was preparing for her shower. Walking over toward the adjustable light switch in her extra large bathroom, she set it to dim. Afterward she placed her silk red nighty on the sink next to her towel. She couldn't wait for Kavon to come through their doors to make love to her. She already knew he'd be intoxicated and extra horny after dancing up on some skeezer vying for his attention. The thought alone made her smile. Something about drunken sex always turned her on.

She ran her hands over her small belly and smiled inside. *Wait till he finds out he's gonna be a daddy.* She thought. *He's gonna love me even more.*

God had been so good to her and sometimes she felt undeserving. It frightened her that before meeting Kavon, she'd led the life of a prostitute. It didn't matter that men and women paid the big bucks to be with her. She knew a hoe by any other name was still the same. And although she didn't divulge all of her secrets to Kavon, she did hint around to her reasons for being in this country. But in Kavon's mind, most of the women he dealt with were hoes they just didn't know it.

Loving music while she showered, she turned on the waterproof radio and stopped when she heard Atlantic Star's "Always." It was one of her favorites. She hummed the words and looked for the soap. She moved the soap briskly over her body until it created a thick creamy foam. She contemplated making herself feel good until her baby got home. Playing with her pussy never hurt anybody.

Just like Kavon, she loved the softness of her skin. But when she thought she heard the front door slam downstairs, she decided to let Kavon do all the work. Normally the alarm would sound but they were changing providers and it wouldn't be reactivated until tomorrow.

She counted down the seconds before he'd enter the shower like he always had after coming home from the club. Like always, the moment he came into the bathroom, he flipped off the light switch and walked toward the shower.

"Home already, huh?" she cooed.

"Mmm Mmmm," he responded.

"Miss me?" Tara giggled.

"Mmmmm Hmmmm."

"You gonna do all those things you did to this pussy last night?"

Silence.

She backed up against the shower curtain so he could reach her. She loved feeling his hands against her body first. On cue he reached in the shower and wrapped his arms around her waist, nothing but the wet shower curtain between them. He placed his hands between her legs and softly touched her breasts. There was something about his touch that felt different. She ignored it.

"Mmmmmmm," she moaned.

She pushed back further into him so she could feel his thickness grow. Her head dropped backwards and she was anxious. As far as she was concerned the game was over and she was ready to get down to business. But *something* felt different about his body too. Not quite right.

"Kavon," she whispered, wanting to hear his voice. "Why don't you cut on the lights and join me inside here. The water is warm and I miss you."

Instead of being taken up on her offer, she felt a force rip her out of the shower and throw her onto the cold floor. The wetness from her body mixed with soap caused her to slide a few feet on her back. For a minute she didn't know what happened because the wind had been ripped from her body. She tried to reach for the door handle. But without warning, she was dragged by her legs into a wider area within the pitch darkness of the bathroom. She heard the door lock. Her body shivered.

"Kavon!" she cried out for help despite knowing he wouldn't be home for hours. "Kavon, help me!"

"Shut up, bitch!" The stranger spoke. His voice muffled.

"Who are you?" she sobbed. "And why are you doing this to me?"

Silence.

"Please don't hurt me. I'm pregnant."

Silence.

The perpetrator said nothing more. He held her down with the force of his large body and she could feel him rustling at his pants. He was getting ready to rape her. All she could think about was her baby and the pain Kavon would feel once he'd learned he lost his unborn child. He wanted nothing more than a beautiful little girl and she prayed everyday that God would bless them with one. It was settled. She had to fight for her life. She had to fight for their lives.

With all the strength she could muster she hit him so hard in the face she hurt her own hand. Whop!

"Ouch!" he responded to the pain as he grabbed her wrist.

This angered her attacker and he viciously took a bite out of her face. She screamed out in agony. A small piece of her skin smacked against the bathroom floor. He pinned her down even harder and pressed all of his weight onto her thin body. He was a monster. She could do nothing but allow him to do what he will. If she fought, she knew things would get worse.

Going against everything she believed in, she widened her legs, turned her head to the side, and let him penetrate her vagina. She wept silently. No fighting. No fussing. No nothing. Her spirit was weak and she was taken back to a moment in Brazil in which a member of her church raped her repeatedly.

For thirty minutes, her assailant went in and out of her body, pushing her into the hard bathroom floor. Although he was obviously someone who didn't care for her, something about him was startlingly familiar. So familiar it scared her even more. Like the preacher at her church, she felt she trusted this person at one time. But the darkness concealed his identity.

When he bent down to turn her abused body around so that her stomach pressed against the floor, she got a whiff of a familiar scent. It was the same scent she smelled whenever she hugged a long time friend of the family. Irish Spring soap. Although she hadn't cried since she made up her mind to let him rape her, the moment she knew who it was, her body shook from head to toe.

With her belly against the floor and his pressure still upon her, she prayed to make it out of this alive. She was so frightened she didn't realize she said his name out loud.

"Shy."

"I really wish you didn't know it was me." He told her, flipping her over entering her anus from the front. Instead of being delicate considering her condition, he raped her harder than before. It was as if he was taking out all of his anger on her body. "I know you like it rough. Kavon told me you like to be fucked like a whore sometimes."

"Why, Shy? *Whhhhy*? I loved you," she sobbed, her chest feeling as if it were caving in.

"Because I'm tired of you teasin' me." He moaned in between his words. "You know you been wantin' me ever since I found yo ass suckin' dick. All them kisses and havin' me fight your battles cuz yo man to weak to do it himself. I'm tired of that shit. Mmmmmmmm." He moaned again. "And then what you do? Have this nigga's seed! Fuck that shit! I'm bout to give you an abortion the old-fashion way. Then you gonna tell his ass you can't be with him no more. You hear me?!" He pumped her harder and harder.

"Please, Shy. I can't do that."

She had never experienced anything so horrific in all her life. The force. The reason. Nothing made sense. Sure, Shy always had come to the rescue when she needed him, but she thought he was family. She thought he loved her.

"What about Kavon? He's your friend."

"What about that nigga? I'm sick of that dude."

This was the worse thing she could've experienced. She would've preferred being raped by a total stranger than by a man she trusted with all of her heart and soul.

"And if you tell him, I'ma kill you," Shy growled. "Shiiiiiittt, yo ass feel as good as your pussy. I see why dude bout to put a ring on dat finger."

She never dreamed confirmation of Kavon's marriage proposal would come by way of rape. He pounded her over and over again before he ejaculated inside of her. His panting was heavy and she could tell he was intoxicated. Finally he flipped on the lights showing his face. She focused on him best she could, due to being in total darkness for so long.

"Now hear me and hear me good. You will leave that nigga or else I'ma come back and kill him and you. You got one week to be ready to bounce wit' me."

He looked like a madman as he ranted. There were wrinkles in his face and he didn't look the same.

Saying nothing else, he punched her so hard she passed out.

KIRK BOWLER CHIEF OF POLICE WASHINGTON D.C.
LIKE TAKING CANDY FROM A NIGGER

Kirk sat back in the large black leather chair in his office and twirled around. He was in full uniform as he glanced down at the four stars, which symbolized his rank. His tanned skin and chiseled bone structure were more fitting of a 29-year-old model than the chief of police.

"Sir...Mr. William Jamison is here to see you." His young white secretary said.

"Thanks, Jessica, let him in."

Williams walked in and for a brief second, they exchanged mental glances. They were victorious. They'd been trying to put Kirk in the mayor's way for a minute and it finally paid off.

"Congrats! So how does it feel to be the Chief?" he asked, sitting in the seat across from his desk.

"You know me. I've always been in charge." He lit a cigar. "Now it's time to prove it."

"I see modesty is not a quality you possess."

They laughed.

"You're right about that...and now that Janice helped expose Gibson's drug use, things are turning out better than ever. All we have to do is form a plan of attack."

"I'm already on top of it. My secretary's bringing me the files of all my top cops. I'll get rid of most of them to make space for our boys in the KYC. It's gonna take some time, but after I'm done things will never be the same."

"It'll be like taking candy from a nigger." Williams said as jovial laughter continued to fill the office.

NYZON PEATE
NIGHTMARES WHEN AWAKE

He was four years old, in the back seat of a car buckled in his seat belt. Rain pounded ferociously against the windows. A woman with beautiful auburn hair talked to him from the front seat of the car as she drove. He couldn't see her face, but her voice soothed him.

"Don't worry, honey. We're almost there." She spoke in an angelic voice. He rested easy knowing that whoever she was, she would protect him. That's all he needed to know at the time. And that's all that mattered. Suddenly the car rocked and the woman who was once calm, appeared on edge.

"Oh, no!" she called out, scaring Shelton. "Shelton…I love you."

The next thing he knew the car windows came caving in on them and the car rolled five or six times and his tooth broke against the door's silver handle. And Nyzon woke up screaming.

"You okay, honey?" Angel, his babysitter asked as she lay horizontally in the bed, rubbing the sweat from his face. Angel watched him whenever his mother worked overtime at DC General Hospital as a nurse.

"I'm fine." He sat up straight and looked at Angel's eyes. His mouth was dry and parched and he felt slightly embarrassed.

She clicked on the lamp and handed him a cup of water sitting on his nightstand. He eyed the cute little red dress set she wore but more importantly her perky breasts which rose slightly from under it like fresh baked bread.

Gulping down half the water, he wondered if his mother told her about his constant nightmares and the fact that he didn't know why he was having them.

"As long as you're fine. You had me scared there for a minute. What were you dreaming about?"

"Nothin'."

She could tell he didn't want to talk about it and she left the matter alone. Instead she adjusted in the bed as if something was on her mind, and Nyzon noticed. He had it for her bad. She had beautiful chestnut-colored skin with the biggest tig-o-bitties he ever laid eyes on. Ironically "Let Me Love You Down," by Ready For The World played on the radio.

"I understand you don't want to talk about it." Angel said looking up at him. "I bet all the girls like you at school."

"Most of them." He smiled unable to look into her eyes. "Why you say that?"

"Cuz you cute and I know you know it." She licked her lips and he looked away.

"I'm a'ight. You win some and lose some you know?" He rubbed his hand over his waves.

Without notice, she sat up straight, reached in and pulled him to her, pressing her titties to his face in the process.

"What was that for?" Nyzon asked puzzled, not wanting her to let him go.

"That was just for bein' you." She responded pulling away. Something about the way she looked at him tonight was different. "Did you like it?"

He nodded yes. She hugged him again but tighter this time.

His heart beat like someone was using his body to play drums and he ran his hands down her back. He was a natural at his game.

"You ever kissed a girl before Nyzon?"

"Once or twice."

"Wanna kiss me?"

Before he could answer she pressed her pouty lips against his. His eyes remained opened as he stared at her closed lids.

"Ummmmm." She nodded her head in approval and smiled. "Nice. Real nice."

"Thanks." He shrugged his shoulders. He was desperately trying to be the Nyzon girls knew him for. All he could do was hope it was working. "I told you I kissed a girl."

She giggled. "You were right and it was just like I thought. I know the girls love you."

"I told you I do a'ight," Nyzon said, feeding his ego.

"Wanna go all the way?" she asked.

"Wh...what you mean?" His eyes looked her over and he licked his dry lips.   "I said do you wanna go all the way with me?"

There was no way on earth his boys would believe this. He didn't even believe it. He needed some proof. But the closest thing to evidence would mean using the fat ass brown tape recorder under his bed. If he pulled it out, she'd spot it from a mile away. He had to rely on his own memory for this one.

"Yeah...I do." He wondered what all the way meant.

She lifted up her blouse and exposed her white bra. This was getting better by the second and he felt a strange sensation between his legs that he couldn't describe. Placing one of his hands over her breasts, he quivered. And when he was ready, she placed his other one on the second. She dropped her head back and moaned giving him the impression she was enjoying herself. He wasn't nervous like he thought he'd be. Until it finally happened.

"I see you watchin' me Nyzon. Do you like watching me?"

Right now the only thing he was watching was titties.

He nodded yes.

"You wanna kiss them?"

His eyes widened as if he looked harder, he'd wake up from a dream.

"I don't know."

"Come on, Ny. Kiss them for me," she urged. "If you kiss them good, I'll kiss you back."   It was settled. He was going to go all the way and if he failed, at least he tried. Nyzon placed his mouth on her nipples and kissed them like he'd kissed his mother's cheek.

Angel giggled. "Open your mouth, Ny." He did.

"Wider."

He did.

"That's it, Ny." She approved. "Now use your tongue."

He did but removed it quickly.

"No silly." She giggled. "Keep it there and move it around and stuff. Like you sucking candy."

He did.

"Mmmmmm. That's nice, Ny. That's real nice. Keep doin' that."

He wasn't quite sure if he liked this part of it or not plus the uncomfortable feeling in his pants had gotten worse. His penis was as stiff as a rock. With all the pussies he fingered, he never got hard. And as if she knew, she reached her hand in his pajamas and touched it gently.

"I see you like me a lot." She giggled.

How she know that? He thought.

She constantly stroked him until he felt a wave come over him. His body shook as she moaned. He was afraid of what he was feeling, but at the same time, hoped the feeling wouldn't go away.

With one last stroke she caused his wildest dreams to come true. It was a tingling sensation and it was the best feeling in the world. He fell into her chest with his mouth still open on her breast. He was stuck. She giggled again and moved him backward.

"You okay, Ny?" she said, adjusting her bra and pulling her shirt down.

Silence.

"That was nice wasn't it?" She asked.

Silence and panting.

If you keep our little secret," she continued. "We can have fun every timeI watch you. It will be just you and me. Would you like that?"

Silence.

"Ny." Angel sounded a little concerned. He seemed stunned and she didn't want him telling his mother. "Can you keep our secret?"

He nodded yes.

"Good." She smiled wiping her hand over his forehead.

"Cause I like you. A lot."

"I like you, too," he answered, still coming off an emotional roller coaster.

"That's good, Ny." She walked toward the door. "I hope you have sweet dreams now."

He nodded again trying his best to maintain his cool.

He was about to let her leave when he remembered something. "Hey Angel, was that your boyfriend who dropped you off earlier?"

"In the Saab?"

"Naw…he ain't even as cute as you." She cooed. "Good night Ny, I'll see you later."

When she closed the door he sunk into his cozy bed reflecting on everything that happened. Prior to then he played with a few girls' coochies but nothing serious. He had to make her his girl. He wasn't even going to pursue Monesha, the girl he met in school anymore. He wanted Angel, and would stop at nothing to get her.

CAROLYN JAMISON
WASHINGTON D.C.
LIKE DADDY, NOT LIKE DAUGHTER

Carolyn and her mother Judge Elizabeth Jamison, were walking on the chilly streets of Georgetown, shopping for fresh fruits and breads. Elizabeth wore a full-length black fur to combat the weather, and Carolyn wore a white, waist length cotton coat with matching gloves.

The streets were packed and the sound of cars driving up and down the wet streets resonated through the small town. Carolyn's arm was looped inside of her mother's while they walked side by side.

"So how's school coming along?" Elizabeth asked as she peered through a few windows for something to catch her eye.

"It's okay...but my Social Justice Professor who is black, hates my guts. At least I think so." Carolyn rested her head on her mother's shoulder as they strolled down the sidewalk.

"Nonsense, everyone likes you. And with as much money as your father and I have poured into that school, they should be in love with you." She giggled at her own dry humor.

"Not her. It's like she thinks I'm going to take all the black men or something. For instance, I requested to work with a partner in class for this project that requires me to work with this non profit organization called "Take Back The Streets", and she gave me somebody I can't stand to talk to, let alone work with as a partner."

"Oh...well who's the partner you wanted? I can make a call and it can happen."

Carolyn hadn't expected her mother to ask her that.

"Oh...he's just a boy. Nothing serious. Don't worry about it, ma."

"Is it, the Moore boy?" She stopped and gazed into her daughter's eyes. "I hear he has an internship lined up with Jenkins and Tony's Lawfirm already. Do you know that company generates over 20 billion dollars in revenue a year?" She rubbed her daughter's hand. "He'll be set for the rest of his life."

"Oh...yeah...he's the one," Carolyn lied. "Well anyway she asked the class who we wanted to work with and I made my selection and instead of honoring it, she gave me some rude ass loud mouthed black girl instead."

"Well you know how it is, Carolyn. You just have to remember what your father says. We have to do what we must to blend in. It'll sharpen your skills to disguise what you really feel because as much as I hate to admit it, niggers aren't going anywhere. We just have to make more opportunities for good white folk."

"I know…it's just frustrating sometimes."

"It's an outrage! Laws are being made everyday for niggers. Imagine if people knew I was married to your father, and he was the head of KYC? I wouldn't be a states judge and they'd probably throw me behind bars. So I play my position, sweetheart and you must too."

Elizabeth did do an excellent job concealing her feelings. Having been a states judge for ten years, no one would've known she was a racist. Still she used her powers on many occasions to sentence people of other races to the harshest of sentences even when it wasn't warranted.

"Just play the game and watch how things will change for the city once Kirk is elected Mayor. You'll see."

They stopped in front of a bakery and looked through the window. "Awww…fresh sourdough bread! It'll be perfect for the shrimp Alfredo I'm making tonight. Let's go in, dear."

"Give me a second, mamma." Carolyn said stopping in her tracks.

"Okay, dear." She looked her over wondering why she wanted to be alone. "I'll see you inside."

Once out of her mother's view, she reached into her purse and grabbed a flask filled with Vodka, downed it and licked her lips. Thinking about her family and how much they differed, troubled her. She knew her mother was right even if she didn't share the total hatred to blacks her parents did. Gulping what was left in her flask, she walked into the store and stood by her mother's side.

The van ride from D.C. to Baltimore was longer than Carolyn preferred. She sat alone in the back seat with her knees uncomfortably pressed against the front seats.

When the car made it to a rundown residential area in Baltimore city, where they had to work, Carolyn gasped when she saw how different the neighborhood looked based on where she lived.

"Here we are," Tina said as they parked in front of some row houses on liberty road. "All we have to do is pass out this literature and remind the kids about basketball camp next year. It shouldn't take more than fifteen or twenty minutes."

Carolyn was zoned out looking at the rundown environment.

"You gonna be okay?" Tina asked sensing her fear. "Cause you don't have to do this if you don't want to."

"Uh…I'll be fine. Why wouldn't I be?" Beads of sweat formed on her head even though it was in the dead of winter. "We just passing out papers. Right?"

Tina and Modell looked at one another and laughed.

"She says she's gonna be okay so I guess she's gonna be okay. Let's go." Modell jumped out the van and opened the door for Tina and then Carolyn.

Carolyn eased out of the van nervous and afraid of *them*...the people she'd been taught to hate her entire life.

"Come on!" Tina said, waving at her. "Stop bein' scared." She thought Carolyn's apprehension was funny especially since she was so big and bold in class.

"I'm not afraid!" She gripped the papers to her closely and walked toward the other side of the van next to them.

Carolyn watched Modell and Tina pass out the literature printed on blue paper. Some people took it, but most told them to leave them alone.

But when they walked up to a row house where six young guys were out on the corner, Carolyn was on edge.

"Fuck ya'll doin' around here?" One of them yelled hopping down off a wall he was sitting on. "I thought I told you not to come around here no more?!"

"You not gonna stop us from comin' around here, Melody," Modell said to him as boldly as he told him to go away. "These kids have a right to know that they're other alternatives instead of slinging drugs and I'm gonna see to it that they know about it."

"You got a fuckin' death wish!" Melody said, so closely to him, he could feel his breath. "I run these mothafuckin' streets and whoever's in em. All you doin' is bringin' unwanted attention round here!"

"Listen...I don't want any trouble, but how many young kids have to die before you realize that there's a problem? I know you don't want no drama around here and I'm not tryin' to bring it. All we wanna do is help."

Another dude stood by Melody's side with his hands nestled inside the thick coat he was wearing.

"I think ya'll should go back to where ya'll came from." The man said smoothly.

"Not until we're done." Tina added looking at them both.

"If I tell ya'll to get the fuck from around here, than believe that I'm doing you a favor. Because there's other ways to make you disappear." Melody opened his coat and revealed his weapon.

"Ohhhh, God!" Carolyn screamed, bringing attention to herself after seeing the gun.

"Who's that bitch?" Melody questioned Modell while glaring at her. Without waiting for an answer, he barked, "J, get her ass out of here."

J-Swizz walked up to her, grabbed her by the arm and took her toward the van. Once there he opened the door.

"Get in." She did. Tina and Modell looked on as he walked her to the car.

"Look…I don't know who you are, but you need to stay away from 'round here. You gonna fuck around and find yourself in a situation you won't be able to get out of."

With that he closed the door.

Carolyn sat in the back seat breathing heavily, trying to focus on what she'd just seen. She was nervous. Scared and confused. And through it all, there was something about him she liked.

"You listenin'?" J-Swizz asked her again.

"Yes…I am." She smiled.

"Good." He said preparing to walk off, stealing another look at her. To him she was beautiful.

J-Swizz returned to the group. And as she watched Modell and Tina talking to the dealers she thought about J-Swizz. There was something that peeked her interest. She was curious. She wanted to know what pulled him to the streets. She wanted to know what kind of person he was. All of these things ran through her mind until Tina and Modell returned to the car. She had to learn more about him, but what she didn't know was how.

KAVON CARTIER
WASHINGTON D.C.
BEST MAN

Kavon sat inside Tara's hospital room and watched Mayor Gibson get dragged away in hand cuffs, after being caught coping drugs from an undercover agent. It was the only thing that played nonstop on the news ever since the operation was blown open a few days ago. As interesting as the story was, all he thought about was his future wife and the fact that she was laying in a hospital bed.

Placing crushed ice over her lips, he thought about the night before, when he realized he didn't have his house keys. And when he thought about losing them fucking with Candy's skank ass, he felt guilty. He still remembered rehearsing his lies over and over as he approached the door to their home. But instead of having to knock, it was wide open. His heart raced and he suddenly felt woozy. His worse nightmares were realized and he knew he'd been robbed, but with his girl inside.

His fighter instinct kicked in and he was preparing to murder whoever had the audacity to step foot into his crib. He had three weapons in his home. One tucked under the bed in his room, one in the kitchen and one under the living room sofa. He dipped in the living room and grabbed the one under the sofa.

He crept through the living room and then up the stairs. All he wanted was for Tara to be okay. They could have everything in that mothafuckin' house but his future wife. But instead of finding Tara safe, he found her bruised, bloodied, and unconscious on the bathroom floor. His body slumped over hers as he gripped her languished body. All kinds of thoughts entered his mind...but it was revenge that dominated his thoughts.

Her legs agape told him off the back she'd been violated sexually. Who would cross him by coming into his home, and raping his girl? For some reason, he thought about everything that happened right before finding Tara in that condition. Kavon didn't know that when Candy dismissed herself from him at the cabaret earlier that night, that she met up with Shy in one of the stalls in the men's restroom.

"You got em?" Shy asked, peering over at Candy.

"Yeah. Here they go right here." She handed Kavon's keys to him. "I told you I'd get em. What you ain't believe me?"

"I know that mothafucka sniffin' behind you." He tucked them in his pockets. "Why you think I had you get em for me?"

She shrugged her shoulders.

"He ain't suspect nothin', did he?" Shy placed his hands on her shoulders and looked into her eyes. "Cuz, I can't have no mistakes," he continued, lines forming in his forehead.

"Look at me...would you be thinkin' bout anything else but Candy?" She boasted.

"You ain't ansa the question. Did he suspect anything?" he was stern with her now. "Did he act funny in any sort of way?"

"No. Trust me, honey. He don't know nothin' and ain't thinkin' bout nothin' but me." She punched her fists onto her hips. "You gotta remember...he don't know you're the reason I left him when I was with him. He's clueless and green. Relax."

"You mean he don't know that I snatched your ass."

"You are so cocky." Her smile told him she loved his attitude.

"But we can never be too sure." Shy wanted her to be a little more serious.

"I know, Shy, but everything went as planned. We're going to a hotel and everything."

"Straight." He smiled devilishly.

"But I do have a question."

"What's up?" He wanted her to cut the small talk and get back to business.

"You want me to fuck him, too?"

"Do what you gotta do to keep his ass busy. I need him gone for at least four hours."

"Cool. So what you gonna do? Rob him?"

Shy contemplated smacking the shit out of her.

"Why the fuck you worried about it?" he quizzed.

He wasn't feeling her bullshit. He knew if he told Candy he was trying to make Kavon stay in the business with him and that he'd been lusting after Tara for two years now, she'd flip.

"I was just askin'." She waved him off. "I mean, I thought ya'll were cool that's all. It don't make me know never mind."

"Good. And just so you know, that nigga's not about business like he use to be."

"Ummm...Hmmmm." She flipped her hand in the air.

She could be a sassy little bitch when she wanted to and Shy couldn't stand that shit about her. On the other hand, she did whatever he asked her to.

"You still gonna stop by and see me tonight—right?"

"It depends." He said looking her up and down like he wanted to eat her alive.

"On what?" she said, growing angry with his lack of attention towards her lately. She couldn't count the number of times he'd say he was on his way over her house and never came.

"On what you willin' to do to convince me to come back tonight."

He stroked his dick. Shy's dick was larger than most women could fathom. And because Candy fucked so much she barely had walls inside her pussy, they meshed just fine.

Knowing what the deal was, she dropped to her knees and placed his dick inside her mouth. She stared up at him. With the power of a Hoover, she sucked him until she made him weak to his knees. As big and as bad as he was, he needed the help of a cane when it came to enduring Candy's sex game just to stand up. He placed his hands on the sides of the wall in the stall and allowed her to go to work. It took all of two minutes before she made him bust, swallowing every last drip.

Wiping her mouth she stood up and faced him. "Is that enough to convince you?"

"What you think?" he smiled as he zipped his white pants. "But if you don't start takin' better care of lil Shawn, I'ma cut you off for good." He continued adjusting himself.

"Don't start that shit, Shy." She put her face in her hands.

"Don't tell me what to start!" he said, grabbing her wrist. "I ain't playin' wit you."

"I got you." She snatched her arm. "I'm gonna always take care of our child. Just as long as you keep givin' me the money to."

With that she extended her hand ready to be blessed.

Shy pulled out the wad in his pocket and gave her eight hundred dollars.

"You got a lot of shit wit you." He tucked the rest back in his pocket.

"And you love every bit of it." She tucked the cash in her bra.

"Shut yo' ass up and get yo' self together." He opened the bathroom door. "And put some more of that lip gloss and perfume on and shit. I don't want him to smell my dick on your breath."

"I got it, baby. Don't worry."

"I'm not, but if you fuck up, you should be."

Kavon glanced over at Tara's battered face. He'd paid the staff over fifty thousand to be sure she was given the best of care. He also requested the best plastic surgeon to repair the damage made from the bite mark on her beautiful face. And to be sure it was money well spent, he found out who the surgeon was and dropped 10g's on him.

As he looked at her, a white nurse walked through the door to check her vitals. She noticed Kavon's eyes were bloodshot red from crying.

"You okay, son?" she asked as she changed her I.V bag.

"I been betta." He took his black Kangol off, and wiped his face with his hands.

"She'll be okay, son. Plenty of people come back from comas. Besides, you have a lot to be thankful for. The baby's doing well." She added.

He grinned when she said those words. Yesterday he found out she was pregnant and he wondered why she hid it from him when she knew how much he wanted a little girl.

"I know." He smiled, focusing on the thought of his baby. He had a name for her and everything. Tiara Cartier. "It still fucks me up that somebody would do this to her."

"I understand, but everything will be okay. Now let me leave you two alone."

When she was gone, he kneeled down by her bedside and kissed her hand. Holding it lovingly he told her if she pulled through, he'd never leave her side again, no matter what. And for the first time since he'd been there, she gripped his hand.

"Baby?" he said as if it were a question more than anything else. He couldn't believe she was showing signs of consciousness. He was told it could take anywhere from a month to a year for her to pull through. "Can you hear me, baby? If you can, grip my hand."

She gripped it again despite her eyes remaining closed.

"Somebody come in here!" he yelled running to the door. "Can I have a doctor please?!"

The same nurse who was just there came running back.

"Is everything okay?" she asked, worried at his outburst. She immediately went to her bedside and observed Tara.

"Yeah! I mean I don't know!" He walked behind the nurse. "She gripped my hand."

"Oh...she gripped your hand. I thought it was something else." She said as if it were a false alarm.

"What do you mean?"

"It happens from time to time with people in comas. It's called a muscular contraction. It's nothing to be alarmed about."

"How you gonna tell me it's a muscular contraction?" he said angry at her response. "I asked her a question and she responded by grippin' my hand."

"Okay, son." She patted his back lightly. "I see you're upset. Let me show you."

"Tara," she said, soothingly by her bed side. She grabbed her hand. "I'm nurse Cassandra Wells. We're pullin' for you, sweetheart, and if you can hear me, please grip my hand."

She waited five seconds and nothing happened. Kavon felt like knocking the bitch to the floor.

"See…it was just a false alarm."

"Whateva!" He brushed her off. "She heard me and I know she did."

"Son, I don't want to set you up for unrealistic expectations, that's all." She tried to diffuse the matter. "Now I have to go, call me if you need me." She left the room.

He looked at Tara, closed his eyes and said a prayer. It was about time for him and God to have a conversation.

"God, I know I'm not the best man. I may even be the worse. I did some things I'm not proud of. A lot of stuff I can't take back. But I love this woman, with all my heart, and I'm askin' that You not punish her for my shortcomings. Please, Father. I'm willing to try my hardest to become a better person. A better man. Amen."

He was finishing his prayer when Shy walked into the room holding a big bouquet of flowers. He strolled in like Big Red at Jimmy's funeral in the movie, *The Five Heartbeats*.

"You a'ight, man?" he asked, placing one hand on his shoulder after placing the flowers on the night table.

The moment Kavon heard his voice he stood up and faced him. His eyes still red and face wet with tears. He was far from a punk, but everything happening to Tara had him fucked up. As if he knew what Kavon needed, Shy gripped him in a manly embrace. Kavon broke down. He hadn't cried that hard since the death of his mother.

"Why, man?" he said, looking at him. "Why would somebody do her like this?"

"I don't know, but when we find out, we gonna murder dem mothafuckas. You hear what I'm sayin', B? We layin' the murder game down." He paced the floor. "And then she carryin' your seed. Is everything okay with that?"

Kavon was still crying when he thought about what he said. How did he know she was pregnant? He didn't have a chance to say anything to him outside of meet him at the hospital, and that Tara had been hurt.

"How you know?" He wiped the tears from his eyes.

"I ain't wanna tell you," he said real low. "But Tara told me in the kitchen the night we went to the cabaret. That's what we were really talkin' about."

"For real?" he said, scratching his head. He heard him, but something didn't sound correct. Why would she tell him before she told Kavon?

"Yeah…she said she had a feeling you were gonna propose and shit cause you kept fuckin' wit her ring finger. So she was going to tell you the night you asked her to marry you. She wanted it to be a surprise."

Kavon smiled when he remembered he may have gone a little overboard with trying to get an idea of her ring size.

"Yeah...I was jive extra."

"I know you fucked up right now, man." Shy said skipping the subject. "But this shit will get handled. You can believe that."

"I know." Kavon confirmed. "They took some cash and some jewelry, too."

"Word? Any idea who did it?"

"None."

"Well I guess you gonna have to stay in the game now." Shy said seriously. "At least until Tara's better."

"For real my man, I'm not thinkin' bout that right now." Kavon thought it a bit insensitive to be talking about business at a time like this.

"I feel you." Shy realized he might have gone too far. "I just want you to know the offer still stands."

Kavon gave him some dap and Shy walked over to Tara's bedside. Wanting to give him some privacy, Kavon sat in the chair across the room.

When he was out of Kavon's earshot, Shy placed one hand on hers and said, "Don't worry, Tara. This shit is almost over. And when you come to, I'ma grab yo ass outta here by your mothafuckin' hair and finish what I started."

All of a sudden Tara's heart monitor sped up. Kavon jumped up and ran to her side.

"What happened?" Kavon pushed him out the way.

"I don't know man. I was talkin' to her and the shit went off." He got out of his way.

Kavon was on his way out to tell someone there was trouble but the doctor and the nurse from earlier came rushing inside. They flew into a frenzy of activity and Kavon was terrified that he had lost Tara for good.

"You two have to leave." The doctor said as more staff members came in.

They didn't move. Both of them wanted to see what was happening. They both had motives. One good. The other bad.

When she opened her eyes, Kavon's heart dropped. She looked scared. It was as if she'd seen the devil. Kavon pushed past the staff members so he could be the first one she saw. She spotted him and reached out for him. The doctors couldn't pull him away if they tried. She had to tell him something and she had to tell him now.

"K...K...Kavon." She said trying hard to speak.

"Yes, baby. Yes. I'm here." He stooped down and clasped her hand. She whispered something in his ear.

The staff members covered Shy's view. He wondered what she was saying. But when Kavon submerged from the hustle of the staff members who were struggling to make sure she was okay, the look in his eyes told Shy everything he wanted to know. And if looks could kill, Shy would be dead. Kavon walked slowly over to him. Shy dug in his coat and put his hand on his heat. Kavon stopped a few feet in front of him when he noticed.

"What she say, man?" Shy asked as Kavon stood directly in front of him. The staff members still on Tara.

"Nothing…she ain't say nothin' man. It's just a muscular contraction." Kavon eyed Shy's hand in his coat pocket.

"Word?" Shy said. "Cause whatever she said can be dealt with right now."

"Naw, main man…there's a time and place for everything." Kavon responded.

"Well, when you're ready for that time, let me know." He said, his hand still on his heat hidden from the average view. He left the room backwards eyes glued onto Kavon's.

"I will see you again."

"Not if I see you first."

"Time will tell." Kavon said. "You can count on it."

CRAYLAND BAILOR
BALTIMORE, JANUARY, 1989
BIRTHDAY BOY

The cool air ripping at his face could not stop Cray from rushing home to see the cake his father got for his birthday. He was so excited he left Markise and Jason at school because Jason had to double back inside to get his house keys and Cray was too anxious to wait.

Once at the door he flew inside leaving the front door swinging.

"Boy what you doin' runnin' in here like that?!" His father was sitting on the couch watching TV with a can of beer in his hands resting on his knee.

"Sorry dad." His breaths were heavy. "Where is it?"

He continued to watch television.

"Where's what?"

Cray thought he was playing with him. He did a little research of his own with his eyes to see if he had the cake stashed somewhere. He remembered he'd tricked him before by hiding the gifts and the cake one year for his birthday.

"Come on, dad." Cray giggled. "Where's the cake?"

All of a sudden, his father burst into laughter. Cray's feet scratched backward confused.

"What was so funny?"

"Nothin'." He started sipping his beer. "I thought I had a son that's all."

Silence.

"Let me find out I'm raising a little girl instead, who's still into cakes and shit! You betta toughen up Cray! You startin' be act weak. Now get the fuck out of my face."

Cray's nose burned a little as he thought about what was happening.

"Now!" he yelled giving him a look that said he was preparing to punch him in his face if he didn't obey him.

Huffing and puffin, Cray bolted through the front door and outside the apartment. His heart ached because his birthday was the one day that belonged to him. He allowed his parents the other 364 days of the year to fuck up his life.

What was he going to tell his friends? They're parents had already gave them the okay to stay over. He hated his life and everything about it.

Once outside Frankie the dog ran up to him. Out of everyone, he migrated to Cray the most. In his mind they were the same. Alone. Unloved and Misunderstood.

Angry and upset, Cray sat on the steps and begin petting the animal. Suddenly he started to think about his fucked up family. His fucked up life, and never having what he wanted. Happiness. Sometimes he wished someone killed him. Better yet, he wished his parents didn't exist anymore. He wished he was strong enough to kill them himself, and then he wouldn't have to wait for them to die. When he came out of his thoughts, he realized he had the dog's neck in his grasp, with both hands. His tongue hung out the side of his mouth and he had squeezed his throat so tightly, he was dead.

Jumping up Cray looked around to see who was watching. No one was. How could he kill the only thing outside of his friends that loved him? His mind raced and he felt worse. He was a killer. He was cold and heartless. He was a little of his father and some of his mother. He made up his mind that he was going for self, no matter what and suddenly a sense of calm came over him.

The dog's death symbolized how he felt about life. The death of Frankie, was just the beginning.

"Cray! Cray!" He heard yelling from his bedroom window.

It sounded like Jason's fat ass.

He walked over to the window and sure enough, Jason was outside staring up at him while Markise was whispering something in some big butt girl's ears. He shook his head at the scene because he felt Markise was worried about the wrong things in life, coochie.

"What?!" He lifted his window allowing the cool air to rush in.

"You comin' out?" Jason asked, his waist-length coat barely covering his stomach.

"Yeah, give me a minute."

"Well hurry up! Yo' cousin Devon out here!"

Devon was his first cousin on his father's side. He was twenty years old and the coolest dude he knew. Devon didn't have as much cash as Melody, but he had enough to floss to be his age.

"A'ight! Tell him I'm comin' out now." He shut the window.

Cray grabbed his book bag and lifted the mattress to grab the gun he found. He looked at it and walked over to the mirror in the aiming position. He knew he didn't know the first thing about using a gun, but if he was scared enough, he ventured to say he would learn. Once the gun was tucked in his bag, he walked out the door.

Outside

Devon leaned against his black Acura Integra and kicked what he thought was knowledge to Cray and his friends. Some of the stories were interesting, but most of them were ridiculous.

The one good thing about Devon coming over was that he always had cash and he was always willing to spend it on them. Devon had his black Eddie Bauer coat on with his Guess jeans and green Gucci sneakers. He was beyond fine and knew it. His deep chocolate skin had a scar directly under his left eye. His hair stayed low and he kept a wave brush with him at all times. The women loved him the moment they laid eyes on him, and he loved them back.

"So we at Crazy John's gettin' some grub, and I'm tellin' dis bitch to get in the car," he started as he ate Shrimp Fried Rice, right out of the Chinese box. "So…she gonna holla 'bout she not ready to go. So I tells the bitch, look bitch, get yo ass in this car or you bout to get left."

He hadn't even gotten out everything before Jason's ass busted out laughing and fell on the ground.

"Yo…what is so funny, dude?" Markise asked as he ate his beef and broccoli with rice. "The man not even finished yet and you laughin'."

Cray shook his head. He knew Jason's beastly ass was more happy to be eating than anything else.

"Leave the lil nigga alone." Devon laughed. "He feelin' me on this shit. So I tells the bitch get in the car. Do you know this broad had a nerve to slap me?"

"For real?" Cray said finally interested. He wasn't into all the stories about the girls and the many ways he fucked them. For real, for real, he thought he was too old to be talking to them about stuff like that anyway. "What you do?"

"I dropped her! Hit her slam in her jaw," he said as if he should've known. "What you think I did?"

"Man, you ain't supposed to be hittin' no females." Markise said shaking his head in disgust before digging in his food. "That's juvenile man."

"Listen to this lil nigga talkin' about somethin' juvenile." He laughed as if he didn't know the first thing about handling women. "Let me school you, lil brother. You gots to keep a woman in check. Got to! Plus, they be likin' that shit."

"I disagree. My father said ain't no man 'spose to be hittin' no woman. We stronger than them anyway. So why put our hands on em?" Markise continued, never backing down from his beliefs. "I mean, let's be real about it. How bad can a girl hurt you?"

"I hit this girl once for poking her finger in my sandwich at lunch one time." Jason responded, desperately trying to have a valuable contribution to the conversation.

"Man, shut yo ass up." Markise laughed. "Hittin' bitches is dumb, but hittin' girls over sandwiches is lame." Markise came down hard on Jason sometimes. He just wanted him to have his own mind, but he never did.

"I don't think so. Sometimes you got to keep yo house in line and hittin' a female is the first step." Cray said. "It's the same thing as if you were disciplinin' a dug. If a dug keep shittin' in the house, you got to keep hittin' his ass. Eventually, he'll get it right."

When Cray finished they were all silent. Prior to now they forgot that his father beat his moms on a regular. Had they remembered, the conversation would've never occured.

"Uh…yeah…you right, lil man." Devon glanced down at his watch. "But let me bounce. I'll get up wit you lil niggas lada. Happy Birthday, Cray, and don't spend all the money I gave you in one place, eitha."

He gave them all pounds, jumped in his ride, blasted "Keep Risin' To The Top" by Doug E. Fresh and sped off. Nobody knew until later, that halfway down the block, Devon would be arrested on drug charges.

The boys were left alone to think about how the convo ended and both of them felt bad for talking about abuse in the first place.

"I'm sorry, man," Markise said. "I forgot."

"I don't want to talk about it." Cray said. "Ya'll wanna see somethin'?"

"Yeah…what?" Jason said, excitedly.

"Come wit' me," Cray clutched his book bag.

They marched further down Liberty Avenue until they saw a little alleyway. Once there, Cray looked all around. When he was sure no one was in sight, he carefully pulled out the gun.

"Oh, shit!" Jason said, totally amused. "Let me hold it."

"Man, put that shit up," Markise said, not feeling the whole gun thing. He backed away a little as Cray held it in his hands.

"Why you scared?" Cray laughed, loving the fear in his eyes.

Markise was tough and it was hard to frighten him, so Cray was getting a kick out of it now.

"Naw, but I know guns are not toys." Unconsciously, his hands flew in the air as if he were protecting his face.

"You sound like one of them dumb ass teachers at school," Jason added. "Let me hold it Cray."

"I don't trust your ass." Cray laughed. "I want Markise to hold it."

"And I said I don't want to!" He fired back. "So put it up, man!"

"Come on," Cray demanded as he walked toward him gun aiming in his direction. "Stop bein' a baby."

Markise backed up onto the brick wall.

"Cray, you actin' real crazy now," he said calmly, noticing his finger was on the trigger. "I don't like guns. So can you please put it up?"

Cray looked at him dead in his eyes. For the first time ever, he had Markise shook. He wasn't a tough kid anymore. He was just a kid.

Cray backed away, preparing to put the gun up when someone said, "What ya'll doin'?"

Cray got so scared that he turned around toward the person's voice and the gun went off with a loud blast. Kris's eyes were wide opened as he held his chest and dropped to the ground.

Cray's heart raced when he saw him fall. For a minute he was filled with remorse and pity. All he wanted to do was show Markise and Jason the gun to make him appear tough. Especially after his birthday celebration was a bust.

Sweat formed on the surface of his head as his mind raced. He wondered what to do next. He couldn't tell people he shot Kris and expect to get away with it. All of a sudden, his fighter instinct kicked in.

"Oh, shit! You shot him!" Markise said as they all ran over to him and got on the ground next to him. "Kris...Kris...you okay, man? Get up. Come on, Kris, get up."

He pulled him by the dirty brown coat he wore.

Jason stood up.

The boys panicked.

This had already gone too far.

"Let's go, man," Cray said calmly, as if nothing had happened.

Cray's knees were on the ground and noticed that they suddenly felt damp. When he looked to his left he saw Jason staring at Kris pissing his pants.

Cray stood up.

"What you mean let's go?" Markise asked, looking up at him. There were tears in his eyes. "We can't leave him here!"

Cray looked at Markise.

"We got to go. If we stay we're gonna all be in trouble."

"We can't leave him, Cray. We can probably still help him? Tell him, Jason. Tell him we can't leave, Kris."

Jason didn't say a word as liquid continued to escape his own body.

"Listen, Markise...he's dead. Look at him. We have to go. Now come on."

Cray said pulling his arm. Markise pulled away from him at first, but when he looked back down at Kris and saw his eyes shut, he reluctantly got up. Finally getting Jason to move too, the three of them took off running back towards Cray's house, the gun still in his book bag.

Once inside Cray's house, he made Markise wash his hands and Jason take off his jeans to wear some of his father's before they even thought about going into his bedroom.

"We can't never say nothin'," Cray advised walking around them, as the boys sat on the floor and looked up at him. He loved the power. He was in charge.

Silence.

"I know ya'll mad at me, but it was a accident."

Silence.

"We have to tell somebody." Markise said slowly. "This is wrong, man. He may still be alive."

"Fuck that...we carryin' this shit to our grave so if anybody got a problem with it say it now and we can handle the shit right here."

Silence.

Jason and Markise looked at one another.

"I guess its official. We can never say a word."

The Next Day

Cray stood outside alone kicking a can on the street. He'd been locked out of the house and was waiting for his mother and father to get home. He was freezing cold. He was just about to walk to the store to shoplift and wait in the heat when Melody's Audi pulled up.

"Get in." He told Cray.

Cray nervously got inside.

"Hungry?" he asked pulling off down the road.

He was comfortable in the heat inside his car as Melody sped down the slushy streets. He took notice at the digital stereo system and brown leather seats. He'd never been in a car like that in his entire life.

"Kinda."

"Open my glove compartment and hand me that cash."

Cray didn't move. Just stared at him. He wondered what he wanted. Just the other day he couldn't stand his guts and now he was being nice.

"You heard me? I said get the money."

Digging into the glove compartment he handed him a wad of money so big, his fingers made a large C just to hold it.

"Take out five hundred and put the rest back."

He handed it to him.

"Naw. Put it in your pocket."

"What's this for?" he asked.

"Nothin'. I like your style that's all."

Cray didn't say much. Besides, he figured he'd impressed him with the way he handled his punches. Or maybe he wanted him to sell drugs for him like Grimy Mike and Charms did. As long as he could be put on, Cray didn't care. He wanted his own money and was willing to do whatever it took to get it.

All of his questions were answered when Melody pulled up to the McDonalds and said, "Get what you want *Shooter*. It's on me."

NYZON
MIDDLE SCHOOL, WASHINGTON, D.C
MONEY, MONEY, MONEY, MONEY

The school party was jammed packed. Even though chaperones were present, most of them were teachers and a few parents who didn't really care what the kids did, just as long as there was no fighting.

The DJ played all the favorites from artists like Erik B & Rakim, EPMD, and The Beastie Boys. Everyone was doing dances like The Runnin' Man, The Prep, and The Cabbage Patch. The party was off the hook. Nyzon had just stepped through the doors when Mrs. Tawney approached him.

"Nyzon, did you ever give your mother the documents to be completed?" she asked with a clear cup full of punch in her hands.

Nyzon looked around to see who was watching. Royala and Lazarick were. Ever since she gave him those papers, he'd been dodging her.

"Uh…yeah." He lied. "She said she'll give em to me later."

"Well we need it by Monday or you won't be able to continue at the school."

Nyzon's heart dropped. "A'ight. I'll let her know."

When she left Royala and Lazarick approached him.

"What she want?" Royala asked dancing to the music. "She been sweatin' you a lot lately."

"She ain't want nothin'. She talkin' bout some papers for my mom that's all. But look, I'm bout to roll. I was just tryin to buy time after moms just dropped me off."

"For what?" Lazarick asked. "The party just gettin' started." Royal, posed on the floor next to them in her jeans, baseball cap and sweater.

"I'ma ask Angel if I can have a chance." He scanned the party.

"Who?" Royal asked.

"Angel." He repeated knowing already they were about to give him grief. They both broke out in laughter.

"I don't know what's funny cuz I already hit." Nyzon replied brushing off his shoulder. "So stop sweatin' me."

"If you gonna ask her right now we goin' wit you." Lazarick said spotting Monesha looking in their direction. "And what about her?"

Nyzon saw Monesha.

"Why have a girl when I can have a woman?" he asked.

Monesha had been putting herself in Nyzon's way ever since they met.

And she rubbed him the wrong way. He didn't understand how you could meet somebody, and sweat them every five minutes. She waited for Nyzon after each class, met him at his locker, and called his phone every five minutes. For real, she was blowing him.

They were preparing to leave the party when they saw Starlette, the girl he fingerfucked on a regular, and her crew walking toward them.

"Are you tellin' people you hit at school?" She asked rolling her neck and popping her gums.

"I ain't tellin' people shit, and if I did what's the problem? I did hit that." He advised wondering if Lazarick said something to somebody like he always did.

That's why he never told him his most intimate secrets because he talked too much. And when he looked back at Lazarick, he was looking the other way.

"The problem is you lyin' Nyzon! Me and you ain't neva got together." She continued.

"Bitch you lost your mind!" Royala added. "I was on lookout when Nyzon hit that in the Freak-Mobile. You betta get out of her wit that bullshit."

Now Starlette was angry. Lines formed in her forehead and Nyzon could've sworn she was preparing to punch Royala. He just hoped for her sake she had enough sense not to.

"Ain't nobody fuckin' wit no broke ass Nyzon!" Starlette spat. "He don't even have a decent pair of shoes to wear." She and her friends pointed and laughed. "Fuck I look like messin' wit him when I got a boyfriend wit money?"

"Want me to slap him?" Rhonda, one of her friends asked.

She loved fighting and that's why her face was so fucked up. She had scars all over it.

Nyzon wasn't scared of Starlette or her loud friends. He just wasn't up for the bullshit. He couldn't understand why this bitch was in his face when she knew he fingered her at least once a week. He figured her boyfriend found out and dumped her, either way, he didn't care.

"I'ma drop your ass if you touch me!" Nyzon said to Rhonda.

"And I'ma get in on that too!" Royala added.

"What the fuck ya'll gonna do?" Starlette asked Royala and Lazarick. "My brothers will fuck you up!"

"Yeah, Joe! How you tryin' to carry it?" Trudy one of her other friends asked.

"Bitch I don't give a fuck about your brothers! I got people too!" Royal responded fully prepared to fight her on the spot. "Ya'll always startin' shit!"

"You got a nerve! My mamma warned me about girls like you! Dyke!"

Starlette smirked.

The look on Royal's face showed her ego was bruised. Not talking anymore, Royala stole her in the face and watched her hit the floor. Everybody started fighting and although Nyzon didn't believe in hitting girls, he did choke a few of them trying to get them off of Royala. But once everyone was out the way, and Royala still had Starlette on the floor, she took a blade from her pocket and sliced her mouth from the inside out. Blood spat everywhere as Nyzon and Lazarick managed to pull Royala off of the girl.

Starlette was crying holding her mouth and it looked like a scene in a horror movie. The chaperones rushed to her aid but it was too late, the damage had begun and Royala had given her a smile four inches wider.

The school called the cops and they took her to jail. A few hours later Mrs. Quick, Lazarick and Royala's mom, picked her up from the holding cell and they dropped Nyzon off at home. It was the first time Royala went to jail, but it certainly wouldn't be the last.

After all that drama, all Nyzon wanted to do was go home. He knew Angel was there because his mother told him she asked Angel to sit with him after the party. So before using his key to get inside, he smoothed his waves with his hand, took off his coat, and pulled his chain out of his shirt so it would show. Finally he opened the door and almost fell back when he saw Angel laying on the couch with a tall dark skin guy straddling her as he titty fucked her.

"Oh, snap!" The man said after he tucked his dick in his pants and closed them up.

He looked at Nyzon and then at Angel. He had two gold chains with large medallions hanging from them. Cray knew right away he was a dealer and the same man he saw drop her off with the Audi.

"I thought he wasn't supposed to be home until later?" the dealer said.

"He wasn't." She adjusted her bra to hide the titties that just a few days ago, he had in his mouth.

Nyzon's heart hurt when he saw her with somebody else, after everything they shared. And in his own house at that.

"Ny...what you doin' here?" was all she could say as she stood up and walked toward him.

"I live here remember?" he said, coldly. "What you doin wit him?"

"Oh...uh...this is my boyfriend Elite." She smiled.

"Your boyfriend Elite? But I thought you said you didn't have one. You told me you liked me?"

Elite busted out in a loud chuckle.

"Like you? Nigga look at your fit? You ain't just young, you's a dusty lil nigga at best! How the fuck you think you can land a girl like her. Tell him Angel," he laughed again. "Before I give this lil nigga a lesson in life."

Angel turned around to Nyzon and said, "Ny, I can never be wit somebody like you. You know that."

Nyzon's limp body fell into the loveseat as he looked at both of them. What did she mean she couldn't be with somebody like him? She was just with him in his bedroom. In his house.

"Come here, Ny." Angel said as she grabbed his hand. She was trying to catch him before he said too much. "Elite, I'll be right back."

"Well hurry the fuck up so you can tend to your nigga."

Nyzon cut his eyes at him until they were in Nyzon's room alone. Both of them sat on the edge of his bed and Angel wiped her face with her hands before dropping them into her lap.

"I know you're hurt, Ny, but this is life. You sucked my titties and I let you." She said as if they were discussing a television show and not intimacy. "But it was nothing more."

Silence.

"Nyzon...I'm older than you and we can't be together. Plus I like nice things and Elite can buy them for me. You can't."

"But I was gonna let you wear my chain." He hoped he could convince her that he was capable of fulfilling her needs and wants.

"Nyzon. It'll never work. You'll probably never be on my level. I like what I like and you are too young to give it to me. Everybody not cut out to be hustlers. And that's all I fuck wit."

So that's what he does. He thought.

"You're cute, Nyzon. And maybe you can find a girl who'll like you for that."

His mind wondered on Monesha. Now he wished he hadn't brushed her off.

"When you're old enough you'll understand what I'm saying. Elite got the money and because of it, he got me."

She paused and put her hand on his knee believing she gave him enough for the night.

"You hungry? Want a sandwich or somethin'?"

He nodded yes just to get her out of his face. He needed to be alone.

"We still friends right, Ny?" Silence.

She hugged him against his will and his heart beat rapidly against her chest. He couldn't lie, he liked her, and he liked her a lot. And it would be a long time before he got over his first heartbreak. But there, in his room he made up his mind to hustle and hustle hard. He didn't want to be like the kids he saw on the block around his way. He wanted an empire. And he'd stop at nothing to get it.

KAVON
Sweet Payback

Shy opened Candy's apartment door off of Maryland Avenue, in Washington D.C as she straddled his body, kissing him aggressively on the lips. Her weight was nothing compared to his brut strength. His dick grew harder as she gyrated against him. She was a freak in every since of the word.

"You know I'ma tare that shit up right?" He unlocked her apartment door. She nibbled a little on his bottom lip.

"You betta!" she demanded. "I want it rough tonight, Daddy. Real rough."

She clarified, biting his ear harder than most people could stand.

"Give it to me like how we use to do it before Lil Shawn came into the picture." She continued.

"Came into the picture?" he said briefly, questioning her use of words.

"You know what I mean...before we had him."

"You need to watch what you say out yo' mouth." He wished she could've been a better mother instead of the worthless bitch that he was accustomed to.

"Well, why don't you teach me about my mouth?" She was looking for any excuse to use violence with sex.

Once inside, he locked the door and she jumped down. The moment he closed the door, she slapped the fuck out of his face. SMACK!

His head moved to the right and when he looked at her, he had a devilish grin on his face. He loved every bit of it. The red bruise from her force showed immediately on his light skin.

"That's all you got, bitch?" he said, wanting to be hit again.

He took his coat off and threw it to the floor. She did the same as they left a trail behind them.

"Like that?"

"You got to come betta than that."

"Oh, for real?" Candy moved away from him backward as he followed her into the bedroom.

She took off her blouse, threw it on the floor and hit him again. SMACK!

"You like that shit, don't you? You like when I beat that ass." She removed her bra, her C cup titties swinging in the air.

"I like when you hit me but you ain't did shit yet!"

He laughed as he contemplated how hard his dick would get after all the pain he put her in. Candy was the only girl he knew who when she said she liked it rough, that's exactly what the fuck she meant. And with Lil Shawn being over her moms, they could get as nasty as they wanted.

Shy had been staying over Candy's house for the past three weeks faithfully, not necessarily to hide from Kavon because he wasn't afraid of him, but because he didn't know where he was. The truth of the matter was that he didn't think Kavon was bold enough to come after him. Shy was more concerned with controlling where the war took in the event he changed his mind. And at the latest, until he found him.

Day and night his crew looked for Kavon, but was unsuccessful. It was as if he had fallen off of the face of the earth. He wasn't at his house. He wasn't with the people he rolled with and neither was Tara. Had it been average beef, he was sure Kavon wouldn't know how to handle it. But since Shy brutally raped Tara and threatened her on her hospital bed, he wasn't sure how Kavon would react.

"How about now! Is that hard enough?" She smacked him consecutively two more times.

His face now inflamed and red. She walked in her dark room and still he followed.

"I ain't feel shit." He laughed standing in the doorway.

"What about now!" an unfamiliar voice said as he stole the fuck out of him.

Shy was caught off guard as he stumbled to the floor. Candy, wearing only her pants, jumped on the bed screaming her lungs out. The stranger turned the lights on and stared them down. She stopped crying momentarily.

When Shy looked up at who just hit him, he saw a man twice his size hovering over his body. And with his build and stature being as large as it was, the man above him was gargantuan. Within seconds, Kavon appeared from the closet holding a 9 millimeter directly in Shy's direction.

"There's a time and place for everything," Kavon said in a low deadly tone, reminding him of the last conversation they had together. "I venture to say that now is the time."

He sat in a chair across the room.

Candy continued to yell and scream.

"Bitch, shut the fuck up fo I pop yo ass first!" Kavon told her.

It was the first time he talked to her so brutally.

"So you found me, huh?" He laughed as he wiped the blood from his mouth and made an attempt to stand up. When he did, he got knocked on his back again.

Whop!

"I think you betta stay down." Kavon's tone was cold and steely.

"Who is this mothafucka?!" Shy asked, looking at the man who hadn't said one word since they met.

"They call him Kurtis Blow and I'm sure you already know why. But we'll get to everything you need to know later."

Kavon remained in the chair letting it be known that he was in charge. Kurtis was a long time friend of his and the one man he knew he could count on, despite it all. Kurtis only flaw was that he stayed in and out of jail. As a matter of fact, this was his first job since he'd been released from a five year bid.

"How did you get in?" Shy asked, looking at Candy as if she'd set him up.

"It's not hard to get a key if you pay the right person at the rental office." He winked. "Ain't that's what you always told me. It ain't a thing in the world you can't buy. The key's to this apartment included."

"What the fuck you want then, nigga? Cause it's obvious you ain't about shit cuz I'm still breathin'."

"For now, Shy. First I wanna know why you pull Tara into our beef?"

Shy looked at Candy. It was evident from the glance he gave her that she hadn't heard the full story.

"You know I was gonna make her my wife and you raped her, beat her and left her for dead." Kavon finished. "Next to me, she loved you the most."

Shy looked at Candy, and then Kavon. She was confused. She had no idea he was going to rape anybody let alone Kavon's girlfriend. She thought it was about money.

"Nigga, fuck that shit! I'm the one who gave her to you. She was a whore when I met her and she was a whore when I fucked her. She wanted it just as much as I did!" Shy sounded maniacal. "I was tryin' to do you a favor by lettin' you see the truth."

"Are you serious? You gave her to me?! You introduced me to Tara to clear up the debt you owed for takin' my money." Kavon let it be known right then that he was aware that Shy held on to the money he stole from Paris. "But I counted as an "L" because she was worth every bit of it."

Shy looked like he seen a ghost. All this time he thought he was fooling a *naïve* ass Kavon. When in actuality, he was fooling himself. That brought him to his next question.

"How you know that?"

"'Cause the folks you got into the money for started askin' a bunch of questions and came for me. I was the last person Paris owed money to. So they put one and one together and got me. You just had to take the entire 100 didn't you?" he laughed. "Greedy ass, nigga. 'Cause of you I made Miami connects. Had it not been for my gift of gab, they would've taken my life. I told them I ain't have shit to do with it, despite knowing it was you. They took me as a man of my word and left it alone. We're still in business to this day."

"So you makin' money on the side?"

"Not as dumb as you thought I was right?"

"And how the fuck you know I was here?"

Kavon laughed before answering this question.

"I knew 'bout you and Candy the second after you fucked her. But bein' the nigga that I am, I was determined not to let a hoe interfere wit business. You couldn't do that. And since it was that easy for her to leave, I felt you did me a favor. I got to admit, I just thought you were fuckin' her from time to time. I ain't know ya'll were in here beatin' each other's asses and shit." Kurtis Blow and Kavon laughed. "Nigga, I knew this would be the first place you'd run."

"I ain't run."

"Shy, you ran. You know how much I love that woman and you ran. You got scared. I coulda smoked your ass a long time ago but I wanted to make sure my Tara was a'ight. And now that she is, I'm here" Kavon smirked.

"Nigga, fuck you!"

"They'll be plenty of time for fucking." Kavon grinned. "Plenty of time."

Shy didn't know what that meant and he adjusted on the floor. He wondered if he could take them out but quickly wiped that thought out of his mind after remembering his weapon was in his coat on the floor and in the living room.

"Why don't you fight me like a man, huh? Straight up!" Shy offered seeing no other ends to the means in sight.

Kavon laughed.

"Shy...Shy...Shy. Have you taught me nothin'? Why do dirty work when I can pay somebody to do it for me? Plus I'm too pretty for this shit."

"That's why you got this nigga here?" he responded. "Cause you can't fight your own battles? 'Cause he your bitch?"

"Battles?" He smirked. "Nigga, I fight wars." Kavon responded in a cold tone. "Main man bout to do everything to you, you did to my wife and more."

Kurtis Blow cracked his knuckles.

The look on Shy's face transmogrified from confidence to concern in an instant.

"Stand up." The stranger finally spoke.

Shy looked up at him and reluctantly stood up. He figured if he was going to die, he might as well go out fighting. The moment he rose to his feet Shy stole Kurtis Blow off the top. Whop!

But Kurtis seemed unmoved. You would've thought he stroked his face instead of hitting him. He smiled and returned the favor by hitting him so

84

hard, he regained his position on the floor again. Whop!

Blow after blow he dealt Shy until his large limp body remained down covered in blood. Candy still on the bed cried her eyes out.

"That's enough for now," Kavon said, stopping him. "Take his pants off."

Shy was still moving, slightly conscious, but barely. Kurtis Blow was trained at this shit. When his pants were off, Kavon threw him the knife and the duct tape he brought with him. Everything was thoughtfully planned.

After Kurtis taped Shy's mouth and hands, Kavon said, "Go in slow."

With his legs bent at the knees, Kurtis rammed the knife into his rectum as Shy screamed out in agony. His voice muted.

"Do it again." Kavon demanded. And again he rammed it up his anus. "That's enough."

With Shy falling in and out of consciousness it was important to Kavon that he got a few things off of his chest before Shy took his final breath.

Kavon walked over to him and knelt down. "One last thing. I know that bastard kid was hers the moment I saw his eyes. Whatever happened to bros above hoes?" he asked sternly. "It don't even matter now though. And don't worry, I'll let the lil nigga call me daddy."

Pop! Pop! Pop!

He shot him three times before he backed away and eyed his work. Candy, now quiet looked petrified after realizing she'd have to be dealt with next.

"I say we kill her," Kurtis said, breaking the deafening silence.

Kavon looked at Kurtis and back at her. He didn't want to kill her because she had a son, and he'd already taken his father.

"Can I trust you?" he said, seriously walking over to the bed.

"We need to kill her man," Kurtis interrupted. "She's seen my face, too."

Kavon looked down knowing he was right.

"I promise I won't say nothin'," Candy interjected. "You know me." She cried, wiping the sweat off of her face with her hands.

That statement almost got her killed.   Everything in him told him to exact upon her the same fate. But the softer side of him, the side that was becoming a father, thought about Lil Shawn. He didn't want him growing up with nobody to care for him even if it was her fucked up ass.

"I'm gonna let you breathe. But if there's a problem, we will come back and finish you off. Do you understand what I'm saying?" he said calmly.

She nodded yes.

"If you ever tell anyone…I will be back."

"I won't tell anyone, Kavon…I promise. You can trust me."

Four Days Later

Homicide Detective Betha knocked on Candy's door with his partner Detective Mesaline. Although Detective Betha was white, and Mesaline was Italian, their beliefs mirrored one another so closely, they could be brothers.

Years of food, alcohol and cigarette abuse showed all over their dried faces and protruding bellies. Homicide detectives had to be tough and diligent. It was rough trying to get people to cooperate with police especially in the D.C, area.

"Who is it?!" Candy yelled on the other side of the door.

"Detective Betha and Mesaline. We'd like to talk to you for a moment."

There was brief silence and they could hear wrestling on the other side of the door. Two minutes later, it swung open and Angel walked over to the couch wearing a pink robe. A cigarette dangled from the corner of her mouth.

"What's up?" Candy crossed her right leg over the left one. "I'm kinda busy."

They looked around. "Well it's obvious you ain't been busy cleaning up."

She stuck her tongue out.

"This'll only take a second." Detective Betha sat in the chair across from her while Detective Mesaline remained quiet and looked around. "How are you holding up?"

"I'm fine I guess! All I really want to do is move on with my life and take care of me and my son." She removed the cigarette from her mouth and emptied a few ashes on the table instead of the ashtray inches from it. "But ya'll keep bothering me like I murdered him."

"We're not bothering you, ma'am." Detective Mesaline said as he looked down at his partner. "But you do seem to be handling this pretty well."

"Where I'm from people die all the time." She looked up at him and back at Det. Betha. "Now what ya'll really want with me?"

"We want to ask you a few questions for starters." He whipped out a small spiral notepad from his inside coat pocket. "Did Shy have any other enemies that you know about? Because like we said earlier, the crime seems hate-related. It doesn't seem like a robbery like you said it was."

She giggled.

"What's so funny?" Detective Mesaline was shocked at her rudeness.

"He was a drug dealer for cryin' out loud! I'm sure he had enemies."

"Did he have any enemies that you are aware of?" Det. Betha asked, frowning at her.

She paused for a second, smirked a little and said, "If he did he didn't tell me."

Realizing talking to her was a dead end, they both decided to leave. There were other ways of getting the truth and it wouldn't be through her.

"We've wasted enough of your time today. But we'll be in touch." Det. Betha said.

"Whatever you say." She threw her hands in the air.

The moment they were outside of her doors, they made a phone call.

"Lieutenant Devely. It's Betha and Mesaline. We're gonna need the search warrant after all. She's not trying to help. I'm positive she had everything to do with this murder. And the wire tap will prove it."

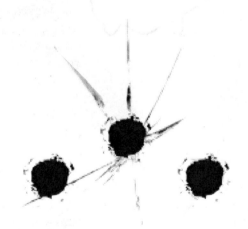

FIRST DISTRICT
WIRE TAP SURVEILLANCE

It had been two weeks since Detective Betha and Detective Mesaline were able to get a warrant and still nothing. They were frustrated as they watched over the machine waiting for evidence of any kind. But so far everything they heard seemed like a waste.

If Candy Brown wasn't talking about going shopping, she was talking about who she would fuck to go shopping. All they were sure of now, was that she could care less about what happened to Shy.

Securing a warrant wasn't easy. They had to convince the judge that Candy had probable cause to kill Shy and that she carried through with it. And after learning that she had a small life insurance policy on his head for $10,000, that she claimed was for their son, they thought it would be easy enough to do.

Before Judge Cheryl Bail signed anything, she wanted to be clear on the conditions. It wasn't too long ago that both Detectives fumbed an entire case by submitting tampered evidence that had been given by an unreliable source. She did not want to have that type of mishap happening again. But the detectives assured her this time was different.

And now with everything in place, they were waiting for that one moment, when all would be revealed.

In The Mall

Candy pulled Lil Shawn by his arm in the Union Station mall, in D.C. She was in the Benetton shop picking up a few shirts, as her five–year-old son begged for food.

"I'm hungry!" he cried. "I want to eat."

"Shut yo ass up!" she told him. "You ate this morning."

It was now 6 in the afternoon. The truth was, she was an awful mother who preferred to spend the remainder of her money on gear instead of taking care of her only child. If it were quiet enough, the boy's stomach could be heard growling from a few feet away.

"But I'm hungry, Mommy."

"I said shut up!" she continued popping him in the back of his curly head.

"I want my daddy!" he cried out.

"Well, yo daddy dead!" She yanked his arm toward the exit.

After hearing what he already knew, the little boy cried even worse. When Shy was alive he spoiled his son rotten. No matter what, Shy spent at least three days a week with him. If Shy was capable of loving someone, his son would've been the only one to receive it.

Candy was fed up with Lil Shawn's whining. She decided to sooth his beastly ass by feeding him. He was chubby like his father was when he was his age.

Walking to McDonald's, she ordered the Happy Meal when the child could clearly eat a regular size helping. But the moment she dipped into her purse, she noticed all she had was five dollars. This was a problem because they still had to catch a train home. So she decided against getting him anything to eat.

That was it! She had to talk to Kavon. It was his fault she didn't have the bottomless pit of dough anymore. Lately, all she had was a steady stream of cops questioning her about Shy's murder. Surely her lazy ass could've gotten a job but why? And yes she spent all of the life insurance money. Still, she wanted Kavon to feed her habit for fly clothes. If he didn't, she had all intentions of doing what she had to do to make him pay. She wasn't afraid of his threats anymore either. She knew him enough to know he had a soft spot and children were it. And as long as Lil Shawn was alive, she'd be safe.

It was settled. She had to make a call.

Kavon's Home

Kavon helped Tara who was walking on crutches to the couch. Despite being in pain, she stayed upbeat. Her courage made him love her even more.

"I can't wait to make you my wife." Kavon knelt down in front of her and massaged her feet.

"And I can't wait to be your wife." She stroked his face softly.

She showed him the rock on her finger as if he wasn't the one who dropped enough cash on it to feed a small city in Africa for a week.

"Get that thing out my face, girl." He joked. "I can't see."

She laughed. He smiled.

"You sure you don't want to go to the Justice of the peace and make this official. We don't need no fancy ass wedding to prove our love to one another."

"No...I want to marry you right." She didn't want to have a rush wedding simply because Shy almost took everything from them.

Kavon looked at her face and noticed it was healing nicely. You barely saw where Shy's teeth had punctured her face. To him she was more beautiful now than ever. As he talked to her, his pager went off on his hip. His heart dropped when he saw the number. It was Candy's home phone.

"Baby, give me a second, I got to make a call."

"Sure honey." She did not question his motive for leaving so abruptly.

Kavon walked to the kitchen, picked up the yellow phone on the wall and dialed the number.

"What, bitch?"

"Now...now...now." She said slickly. "Is that any way to talk to someone who can keep your secret?"

His heart dropped. The bitch was threatening him.

"I thought we agreed that our arrangement was done." He said angrily.

"We did." She laughed.

"So what the fuck you want from me now?"

"Fifty thousand dollars...cash." She told him right off the top. "And that's an easy price to pay for me not to tell the cops you killed Shy."

"You dirty, whore."

"Kavon, please! Stop with the compliments. You are the one who took everything from me. I barely got enough money to feed my kid! Either you pay up or I'ma tell everything I know. And I do mean everything. You got five hours to think about it. When your decision is made, meet me at Haines Point to drop off my cash." She hung up.

He had to think. If he paid her, he might as well open a bank account in her name, because the threats would never end. But if he didn't, he was going straight to jail. As far as he saw it there was only one choice, he had to put her to sleep. He was a fool for not doing it in the first place.

"Is everything okay?" Tara asked, limping into the kitchen after seeing him hang up the phone.

"Not really, baby," Kavon said. "I need to know if you could take care of yourself if somethin' happened to me."

"What?" she said as if the thought alone was unimaginable.

"Can you take care of you and our baby if somethin' happened to me?" he repeated with more clarification. "I need to know."

Tara walked a few feet away. It was as if she wasn't sure.

"I don't know." She shook her head. "I don't know."

"Well, I need you to prepare for the worse."

"Why?" She hobbled over to him hugging him closely. "You can't leave me, baby. I'll die without you."

His question was answered.

"Tara," he said, picking her up and walking her to the couch. "You have to be strong. I just talked to Candy and I'm not sure what she's gonna do right now. There's a good possibility she'll tell the cops."

"No!" Tara sobbed heavily. "Kill her! Kill her now."

"I know what I have to do Tara. But I'm more concerned with you and our unborn child. This baby means more to me than anything and I haven't even met her yet. So I'm askin'…can you be strong for me? For the three of us?"

"I don't know, Kavon…I'll try."

It was as good as it was going to get.

KAVON
DISTRICT OF COLUMBIA COURT HOUSE
Minutes Before The Verdict

Kavon sat in a crowded courtroom six months after the murder, wearing a three thousand dollar suit. The heat seemed unbearable and he adjusted his tie several times trying to get comfortable. But how could he? His future, his life and everything he wanted to keep rode on the verdict.

His beautiful wife sat behind him and her fear of losing him weighed so heavily on his shoulders, that they drooped. Although they didn't get a chance to have the dream wedding Tara wanted, he was able to make her his wife by marrying her at the Justice of the Peace a few days after Candy's call.

He felt stupid! How could he have a conversation about something so important on the phone? And above everything, on a phone that was tapped. It angered him that Candy had gained immunity for her testimony, while he sat on trial for his life. And as she ranted off her testimony against Kavon, she never mentioned Kurtis, for fear he would come after her later. Kavon wanted it that way. Murdering Shy was his call and Kurtis shouldn't take the blame. So he didn't mention him either.

"All rise! The honorable Elizabeth Jamison presiding."

The middle aged white judge walked into the courtroom slowly. Her presence put Kavon on edge. What was even more eerie was that she looked familiar. Where had he seen her before? Paper rustled throughout the courtroom and eventually everything was deafly silent. For a second, he saw his future in her eyes and got a glimpse of his fate. Guilty.

"You may be seated." She stole a few stares at Kavon who sat in the defendant's section looking as handsome as ever. "Jury, have you reached a verdict?"

Kavon turned around and smiled at Tara, their beautiful baby girl Tiara, in her arms. He was hopeful. Hopeful that he would be able to remain with his family. He knew Tara wasn't strong enough to take care of them on her own. He prayed that the high priced lawyer he hired was worth his weight in dough.

Phillip Croones was the best defense attorney in the business. His clients got off, and it was as simple as that. Out of one hundred cases he tried, he lost ten.

"Yes, your Honor. We the people find Mr. Kavon Cartier guilty in first degree murder."

The courtroom erupted in loud babble and the prosecutor smiled slamming his briefcase shut.

"Great, we'll reconvene for sentencing in two weeks." she continued.

Kavon's shoulders collapsed and his head fell. How could this be? His lawyer assured him he could beat this case. All he was doing was protecting his wife! Didn't they understand that? Nothing about his core was violent and nothing about the man he was wanted to hurt another human being, except when the lives of his family was endangered. And Shy's carless act could've taken the lives of both his wife and daughter.

"Settle down!" the judge yelled striking her gavel several times.

The courtroom grew quiet.

Kavon tapped his lawyer on the shoulder and whispered in his ear. The attorney looked at him as if he'd lost his mind.

"Are you sure Mr. Cartier?" He nodded yes.

"Your honor. My client wishes to waive his rights and be sentenced today."

The judge smirked but Kavon didn't care. He couldn't put Tara through more than she'd already endured. He couldn't get over not being able to make love to his wife or of being able to hold his baby girl. His mind wandered to the last quality time he spent with Tara when they hung a wooden sign on their daughter's bedroom door which read, Tiara.

"Noooooo!!!!" Tara cried out, thinking she failed to explain the brutality of the rape properly.

Perhaps if she did a better job, their decision could've been different.

The courtroom erupted into *Oooohs*, and *Awwsss*.

"Quiet in the courtroom!" the Judge ordered, pounding her gavel again. "Mrs. Cartier, one more outburst like that and you're out of here!"

Tara's on and off again friend, Brook White, rubbed her arms and tried to console her.

"Mr. Cartier, there's no mistaking the brutality that the victim experienced in this murder. It was of a vicious and heinous nature. You were cruel, calculating and thoughtless. Therefore, I sentence you to 40 years in prison wIthout the possibility of parole. Court is adjourned."

It was over. His life was gone. He turned around and looked at his fiancé who was emotionally beat. Her eyes and nose red and her spirit broken.

"Be strong, baby!" he yelled as the bailiffs handcuffed him. "I need you strong Tara."

"I will!" she sobbed still holding their child. "I'ma be strong for us."

"I love you Tara, and if I could've murdered that mothafucka again I would."

There was love in his words despite the seriousness. The Bailiff hearing him got rough by squeezing his arm. Kavon didn't care. He meant every word.

"I love you, Tara! You and Tiara are my life!" The officers pushed him toward the back.

He struggled desperately to say one last word to her. He was unsuccessful.

And just like that…he was gone.

Six Months Later

Tara was nervous about what Kavon wanted to talk to her about as she sat in the waiting area in DC prison. Lately he forbid her to bring his child, not wanting her to have any memories of him behind bars. It didn't matter that she was just a baby and probably wouldn't remember anyway. The decision was made.

The first month in prison was the worse he'd endured in his entire life. He stayed to himself and thought often of Tara and his baby girl Tiara. The second month he stopped being a loaner, and kicked it with a few dudes he knew from back home.

But it was a conversation that he had with a prisoner named White Boy that changed both he and Tara's life.

"Let me spot you." The muscular light skin man said as he lifted the barbell off of the hook and handed it to Kavon.

He looked like Kid from the group Kid and Play.

Kavon accepted.

"So how you holdin' up?" he asked as Kavon exerted energy to lift his third one.

"Hold up…you ain't no faggy, are you?" Kavon placed the barbell back on the hook. "Cuz I don't play that bullshit!"

He waited for his answer.

"It's a good think you got up cause I was bout to drop that shit on yo head, nigga. Don't insult my fuckin' intelligence."

Kavon liked him immediately.

"Just checkin'." Kavon lay back on the bench. "What's your name?"

"They call me White Boy," he said, giving him back the weights.

"I can see why." Kavon joked.

"Most people do." He laughed. "My man Kurtis told me to look out for you."

"I'm good." Kavon advised as he worked on his second set. "I can handle my own."

"Out there that may be true, but everybody needs somebody watchin' their back in here."

Kavon didn't respond because prior to now, he always beat his charges. I guess things were different when murder was involved.

"I hear you got a baby girl out there." White boy added. "I got one too." Kavon smiled. He kept her and Tara's pictures up on his cell wall.

"Yeah...they're my reason for breathin'."

"It's a shame you got to get over em if you wanna make it." He placed the barbell back on the rack.

Kavon sat up straight.

"What you talkin' bout get over em?" he asked. "That's my wife and kid."

"There's no way you can make it in here thinkin' about them. Every little thing she do you gonna analyze. It's gonna drive you crazy."

"That's not true!" he said breaths still heavy from lifting.

"Yeah okay." He laughed. "Every one of us made a phone call home and wondered why it wasn't answered. You gonna start thinkin' bout who she fuckin...who she wit...and all that otha shit. It's life."

Kavon didn't want to tell him it happened already. He'd called home and couldn't reach her one afternoon. The messed up part was that he told her that he would be calling home at that exact hour. When he finally got a hold of her, she claimed she was out with Brook, a friend of hers he couldn't stand who snorted coke. They supposedly took the baby to the park. It killed him not having her so accessible. Hell, it was her fault he was in there to begin with.

"Well, I ain't forgettin' my family." Kavon wiped his face with the towel in his lap.

"Well get ready to do HARD time." He gave him dap. "Cuz if you really loved em, you'd let her move on. I'll get up wit you lada, partna."

Ever since he had that conversation he thought about Tara. As much as he hated to admit it, White Boy was right. Tara was beautiful and she deserved to have a good man. A free man. He decided to break it off from her once and for all.

"Hey, baby!" Tara said, touching the glass. She had just gotten her hair done and it was extra bouncy. A few dudes who should've been looking at their own visitors couldn't help but stare at her. "I miss you."

Kavon was being transferred to Lorton in a month.

"I miss you, too." He smiled, mad grillin' the dudes who were captivated by Tara's beauty before looking back at her. "Your hair is nice."

"Thank you." She ran her fingers through it. "You like it?"

"I love it, beautiful."

"I love you more, honey." She touched the glass.

She couldn't get over how handsome he was in his prison uniform. His muscles had become more defined and although he was in prison, he looked better than ever.

"Not as much as I love you."

She blushed.

"I got the money from Kurtis. He's really good about looking out for us."

He didn't doubt that Kurtis would be down for business. He had given him access to his stash and still had dough put up that know body knew about. In total he had 3 million at his disposal.

"That's good." Kavon prepared to break the bad news.

"Is something wrong?" Tara asked, seeing his mood. "Did I do something?"

"No...you didn't do anything."

"Okay." She smiled. "Cause I'm trying to be strong for you, baby. I really am. Like you asked me to."

"I know." He affirmed. "I know. How's Tiara?"

"She's so pretty!" Tara lit up. "She looks just like you. It's funny. I never saw a baby with chocolate skin and golden hair."

"Yeah...she's gonna have me kill somebody one day," he responded, grinning. His expression changed when he remembered he would be in for 40 years of her life.

"What's up, K? Talk to me."

"It's over, Tara." He looked at her through the smudged glass.

"What?"

"I said it's over," he said seriously. "Don't come here anymore."

"Why, baby? Why?"

"Cause I can't see you like this! This shit is killin' me." He hit his hand on the counter. The officer approached him and he took his anger down a notch. "I'm sorry, man," he told the officer.

"Kavon...please don't do this to me! Do you want me to die out here? Is that what you want? Cause if you leave me, that's exactly what I'm gonna do!" she cried, large tear drops leaving her eyes and falling on the counter.

He hated seeing her cry especially when he knew he was to blame. But he wanted her to move on, and land one of them doctor or lawyer types. She deserved happiness not a man behind bars.

"Tara, stop saying that!" he said. "You know I want you alive to care for our child."

"So all you care about is her? And not me?" Tara wiped some of her tears.

"I care about both of you. You know that."

"Then I don't understand why you're doing this?!" she begged. "Please...don't leave me....don't leave us. I can wait for you. I promise! We got the lawyer looking at the court documents again, baby." She smiled trying to maintain her composure. "He's gonna find somethin' I just know it! Please Kavon! Stay with me baby. Stay with me."

"It's over." Kavon's voice remained firm. "And you are not to come here anymore."

"But I will." Tara sounded adamant. "I will anyway."

"I put in a request to have you removed from my visitor's list." He looked into her eyes.

He wanted her to hate him. He wanted her to get angry and prove to him that she could do it on her own.

"Why would you take the one thing from me I need?"

"What are you talkin' about?"

"You."

"It's over."

"I see. It looks like your mind is made up." Tara said, removing a piece of tissue from her pocket. She blew her nose and wiped her eyes causing her mascara to smear. "Remember you wanted this not me." She stood up. "I'm only as tough as I am with you. Alone I'm not the same woman. Remember that, Kavon. Good bye." And just like that, she walked out his life.

CAROLYN
MOTEL – WASHINGTON, DC
ONCE YOU GO BLACK, YOU NEVA GO BACK

Carolyn lay on the hotel bed looking at the ceiling light. The more she stared the harder it was to focus. Her naked body drenched from the sweat shared between their bodies during lovemaking.

She was addicted to everything about him. The way he held her, the way he smiled and the way he was as different from her as night is to day.

"What you thinkin' bout?" Ozim "J-Swizz" Daye asked as he returned from the bathroom, nude, his limp penis dangling before he cupped it. "You ready for another round?"

Carolyn's desires to live her own life, manifested itself into bittersweet rebellion and poetic justice. She had a tendency to be pulled to what was forbidden. Even in her earlier years, her father told her never to eat strawberries because she was allergic. For years she did as she was told, until one day his forbids got the best of her and she ate six of them and almost died. In a lot of ways, J-Swizz was her strawberry.

So after weeks of riding to the neighborhood with Tina and Modell, even after J-Swizz told her to stay away, she finally got the courage to come back alone one night. There was something about the way that he looked at her that had her intrigued. But when she pulled up on the block, she couldn't find him. She was stupid for thinking he'd be interested in a white girl who grew up privileged all her life, while he had to neighbor with the cold hard streets. Besides, outside of a few glances, there was nothing she could say to him that he could relate to.

It wasn't until Tina joked that someone called "Take Back The Streets", requesting the only white girl there that her wishes came true. She answered the phone and J-Swizz was on the line and offered to take her out. She accepted. And from that moment on, they'd been kicking it ever since.

When he eased into the bed next to her, she rolled over and looked at his dark handsome face. She was a woman. He was a man. She longed to get away from her father and his unreasonable beliefs, and the streets were taking a toll on him and she was his escape. What they didn't speak out loud was that through it all, he was a drug dealing black man, and she was Carolyn Jamison, the daughter of an extreme racist.

Things were even more complicated than when they first began.

Because now she was in love with a man that knew nothing about who she really was. It panged her heart that all her father cared about was the racist chief of police he got elected on his payroll when all she cared about, was J-Swizz. She wanted to introduce him to who she loved, but she feared for both of their lives.

"You are always ready!" She grabbed the cup filled with Vodka on the nightstand, before downing it all.

Lately she relied on alcohol and her addiction for sex to take her mind off her life.

"I am when it comes to you."

"I figure you'd be tired of me by now."

"How can I get tired of this?" He pulled her to him and placed his hands on her ass, before gyrating against her until he was hard again. "You're the best thing that has ever happened to me."

"Good...cause I want it to stay that way."

She kissed him softly on the lips and wondered why he looked as if something was on his mind.

"What's wrong?" she asked with puppy dog eyes.

"When are we going to talk about your family?" His questions caught her off guard. "It's like you don't want me knowing nothin' about them."

"I can't talk about them J." Carolyn lifted up and lie beside him. "And I really don't want to go through this again."

"Look...we been together for months now and I have a right to know everything about you. So if you don't want to tell me, it makes me think you're hidin' somethin'. Are you adopted? Is that it?"

"I can't talk about them, J. I wish I could but I can't and I'm asking you to respect that."

She sat up on the side of the bed.

"You should really trust me more, Carolyn. I haven't let you down yet."

"You don't understand. My family's different. There are a lot of things going on in my life that I can't even understand. And I'm afraid if I tell you, you'll feel differently about me."

J-Swizz sat up, moved behind her and massaged her shoulders.

"I don't care what you tell me...I ain't gonna stop dealin' wit you, Carolyn."

Carolyn looked behind her at his face and smiled.

"I wish I could believe that."

Outside the Motel

Todd Jamison sat in his green Ford Wagon looking at the motel his sister was in. He'd been following her for months now. The hate he felt for her was starting to consume him. How could she deal with a nigger, knowing full well what their family stood for? Todd also battled with the fact that no matter what he did, his father always took to Carolyn more. He was jealous of the relationship she had with their father.

His eyes were wide as he took a knife repeatedly to his thigh over and over again. Blood soaked his dingy jeans and fell into the burgundy seats. Whenever anger consumed him, he took it out on his body. It was as if punishing himself, made things easier to deal with. The stinging sensation running through his thighs acted as a release and in a way gave him complete power over the situation.

For now he would say nothing to her. Everything would be done when he was ready. But when the time was right, he would make sure she'd know exactly how he felt.

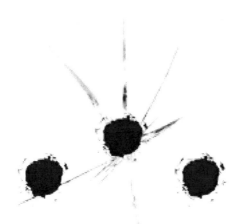

Yo Yo J-A-Y, I flow sick…
Fuck all y'all haters blow dick…
I spits the game for those that throw bricks…
Money cash hoes money cash chicks what…
Sex murder and mayhem romance for the street…
Only wife of mines is a life of crime…
And since, life's a bitch in mini-skirts and big chests…
How can I not flirt with death?...
-Jay Z

CRAYLAND
(SEVENTEEN YEARS LATER)
WEST BALTIMORE, SUMMER OF 2006
MENACE TO BMORE

It was a hot summer day and twenty-nine-year old Crayland was watching his boy Markise run niggas on an outside basketball court in East Baltimore. Sitting in the stands, he sipped on a Corona as he sported a pair of green army fatigues, and a white wife beater. His hair was bleached blonde and he kept it low to prevent it from curling up too much. A few feet over, someone blasted, Tupac's "Hail Mary" from radio speakers.

"Markise is killin' they asses out here!" Jason said as he sat next to Cray.

He'd lost all his baby fat and hit the weights so hard that you could see his build under a coat. As strong as he was, he was still weak without Cray.

"You tellin' me." Cray confirmed. "Dat nigga's vicious."

When Cray's phone vibrated, he frowned when he saw it was Melody. Whenever he wanted somebody to disappear, he hit him with all 9's. Ever since Melody told Cray he saw him kill Kris, he'd been putting in work for him. And over time Melody respected how tough Cray was. Cray was fine with their business arrangement until he realized the money wasn't long enough to get the thing he wanted...POWER. The only way to get really paid was to involve himself in the distribution part of the business, and he was ready. In fact, he wanted Melody's operation.

"What up?" Cray asked.

"He's at a cookout at Druid Hill Park," Melody went straight to the point. "How long will it take you to get there?"

"Cray glanced at his watch and said, "Thirty minutes."

"Cool. Handle your bizness."

"I always do," Cray reminded him. "But when I get back I want to holla at you bout somethin'.""

"Before we do all of that, take care of my biz." Melody hung up.

Punk ass mothafucka! Cray thought.

When he put his phone back in his pocket, he saw Markise get close lined by a nigga on the basketball court. Without even thinking, he hopped down eight and nine benches at a time to get at him. From his peripheral vision, he saw his boys were running in that direction too. They were twenty deep! Cray led the pack as he ran up to the dude who momentarily put Markise on his back.

"You a'ight, man?" he asked helping Markise up eyeing the perpetrator the entire time.

He nodded yes.

"You must've forgot how to play the game, dude." Cray said, looking for a reason to lay the tall lanky man on his back.

"I ain't forget shit! He traveled." His four friends hesitantly moved behind him.

But the look in their eyes showed him that they were praying things were resolved civilly. To say that they were outnumbered was an understatement. Cray had over twenty men behind him.

"Yo, got mouth!" Jason added. "Let's bank this mothafucka!"

That was all he needed. Cray hit him with a two-piece. His friends tried to run but were caught a few feet out by Cray's goons. It looked like a riot on the basketball court. The dudes were getting stomped out by three and four niggas at a time! As always, somebody watching from the sidelines called the cops. And when they heard the sirens, everybody bailed. Cray and them didn't relax until they reached Cray's car.

"Yo, got his shit cracked!" Markise said, jumping on his 900 red Suzuki motorcycle. "Good lookin' out." He continued putting on his helmet.

"You know how we do." Cray laughed giving him dap.

"I'll get up wit ya'll tomorrow though. I got to grade these papers."

Markise was a teacher at a community college and played basketball overseas. Nobody even knew he had skills until he got to high school. But it wasn't until Markise picked up a ball that he knew himself.

"A'ight, yo!"

Zoom...ZOOM...ZOOOOOOOOOOOOOOOOOOMMMMMM!

When Markise sped off Jason and Cray jumped into Cray's white Crown Vic. His ride was beyond clean even though it resembled a police car.

"That shit was wild, yo!" Jason laughed, firing up the bob.

Cray watched him carefully from the corner of his eye. He didn't mind smoking in his car just as long as he didn't get shit all over his seat skin covers and shit. He was a neat freak to the ninth degree.

"You rollin' wit me?" Cray asked. "Cause I ain't goin' straight home."

"Where we goin?"

"I got to handle somethin' right quick."

He gave him the look that said murder was on his agenda.

"I guess I'm rollin' wit you then."

At The Picnic

The park was crowded with families there for the big picnic. Cray scanned the area for the police and didn't see any nearby. There were so many people out there he could barely drive. So he parked, got out, and looked for Tip, the dude who owed Melody money. He didn't understand why people didn't get it through their heads that Melody wasn't playing when it came to his dough. He couldn't count the number of bodies he dropped.

Although the park was jammed pack, he knew Tip wouldn't be hard to spot. And just as he thought, he stood out as he groped some short girl with dark blue hair. Cray hoped for her sake that she could carry his weight when he popped his punk ass.

Carefully he approached his target, heat in hand. He had to be quick because there were already a few people who recognized him. Cray's rep whistled throughout BMore and he'd earned the name the Reaper.

"Main man, you got change for a ...POP!"

He hit him in his head with a hot slug and watched him fall onto the girl in front of him.

When she moved he toppled to the grown eyes wide open. His body started shaking violently. And to be sure he was dead, Cray walked up on him and...Pop...Pop...Pop! Three more into his body.

Kneeling over him he said, "You shoulda paid up. Now you're number 128." He continued referring to how many people he killed in a lifetime.

With his work now done, he calmly walked away.

On His Steps

"You sure you can handle this?" Melody asked him after Cray told him how he felt about wanting a change in position. "Cause I don't like my money fucked wit."

They were outside, in the same place where seventeen years ago he knocked the wind out of his undeveloped chest for touching his car.

"Positive." Cray said with his hands in his pockets rocking from side to side.

Melody exhaled, walked a few feet away, and went back over to Cray.

Cray wanted to be put on but he wasn't about to beg his bitch ass either. If he didn't put him on, he had plans to be his worse enemy.

"You can trust me." Cray offered hoping it would be the deal breaker.

"A'ight, Cray," Melody said as if he should rethink his decision. "I'ma try you out tonight with my D.C. folks who move my product from NY. He's the only one I trust outside of J-Swizz to handle biz. Normally, I meet him myself, but since you want it, I'ma give it to you."

"I got…"

"I'm not finished," he said, cutting him off. "If everything goes as planned, you'll get more work. Got it?"

"Yeah," Cray said, trying not to be too anxious even though this was the break he needed. The only problem was he hated DC cats to the core!

"If my weight's off just a little, you might as well put a bullet in your head, cause what I'll do to you will be far worse."

Cray shook his head.

" I'm the same dude who cracked your chest back in the day, lil nigga. Remember that." Melody stated staring him down.

Cray listened but he had a news flash for Mr. Melody. He may have been the same dude who cracked his chest, but he wasn't a kid no more. He was a cold-hearted killer who wouldn't hesitate to put it to anybody who tested him. And that included the nigga who put him on.

At Home

Cray was returning home from D.C early in the morning, half sleepy after being in the hospital with Markise who had just gotten into a motorcycle accident. He'd already dropped Melody's dope off at his house but had to dip right back out after receiving the call from Jason that he was hurt. Nobody said it, but his ball playing career was over. Luckily for Markise outside of a few broken bones, he would be alright and still able to walk.

He almost dosed off on the road when he heard a cab driver pressing repeatedly on his horn behind him at the light. The cab driver had long blond hair and was swearing at him out his window. Just to fuck with him, Cray looked out his window and pointed his weapon in his direction. The cab driver through his hands up in the air and shook his head pleading with him not to shoo. Cray laughed and pulled off.

But the moment he entered his house and the hallway leading to his room, he couldn't help but feel that something was different. Turning the doorknob, he removed the gun from his waist, and tiptoed stealthily inside. Once inside, he saw his father kneeling on the floor peeling the plastic back off of one of Melody's keys. He was enraged. All his life his father violated him and he was tired. Aiming at him he cocked the hammer and saw his life flash before his eyes.

NYZON
WASHINGTON DC
FAMILY TIES

Nyzon was laying in Gabriella's bed, trying to think of the right thing to say to convince her to slide out of her panties. It was late in the afternoon and he was hoping to get some pussy before handling his business. It was hard for her to resist because Nyzon was finer than ever. He wasn't sportin' the waves anymore, but he did keep his hair in a low cut and knew how to wear his clothes. Not to mention, he was getting a little money from transporting some of the best heroin from New York that the east coast had ever seen..

"Gabriella...you know I'm feelin' you, right?" he said, laying on his side looking into her eyes. They were facing each other.

"I guess." She shrugged her shoulders playing with his platinum diamond chain. "But you like my best friend too." She grabbed a pillow, placing it between her legs.

"I know, but she ain't as sexy as you." He dug deep into his Game database. "I can see spendin' the rest of my life with you." He went too far, and he knew it.

"Monesha told me you said the same thing to her."

He was becoming sloppy with the game he ran on chicks but he wanted to fuck her so badly, he didn't care. He loved the chase and he broke hearts on a regular. It was all about fucking, getting money and flossing. Besides, he'd been with Monesha since high school and she still hadn't put out.

"I don't remember sayin' all that." He lied. "I'm serious, Gab, I'm tryin' to get to know you." He touched her face.

"Nyzon...," she said softly letting her guards down. "You messin' wit my head."

"I don't mean to be." He pulled up her shirt. He licked his lips when he was able to see the brownness of her nipples. "But you shouldn't be so fuckin' sexy."

The next thing she knew he had one of her titties in his mouth. He was quick and then his phone vibrated.

"Shit!"

He was about to ignore it until he remembered he needed to meet with Melody to deliver the keys.

"Hold on, shawty." He looked at the number. "Give me a sec."

"Go 'head." She pouted. "I guess I betta go to the bathroom and wipe myself off. And to think…I was gettin' real wet."

After hearing that he wanted to punch Melody in the throat for interrupting.

"What up?" he answered the phone watching her sash-shay away with that phat ass toting behind her.

"Change of plans. Same place. Same Car. New Person. Blonde Hair."

"Got it." He hung up. Nyzon never said too much over the phone.

When he looked at his Rolex, he saw he had thirty minutes to make it home, grab the Keys and pass them off. And then he'd have to rush to the bank to drop his dough off in his safe deposit box. Judging by the description, it would be a white dude, with blonde hair who was driving the rental car Melody usually used that was in a crack head's name.

"Gab, I got to go. Can I come through later?" He walked up to her and palmed her ass.

"It depends."

"On what?" Nyzon asked, kissing her forehead.

"On if you bringin' me a five piece chicken dinner with fries from Eddies. With mumbo sauce too."

"Got it, shawty."

"I'm serious, Ny. Don't' come back here without my food."

"I won't."

With the confirmation, he jetted out the door.

"Call me when you on your way," Gabriella yelled in the hallway. "I don't play that pop up shit!"

"No doubt."

In Her Apartment

"Girl, he fell for it." Gabriella said watching him jump into his car from her bedroom window.

"Stop lyin!" Monesha cried.

"Nope, I asked him to come over and he came. I told you he ain't shit!" Monesha cried harder.

"Did you fuck him?"

"No. I wouldn't do that to you."

"Did he suck your titties? He likes to suck titties."

"Didn't let him touch me."

"I'm so mad with him! I love, Nyzon."

"I'm so sorry, Monie. If you want to, you can spend the night with me." She hoped to get her in the bed again. She missed the softness of her skin against her own. They'd been playing the *Kissing Game* since high school.

"Maybe," Monesha said, breathing hard due to being angry. "I want to catch him in the act first."

"I can set it up!" Gabriella told her excited at the idea of him finally being gone from their lives.

"How soon?"

"Tonight! It ain't nothin' but a thing. Maybe now he'll finally get what he deserves for hurting you."

In Nyzon's Car

With the keys on him in a blue book bag, he waited patiently in his black Acura Legend for Melody's rental. Five minutes later the rental car pulled up. When he saw the blond hair Melody was talking about belonged to a nigga, he laughed. *These Baltimore cats be killin' me!* He thought.

Nyzon got out of his ride and jumped into the rental. They stared each other down for one minute. For some reason, there was immediate tension between them.

"Are you gonna suck my dick or give me the keys?" Cray asked.

"Naw shawty, but with all that beautiful blonde hair, I might let you suck mine." Nyzon retaliated.

Both of them reached for their birds and aimed them at one another. Had anybody flinched, the entire car would've been riddled with bullets.

"Do you really want it with me?" Nyzon asked, still aiming in his direction.

"Where are they?"

"Here." He threw the book bag at him with his free hand.

Cray opened the bag and briefly inspected the contents. "Now get the fuck out my car."

Still aimed.

Nyzon exited backward and slammed the door extra hard.

"Bamma mothafucka!"

"Fuck your slouch-sock-wearin-country-bumpkin, ass!" Cray called out.

When he pulled off, Nyzon hoped he'd never see his ass again.

At The Bank

Nyzon didn't go straight back to Gabriella's like he wanted because the moment he went home, the police surrounded his neighborhood on a drug sting. So he stayed over Royala's crib since the bank, which held the safe deposit box he used, didn't open until morning.

The moment it opened, he called Gabriella and offered to bring her some breakfast instead, before dropping off his money. He had thirty minutes before Gabriella said she'd lock the door. He rushed through the banks doors and the moment he saw an available attendant, he ran up to her.

"Excuse me, can you get somebody to let me into my safe deposit box?"

"Excuse me young man but I was next." A man said in a black shirt and blue jeans.

"I'm sorry sir...but if I don't get in there right now, I'll lose out on a woman I've been tryin' to get at forever."

The stranger smiled and said, "Go head. I know how that is."

"Thanks." Nyzon smiled as the attendant instructed him to sign in and escorted him to the safe.

The way he saw it in less than twenty minutes, he'd be having the time of his life, and that's all that mattered.

Back at Gabriella's

Nyzon sat in his car for a minute adjusted his chain, looked in the rear view mirror and approved of how he looked. But the moment he walked up to Gabriella's building, two dudes jumped out from the corners and grabbed him. They punch and kicked him all over his body. The oldest one of the two stood him up straight and was preparing to hit him again until he looked at his face.

"Hold up," he said, eyeing him closely. "What's your name?"

"What, mothafucka?" he yelled, blood in the corner of his mouth.

"I said what's your name, lil nigga?"

"Fuck you!" Nyzon yelled. "If you let me go, I'd punish your bitch ass."

Nyzon boxed at the local gym everyday and was good at it. So good he was only a few fights away from going professional. But what he really wanted to do was reach for the weapon in his waist.

"Put this nigga in the car," the oldest one said to the other one.

"Why?"

"Just do it!" he demanded.

"Where the fuck ya'll takin' me?" he asked growing irritated at what was going on.

They threw him in the back of a white Suburban next to Monesha. His arms and body ached all over. The moment he got in he looked up at her.

"Why ya'll bring him in here?" She looked at them like they were crazy. "You were supposed to fuck him up and leave his ass out there!"

"Be quiet, Monie. I'll tell you in a minute," the oldest said, pulling off.

Judging by the way they interacted, he figured they were all family. But he couldn't be sure because she never introduced him to any of her people. She swore she never would until they were married. So it was messed up they had to meet like this.

Family or not, once they took him out the car, he had plans to pull his weapon. He would've done it then but he was worried for Monesha. He didn't want her to get hurt in the process.

"I'm sorry, Monie," he said, softly.

"Fuck you! It's over." She started crying and turned toward the window.

"I know…but I'm still sorry," Nyzon said. "I fucked up. But what your peoples doin' right now is wrong."

"Look…I don't want to hear that shit," the oldest man yelled from the front seat. "Now shut the fuck up before I pull this mothafucka over and finish yo ass."

When the truck finally stopped he noticed he was in front of an old brick house in Fort Washington Maryland. Something about it was eerily familiar.

"Grab his young ass," the oldest directed.

All four of them walked into the house. Only the oldest knew the plan.

"Mamma," he said, placing his keys on the kitchen table. "Come in here! I got somebody I want you to see!"

"Boy, why is you yellin' in my house?!" she screamed from the living room.

With the lights all on, Nyzon stared at all of them closely. Something was very familiar about them, too. What was going on? He'd been in this house before. He just knew it.

After a few minutes, an older chubby woman wobbled into the kitchen. She was wearing a black silk robe and a black silk cap on her hair. Her feet could be heard slapping against the kitchen floor as she walked toward them. And the moment she saw Nyzon, she froze.

She couldn't move.

"Oh my, God!" She called out. "Oh my God!"

She dropped to her knees and prayed.

"I can't believe you're here." She yelled. "I can't believe you're really here!"

CAROLYN
GEORGETOWN, D.C
UNFAITHFUL

Carolyn sat at the dinner table with her father, brother, mother and fiancé, Conroy Moore, the man her mother always wanted her to be with since college. They were in her parent's home in Alexandria, Virginia. And the queasiness she was feeling was unbearable. All she wanted to do was get through dinner, look at the pregnancy stick she peed on just fifteen minutes earlier, and lay down.

"The campaign is already taking off to a good start, honey! Congrats!" Elizabeth said as she took the baked chicken casserole from the real china dish and placed it in the plates in front of her family. "You guys worked so hard and it's finally paying off!"

"Thanks, but we're far from where we need to be. Kirk needs our support more than ever if he's gonna win against Don Borslow. That nigger has backing from the major districts and major government officials. It's no other way to say it. D.C. wants a black mayor."

"Well I have an inside track that Don Borslow is shivering in his shoes." Conroy offered.

Although he was rich beyond belief, Conroy was nothing to look at. The only reason Carolyn kept him around was to take attention off of her true love, J-Swizz. J-Swizz of course didn't know about her fiancé. Conroy's nose seemed extraordinarily too big and his face was riddled with dark brown freckles.

"I don't think Kirk will have any problems winning the campaign to become mayor this time." He smiled rubbing Carolyn's hand.

She quickly snatched it away, and everyone tried to act as if they hadn't seen it.

"Thanks son, but I've been hearing the opposite. I think Kirk has a lot to worry about if he doesn't sway the votes."

"I don't mean to be rude, but I need to go to the restroom." Carolyn felt a gagging sensation take over her and unconsciously made a moaning sound.

"You okay, honey?" Elizabeth placed one hand on her shoulder.

"Is there anything I can do sweetheart?" Conroy asked, his breath smelling like hot shit.

"I'm fine." She turned away from him slightly to breathe. "I'll be fine."

Here she was a successful woman, with a college degree and high profile job as a partner in Barks and Smiths, and still she was afraid to tell her father that she was in love with, J-Swizz, a black man."

"You sure you're fine?" Todd asked, looking over at her with his wild eyes. Although he was asking her, she could tell he was being sarcastic. After all these years Todd still lived under their parent's roof and acted as the microphone for everything his father believed. Todd stayed in and out of jail and the Jamison's never knew what would happen with him on any given day. If he wasn't fighting, he was caught expressing his views in the public eye. For a while, William had to disassociate himself from his own son just to see Kirk through the election.

"Like I said I'm fine." She frowned looking at him. It was obvious that he didn't like her and she made no gripes about showing she couldn't stand him either. "And I'll be right back."

"Hurry, Carolyn, we have to discuss the details on how you can help with the mayor election too. I need everyone in this family on board."

"I understand, Daddy. Just give me one moment."

Lately, it seemed as if all he cared about was strategy, and getting Kirk into office. Here she was sick and he didn't bother asking if there was anything he could do.

Pushing open the door to the guestroom, she made her way to the private bathroom. The moment she did, she saw the stick she peed on ten minutes earlier missing.

She searched the floor, around the sink and even in the trash. Nothing. Where had it gone? Reaching into her pants pocket she pulled out her phone to call J-Swizz. She needed someone to calm her down. The moment someone answered, she noticed it was a female's voice.

"Hello?" the caller said with a slight attitude.

Carolyn looked at the phone sideways. Without responding, she hung up blocked her number out and dialed again.

It must be the wrong number. She thought.

"Hello? Who the fuck is this? Dis bet not be another one of J's bitches!" the girl screamed from the other end of the phone.

Carolyn fell up against the sink. She'd been with him for so many years! How could he do this to her again? She put everything on the line for him! Her family. Her life and now her body! And this is how he repays her? She didn't even care about the pregnancy stick anymore, she already knew the answer. She was pregnant and with their first baby.

With the phone still against her ear, she finally heard his voice.

"Yo give me my phone and stop trippin'."

Silence.

"Who is this?" he asked.

She said nothing. After all, what could she say?

KAVON
WASHINGTON, D.C.
BABY I'M COMING HOME

The cab ride from Lorton to D.C. was the longest ride Kavon had ever taken in his life. Everything he'd known for sixteen years had changed. Everything! Even the cars were different and he sensed a different atmosphere in the air. He was still thinking about everything that faced him ahead when the white cab driver with long blond hair pressed on his horn. He sat quietly in the back seat wearing a thin black shirt and blue jeans wondering what was up with the commotion.

"What's goin' on?" Kavon asked looking up at him.

"This fool is sleep at the wheel! I tell you they shouldn't give everybody licenses these days!"

Kavon and the driver laughed until a young boy with bleached hair stuck his head out of the window and pointed a gun in their direction. There was a devious look in his eyes and it set uneasy with Kavon. For some reason, he reminded him of Shy.

"Dear God, please don't let me go out like this," the cab driver prayed with his hands in the air.

"Just be easy...he's just fuckin' wit you." Kavon had seen enough of bluffing in his days to know one when he saw it.

And just as he thought, the white Crown Vic pulled off. It took the driver three minutes to regain his composure

"I see the world hasn't changed much." Kavon adjusted in his seat, relieved the close call was over.

"The hell if it ain't. I don't know how long you been in, but everything's changed. After they impeached Mayor Gibson for finding out he smoked cocaine, they got mayor Lavern Watts who didn't know her ass from her elbow. She lasted all of one term before they got Mayor Bordell Holds. Now he's good, but far from perfect. I think Kirk Bowler is gonna shape this city up just fine. You'll see."

"I don't know about that, I mean, I been in jail but I ain't been out of it. They say more white people in the police force than ever before. Naw...I think if Kirk Bowler runs the city, we're all in trouble."

The cab driver continued to talk and Kavon allowed him, but he had other things on his mind and he zoomed out.

It had been seventeen years since he'd seen or heard from Tara or his daughter. And after he dissolved their marriage, for the first few months she called the prison every night trying to get a hold of him. When that didn't work, she wrote a letter a day without fail. He never opened a single one of them.

He wanted them to be happy and to have a chance at a future, not stopping by once a week to see him behind bars.

And then his lawyer came to visit him on a rainy day in April last year. It was the day that changed his life.

"Kavon...I think I found something." He said.

Kavon sat on the other end of the table looking at him hopelessly. Phillip had said those words at least three times before and every last one of them went nowhere.

"Phil, please. How many times I got to hear that? I think you just ridin' on my money while I'm rottin' behind bars. I'm in here for forty and I have to accept that."

"Kavon...the detectives exceeded the amount of time they were supposed to listen when they tapped the phone." Phillip Croones sat his brown leather briefcase on the table and popped it open releasing a white piece of paper. He handed the report to him. "The tap was only supposed to last a minute. If they didn't hear what they needed to by then, based on the warrant, they were supposed to terminate the tap. You didn't say what you did until one minute and thirty seven seconds into the conversation. It's inadmissible, Kavon. In your words, they fucked up."

Although he fought it, he couldn't help but smile. He'd studied enough law books to know that this time, Croones was on to something. What he really wanted to say was, how come he didn't point this out before. He was supposed to be the best of the best. But because he needed him focused to get him out he let it ride.

"And this isn't the first time Detective Betha and Mesaline have messed up. They have ties to a racist organization called the KYC. These people live their lives trying to persecute black people. This is the moment we've been waiting for."

Those words played in his head for over a year until he was finally released. Once a prisoner, now he was a free man based on a technicality.

"That's it right there." He pointed to Nations Bank in Southwest D.C. "Keep the car running, I'll be right back."

When he got out he grabbed his book bag and opened the bank door. There were a few people standing around handling business. It took ten minutes to get the attention of one of the bank employees. But he was patient because he'd just done more time behind bars. Finally a thin black woman asked if he needed help when a young man bolted pass him.

"Excuse me, can you get somebody to let me into my safe deposit box?"

The young man appeared to be in an extreme hurry.

Kavon remained calm.

"Excuse me young man but I was next." Kavon replied.

"I'm sorry sir…but if I don't get in there right now, I'll lose out on a woman I've been tryin' to get at for a minute!"

Kavon smiled and said, "Go head. I know how that is."

"Thanks." He smiled before the attendant let him in the back.

Kavon waited for ten minutes before the young man thanked him again, ran passed him and out the door.

"Right this way, sir." The attendant said walking over to Kavon. He followed her to the back signed in and proceeded to his safe. "Let me know if you need anything." She said as she gave him some privacy before closing the door behind her.

When she was gone, he removed a shoebox from the safe and placed it in his book bag. Judging by its weight, it was all there. He wouldn't bother counting it at the bank. He'd do that in the car.

He walked back to his cab and paid him handsomely for waiting. Then he opened the shoebox and checked the contents. Yep, it was one million in cash. Before he went in he gave Kurt access to the other key and told him to handle two million dollars. Five hundred thousand was for him the other money was to care for his wife and baby. The only thing Kurt took off the top was his share. But with all of the drama he experienced with Tara trying to get more than Kavon allowed her to at one time, he was certain, the 500 thousand was not enough.

People were telling him all kinds of shit about his wife when he was locked down. He heard everything from her being on heroin, to her selling her body for crack. At one point he tried to reach her but the phone was turned off. And he wasn't able to get a confirmation from Kurt, because he was doing time on a manslaughter charge, unrelated to anything he did for Kavon. Instead of believing rumors, he wanted to see her for himself. He couldn't believe Tara would go that route. He knew the moment he laid eyes on her he'd be able to tell if everything he heard was true.

The cab driver stopped in front of his old house. He shook his head in disgust after seeing how unkempt the grounds were. A few of the windows were boarded and the others had cracked glass. What hurt even more was that it was the only house that was uncared for on the block. When he saw a black woman tending to the small garden in the front of her home, he knew the white family who lived there had moved on, probably cause of whatever Tara had going on.

The woman rolled her eyes at him, and he imagined how many had traveled in and out of his home.

"Keep it runnin'," Kavon told the driver. He grabbed his book bag and walked to the house.

When he approached the door, he was surprised to see the key still worked. But the moment he opened it up, a gust of foul smelling wind hit him. The door could hardly open due to all the clothes amongst the floor. All of their furniture was gone. The brass table that cost him over four thousand dollars and the frames on the wall were all gone. He held his nose as he pushed past all of the junk.

Looking at his daughter's bedroom door, he noticed the wooden sign that spelled Tiara was missing the T. And when he opened it, he saw a dirty mattress on the floor covered with filthy clothing.

A dim nightlight lit the room, just enough for him to see her face. When he walked toward the bed, he stared down at his daughter. Tears filled his eyes. How could he do her like this? How could he abandon his only child? He knew Tara wasn't strong enough. She told him. The child he prayed to God for every night, in the end, he abandoned.

Kneeling by her bedside, he looked at her some more. Her beauty surpassed even that of her mother. Her chocolate skin belonged to him, yet her eyes, hair and even her nose were all Tara's. Her eyelashes were extremely long and her face was clear and without flaws although she was too frail and skinny to be seventeen.

It was settled, he was taking her out of there. When he touched her gently, a teardrop fell from his eyes and onto her cheek. She opened her eyes, smiled and hugged him tightly. She knew him. But how? He had no contact with her in all these years.

"Daddy...I knew you'd come for me!" Tiara said, hugging him closely.

He was speechless.

After twenty seconds he said, "I'll never leave you again."

"I know, Daddy." I prayed for you. Every night."

"Get up, we're leaving."

With her hand in his, he moved toward the front door. When he did, he saw a tattered picture of himself and Shy at the cabaret the night he raped Tara. That's how she knew it was him. He told her to leave it wanting no memories of that beast around her.

When he walked to the front door, Tara appeared from her bedroom. He turned around and faced her.

"Daddy, please...let's go," Tiara begged, trembling. "I don't want to be here anymore."

What had her so frightened?

"Kavon!" she said, softly. "Oh, my God, you're finally home. It's really you."

Despite years of drug abuse, she was still beautiful to him. Her skin looked dry and she had a small cut in the corner of her mouth.

He heard of people recovering from drug abuse and getting back on track. Maybe with a little help, he could see her through this. At the same time, she did a terrible job as a mother. He looked at Tiara who was almost as tall as her mother and decided to go with his heart. He just hoped that he'd make the right decision.

KRISTINA'S DINER
CURRENT DAY

The girl sat in amazement at the stranger's story. Although the restaurant was even more crowded than when he first started, to her it seemed as if they were alone.

"Well?" she asked as she occupied the seat between them that at once held her purse.

"Well, what?" He laughed as he sipped on his hot chocolate before ordering another one. "I'm gonna tell you, Tammy." He laughed at her apt attention.

"Tammy?"

"Yeah...that is your name right?" He knew she lied from the beginning.

"Oh...no...sorry. I thought you were trying to come on to me earlier. My name is Beliza. Sorry for lyin'."

"Not a problem, shawty. I rarely use names anyway, but if I'm gonna tell you the rest, I need to know who I'm talking to."

She smiled to shield her embarrassment.

"Sure. I'm just happy to know it's not going to end there. You have to tell me the rest!" Beliza was definitely interested and it amused him. "So what happened next?"

"There is more...a lot more." His voice was serious but calm.

"Oh, no! Please don't tell me something happened to the Tiara!" she placed her hand over her mouth and looked at him with saddened eyes.

"Let's just say this. Before anything good can happen, tragedy has to take place so that it can be appreciated. And this story is no exception."

THE SAGA CONTINUES

What's beef? Beef is when you need two gats to go to
sleep
Beef is when your moms ain't safe up in the streets
Beef is when I see you
Guaranteed to be an I.C.U, one more time
What's beef? Beef is when you make your enemies
start your Jeep
Beef is when you roll no less than thirty deep
Beef is when I see you
Guaranteed to be an I.C.U, check it.

-Notorious B.I.G

NYZON
WASHINGTON, D.C., 2006
EVERYTHING KNOWN WAS A LIE

Nyzon stared at the woman in the kitchen and wondered what she meant. He watched as the niggas who kidnapped him moments earlier helped her up from the floor. Her eyes were filled with amazement as she shook them off to let her go.

"Look at you....you're so handsome."

His head was between her large soft hands as she examined every inch of his face. Any other time he'd be apprehensive about someone touching him but this was different.

"And...what happened to your face?!" she asked briefly skipping the subject. "Which one of you niggas beat this chiyald?" She looked to them for answers but they kept their heads hung low.

"We found him like that." The oldest one lied giving Nyzon the look to keep their secret.

"Yeah right! Hand me a napkin and some water." She directed everyone around her. "And Monesha, go in the bathroom and bring me the peroxide." When Monesha left she remembered something else. "And the Band Aids too!" her outburst rocked Nyzon's eardrum.

With everything sitting neatly on the yellow kitchen table, she went to work at once on his bruises.

"Sweetheart, I'm your aunt Jackie." She dipped the napkin into the per-oxide and tapped his face. It stung slightly. "And I've spent most of my life looking for you."

"My aunt? I ain't got no folks out here." Jackie patched his face up with a Band Aid.

Her eyes widened at his response.

"Baby...I don't know what you've been told, but you have a huge familee in D.C., Maryland' and Virginia!"

Nyzon sat down at the kitchen table, rubbed his head and unconsciously placed his gun upon it. Her statements confused him. Family? Locally? If what she was saying was true, it meant everything he'd ever known his entire life was a lie. Than he remembered all the times his mother moved him from school to school almost as if she was running from something or somebody.

He was still taking everything in when she screamed, "Oh my LAWD!" She jumped back against the refrigerator rocking the entire unit.

Nyzon realizing what upset her tried to tuck his gun back in his pants. "My bad."

"Get that shit OUT my HOUSE! Jesus…my Savior….thy God! Help me please Father God!!!"

"Let me get that up off you." The oldest one said walking over to him, his hand extended for Nyzon's heat.

He handed it over to him willingly and he walked it outside.

"Listen son…now I know ya'll gots to do what ya'll gots to do when you out dere in dem streets, but don't ever bring no weapons in my house again. You hear me?"

He nodded yes.

He'd only been in her presence for only five minutes and already he had Great respect for her. When she felt he knew how serious she was, she said, "Let me introduce you to the rest of the familee." The older one walked back inside. He made mental notes to check him for his piece before he left. "This here is your cousin Dyzell, he's my oldest son."

"But everybody calls me Cooks."

Cooks was so tall he had to stoop down just to walk through most door-ways. With medium length dreads, you could see the streets written all over his face.

"Everybody but your motha!"

"I know ma." He said under his breath. "Ever since they been callin' you that you been in and out of trouble!"

Silence.

"Now this one right here is my second to the oldest son Simon." She pointed.

"And they calls me Simon." He responded laughing at his own joke. Simon was a little shorter than Cooks, with a ball head and chubby waist.

"Shut up fool!" she gave him a serious look. "Lastly this is Monesha, the only girl of the family. She's like a daughter to me."

"Stop playin' ma! I am your daughter." She giggled.

Hold up. He thought. *Her daughter equals my cousin. Fuck!*

Jackie gripped her while Monesha and Nyzon's eyes locked. If they were really family, that would be the worst part about it.

"She lives in D.C. with her father and my ex-husband Rob. Have you two met?"

There was no way he could tell her yes when just last month, Monesha had his dick in her mouth.

"Naw…they don't know each other." Cooks interrupted. "He knows one of my friends, and I was bout to give him a ride home when I noticed he looked familiar."

Nyzon breathed a sigh of relief.

"Oh. I see." Her face softened as she looked at Nyzon again. "I still can't believe you're here. My baby sister's only son." She wiped her sweaty face with a napkin from the table. "I miss her so much."

She became dejected as she thought about her sister.

Cooks consoled his mother by rubbing her back softly.

"If what you sayin' is true, and your sister is my mother, she's still alive." He said although his gut told him something was up with his mother's story. He'd always believed that the woman he knew all his life, was not his mother. "We live in Southeast."

They looked at each other like he'd lost his mind.

"Son what are you talkin' about?" She walked up to him. "I buried my sister many years ago."

"I guess we're not related then." He stood up. "Can somebody take me to the city please? Cuz I gotta get my ride."

"Get the photo album Monesha." Her eyes were planted on Nyzon. "And sit down, son."

Nyzon obeyed.

Monesha returned a few seconds later with a huge yellow photo album and placed it on the table.

"Open it, Shelton." She was speaking to Nyzon.

"Shelton?" he repeated raising his brow. He'd heard that name before, but where? "I mean…open it, son."

His expression told her he was unaware of his birth name.

When he opened the album, the pages made the crackling sound most photo albums due when it hasn't been opened in awhile.

"Keep flippin' son."

He continued to turn the pages until she stopped him by placing her hand over his.

"There. We took this on the day you were born."

A sparkle entered her eyes as she stared at the photo. "The doctor told your mama she couldn't have kids. They were wrong." She touched his face again with the back of her hand.

Nyzon slowly pulled the plastic back, removed the photo and stared at the picture closely. The baby in the photo looked like him, but it looked like it could've been any one of them.

"And this is your mother."

The woman in the photo had auburn colored hair. He examined it closely. A sporadic smile spread across his face. She was exquisite. Her large eyes matched his perfectly. Suddenly the room began to spin as he realized, she was also the one from his nightmares.

"She died in a car accident." Jackie continued. "I was the last person to see her alive. Alls I really remember, is that she was upset about somethin'.

She never told me what. I shoulda forced her to stay, but I didn't. Hours after she left my house, her car was demolished in a car accident. We found her body, but couldn't find you anywhere. They formed a search party for months and when they stopped, our family kept looking. Somethin' in my spirit knew you were still alive." Suddenly she gave him a look as if she remembered something extremely important. "Where have you been, Shelton? Where were you all this time?"

Her mouth was moving but he could no longer make out the words. Too much was revealed at one time. He went to stand up, wobbled, and fell to the floor.

CRAYLAND
FUCKED UP LIFE

Cray couldn't believe his father had the nerve to peel back the plastic off of one of Melody's keys. To say he was angry was an understatement. Right before he was about to click, pop on his ass, he felt his mother come behind him.

"Don't do it, baby." Her arms wrapped around his. "It's not worth it."

On his knees, his father cowardly remained with his arms in the air. His once muscular body now frail and thin from drug abuse. His fright pleased Cray. He was sick of telling his ass over and over to stay out of his space. His lack of respect for him got the fuck on his nerves. And as far as he was concerned the world would be better off with one less junkie roaming around, especially one who wasn't paying him.

"Don't do it, son." he pleaded shaking. Cray smelled a faint stench of shit in the air from his father's bows releasing. "Please don't kill me."

He was angry that a part of him, the part that wanted a father, still cared. The gun shook in his hands. He wanted to do it. But was he really worth it? The bottom line was, from the moment he could walk he'd been doing it alone ever since.

As he decided his father's fate, his phone rang. It brought him back to reality. Cray's arms dropped as he watched his father fall up against his nightstand in relief. It was Melody.

"Get off me, bitch!" he said to his mother after placing the gun in the back of his pants, covering it with his shirt. "Don't ever put your fuckin' hands on me. I wasn't bout to waste a bullet on his ass anyway."

With a closed fist, he walked up to his father who smelled worse than the New York City sewer system and knocked him out. With his father stretched out at his feet, Cray reassembled Melody's product, put it back in the bag, and answered the phone.

"Melody, where you want to meet?" he asked seeing his mother kneeling down, trying to help his father off of the wooden floor. She almost toppled over when all of his weight rested on her thin body. "Hey, yo! Hurry up and get that nigga out of here!" Cray interrupted Melody before he could answer.

After all the shit he did to her, you'd think she'd be happy I stole his ass. He thought.

"Where you at?" Melody asked.

"Home."

"I'll be at my crib lada. But knock on the door and give my shit to J-Swizz."'"

"You sure?"

He wasn't feeling handing product to a third party before Melody could inspect it.

"Positive. Did everything go okay wit Nyzon?"

"Oh that's that nigga's name?"

Melody laughed.

"You know I don't fuck wit' DC cats! But it went a'ight if that's what you want to call it."

"Well get over it." Melody responded singing the rest of the words. "Because if I continue to use you, that's who you'll be dealin' wit for now on."

I'm sick of this nigga's shit! Cray thought.

"It is what it is." Cray responded.

"Lada."

When he hung up, he rushed out his bedroom door with the bag in hand. He was moving out of the house and leaving everything behind. He'd buy all new shit once he got situated.

"I'm movin' out." He told his mom walking past her in the living room.

No details were necessary. With him gone, he was sure they'd lose the house. He financed everything, their drug habit included. But he was tired of having to hide his possessions every time he left the front door. The cash he wasn't worried about because he never kept more around than he could stand to lose. And he wasn't blind to it missing money despite tucking it under his mattress. Besides, if they took it, he wouldn't have to give it to them if they asked.

"I know you're leaving, baby. It's time." He stopped and turned around. And the moment he did, he noticed something different about her eyes. He couldn't place his finger on it.

Was she clean? He thought. *Fuck naw!*

"And I know you're disgusted with everything we did to you over the years."

"You don't know nothin' bout me." He was angry and hurt.

"Cray, please. I might never see you again and I want you to hear me out."

He stopped, his breaths heavy.

"I know you're disgusted with me. But I swear to you…on what's left of my life, that I'm gonna get better. And if it's not too late, maybe I can learn to be a mother to you again. If nothing else a friend. I haven't gotten high in over a month." She *was* clean.

Still, her body was beyond thin and the scars from the many years of drug abuse shown all over. He hated her! He hated them! He decided to put her to the test. And if she passed, who knew what life had in store for their relationship.

"You really clean?" A maniacal grin took over his face.

"Yes, son. I am." She smiled proudly.

"So you don't want dis new shit I got in my pocket?"

Her eyes widened a little, still she shook her head no.

"You passin' up on some good shit. I got this from New York and every-body hittin' me up. You ain't heard? These feens goin' crazy 'round here. You sure you don't want it?" Silence.

He witnessed her body shake as the desires of her mind battled with those of her heart.

"I...can't...I'm...tryin', Cray. Don't do this to me because I'm tryin' so hard, baby." She cried. "Please don't make me choose when I'm not strong enough. Let me fight this thing some more."

"You want it or not?!" He screamed. "I ain't got time for this shit!"

She dropped to her knees and sobbed heavily. "Cray, please stop. Don't do this."

"Fuck it I'm out of here!"

He was halfway to the door until she said, "Don't leave, Cray. P...Please don't go."

His heart raced.

He wondered if she wanted *him* or the dope.

"I need the drugs."

She lost the battle and she lost him.

He laughed although his heart broke inside.

"That's what I thought. I neva had a mother, bitch! So don't waste your time."

He went down the steps and out the front door. Leaving her empty hand-ed.

KAVON
WASHINGTON, D.C.
DADDY'S LITTLE GIRL

Kavon hadn't planned on seeing Tara. And most of all, he hadn't planned on her looking as badly as she did. But it was time...time for him to deal with what he'd been running from for so many years. His failure as a husband, father and man.

"Tiara, honey," He looked down at her bare feet. "Run to your room and put on your shoes." He voice was soft. The foul smell inside of the home was so strong it weakened his stomach.

"Okay, daddy. Don't leave me okay?"

"I won't."

Tiara looked at her father and walked carefully past her mother. Then she jetted toward her bedroom

"Tara...what happened?" he pushed past the dirty clothes on the floor to reach her. And the only thing that resembled the woman he knew was her eyes. "Look at you."

"Yeah...look at me." She raised her arms and dropped them by her sides. "What did you think would happen, Kavon? You were the only thing I had in this world, and you took that from me."

"Tara...I wasn't trying to leave you. I was tryin' to give you a chance at a life. I ain't want you bein' stuck wit a nigga behind bars for forty years! I wanted you to be free."

She laughed heavily. "So is that what they're callin' it now in prison? When you run out on your family?"

He couldn't come back with a response.

"I loved you, Kavon. I didn't care if it meant seeing you in jail all 2,080 weeks." His eyes widened in surprise at her accuracy. "Yeah I counted them. When you got locked up, I thought I would die. And then I realized, I'd still be able to see you. I still be able to see the face that got me through so many days. So I counted the weeks I'd be able to see your face. And when you left me I recounted the weeks I couldn't. All I wanted was you. And the drug was the closest thing to you. I traded one addiction for another." She cried rubbing her arms. "But you know what, I'm still in love with you now."

Her words hit him like a ton of bricks. This was all his fault.

"Tara but," he was interrupted by Tiara walking out with two wrong shoes. Her beauty stung him every time he saw her. She looked like a model. She was holding a burgundy diary with a gold lock. It was the only thing consistent in her life because she wrote in it everyday.

"Tiara," he laughed lightly as not to embarrass her. "They don't match, baby. Your shoes don't match."

"These are all I have."

His heart fell to the pit of his stomach. He looked at Tara and back at his daughter. A wave of temporary anger overcame him.

"Okay, honey…go get in that car outside." He opened the front door and pointed to the cab. "I'll be out in a minute."

"You promise?" Tears escaped her eyes.

"Listen, sweetheart." All Kavon wanted was for her to look into his eyes. He felt if she stared hard enough, she'd see and feel how much he thought about her every day he was locked down. And that no matter what, he was never leaving her again. "My breath would have to be removed from my body before I ever left you again. You hear me?"

She smiled and threw her arms around him. Believing she understood him, he breathed a sigh of relief.

"Now go to the car. I'll be out in a second."

She opened the front door wider and ran to the car, looking back once before she jumped in. Once she was inside the cab, he adjusted his book bag and faced Tara. Walking over to her, he tried to hold her but she pushed him away.

He tried again.

She pushed harder.

He tried one last time and she gave in.

Tara broke down in his arms crying her heart out. And the tears from her pain drenched Kavon's shirt. He held her tighter. She hadn't had an emotional release since he was locked up, and he felt she deserved it. When her cries subsided a little, he released her slowly.

"We're gettin' out of here so I can help you." Kavon's voice was mellow yet authoritative.

If she was half the woman she used to be, he knew she'd appreciate him taking charge again.

With one hand on her shoulder he said, "You're still my wife and I still have a commitment to you."

"Commitment?" She repeated with sarcasm. "Why does that matter now?"

"It always mattered. That's why I let you go."

"Why?" she asked wiping her tears. "I mean look at me. Look at Tiara!" she pointed toward the door. "I didn't even keep our home together. I'm nothin'."

"Tara…I don't care. You think I give a fuck about this materialistic bull-shit?! I was willing to give it all up for you! That's why I told Shy I wanted out of the game."

Her eyes widened because she didn't know that.

"Yes, baby. The night he," a lump formed in his throat. "The night he raped you, I told him I wanted out. So I could care less about the money or these things. They're meaningless! I'm not gonna lie to you. I never have and I never will. So let me say, I did come here for Tiara at first."

"I knew you did." She turned away from him and walked toward the hallway. "She's the only one you ever cared about. Now that you have her, why are you still here?"

"Tara…please. I need to be honest with you always." He gripped her hand softly and pulled her toward him. "At first I did come for Tiara. But the moment I saw your face, I knew I was still in love with you. I guess what I'm tryin' to say is, I never got over you. And I doubt I ever will."

She cried.

"Come with me, baby." He wrapped his arms around the lower part of her body. "Come with us. Let's be a family. We've lost so much already. We can make it if we do it together."

"I don't believe in fairy tales."

"You use to." He smiled. "Remember?"

"Not anymore."

"Well I'm still your night and shining armor. I'm still that nigga who can make that pussy jump and your body tremble. I'm still the nigga who would lie down his life right here and now to prove how much I love you. I'm still that nigga who realizes that there's not another woman alive out here for me. I'm still that nigga who commited murder for you. Do you believe in fairy tales now? Do you believe I've come to your rescue?"

He got on one knee, as if he was proposing to her all over again. And in a sense, he was. "I fucked up, but I'm here, askin' you to let me make things right by you. I'm sorry baby. Give me a chance."

She didn't answer.

Her silence was killing him.

Next to his freedom and being with his daughter, he wanted nothing more.

"Okay."

"Okay?" He stood.

"Okay. I'll go with you."

"Me and you against the world?" He joked.

"Always."

He led her to the door and she followed holding his hand. Kavon looked back once to be sure she was really there. She was. He knew it wouldn't be easy to help her get over the addiction, but he was willing to do whatever it took to fight for his family.

He'd start by getting both of them fresh clothes and then they'd stay at a hotel until he found a new place for them to live. He had enough cash to make everything possible. He already worked out the details to sell their home in his mind. There was no way on earth he would keep his family in Georgetown, even though it was the ritzy part of D.C. Kavon was positive that whatever she got tied into, would find her again if they stayed there.

Once in the cab he released Tara's hand and slid into the backseat next to Tiara. After all these years, his family was finally coming together. And the moment he sat next to Tiara, he kissed her gently on the cheek. To have gone through so much, she had so much love in her heart.

"I love you, daddy."

He winked and said, "And there's no one I love more than you."

With the door still open, he waited for Tara to get in next to him, but there was something in her eyes. It was as if seeing them together, made her jealous, and instead of getting in, she slammed the door shut.

"I can't go with you." she sobbed looking through the rolled down window. "I'm not ready, Kavon. I'm sorry."

"Why not?"

"Because I can't feel the way I did when you left me. I just can't. I'm sorry, Kavon. Take care of Tiara. Goodbye." She took two steps back from the cab.

He was silent as he pushed out the feeling of hate that tried to overcome him. *How could she do this? How could she not want to see their daughter grow into a beautiful young woman?*

"You could leave Tiara so easily?"

"I already have."

He was sick. Everything in him wanted to get out the car and force her to get in. He envisioned grabbing her by the back of her neck and pushing her inside the car. He'd be damned if he'd allow drugs to maintain its hold on her life.

In fact, he moved to do just that until Tiara gripped his arm, reminding him of his original purpose. He turned around looked at his daughter and just like that, his heart softened and his chest hardened. He had to protect Tiara and getting her away from Tara may be the best thing for her.

Turning back around he faced his wife and said, "It's your call."

With those words he told the driver where to go and looked at Tara one last time, until she was out of sight.

CRAYLAND
REISTERSTOWN, MARYLAND
BEAUTY IS HER NAME

The temperature was hotter than normal outside. Any other time Cray and his boys would be in the house until it cooled off, but today was different. They'd just finished lugging Cray's stuff into his boy Blunt's crib, and was in the garage sipping beer. He decided to stay with him in Reisterstown, Maryland, until he figured out his next move.

Vic who was now called Blunt, had been cool with Cray ever since he warned him against going to Hammerjacks, a nightclub in Bmore. Turns out this nigga name Greedy Gary was after him after he murdered his friend who really was his gay lover. But instead of Greedy Gary poppin' his head, the moment Greedy's timbs touched the curb, Cray unloaded so much lead into his skull, the morgue technician gave up trying to take it all out.

Blunt was a hand to hand cat most of his life. He dropped out of elementary and worked for a few small time dealers around his way. Before he saved his change, he lived in a fucked up row house off Freemont avenue in West Bmore. He had no electricity but stole some from his neighbors by connecting to their power lines. To top it all off, he took care of his four brothers because his mother left them alone the day he turned twelve.

So Cray knew he needed all the extra cash he could get just to survive. And when things worked out later, he had plans to make him a lieutenant, finally putting him where he deserved to be, in his army.

Blunt also knew more about automobiles than the people who made them. If you wanted something fixed on your ride, and you wanted it done right, Blunt was the man to call.

As he blasted NWA's "Dopeman", he smoked a blunt while he worked on Cray's car. He use to smoke cigarettes all the time but traded them for weed. Nobody ever saw him without a blunt in his mouth, hence the nickname.

"So let me get this straight, you fucked this broad in the bathroom at Giant?" Blunt asked as he looked under the hood of Cray's car, tools in hand. He looked so much like DMX they could be twins.

"I know ya'll niggas don't believe me, but I ain't got no reason to lie on my dick. Yo ain't give a fuck! She was straight up like, you tryin' to see me now or what. I had to push off."

"That's some nasty shit!" Markise sat in a green plastic chair and sipped on a Bud. "Niggas is gettin' reckless wit they fuck game nowadays. Too much shit out there and I bet your ass ain't wear a condom either."

"Don't be mad cause you can't fuck girls like Cray! He the man!" Jason stayed jocking Cray's dick.

It was pitiful and Markise never gave up hope, that one day he'd be his own man. Jason and Markise had gotten closer over the years, and the only time they fell out was when Cray was involved.

"This nigga sound dumb!" Markise shook his head in utter disbelief. He tried to position himself to sit comfortably in the chair with his leg cast on. Luckily all he had was some broken bones from the motorcycle accident. "You must be fuckin' him too?"

"Leave dis nigga alone! He know I be gettin' mad pussy. But that shit today proved my point that these females ain't good for shit! I would neva wife one of these hoes out here!" Cray said downing more of his beer.

"You say that shit now, but one day you gonna meet the right girl to change all that shit!" Markise said as he got up, hobbled over to the cooler and grabbed another beer. "It's just a matter of time." He sat back down.

"Naw...not me! All I care about is gettin' this cheddar! Why you think I keep handin' bitches off to this nigga?" He pointed to Jason. "Bitches come a dime a dozen."

"Since you wanna hook a nigga up, what's up with Jasiya?" Blunt dropped the hood and rubbed his hand on the white oily towel. "Cause you actin' stingy as a mothafucka wit that one."

They laughed.

"That's cause I ain't smash yet! Greedy ass nigga tryna get the pussy before me." Cray raised his arms up in the air with his beer in hand. "When I'm done she's yours."

"A'ight...but remember however you treatin' these broads, somebody could be doin' yo mother the same way." Markise was so dead set on proving his point, that he didn't care about who he was talking too. One crazy ass mothafucka.

"What you say, nigga?" Cray asked approaching him.

"Aw shit!" Blunt said wiping his hand on the towel before dropping it to the ground. "Come on, man. Ya'll peoples."

Every now and again Cray liked to fuck with Markise because after all these years, he still couldn't get him to follow his lead the way he could with Jason. Markise always stood his ground and today was no different.

"Oh so you gonna hit me while I'm down? If I wasn't in this cast, you couldn't go one round with me."

"Is this nigga serious?" Cray looked around for backup. "I could sit in a chair with one arm strapped behind my back and still kick yo ass."

Cray was high and mad about everything that happened at his crib. He was angry for putting his mother to the test believing had he not, she would've really tried hard. He was mad at having to work for Melody and he was mad at the world. So for real, now was not the time to go toe to toe with him.

Instead of responding, Markise laughed.

Blunt and Jason looked at him wondering what was funny.

"Yo, love showin' off in front of niggas. I been tired of yo shit since we was kids. Hate for a nigga to speak their mind. I put this on everything, weapons down, I'd knock your block off if I wasn't hurt." Markise added shaking his head and sipping his beer.

Without warning, Cray took the glass bottle of beer in his hand and smacked Markise so hard against his head it shattered on his face. Blood was everywhere.

"Oh shit!" Blunt yelled out. "Cray what the fuck you doin' man? That's your boy!"

Markise placed his hand on his head and held his eye. He would definitely have to go to the hospital behind that shit. Cray was about to swell on him again when he saw this girl getting out of a car a few doors down. Her golden hair and chocolate skin caught his attention. Who was she?

"Fuck! Now my neighbor's home." Blunt said holding his head. "This a respectable community, man. You can't be doin' shit like that 'round here!"

"Nigga, this Reisterstown, Maryland! It's still the ghetto!" Cray corrected him.

"Man, you can't be doin' that east Baltimore shit out here like that!" Blunt continued. "Yo Jay, take this nigga to the hospital. I can't stand niggas sometimes! That's why people want to live with the white folks! As a people we don't know how to act. Damn!"

"Shut yo, Do The Right Thing ass up!" Cray continued.

"I'ma get your ass back nigga!" Markise promised. "I put that on everything!"

As Jason lifted Markise off the ground, Cray's attention remained fixated on the girl. And she didn't see him until after her door was open, and she smiled.

"Yo, Cray?" Blunt yelled brining him back to reality.

Cray turned around and looked at him.

"What's up?" He finally remembered what happened as he saw Jason pull off, with Markise in the back seat holding his face.

"That was fucked up, man. You know that nigga ain't mean it like that."

"Fuck that shit! I ain't neva fuck wit him for real for real." He lied. He wished he hadn't took it that far with Markise but the damage was done. Literally. But outside of Jason, he was the only family he had. "I was tired of his shit."

"I still think you were wrong. Man, I'm goin' in the crib. I need to fire up after that shit."

When blunt left he looked back at the house and the girl was gone.

"You gonna hit this?" Blunt asked returning with some bomb ass weed from Jamaica.

"Naw...but I do wanna hit that girl. Who is she?"

MONESHA AND GABRIELLA
WASHINGTON, D.C.
LET'S WAIT AWHILE

Gabriella opened the yellow chiffon curtains to let the afternoon sunlight inside of her one bedroom apartment and pulled her long brown hair in a ponytail out of her face. The music was so loud she could barely hear her footsteps. She looped Janet Jackson's "Let Wait A While", a thousand times because that's what Monesha had always told her, and she was tired of waiting. Gabriella was hopelessly in love.

She was just putting her lunch sandwich, lemonade and chips on the living room table when Monesha came bolting through the front door with her keys. Flinging her red Prada purse on the couch, she threw her weight down next. It had been a month since she'd heard from her.

"What's wrong? Are you okay?" Gabriella asked frightened at her distorted angry face.

Her beautiful skin flushed red.

"He's related to my family."

"Who's related to your family?" Gabriella stooped down in front of her and caressed her knees. "What's going on?"

"Nyzon. I can't believe this shit! All this time and he's related to my family! He won't answer my calls or nothin'. I don't know what to do."

A sigh of relief overtook Gabriella because maybe she'd finally give him up. "You say it's over anyway."

"I know. Still!" Monesha folded her arms against her body and dropped her head back. "I can't get over him."

Her words hit her like a ton of bricks. No matter what Gabriella did, she couldn't make Monesha love her, and she'd tried so many times.

"Maybe he still wants you. I know I would." She let out slowly.

"You think so?" She was thrilled and appeared hopeful.

"Maybe." She sat next to her. "But I miss you Monesha. Let this thing with Ny go. Please."

"I miss you too but there's so much going on right now. You have to wait awhile with me, Gab."

Gabriella sighed.

"I need your friendship." She touched her face lightly and Gabriella's pussy jumped. "Can I count on you?"

"You know you can."

"Cause I have a plan." Monesha grinned. "And it's one that'll lock him down for good."

NYZON
BALTIMORE WASHINGTON PARKWAY
A FUCKED UP MIND

Nyzon stood in the ring of the sweaty boxing gym as his trainer Bowman yelled from the outside as he sparred with Shavel. Shavel although a good boxer, could never get his breaks as a professional because he failed to get his endurance up. Still he did an excellent job working with other boxers.

"Nyzon, stop being a counter fighter! You waitin' until a mothafucka throw a punch before you throw one. You'll never win a decision like that!"

Nyzon heard him but his mind was on his mother, or the woman he thought she was. Between her lies and Monesha still trying to get with him, he wasn't on his game. Everything was fucked up in his life!

Shavel was still punishing him this round.

"Ny! Lead with your jab and stop sittin' on your punches!"

Bowman was the most sought after coach on the east coast. He recognized the potential in Nyzon and wanted to grab him before someone else did. But today Nyzon was jabbing but not landing shit. And when he stumbled, Shavel knocked him down with a firm right.

"That's it!" Bowman yelled. "The man took enough beatin' today."

Nyzon got up, hopped out the rink and walked over to Bowman.

"Son, I don't know what's on your mind, but get it off, or don't come back in my gym. I only work with the best, you know that. How are you gonna think about fightin' internationally if you're movin' like this?"

"I know, sir." Nyzon said wiping his face with a towel Bowman handed him.

"Now, on the other note, if you need to talk to me, I'm here."

"Thanks, man." He took off his gloves, "but I'll be fine. I just have to work some shit out on my own."

In His Car

Driving down the BWI parkway drunk out of his mind, he tried to reach Melody again. He hated to admit it, but he was sure he was dodging him. He owed him ten thousand dollars from the last drop off and hadn't paid him. With him staying at the Holiday Inn, in Laurel Maryland, he needed all the money he could get.

He wasn't even thinking about spending what he had saved because he had plans to buy a package from the connect Melody used. He wanted his own operation. But the last time he approached Juarez, the Columbian connect, he told him don't even think about stepping his way with less than a million. He only dealt in major weight. Calling one last time with his number blocked, he wasn't surprised when he finally reached him.

"Melody, it's Ny…where's my dough man?"

"Your what?"

"My cash!" Nyzon was heated. He knew his bitch ass heard him the first time.

"I'll get it too you when I get it to you."

"And when is that?"

"Next week."

This was the third time he changed up. This nigga just bought a Yacht so he knew he had his money.

"What's wrong wit now? I can roll to Bmore."

"I'm in Hawaii."

How the fuck can he run and operation when he ain't ever here? He thought. It had gotten to a point when instead of dealing with him, he had to go through J-Swizz.

"Man, I'ma need my dough now. I'm gettin' the strange feelin' you tryin' to bullshit me."

"Bullshit you? Lil nigga, you done lost your mind! When I get back you'll get your cash but afta that you cut! I'm sick of dealin' with ungrateful mothafuckas like you!"

"Shit!" Nyzon hit the steering wheel.

Melody had him on some whole 'notha shit, and he was getting ready to deal with it. Straight up. He just didn't know how.

He needed to talk to somebody so he called Royala. Ever since they graduated from high school, they became closer. And if anybody could calm him down, she could.

In Royala's 1991 Cadillac Coupe Deville

"Yo suck that shit right!" Royala told her girlfriend Simple as she bent over in the passenger seat of her car and sucked the dildoe she had strapped on. Royala had it in her mind so much that she was a guy, that she wore her strap all day everyday. This was not common for most dominate women.

Slapping her vanilla colored ass, she encouraged her to take it all in. Although she was sucking the brown colored dildoe and not her, Royala was still getting aroused. So when the phone rang and she saw it was Ny, she couldn't answer it. At least not right now.

"Who that?" Simple asked as she looked up at Royala holding her cell phone.

"Don't worry about that," she said tossing the phone down. "Worry 'bout this dick."

With that she continued to suck it.

Back in Nyzon's Car

Nyzon slammed his RAZR phone shut when Royala didn't answer. Grabbing the half empty Hennessy bottle in his seat, most of which he'd drank on the way from the gym, he almost missed his phone ringing. Without seeing who it was first, he answered.

"Ny...its Monesha."

"Fuck you want, Monie? Cause I ain't got time for no shit." he slurred. He was drunk as shit.

"Can I see you, Ny?" she said softly. "I mean I finally understand we're family and what we had is over. I just really need a friend right now."

Had he not been drinking, he would've probably said no but between her, his mother and Melody fucking with his money, he needed some company. So he gave her the address to the hotel he stayed in.

"I'm on my way." She hung up before he changed his mind.

In the Hotel

The clock radio blasted with 95.5 as they talked about old times. The liquor was still in his system and he hadn't had that much fun since the last time he was with her. And he missed that.

Two brown paper bags dressed the bed filled with the remainders of the cheese steaks they ate fifteen minutes earlier.

"Ny, you are so silly! But please tell me you remember running into my head knocking me over at school."

"What?" Nyzon laughed looking at her sideways. "I ain't never knock you over at school."

"Boy, you must've bumped your head for real!" she giggled. "We were in middle school and you bumped into me. That's how we met!"

"Oh shit! I remember now." He rubbed his head finally recollecting. "I had to help your lost ass find the office. Tell the truth, you were just tryin' to get my attention right?" Nyzon joked.

"Boy, whatever! I already heard about you."

"That's cause they all wanted me."

She got up, cleared the bed of the bags and plopped back down.

"I ain't want you. For real...I was feelin' Lazarick."

For some reason when she said that, his stomach turned.

"Yeah right! You was always on me."

Silence.

They stared into each other's eyes. She was moving in to kiss him and he stopped her.

"We can't...we're family, Monie. Let's leave it like that."

"What if I told you we aren't? Would it make a difference between us?"

"Naw...cause we're better off as friends."

Nyzon didn't want to play games with Monie even if they weren't related because he couldn't be faithful. She deserved somebody good and he wanted her to have that.

She frowned and instead of understanding, she thought he wasn't drunk enough.

"Now you can sleep here," he said seriously. "but in the morning, you have to leave."

"A'ight, Ny. A'ight."

Later That Night

It was pitch dark in the room when he felt the covers pull back from his body, and the cool air move over him.

"Monesha, what are you doin'?" he asked pushing her away looking at the red glare from the clock radio.

It was 3am.

"You know what I'm doin' Ny." She kissed his lips. "Stop playin' wit me."

"Monie...we can't do this shit."

"Yes we can." She rustled with his boxers. The alcohol was still in his blood.

"Have you been payin' attention?" he asked as he grabbed her wrist and held them firmly in his hands. "Whateva we had is through!"

Just a few months ago he would've given anything to fuck her, but now since he was 99.9% sure they were family, he just couldn't do it.

"Fuck that shit!" she said getting louder. "I still love you, Ny! Why you think I'm here? Make love to me, please."

She was crazy...out of her mind. But the mere fact that she was begging him turned Nyzon on.

"Monie, this is fucked up!" he continued, now kissing her gently. His body was doing the exact opposite of what his mouth was saying. "I'm...your...."

"Man." She continued as she slid her slippery wetness onto him.

One thing for sure, the bitch wasn't the virgin she proclaimed to be. She bucked her hips with the moves of a professional.

"Monie, fuck this shit!" he yelled lifting her up off him. He paced the room with his dick rock hard and sticking out of his boxers. "I can't do this! You hear me? I can't! You gotta leave."

"Yes you can baby." Her knees hit the floor as she put him into her mouth. She wanted to catch his thickness before it went back down. "Just try. I won't tell nobody. I promise. It'll be our little secret."

Her tongue moved ferociously over his penis and she could taste her bittersweet wetness mixed with his juices.

"Ahhhhh… shit," he cried out as his head fell against the wall. "You feel so fuckin' good. We shouldn't be doin' this shit!"

Before he knew it, she bent down in front of him and wiggled her ass onto his dick again. It was over. He was no match for her seduction. Monie's hands covered her toes as she whined her hips against him. When he looked down all he saw was ass.

"You like that shit don't you? Tell me how much you like it?" She demanded.

He was silent. This was fucked up enough without the adlibbing.

"I know you do." She continued pushing against him harder, squeezing her inner walls each time. "Ohhhh, Nyzon….I'm about to…."

"Me too. Oh my goodness….I'm about to cuuummm! Shit!" he whimpered as he released himself inside of her holding her hips in place.

And just like that, the moment he came it was over. And he was back to reality. How could he live with himself having fucked his cousin?

"Monesha, this was my fault." Nyzon took the blame. "but this will not happen again."

"That's not what I had in mind."

"I'm serious. I'll spend the rest of my life makin' it up to you, but that…what just happened…can never go down again."

"So you would sleep with me, let me suck your dick and tell me I'm not good enough for you? Is that what you're sayin'?" she asked looking as if she'd been possessed.

"I'm sayin' you're my cousin, and it was wrong. Please leave, Monisha."

"You're gonna regret this, Shelton, Nyzon or whatever your damn name is!" She said calling him by his birth name. "I put that on everything you're going to regret this."

She collected her things, got dressed and left.

With her gone he beat himself up mentally for making such a major mistake, and he was sure she was true to her word that he would regret every bit of it.

But for now he would go to sleep.

CRAYLAND
ARUNDEL MILLS, MD

Jillian's in Arundel Mills mall was crowded but Nyzon wanted to meet with Cray to discuss business. He sat nervously at the bar trying to figure out what to say to convince Cray to cross Melody. After all when Cray stepped to him a month ago about doing business since he had access to the connect, Nyzon denied him.

One Month Earlier

Nyzon had been waiting for Cray for thirty minutes when he finally strolled up to their usual location. He was late as rain.

Mad as shit, Nyzon jumped into Cray's ride and unleashed.

"Fuck too you so long?" He threw him the duffle bag with the weight, looking around to be sure no one was watching.

"I'm here now so calm the fuck down." Cray said checking the contents of the bag before closing it shut.

"Next time you waste somebody's time, make sure it ain't mine."

Nyzon was exiting the car when Cray said, "Give me a few ticks. I want to talk to you bout somethin'."

"What?"

"I'm sorry...how do you DC boys say it...let me rap to you for a sec." he said in a condescending tone.

Nyzon smirked, but sat down and closed the door. He was curious. What could a D.C. dude and a Bmore cat possibly have in common? But he have a few minutes to spare so he gave it to him.

"Make it quick."

"How long you been workin' for Melody?"

"Long enough." Nyzon responded wanting him to get to the point. He was sick of looking at his gold hair wearin', burgundy timbs lacin', Baltimore bamma ass.

"Okay...okay...," Cray responded sensing he'd better speed it up. "I'ma come straight out wit it."

"Please do."

"Do you have access to Melody's connect?"

"Are you serious?" Nyzon said staring his ass down. He sat back in his seat and laughed in his face. "If I did why in the fuck would I tell you?"

Cray looked out his window and back at Nyzon.

"Don't you get tired of being a mule? A fuckin' flunkie?"

"Don't you? As far as I can see you pick up and drop off just like me."

"I'm serious! You can't be gettin' more than I do and I know I'm not gettin' enough."

"The only thing I'm tired of is listenin' to this shit. And as long as he's payin' me, I'm good."

"That's just it, from what I hear, he ain't even payin' you. That niggas tellin' everybody he pay you when the fuck he feel like it. And how you be beggin' him for your money like one of his bitches."

Silence.

"So you do wanna make some real money right?" Cray laughed and said, "No scratch that, do you want to make *any* money."

"You already know the answer." He said irritated that Melody was playing him, and telling everybody about it.

Cray took a deep breath, grabbed his chin and said, "If a situation presented itself...and we stood to gain way more than we'd lose, would you go for it?"

"With who? Your bamma ass?"

"Let's stop wit the compliments, country ass nigga." He said talking calmer than he usually would have under the circumstances. "Would you do it or not?"

"It depends." Nyzon said looking out the window before unlocking the car door.

"On what?"

"If I'm ready to die." With that he jumped out the car and walked toward his.

Cray backed up the rental and said, "In that case this conversation never happened right?"

Nyzon pulled off without answering his question. To this day Cray never knew why Nyzon kept his secret. He just did.

And now that the tables were turned, it was Nyzon who needed Cray's help. And without hesitation, Cray agreed to meet him.

Nyzon had just ordered a vodka and orange juice when Cray walked into Jillian's, late as usual.

"What up, nigga?" Cray said giving him some dap.

"Ain't shit!" Nyzon said.

"Aye, yo...give me two of what he just had." He told the bartender.

"You can't handle this shit, youngin'. You betta stay in your league."

"Yeah a'ight! I drink this shit in my sleep, partna." Cray drank both drinks and asked for another.

"I bet." Nyzon said sizing him up.

Can I trust your ass? He thought.

"Where you rollin' to tonight?" Nyzon was trying to make small talk because outside of handling business with this mothafucka, for real he didn't know him.

"My man's throwin' somethin' at this place in the city but I got to pick up my new ride first." Cray downed his entire drink and flagged him for another. "You should come through."

"Me get down in Bmore? Wit' all that club music and shit? No thank you."

He could tell Cray was a little salty but he was speaking the truth. His truth.

"Like Go-Go music much betta. Come on now, *must* ya'll niggas steal every song that come out?"

"Steal it? We empower it, man!"

They both laughed at that bullshit.

"No seriously…what's good? I know something's up." Cray asked.

"Yeah…that nigga Melody done me greasy, and I'm ready to take you up on your offer. That is if it's still available."

Cray smiled slyly.

"What's funny?"

"Nothin, that nigga's reckless wit' his operation. Plus I ain't gettin' enough for the things I want to do." Cray confirmed. "I been lookin' for a reason to cut him off."

"Well here it is. You still down?"

"You still got access to the connect?"

"I know who he is, but we need distribution. My cousin got a few cats in DC who can move it no problem. But the connect don't fuck wit nobody without real money for real weight. So the folks I got in Southeast and Southwest ain't enough to move it."

"How much he askin' for?"

"A mill." Nyzon confirmed.

"I can get the cash no problem. I'll have to hit a few niggas heads but it'll be all good."

"So what's up? When can you come up wit your cake?"

"Give me two months. I have to handle a few things, but I'ma hit you back. Be gettin' your starting line up together and I'll be getting mine. If you're really serious, I'll know then."

"You ain't said nothin' but a thing." Nyzon said eager to stack his chips.

"Imagine this," Cray said.

"What?"

"Two enemies uniting."

"Unlike niggas who smile in your face, at least we've always known where the other was coming from."

"No doubt."

INTRODUCING...TIARA CARTIER REISTERSTOWN, MD

CRASH

Kavon sat at the kitchen table with his real estate books and papers spread out. For the second he put his work aside and focused on his daughter's. Tiara stood over him as he looked at the homework from high school in his hand.

Six months had passed since they moved in a small two-bedroom home in Baltimore county. He moved from DC hoping to get her away from the lures of the street. What he forgot was that ever city has a corner.

"Well, daddy? Is it okay?" Tiara asked standing over him, her beautiful golden hair in a long ponytail.

Silence.

"Its okay, Tiara, but I still feel you're rushing. Now I know you wanna roll wit them skanks you got for friends, and that's all well and good, but I want your focus to remain on school."

She sighed.

Yolanda and Felecia were the only friends she had and he hated them both.

"I'm serious! You're going to college so you don't have to worry about these niggas out here takin' care of you. And I'ma see to it."

"I know, daddy. You tell me that everyday."

"Don't sass me."

"I'm not trying to but I'm working hard."

Kavon handed her back the assignment and opened his books. "Not hard enough."

Tiara remained over him.

"Now what's up?" he asked when he noticed she hadn't gone to her room.

Tiara was hesitant. He'd just finished expressing how he felt about Yolanda and Felecia so how could she ask him to go out with them?

"Felecia and Yolanda want me to hang out with them at..."

"Not tonight. You have an exam tomorrow." He cut her off.

"But, daddy...."

"No, Tiara! They're just using you for your car. Now let me finish my work."

Tiara walked away, defeated.

Two Hours Later

Tiara sat in her room with Felecia and Yolanda. Her wooden canopy bed sat in the middle of the floor and the white chiffon curtains were drooped along the sides. The dresser matched the light colored wood and had a mirror large enough for her to see her body if she stepped a few feet away.

"So we goin' out tonight?" Felecia asked as she strutted in front of the mirror with her tight jean shorts and her red halter top.

Felecia had a beautiful dark chocolate complexion and a shapely body but her poor taste in clothes made her look cheap. "Cause I ain't had no dick in days!"

"Bitch you was just fuckin' Kenny's ass last night." Yolanda reminded her.

She was more conservative in her blue jeans and her white Armani Exchange t-shirt. Yolanda had a vanilla milk complexion and a body that still expressed her adolescence. She didn't feel out as well as Felecia and Tiara. She was just a cute girl.

"I meant good dick!" Felecia looked at her and rolled her eyes. "Everybody not like you Yolanda...some of us need a good man up under us."

Her need for a man was probably why her snatch was always funky. It seemed like Felecia had a new man every other day. And with her mother being the church's jezebel it's easy to see how the apple didn't fall far from the tree.

"I can't mess wit it tonight." Tiara said walking to the mirror. Although they'd known her for months, every time she moved, they had to look at her. They figured if they stared at her hard enough, they'd could find one flaw on her beautiful body. But from the top of her beautiful golden hair to the bottom of her tiny little feet she was perfect. "I got an exam tomorrow."

"What is up wit you and school?" Felecia was the troublemaker out the group but she didn't see it that way.

"You know how my father is about school."

"Come on, Tiara...Kavon is fine and everything, and he maybe your dad, but tonight Hammerjacks is gonna be jumpin! You gotta roll wit us. You need a man. If your father had it his way you'd be fuckin' him."

"Don't say that!" Yolanda defended.

"It's true! I wonder if you look like your mother because he be obessesing over you hard!"

"Please don't say those things about my father."

"Please don't say those things about my father," she teased.

"I can't go. He told me no and I can't lie to him. Maybe we can go to the movies or somethin' tomorrow."

"Movies?" Felecia laughed in her face. "Bitch you is soooooo green!"

"Don't ask her to do nothin' you wouldn't do." Yolanda sat down on the soft bed. "On second thought, don't ask her to do nothin' at all."

They all laughed because they knew full well Felecia was without limits.

"I'm tryin' to get her out the house for a change. That's why people think you a joke cause you never go nowhere!" Felecia was trying her hardest to play on her emotions.

Although Kavon instilled virtues in Tiara, she didn't have a backbone. There were plenty of times Felecia threatened not to be her friend if she didn't do what she wanted. Because after all of the years of having no security, all she wanted was acceptance.

"I hope yall have fun, because I can't go." She was trying to talk calmly to Felecia because she knew she could say things to instantly cause her to cry. "Just tell me how it is."

"You know what…you gets the fuck on my nerves! That's why don't nobody hang wit you but us 'cause you slow." She gathered her things preparing to leave.

"You comin' wit me Yolanda?" she asked approaching the door.

Tiara knew Yolanda knew Felecia longer so by default, always took her side.

"Call me later Tiara." She walked behind her.

When they left she through herself on the bed and cried.

Even Later That Night

After Tiara kissed her father good night, she sat on the edge of her bed looking at her phone. Now what was she going to do? Be bored all night?

"I'll just call them and see what they're doin." She picked up her phone and called Yolanda.

She chose her first because even though she followed behind Felecia, she was always easier to talk to.

"Yolanda…what you doin'?"

"Gettin' ready to go out." The music was blasting in the background.

"Ya'll goin' to the club anyway?"

"Yeah…we gettin' dressed now." Tiara tried to prevent the wave of jealousy from taking over.

"Who that? Tiara?!" Felecia's voice came bellowing through the phone line. "Cause tell her we ain't got time for no green ass females."

"Tiara, we 'bout to roll." Yolanda's voice was sympathetic and low. "I'll call you tomorrow."

"Uh…well…how you gettin' there?" Tiara was doing her best to maintain hold of her friends. "Cause I was gonna meet ya'll up there."

"For real! Don't play if you not comin!" Yolanda's voice was heavy with excitement.

"Yeah…I'm not worried bout my father. He gon be a'ight."

"Tiara, said she meetin' us down there." Yolanda informed Felecia muffling the receiver so Tiara couldn't hear if she said something bad.

There was some slight commotion before Felecia got on the phone. Tiara's heart sped up as she wondered if Felecia would be okay with it.

"You finally come to your senses?"

"I guess…ya'll need a ride?"

"No…we good."

Tiara felt an instant sense of lost.

"But….my suga daddy was gonna get on my nerves anyway. So if you want to roll, we'll be over there in fifteen. We'll let you take us instead."

Tiara quickly got off the phone and rummaged through her closet. She had to look fly if she wanted to be seen with Felecia. Because although Tiara was beautiful, she didn't have any taste in clothing. Kavon did a good job of buying her things that were cute, but not sexy.

She settled on the black skirt she wore for church, which covered her knees, and a button down white blouse, which she also wore on Sunday morning. The moment she came outside, Felecia ate her up.

"Yo…what the fuck do you have on?" she laughed so loud Tiara was sure her neighbors heard her. And sense it was 11:00 at night, she worried her father would too.

"Come on, Felecia…my neighbors might hear you." She whispered as she unlocked the car doors of her blue Nissan Sentra and let them in. "This all I got."

"Girl…they gonna laugh your ass out the club! Why you ain't tell me you ain't have shit? I coulda bought somethin' out for you to wear."

"She can't fit none of your stuff." Yolanda reminded her. Tiara turned on the ignition and pulled out the driveway, trying to focus on the road instead of her friends. But being a rookie driver, this was not an easy feat. Kavon knew it that's why he forbade her to drive alone at night.

"I was just gonna play the sidelines anyway. I'm not lookin' for nobody." Tiara responded.

"Are you gonna turn out to be a lesbian or somethin'? Cause I never met a bitch who didn't want a man." Felecia adjusted her hair in the mirror.

"I didn't mean it like that. I'ma get a job this summer anyway and buy my own stuff."

"I be glad when you do…I can't stand going nowhere wit no body lookin' like a bum bitch. And why you drivin' so slow? We gon miss half the fun."

Felecia's complaints were making Tiara uncomfortable and she was starting to sweat. It was bad enough she was lying to her father, something she never did, but then Felecia's hoe ass was fucking with her. Her stomach felt queasy and she wished she wasn't so far away from her house because for real, she would've turned around.

"Can you hurry up please!" Felecia continued to scream and act like a stone cold bitch in the back seat of the car.

"You okay?" Yolanda's voice was soothing but not enough to break her nervousness. "I can drive a little if you want me to."

"She fine!" Felecia yelled from the back seat of the car. "Let her drive."

Tiara did her best to drive until she slammed in the back of a brand new black Lexus with paper tags, tearing the entire back bumper off.

"Oh shit!" Felecia gripped her mouth after seeing the car.

"Oh no!!!" Yolanda screamed.

The driver of the car got out fuming mad! He examined the damage and placed his hands on the side of his head before dropping them.

"FUCK!" He screamed,

They could tell from his reactions that he was going to be a handful.

"Get out and talk to him." Felecia told Tiara. "Cause that nigga looked pissed."

"I can't...I can't." Tiara was in tears.

She saw her whole life flash before her eyes and her relationship with her father out the window. He was the only person consistent in her life and now she ruined it. What if he sent her away for being disobedient like her mother promised to over and over again when she was little. She was an emotional wreck.

"Well, somebody betta go talk to this fool." Felecia offered.

"If you got so much mouth why don't you talk to him?!" For the first time all day Yolanda let her ass have it.

"It ain't nothin' but a thing."

Felecia strutted out of the car as if she wasn't petrified.

I'll just flirt with this nigga and all debts will be paid. She thought.

"We are so sorry about your car." She approached him running her hands down her body. "My friend's a new driver and she..."

"Bitch, I don't want to hear that bullshit! Ya assess betta pitch in and come up with enough cash to get my shit fixed!"

He was so angry the lines in his forehead looked like roads on a map. Felecia was terrified after seeing the look in his eyes. Offering him some pussy wasn't going to cut it...he wanted to be paid in cash, not licks or pumps or fucks.

"I see...let me get the person driving cause it wasn't me." Felecia hurried back to the car trying to get out of his path. "Tiara you gonna have to talk to him." She said once she was inside safe. "Cause if that nigga not tryin' to fuck me, he don't want shit but his money! Believe dat!"

Tiara had never been more frightened in all her life. Had she listened to her father and not the freak bitch in her car, this would've never happened. And now not only would she have to tell him about the damage done to her car, she'd also have to tell him about the damage done to the stranger's.

Slowly and insecurely she stepped out of the car. Her beautiful golden hair laying against the old style blouse could not take away from her beauty. Even while looking homely, she looked better than any woman he'd ever seen before. And then he remembered, he saw her before.

"Hi...uh...I'm the driver and I'm so sorry for what I've done to your car. I'll pay you back everything I owe. I promise."

He was stuck. And it wasn't just her looks that had him in a zone, he could tell the moment she opened her mouth that she was untouched by the cold Bmore streets.

"What's ya name?"

"Tiara...Tiara Cartier."

"Well, Tiara...I'm Crayland Bailor, but my friends call me Cray."

He gave her his government name. He was really feeling her.

"Cray?" she repeated. A light smile spread across his face and suddenly he didn't seem so mean. "It's nice to meet you."

She extended her hand out to his and saw the watch he was rocking loaded in diamonds. She couldn't help but wonder what type of girls he was into. Tiara knew that he'd never be interested in someone like her because like Felecia said, she was way to slow.

"So how about we do this...give me ya info, and I'll call you tomorrow. No need in worryin' about the damage right now."

"No!" she yelled putting her hands out in front of her. "I mean...you can't call because my father is going to flip."

"You live with your pops?"

"Yeah...just me and him."

A look came over his face and Tiara was trying to figure out what it meant. In Bmore it was rare that a father took care of his child alone.

"You wasn't 'spose to be drivin' huh?"

She shook her head no.

"How bout we do this then, let me call my mans right quick and this will all be taken care of."

Tiara let him excuse his self but wondered what he had in mind as he talked on his cellphone, a few feet away from her. She looked back at her car once. Felecia and Yolanda had their hands raised like, *what's goin' on?* She shrugged her shoulders. She was as clueless as they were. But as long as he wasn't concerned about the damage to his car, for right now, she didn't care.

"This what we gon do. My man runs an auto body shop out his crib. He gon get two of his tow trucks to come out here and hall both of our cars to his shop."

"But...I can't be without my car."

"Listen...don't worry...I got you." He extended his hands in front of him for her to slow her roll. "Where were ya'll goin' tonight?"

"To Hammerjacks."

"Fuck Hammerjacks...I got a limo on the way to scoop us up. We gon kick it at The Red Maple and get some drinks."

"But I'm only seventeen."

"You old enough when you wit me." He winked. "By the time we leave, he'll have your car repaired enough to hide the marks. Then tomorrow I'll have him do a betta job on it before your pops even wakes up."

"I don't understand. What about your car?"

"I got that shit. Ain't nobody trippin' off no car. For real I might buy anotha one."

The way he brushed off the damage to his ride turned her on. Not so much that he could afford to fix it and hers too, but because he seemed to let things roll off his back. His power and strength turned her on, and it had been the first time a man had done that too her.

They waited fifteen more minutes talking and laughing outside the car while her friends looked on in disbelief. When they saw the two tow trucks followed by a black Lincoln Navigator stretch limo pull around the corner, their mouths dropped. A white chauffeur hopped out of the limo and walked toward Tiara's car opening the door for her friends.

"Ladies...this way please."

Without hesitation Felecia's freak whore ass and Yolanda jumped into the limo. The chauffer was preparing to let Tiara in too when Cray stopped him.

"I got it from here main man."

The limo driver knew the deal and walked to the driver side of the car while Cray escorted her inside. Tiara blushed at the attention she was getting from him.

Once she was inside, Cray slid in the row seat in front of Tiara, Felecia and Yolanda. They stared at him in awe. He was young, black and rich and they were loving it. Tiara was gushing over his swagger, and was eager to see what the night would bring.

Suddenly, she was happy she defied her father.

CRAYLAND
BALTIMORE CITY
MY SHAWTY

The Red Maple was jumping when Cray walked in with Tiara and her friends. The cherry wood floors and dark furniture added to the ambiance. Cray and his boys had rented out the entire club and all you saw was a bunch of thugs with money.

"Where you been?" Jinx asked approaching Cray the moment he hit the door. He looked just like Pharrell from the Neptunes. "I was bout to come lookin' for yo ass."

Jinx was his man and a future part of his starting line up. Cray never forgot how he gave him his props years ago when he stood up to Melody. The story on Theodore "Jinx" Carter is this…he spent most of his life inside of jail than he did out. Despite his bad luck at always getting caught, thus resulting in the name Jinx, his aiming and firing skills were impeccable. With everything working out the way that it was, he'd already gave him a secure position as his muscle. Plus Jinx reminded him of himself.

"I got into an accident kinda. Blunt got my shit now"

"Well I know that nigga heated cause he been talkin' bout comin' to this joint all night."

"He still comin' through…he just puttin' the cars in his lot."

"Yo!!! Who is that?" Jinx asked eyeballing the hell out of Tiara.

"Naw, yo." Cray put his hand in front of him even though he didn't have the authority to do so. "I got that."

"Oh…that's you?" Jinx asked for confirmation. Cray never claimed a female so this was unusual.

"Naw…but they my folks."

"I heard that…well your table's over there. We got the Hennessy on ice and niggas is gettin' twisted!"

As Tiara and her friends moved through the club, Cray caught all eyes on Tiara. Even though she looked like a church girl, he knew they all were thinking the same thing, with a little financial backing, she could be one of the baddest, if not *the* baddest bitch in Bmore. Hands down.

Once they made it too the sofas Cray was trying to think of a way to get them off his couch so he could be alone with Tiara, and then Jason walked up.

"Yo, Jay...won't you make sure my peoples is good." He pointed at Felecia and Yolanda standing around looking stupid. With all that shit Felecia talked, now she was amongst men, and didn't know how to handle herself. "Get em whateva they want."

When they laid eyes on Jason, Cray knew things would work as usual. He was always good with the ladies.

"Not a problem." Jason smiled letting him know he'd provide ample blockage. "You ladies wanna come wit me?" he extended his hands and Felecia jumped up so fast to get at him, she almost put Yolanda's eyes out.

"And later I'ma need to holla at you about somethin' serious." Cray yelled over the music.

"Aight."

When they were alone Cray fought with what to say. Any other time he'd be telling a bitch to meet him out back to suck his dick but this was different. He felt Tiara's innocence and he wanted to preserve it.

"So...you live around here?" He started off slow and wrapped his arm around the back of the couch so that it was behind her.

He already knew she did.

He'd seen her before.

"Yeah...in Reisterstown with my father. He's like my best friend." She fiddled with her skirt unable to look into his eyes.

While they sat on the sofa, Cray couldn't help but notice other niggas were still breaking their necks to get a good look at her. Her beauty was crucial.

"Sounds like you really close to your father. That's love."

"He's all I got. You close to yours?"

It bothered Cray that the mere thought of him brought up hate, pain and disgust. The last time he heard about his father they said he was so skinny, he couldn't be recognized and his mother had fallen off the face of the earth.

"Naw...I don't know my dad." He switched the subject. "So look...what you do for fun besides knock into people's cars?"

She threw her head back in heavy laughter revealing her extra white teeth. Thinking she must've looked stupid, she tried to conceal her smile.

"Don't do that..." his voice serious and seductive.

"Do what?"

"Cover your smile. I like it."

She blushed and threw her hands into her lap.

"You got a man? Cause I know somebody has to claim you."

"No...I'm too busy working on trying to get into college. My dad says the streets will always be here so I need to focus right now. He's smart like that."

"Word?"

"Yeah...he's the best. I just love him so much."

The way she used words was funny to him. She acted like a church girl. And the more she mentioned her father, for some reason, the angrier Cray became. The love she had for her father was as visible as a brick wall standing between them. He would have to put in work on top of work if he wanted to get through to her.

"I heard that...well you got to get out sometimes. I mean, all work and no play makes you mad."

"No, I'm fine. I just hang with my friends."

"You real close to them?"

"Kinda."

"Cause I've heard about Felecia. You gotta watch who you role with."

"I know."

"So even if I want to take you out you wont' let me? Even after you banged up my ride?" He laughed although deathly serious.

"I can't mess with hustlers."

"How you know I'm a hustler?"

"You not?" her eyes lit up and she hoped he would tell her he was in real estate like her father. Because just being in his presence made her feel stronger.

"I mean...I know a lot of cats that get down like that but not me. My grandmother left me a little money when she died and I been ridin' on that for the longest."

He was lying to this female and he couldn't believe it. All he knew was that he had to have her. A woman as beautiful as her who was also untouched was uncommon.

"I'm sorry to hear about your loss."

"I'm fine. We weren't' even that close."

"Can I get you guys something to drink?" a black young waiter asked approaching them. His eyes were fixated onto Tiara.

"We good." Cray said shooting daggers even though the waiter couldn't see him from all the staring at her.

"Okay...let me get some of this out your way." He picked up some glasses left at the table from when Jason and the crew sat there. As he picked them up, one of them fell to Tiara's feet because he wasn't watching what he was doing. Her beauty captivated him.

"My, man...you doin' extra and I'm five minutes from breakin' ya shit. Now bounce."

Hearing the seriousness in Cray's voice the young inexperienced waiter picked up the glasses and hurried out of their way.

"Sorry about that." He said hoping he didn't scare her off.

"That's okay." She hunched her shoulders and dropped them by their sides.

"I'm happy that you don't sell drugs." She jumped right back on the topic. "Something about my father and hustlers rubs him the wrong way."

That nigga use to deal. He thought.

He was positive that Kavon being in real estate and his hatred toward the game proved he was once involved. *Smug mothafucka turns his back on the entire industry.* He was really starting to despise him. But the more he talked to her, the more he understood what needed to be done. Her father was her strength and he had to break the chain. But coming at her full force would only push her away. He had to play the backfield, and bring her to him.

"Look, I see you a nice girl and I respect that. How bout me and you just be friends."

"Really?"

"Yeah…I can't have friends?" he took his arm and gripped it around her shoulders pulling her toward him.

When he made her smile he released his hold.

"I am capable you know."

"I'm sure a guy like you can get any girl you want."

"I can…the thing is…I don't want, every one I see."

What he didn't know was the way he said those words sent shivers through her spine.

"I'm patient…above all. Feel me?"

"Yes." She nodded slowly.

"So for now…let's enjoy our time together.

NYZON
FORT WASHINGTON, MARYLAND
GET MONEY, NEW MONEY

The weather was perfect for the cook-out. The sun was shining and a perfect breeze comforted the guests. There were so many people in the backyard that it was hard to move. Yet people were dancing to the music, and having a good time amongst family and friends. Jackie prepared hot dogs, hamburgers, grilled chicken, potato salad, and coleslaw. She was proud to introduce Nyzon to his family and he felt the same. The only thing that bothered him was the constant questions everyone had. They all wanted to know where he'd been and who he'd been with. But until he sorted things out, he wasn't prepared to answer.

"Ask Cooks." Lazarick said after listening to him going into business with Cray. "Cuz I wouldn't fuck wit it."

"Why you even bringin' it up?" Royala questioned with her hat tilted to the side, face still pretty like a girl's should be. "The man has made his decision."

"Shut yo bitch ass up! Ask him Ny."

"Nigga, fuck you!" She threw out a queen of hearts.

Telling his cousin about what he was about to be involved in was too much right now. He wanted to do it in a private setting.

"What's up, youngin?" Cooks asked as he took a bite of the barbeque ribs on his plate, threw out a deuce of spades, and grabbed his book. His dreads pulled neatly away from his face.

"It's like this...I might be doin' biz wit somebody I don't know that well. But for real, I'm runnin' out of options."

"Out of options huh?" Cooks asked looking into his eyes. "There's always options."

"I know. But I'm bout to put work in wit this dude from Bmore." Nyzon sipped on his Sprite looking through his cards for the right choice.

"Is there anything about this Bmore nigga you trust?"

Nyzon laughed. He couldn't say he trusted anything about Cray outside of his hustle spirit. And Nyzon was more interested in getting back at Melody than anything else. Even though he met Melody years ago through this girl that was originally from Baltimore, Melody never respected him. Back then Melody was looking for someone to transport his product from

New York to D.C., and she recommended Nyzon cause he was eager to be put on, his record was clean and he'd been doing it ever since.

"No...but I can't say I don't trust him either."

"I'm not gonna lie cuzo." He said as he moved over on the picnic bench so that Simon could sit down. Simon's stomach protruded a little, but to be a big dude, he stayed fresh. "Anything involvin' money is gonna involve risks. That's life."

Nyzon took what he was saying to heart and respected the truth.

"What about you? Would you be down?"

"Dependin' on how big the score is...I might be tempted to get in on that action too. Then again, I'm always lookin' to get paid."

"I guess it's settled." Nyzon responded.

"You offering?"

"Wouldn't want to do it without you. That brings me to my next point, he told me to get my starting line up together and we're askin' everybody to put in on the initial package. He's gettin' his money together on his end and Simon already said he'd be down wit it yesterday. We need a half of mill and we almost got it. Just fifty grand short."

"Nyzon, why we need them?" Royala asked. "You got the connect info."

"Cause the type of weight we buying we need major distro to move."

"I see." Cooks said looking at him intently.

"Do you still fuck wit them block niggas in Southwest and Southeast, Cooks?"

"No doubt."

"Well let's get money." Nyzon responded. "That's the last missing piece."

"Ya'll can leave me out of it." Lazarick said. "I like my freedom."

Nyzon thought his comment was funny because nobody planned on asking him anyway. Everybody knew he loved his job at Verizon, the local telephone company. He was about to tell him just that until Monesha strutted to the table and everyone grew silent. It was obvious from the moment they found out they were family, and since they fucked, that they'd been avoiding each other.

"Mamma said the steaks are ready if ya'll want some." She walked off not really acknowledging anybody in particular.

Lazarick shook his head in disbelief after seeing how fine she was.

"I'ma leave that one alone." Lazarick said looking at Nyzon and than back at her.

Simon and Cooks remained silent. They knew that at one point they were together but what they didn't know was how far they took it.

"Yeah...leave it alone!" Royala responded shaking her head at her brother.

The conversation quickly returned to money until Angel, his old babysitter strutted through the party. She was sexier than he remembered. Her natural coal black hair fell on her shoulders. And her fat titties and round hips filled out the white BeBe cotton dress she wore. She looked better than ever, and he hadn't seen her since he was a kid.

"Please tell me she's not related." He pointed at Angel who was standing beside a cute girl with braids.

"No…I never saw her before until now." Cooks squinted his eyes to get a look at her frame in the sunlight.

"Hold up! That ain't Angel is it?" Royala asked staring her down.

"Fuck yeah that's her!" Lazarick yelled. "Damn dude…she lookin' betta than the last time she dropped your ass!"

"You know her?" Cooks asked. "Please tell me you hit that cuzo."

"Naw…she was his babysitter." Lazarick joked. "All he did was suck some titties and shit."

Everyone laughed.

"You's a hatin' ass, nigga!" Nyzon spat. "And how the fuck you know I ain't hit?"

"Cause for starters you still had that weak ass baby chain a day afta you said you was gonna give it to her."

Lazarick was laughing so hard he could barely sit in his seat. He was playing him in front of his family and Nyzon hated that shit.

"I don't tell you everything nigga!" Nyzon advised squirming in his seat. "So you don't know what I do wit my dick."

"You ain't got to tell me everything cause Angel only fucks wit ballas!" He continued egging him on. "So you might as well get her right out ya mind."

"Nigga, shut the fuck up and throw out your card." Royala said to her brother, getting the attention off of Nyzon and back on the Spades game. "And you bet not renege either. Don't even think about askin' what led."

Nyzon tried to brush Lazarick's comments off his shoulders, but he was still thinking about Angel. And although it was good seeing her again, he never got over how she played him. Suddenly he had an idea on how to pay her back and revenge never sounded so sweet.

CRAYLAND
THE SET-UP

Cray sat in Blunt's basement with Jason, Jinx, Blunt, and Blunt's two cousins Tony and Larry. He was discussing the details of his new plans to take over Melody's operation.

"Thanks for comin', yo." Cray started sipping his Corona after topping it off with Vodka. He had a black skull cap on his head. He was recruiting his starting line up.

"I called ya here on some serious bizness. There's bout to be a shake up in Bmore unlike any ya'll ever seen. Now I'ma be honest, a lot of niggas gonna buck cuz they not gonna be ready for change, but I venture to say many more will be down cause there's a lot to cash to make out here and fuckin' wit me, everybody gonna eat." He continued turning around briefly to look at their faces. "Befo I began, any nigga who feels like they may not want to hear this shit, leave now or forever hold your piece." He referred to their weapons. "Cause if I discuss this shit in front of you, and you cross me, it's ova." He waited on their move.

"A'ight yo!" Tony said giving his cousin Jinx some dap. "I'll get up with ya'll lada.

"No love lost." Cray said.

Larry left too.

After they exited, Cray watched them close the basement door before he began again. "Anybody else?"

Silence.

"Cool. It's like this…the nigga Melody got West Bmore locked down, and most of East. But I got a plan, on makin' this dude fall. And I already got wit my nigga from DC, so we gone eat regardless."

"So we dealin' wit DC niggas now?" Blunt asked.

"Yeah…cause the dude Ny got access to the connect, but I'ma always make sure my peoples eat first. I put that on everything." Cray nodded.

"So what's your plan? I mean, Melody got everybody on payroll." Jason questioned looking at him sideways.

"We gonna try to bring most of his dudes on board because they got the distro, but if they buck, we comin' out blazin." '

"But we don't even know everybody he got on payroll." Jason continued.

"I got that covered too. J-Swizz is his right hand man. He stay by his side but he's weak. Niggas been talkin' from miles around about their ship not bein' tight. And if it wasn't for a few cats on his squad, Melody wouldn't even have an operation right now." He continued sipping his beer.

"So what's up, chief? How we gonna do this?" Jinx asked.

"I was gonna say the same thing." Blunt said more than ready to get down with business.

"J-Swizz keeps this white broad close. I mean real close. This nigga Bloc said he saw him followin' her ass one day afta she cut him off for messin' wit Bloc's sister. I think the girl answered the phone one day when the nigga was sleep and the white broad flipped. So now he wants to marry her."

"That niggas a bum!" Jinx yelled. "

They all laughed.

"Exactly." Cray responded. "I figure if she be wit him like they say she do, she'd have access to information the rest of our asses ain't privy to. If nothing else, she'd be able to find out if put in the right position. Now what we got to do is put ourselves in this bitch's way, you feel me?" he advised looking around for confirmation. "Once I have all the info I need, there won't be any need for J-Swizz or Melody. You got me?"

"And if the block niggas on the payroll not down we're knockin' their blocks off too?" Jason said finally seeing the big picture. "Brilliant yo!"

"Right! And that's where ya pretty ass come in at. Since she's into niggas I figure it wouldn't be hard for you to get at her. With a little persuasion she'll be willin' to tell you everything we need to know. Plus I hear she's loose when she's drinking. They say that thang been all over West Baltimore and half of the county."

"Damn!" Blunt laughed.

"And you want me to bang her white ass?"

"You fucked worse." Cray said firing up a bob before leaning back in the recliner. He took a pull and blew the smoke into the air forming a circle.

"But what if she notices me? I'm around the way all the time. Plus I was tryin' to be more hands on." Jason interjected.

"You never got out of my car when she was around." Cray assured him. "And trust me…this is as hands on as it gets."

"You sure?"

Cray looked irritated.

"Positive! I been plannin' this shit for a year. Trust me…neva." He affirmed.

Silence.

"So who's down?"

All raised their hands and Jason also, he just raised his a little more slowly.

"How soon this 'spose to get started?" Jinx questioned.

"Today my niggas...we need to get rollin' on this plan today."

"Count me in!" Blunt responded ready to get blazing.

"Hold up...there's a bad side to this too. Certain dudes not gonna give in easy so shit's gonna get violent. Particularly Grimy Mike and Charms. I just hope ya'll up for the challenge."

"I was born challenged," Jinx laughed.

"Damn yo!" Jason yelled shaking his head.

"What?" Cray asked.

"Heavy is the head that wears the crown."

"Tell me about it."

TIARA
REISTERSTOWN, MARYLAND
ROCKED FROM UP UNDER

Tiara sat on her bed with her books open. She'd just finished writing an entry in her diary about Cray and she was staring at his name. It was already midnight and she didn't write word one for her homework. She couldn't concentrate...ever since she met him, she wanted to be with him. It didn't help that he wasn't perusing her or trying to get with her like the boys in her school. His age made him more appealing. He did everything he said he would last week. Came by the next day, fixed her car, and left without so much as asking her to call him. She waited everyday just knowing he would ring her phone, but it never happened.

"Tiara...you okay?" Kavon asked walking into her room.

His real estate business was doing pretty well but he found himself out later than he wanted to be. A key connected to a silver chain hung around his neck. He never took it off and when Tiara asked about it, he told her it held her future.

"I'm okay, daddy...just doing homework."

"Don't look like you're doing much to me." He stood over her and noticed nothing was on the white notebook paper. "You need anything?"

"No...I'm fine."

Kavon was just about to walk out and get some sleep when she said, "Daddy, how did you know when you were in love?"

"With your mother?"

"Yes."

"I knew the moment I laid eyes on her."

Tiara thought about Crayland, and how he moved her. Her virgin body longed to be with him. Could she be in love too?

"I see."

"But Tiara...sometimes people mistake lust for love. You'll know its right when your world is knocked from up under you and the feeling is mutual. When that happens, you won't be able to go back to your regular life."

Tiara giggled when she remembered ramming into Cray's car. In a sense, both of their worlds were rocked.

"Should I know something? You got a boyfriend?"

"No. Just asking. For this project I'm doing." It was the second time she'd lied to her father. She was changing for the worse and didn't like it.

"Okay, sweetheart. Good night."

When he left she thought about what he said. She never thought about a man the way she did Cray. She had to talk to him and she had to do it now.

Picking up the phone she slowly dialed his number.

"What up, beautiful?" His voice set her heart on fire.

The way he answered it, you would've thought he was thinking about her as much as she was thinking about him.

"Hi! Why you answering the phone like you were thinkin' about me?"

"How you know I wasn't."

"Were you?"

"If I told you I was would it make a difference?"

She couldn't' answer the question. Everything in her spirit told her she was out of her league, but still, she wanted to play.

"I don't know."

"What you doin' now? Playing Yahtzee with your father?"

"Stop playing boy! I'm supposed to be doing homework but I can't concentrate."

"Let me come scoop you up. Hang out wit me."

"I can't."

She thought about her father and felt bad enough lying to him two times in a month's timeframe.

"Okay…well let me handle some things on this end. I'll call you next week."

Next week? She repeated to herself. It was hard enough for her to go a few minutes without talking to him let alone another week.

"What time can you be here?"

"Quicker than you give the word."

Columbia Lake

The water looked beautiful even though they watched it from the car. Cray chose to take her to the lake in Columbia, Maryland to spend some alone time with her. Plus her gear needed work if she was going to be seen with him in public. Sure he could've taken her to a hotel, but he wanted her mind not her body. Once he had that, he was confident that everything else would follow.

"How many girlfriends you got?" she asked as Raheem Davaughn's CD played.

"I ain't got no girl." He turned around and looked at her.

She wore a plain red skirt and a black blouse.

"But why are you so beautiful?" he asked as his eyes roamed to her thighs.

"Stop sayin' that."

"Okay." He turned around.

"Okay what?"

"I'll neva say it again."

"Stop playin' wit me, Cray!" She hit his arm. "And I know you got somebody."

She didn't realize she sounded childish. He was trying to make millions yet her young mind couldn't conceive anything outside of a boy and girl-friend relationship. Kavon sheltered her too much. He hid her from the world trying to protect her when all he really did, was make her more vulnerable.

"I don't believe you're a virgin." He said totally from left field.

They weren't even talking about sex. It was time that he kicked his control game into full gear.

"I am! I swear it." She nodded her head up and down.

She didn't want him even thinking that she was a freak. "I've never been with any body in my life. Why you say that?"

"Cause you hang wit Felecia. I heard about her. My man Blunt stay over her crib beatin' that pussy up."

"But I'm not the same way." She pleaded. "I wish there was some way I could prove it to you."

"There is." He said devilishly. "Take your skirt and panties off."

She quickly did as she was told and sat naked from the waist down in his car seat. She didn't bother asking for his reasoning.

He positioned himself to get a good view and said, "Now put your finger in your pussy. If it goes too easy, I'll know you a liar, but if it don't I'll know you're tellin' the truth."

She eased her fingers inside of herself and tried to provide traction. She couldn't tell him that this wouldn't prove a thing considering she stayed playing with herself on a regular.

He knew she was telling the truth but liked the control.

"I can't believe you just did that."

"Did what?" she asked looking around.

"Took your clothes off just cause somebody asked you. If you were a real virgin, you'da neva gave in so easy. Put ya shit back on yo, I'm takin' you home."

Without saying anything else he pulled off on the way to her house. She rustled to put her clothes back on and tried finding her dignity. She was pouting the entire way and he saw remnants of tears falling down her face. He loved it.

Once he made it to her house he stopped and said, "Get out my car."

She grabbed the door handle and said, "Cray, I know you don't believe me, but I'm tellin' the truth. And I really like you. I've never been with anybody before and I hope I can see you again."

"Maybe, maybe not." He pulled off.

Tiara cried as she walked into the house. She had no idea that his mind games were just getting started.

JASON
PLAYA, PLAYA

Moe's, a seafood restaurant off of Eastern Avenue in Bmore was were the players roamed. Fly rides dressed the outside of the spot like a thousand dollar suit and anybody who wanted in the game or wanted to be around others who were, chilled in Moe's.

People were running in and out of the restaurant when Jason hopped out of his green Honda Accord. He knew who she was because he'd been tagging her around ever since the meeting adjourned with Cray last week. The moment he saw her walk out with two black chicks, he rushed in the restaurant brushing her lightly with his arm.

"Oh shit!" she looked at him.

She and her friends smiled at how fine Jason was. He was looking hot in his Evisu blue jeans, black belt with a silver skull head buckle. And he completed his look with a plain white t-shirt. He dressed simple but smooth.

"How you doing?" she said running her hands down his arm, clearly intoxicated.

"I'm cool...just 'bout to grab somethin' to eat." He pulled away as if he wasn't interested.

"Got a second?" She asked.

Her friends stood on the sidelines ogling him. One was wearing a red cotton mini sport dress from Gap, holding her green Gucci purse. The other wore a pair of fitted blue jeans and a pink top. She was carrying the traditional brown and tan Louis Vuittton bag.

"I got a few seconds for you, ma." He said giving her a seductive smile while allowing the door to close without him going inside the restaurant.

"So where you goin tonight? To your girl's house or somethin'?" Carolyn asked.

"I am if you goin' to your man's crib."

"I'm single."

For a second she appeared hurt. Jason had no idea that just last week she aborted J-Swizz's baby because she was tired of him cheating.

"Oh really? Why do I find that hard to believe?"

"I guess because of the way I look." He eyed her fat titties.

She looked cute in her black halter top and white kakis.

"So are we done playing games or are you coming with me?" She persisted.

Ever since J-Swizz did her wrong she'd been running around town sexing in and everybody. And now she was beyond intoxicated so that meant Jason was next.

"I guess I'm rollin' wit you then." He said as he ran his hand down her back.

"I feel bad you didn't get anything to eat. I mean, you want to exchange numbers and hook up later?" she offered as she used his body to prevent from toppling over.

"Why eat in there if I can nibble on you?"

She laughed.

He winked.

She blushed.

"Let's get out of here." She gripped his hand.

This was too easy. Jason had hoped there'd be a slight challenge since he had to take one for the team. But the way she was throwing that thing around, he was confident he'd have his dick in her mouth within the hour. And shortly after that, she'd be telling him everything he wanted to know. He wanted things to go smoothly because he knew Cray didn't have any respect for him. He called him weak several times to his face and he wanted him to know he could be counted on.

"Ya'll go head without me." She threw them her car keys. "I'll meet ya'll back at my place."

When she said that, he got a *good* look at the other two. When he did he noticed the one with the jeans was bad as shit! And with Baltimore being so small, he wondered why he didn't see her fine ass around the city before. They were a little more reserved than the women he was accustomed to, all three of them. They reminded him of sophisticated businesswomen who were trying to be down.

"You not gonna introduce me to your friends?"

"Oh…," she swayed from left to right. "This is Angie," she continued pointing at the one he wasn't interested in. "And this is Lisa."

"Lisa huh?" He repeated her name and licked his lips.

Lisa was 5'5, with a peanut butter complexion. Not to mention she had a waist so small it made you wonder how it connected to an ass so fat.

Jason knew he was going way against everything Cray told him to, but there was no way he would not hit that pussy.

"Nice to meet you." She extended her hand before rubbing her index finger inside his palm. This was the universal sign of sex and Jason had all intentions of connecting with her as soon as possible.

"Well girls," She pulled him away from her friends, catching their glances. "I'll get up with you later."

They waived and jumped in her white Lexus as Carolyn went with Jason.

He winked at Lisa before walking off.

"So where we goin'?" he asked, stuck with the one he didn't want to be with.

"I'm coming with you."

"Let's not waste time then. Straight up, are you tryin' to get a room?"

Jason was trying to irritate her so he could meet up with Lisa but it wasn't working.

"Sure." She smiled pleased and without hesitation.

"You neva did give me your name." he told her trying to follow Cray's plan.

"Carolyn.

That's all you need to know." He opened her car door and walked around to the driver's side.

Five minutes into the drive he jumped back on script.

"Shit!" He hit the steering wheel.

"What? What's wrong?" she asked thinking he was about to go crazy on her.

"I can't tell you." He said under his breath. "You got me so fucked up that I forgot I had somewhere to be tonight."

"Is it top secret?"

"No…it's just that most females don't like to hear certain shit. So I refrain from tellin' em."

"I'm not most females either." She told him rubbing his thigh, afterward pulling up her blouse to expose her large breasts. Suddenly, she started to look better to him. "Now tell me what's up." She said stroking his shoulder as he turned down the roads, leading to the hotel in on Baltimore Harbor.

"Naw…I don't want to fuck up." He said shaking his head. "I'm already feelin' you and I know if I tell you what I'm into, you gonna go the other way." He continued as her hands moved up his six-pack abs.

"If you knew the kinda of stuff I see you wouldn't even say that. Besides, I already know what you in to. I got an eye for those little details."

"Oh really?" he said looking at her as she spread her legs, lifted her skirt and fondled her pussy. "Now tell me what I'm in to." He continued as he took his free hand and pushed a finger within her wetness. Her walls contracted on it.

"Let's just say this…you're not a choir boy."

"And how you know I'm not?"

"'Cause choir boys don't look like money. And I associate with somebody major out West and know how ya'll get down."

She began to gyrate onto his finger and there was no way in hell he'd be able to operate a motor vehicle under those circumstances. If she kept it up, he wouldn't have to waste any money on a room either. Jason decided to pull over and watch the freak show.

Jason slid his finger out, laid back against the window and busted out laughing. Mentally he kept a record that his right index finger went into her, that way he wouldn't put it in his face.

"What's so funny?" she asked looking down at herself and than back at him.

"Somebody major out West huh?" he laughed harder. "You don't know nothin' bout dese streets out here. You probably from the county. Where you live at? Owings Mills or somethin'?"

"I do know about these streets!" She pulled her dress down looking at him seriously. "Don't let the white face fool you!"

"Hold up." He said getting serious. "You don't smoke that shit do you? Cause when I was talkin' bout knowin' the streets I'm was talkin' bout bizness, not getting' high."

"I don't smoke!" she said getting angrily. "Why would you even say some shit like that?"

"Cuz don't no white broads be in the streets that's why…unless they on that shit!"

She looked at him and laughed. "Honey my father may be well connected, but I'm not. I know more shit than you think I do. Trust me, and I'll leave it at that."

He'd heard enough. She would serve her purpose. But first, he had to make her fall for him and be willing to tell him anything he wanted to know. The easy part was getting *confirmation*, the tough part was getting the *information*.

"I'm sorry." Jason said rubbing her thigh. "Let's not talk about that bullshit no more. I'm tryin' to get to know you."

"I thought you had somewhere to be."

"I do, but what's important right now is you and findin' out where your head is at. And right now I'd like it to be right here," he said pointing to his dick. "You cool wit that?"

"Yeah." She rubbed his abs again.

"Damn…your lips look soft." He lied.

"They are." She smiled making them perky.

"Why don't you prove it…show me how soft they are."

She went in to kiss him and he gently pushed her head into his lap and unzipped his jeans.

"Show me right here."

Without hesitation, she removed his dick and sucked him like a pro. His head fell back into the headrest as he pumped in and out her mouth. Placing his penis in her hands, she licked the sides of it, and circled her tongue around the tip. When she got his entire shaft wet, she took as much of him into her throat as possible, without gagging. Jason felt a wave coming over him as he held her head in the palm of his hand like a basketball. She was bobbing up and down like she was loving it, and she was.

"Oh shit!" he moaned as he opened his eyes briefly to see a few cars passing by. "Keep dat shit right there."

Up and down she moved until she could feel him pulsating in her throat.

"Ahhhhhhhh shiitt!" he moaned exploding on her lips just seconds after she closed her mouth. "Fuck! Dayum girl!!!" he said adjusting his pants. "You gonna make a nigga marry yo ass."

"I bet a county girl don't know how to do that shit." She bragged wiping her mouth with her hands. She swallowed every drip.

"You ain't lyin' bout that. I'm keepin' ya ass around."

"And why is that?" she smiled.

"'Cause I got to."

Jason knocked on Blunt's door waiting to give Cray the details on his case like he asked him to. A few seconds later Blunt opened the door and gave Jason a pound.

"Dat nigga's downstairs." Blunt said as Jason followed.

Once in the basement, he saw Cray rolling a blunt and running a lighter under it to harden the surface. Blunt plopped down on the recliner.

"So what happened?" Cray asked.

"You was right. That bitch knows everything."

"Cool. You stuck to the plan right? Didn't do more than you had to?"

Jason remembered introducing himself to Lisa, and how he was sure to fuck her but didn't think that counted.

"Naw, yo." He said looking at the TV. "I stuck to the plan."

"Don't play games, Jason. Did you do everything like we talked about?" he asked pointing at him.

"Yeah, man! Everything went smooth."

"Cool…cool."

"So afta I get everything, what you got for me next?" he wondered.

"Nothin'. I'm keepin' you on her as long as possible. Once she gives you names spots and locations, play her even closer. We don't want her thinkin' that's the only reason you stepped to her ass. I don't need Melody's ass expectin' shit until it's too late."

"But when do I get to be more hands on with ya'll?"

"What the fuck is this hands on shit you keep talkin' about? You obsessing over this shit." Cray laughed. "Cuz without the addresses and locations, there's nothin else to plan. Now step."

"So, this all you want me to do? Play babysitter? I'm the only one wit time served on them streets. Let me help wit the set-up or somethin', man."

He was desperately trying to prove to Cray he was tough, but he could see right through his cookie dough exterior.

"Not until you're ready and I'll know. For now…stick to the plan. Get as much info as possible. And when it's time, I'll give you something else. Got it?"

"Got it." He said as he walked hurriedly up the stairs.

But inside, Jason was furious.

NYZON
BWI PARKWAY
HALF CRAZY

Nyzon was driving down the street leaning to the side. He just hooked up with Angel and everything was good. He took her shopping and pretty much bought up Georgetown. He dropped at least five thousand on her. Although he was kicking dough, it wasn't to buy her time. It was to make her see what she'd lost once he was gone. He had plans to get her so mentally fucked up that she'd crawl on her hands and knees to be with him. He always believed the girl of his dreams would drop to their needs one time or another.

Things were looking up for Nyzon. The meeting with Cray was tomorrow and he had his crew and money together. It was just a matter of time before he'd be paid in full. He pulled into the gas station to fill up and was on his way to see Angel when the moment he swiped his debit card, he saw Monesha leaning on his driver's door.

"Where have you been?" she asked staring him down, arms folded. She was wearing a black hoodie.

This bitch is trippin'! He thought. He wondered how she knew where he was. His skin crawled when he realized he must've been followed and he didn't realize. In the game he was in, this was a major no-no.

"What are you doin here?" he was five seconds from cussing her out.

"I'm askin' the questions!" she told him eyes red from crying. "I've been calling you for months now! Everybody in the family's heard from you but me." She walked over to him, hands tucked inside the pockets of her hoody. "So why are you ignorin' me, Nyzon?"

"I'm not ignorin' you." He lied. "At least I'm not tryin' to, but what you want me to do? Every time I try to talk to you, you're pressuring' me about comin over to your house and shit. It's over between us."

"It's over?" she said her voice lowered and her fists balled up.

"Yeah...we're through." He was serious.

"Not if I'm pregnant we not." She smirked.

"Come again." he gave a look like I know she didn't just say what I think she did.

"I'm having your baby." She loved the fear in his eyes.

Nyzon felt his heart beat within his ears.

He took two steps back, looked up at the sky and dropped his head.

"I'm sorry, Monesha." He said walking over to her and hugging her. "I been iggin' you and I'm wrong. You shoulda told me." He gripped her closely. "I'm gonna stay with you through this okay? You won't be alone."

"For real, Nyzon?"

"Fuck yeah. I wouldn't have you going through something like this by yourself."

"You don't know how good it feels to hear you say that." She wrapped her arms around him. It felt so good for her to finally be accepted by him. "I love you so much. I'm sorry for blowin' up your phone too. I just wanted to talk to you and you wouldn't answer my calls."

"I'm sorry, Monie. Everything gonna be straight."

"You sure?"

"Positive, baby girl. So when you want to have it done?" he asked looking into her eyes.

"What done?" she wiped the tears and looked up at him.

"The abortion." He said still holding her.

"I'm not having an abortion." She pushed away from him.

"Well you can't keep it either." He told her angrily. "So you might as well get that shit out ya head!"

"I'm having our baby, Nyzon, whether you want me to or not. So is it over now?"

"What the fuck is wrong with you, Monesha?!" he yelled grabbing her arms. "What the fuck you gonna tell people when they ask you who the father is?" He squeezed her arms harder. "This some bullshit! You shoulda neva came to my hotel room that night!"

"You wasn't sayin' that when you put your dick in my ass and mouth!"

"Monesha...people are gonna trip out if you have this baby. And what if it ain't healthy? We cousins! We're not supposed to be fuckin' each other! You can't do this!"

"I don't care what people think!" she told him hitting his chest forcing him to release her. "I knew you before I found out you were my cousin. It's hard for me to just shut my love off like that! But I'm glad to see you can."

"Listen, none of that shit changes the fact that we're still related."

"I'm havin' our baby, Nyzon!" she said getting in her car. "So get use to it. Cause you gonna be a daddy and you gonna be a daddy to my baby!" She backed her purple ford Taurus up, and pulled off.

"Monesha, wait!"

It was too late.

She was gone.

CRAYLAND
BALTIMORE
A Soldier Above All

Cray sat outside of his old house watching Tiara blow up his phone. It had only been a little over a month and already she was on it...and hard at that. He smiled when he realized that he hadn't even put his game into full player mode. After the car game he ran on her, he showed up at her school to drop off another girl. Her heart dropped when he looked her dead in the eyes and didn't speak. He had her just where he wanted her. Tucking his phone in his pocket, he proceeded up the steps leading to Melody's.

Once at Melody's door, he glanced over at his old house. He thought about his folks all the time but could never bring himself to reach out to them. What was done was done, and now they were on their own.

When he knocked on the door J-Swizz opened it and walked away. *I can't stand this bitch ass nigga!* He thought when he walked into the half lit living room. The TV was on but the volume was down low. A worn out old red velvet couch sat against the wall and J-Swizz and Carolyn sat on it. He could tell they'd been arguing. Little did J-Swizz know but Jason had been all in that pussy.

"Where Melody at?" he asked stepping in front of the TV.

"In the back." Cray smirked looking at the girl. "Now get out the way."

"Make me, nigga." It was obvious J-Swizz was showing off for his piece so he wanted to call him on it. Cray wanted a reason to put him on his back. He never did get over how he grabbed him up when he touched Melody's car years ago.

"Whateva, man."

Cray smirked. "That's what I thought. Punk ass mothafucka."

"We'll see who's laughin' in a sec." J-Swizz retaliated.

Cray didn't know what that meant so he kept it moving.

"Yo, Melody. What you need man?" he asked knocking on his door once before opening it. He stumbled when he saw his father on his knees, asshole naked, sucking Melody's dick.

When Cray turned around, he saw J-Swizz put his head down in laughter. The shame and embarrassment Cray felt was unparalled. He knew J-Swizz knew his father was in there but wanted to see his reaction.

"I thought I told you to tell him to wait out front!" Melody yelled.

"I forgot, man. I'm sorry."

He felt a heat wave take over him as his piercing eyes fixated on his father. He was just about to pull out his weapon and shoot them both when he remembered. He was Crayland Bailor! A loaner and above all, a mothafuckin' soldier! Why let his weak ass father come in the way of his fortune and his plan?

He looked at his father, strolled up to Melody and said, "What you want, man?"

They were shocked. Cray acted as if he'd seen nothing.

His father stood up, covered his own dick with one hand and touched Cray on the shoulder with the other. "I'm sorry, son."

"Nigga, do you know me?!" He waited for him to say something displeasing so he could punish him.

Silence.

"Den get ya hands the fuck off of me!"

His father grabbed his pants and ran out the door. Cray heard stories of Melody going both ways but never had proof. Now he did.

"Man, it wasn't how it looked." Melody offered.

"Nigga, let's get down to business." Cray retaliated.

He didn't want to be put in a position to discuss the matter. Because if he did, Melody wouldn't like what he'd have to say.

"A'ight then." Melody adjusted his clothes. "Give me five minutes."

He left Cray alone with his thoughts as he walked to the bathroom. Cray allowed Melody the time he needed to get his self together, but trust and believe he'd never forget this shit. And neither would he.

NYZON
BLADENSBURG, MARYLAND
The Pact

Nyzon, Royala, Cooks and Simon jumped into his car to meet Cray at a secluded spot. It was quiet as they drove down the street. No one said it but everyone was thinking the same thing. Could Cray be trusted? And why the desolate place?

Once they pulled up to the address on the paper, near a railroad track, all they saw were warehouses.

"This is it." Nyzon said looking at his crew.

"You sure about this?" Cooks asked in the passenger front seat.

"To be honest, I can't call it. I mean, why would he try somethin' when he ain't got access to the connect? Plus he told us to come strapped."

His trunk held their portion of the money for the weight. In total, they had half a million dollars on them, and Cray and his boys were supposed to come up with a half too. With all that cash, he didn't want to bring up the possibility that Cray could be robbing them. It would put a damper on the evening.

"Are ya'll wit me?"

Royala with her baseball cap pulled over her eyes said, "Fuck you think?"

Cooks and Simon nodded. They got out and walked to the door.

As instructed, Nyzon knocked on the steel door five times, waited ten seconds and knocked three more. The door opened and Cray was behind it.

"Glad you made it my, nigga."

"What's up wit the lights bein' out in here?" Nyzon popped off.

He could barely see Cray's face it was so dark. Dude was giving him the creeps for real. If something didn't give in a few seconds, all of them were about to unload on his Baltimore ass.

"You'll see in a minute."

He led them to a larger room within the warehouse. There was one light in the ceiling, which moved a little from side to side, and Nyzon was able to see the rest of Cray's crew. It would be the first time they met. Cray had three people with him but what really had Nyzon fucked up was the person hog tied on the floor, with a pillow case over his head.

"Hey, dude, you betta start talkin'." Royala said slightly nervous at the scene. "Cause I ain't sign up for no bullshit."

Cray looked at Nyzon and than at Royala.

"A broad on your team? Cute." He smirked rubbing his chin.

Royala aimed her 45 in his direction and on instinct, they all aimed at one another. Baltimore against DC in a closed space. If they were to fire on one another nobody would find their bodies for days. There was so much tension in the air it was hard to breathe. One wrong move and everything would be over.

"Aye, yo, I think we need to start all over." Cray said looking at the weapons thrown up in the air like gang signs.

Nyzon with his heat pointed directly at Cray, told his crew to lower their weapons. They obeyed.

"What the fuck is goin' on, young?" Nyzon asked.

"If we gonna unite," Cray started, tucking his weapon in the back of his pants. "I need to know you got our backs, like we got yours."

"We here ain't we? So get to the point." Cooks said focusing on the person squirming on the ground.

"Take the hood off." Cray instructed Jason. When he did Melody was revealed, his face swollen from all the blows he'd endured.

"I'm not down for this shit." Nyzon wasn't feeling the murder game. All he wanted to do was get paid.

"This nigga can't live if we gonna get the money we bought to make. We gonna have to put him to bed. We ain't makin' new blocks, we takin' his!" He said pointing at him with the barrel of his gun. "This the only way, DC. He...CAN NOT...live! Besides, there's no turning back now. This nigga gonna die whether you want him to or not. The only question is, are you with me?"

Nyzon thought for a second. Long and hard. He looked at Cooks, Simon and then Royala. They all gave him the nod of approval.

"So what's your plan?" Nyzon asked Cray after gaining agreement from his squad.

"We bust his ass together. We trust, like you trust." Cray replied.

Silence.

"If we do this, don't ever test me again."

"Never," Cray said.

Without saying another word they all aimed, pointed and unloaded.

The pact was formed.

TIARA
5 MONTHS LATER
TOO YOUNG FOR THE GAME

Tiara leaned against the cold brick wall in the back of her school as she wiggled out of the Baby Phat outfit she wore, to put back on the boring blue jeans and white t-shirt set her father bought. The moment she got dressed and walked toward the front of the building, instead of seeing Kavon she saw Cray's car. It was her birthday and Kavon said he'd be there to take her out. Still she could not have been more excited that Cray was there. Time with him was precious because sometimes he didn't come around.

"Get in." Cray said pulling up on the curb.

She couldn't prevent the smile from shining on her beautiful face. Her long hair bounced as she jogged toward his car. Since he met her he always seemed elusive. It was like he wasn't allowing himself to get close to her and Tiara hated it. All she wanted was to be in his company.

"Why you wearin' that shit?" He looked her over disapproving of her gear. If she was going to ever be his girl, she had to look the part. "Where the clothes I got for you?"

"I couldn't wear them, Cray." She stuffed his clothes in her black book bag to conceal it from her father, sat back in the seat, and put her seat belt on. "You know my dad was supposed to pick me up today. So I had to change them before he saw me. It's like lately he's starting to trip about me hanging out. I don't think he trusts me anymore."

"Why should he? You lie to him right? You still afraid to tell him about me aint you?"

Silence.

"I don't want to make him angry."

"What about me?"

"I don't want to make you angry either. I'm confused."

He stopped his car and said, "Get out! Go be with your father then."

"No. Please! Don't do this to me. Please."

She closed the door and he continued down the road. Tiara couldn't help but feel like Cray wanted her to choose between him and her father sometimes. And that scared her.

"If you gonna deal wit me, you got to stand up to your pops." He said looking at her seriously.

His once gold hair now back to it's original color of black. He had a little length on it so now it curled up.

"I will, Cray! I promise. Just give me some time."

She told him that many times before and sometimes, he just set her off to hear her say it. It sounded so sweet coming from her young lips.

"Yeah whateva! You betta start actin' like it then."

When she saw him past her house she wondered where he was taking her. She couldn't go too far because her father would be pulling up at the school in about fifteen minutes. It was bad enough her car was still left up at the school so when Kavon rode by, he'd definitely see it.

"Where we going?"

"Why? You don't' want to roll wit me?!" he shot back.

"Cray are you mad at me? Did I do something wrong?"

"I'm just tired of playing games with you, that's all. Now you rollin' wit me or not?"

"I'm going with you."

"Than fall back and relax."

The Hotel

It took them twenty minutes from leaving her school to pull up at the Embassy Suites in Linthicum heights. He guided her right past the receptionist desk and right toward the elevator. Her heart beat rapidly as she stood in the corner looking at the buttons light up.

"You okay?" he smiled.

"I'm fine." She was still trying to get over how he treated her earlier.

She didn't understand how to deal with his mood swings, but she was willing to learn.

"I'm sorry, Tiara. I just wanna take care of you and I get frustrated when I can't. You understand what I'm sayin'?"

She nodded yes.

"And don't worry, baby, just cause we're here don't mean nothin's goin' down."

She knew he wouldn't do anything sexually she didn't want. He'd been dodging her since they met. The moment they walked out of the elevator and to room 288, he slid his key in and she caught a glimpse of him from the side.

Damn he's fine. She thought.

The moment the door opened, she saw boxes everywhere. She wondered when he had all the time to do this. Rose peddles filled the room and the scent of vanilla candles teased her nose.

"I hope you like some of the things I bought. It's for your birthday. Open 'em up and tell me what you think."

"All of this is for me?" her eyes wide with surprise.

"Every last box."

Tiara ran through the room touching everything at first before she ripped open the boxes. He bought her Gucci outfits, Louis Vuitton purses and a few labels she didn't recognize. She immediately rushed up to him and wrapped her arms around his neck.

"What are you doing to me?" she asked kissing him all over his face.

"I'm trying to take care of you. You gonna let me?"

"Yes!" she exhaled! "Yes I will!"

She gave him a sweet kiss. This time it lasted a bit longer. He pushed her away.

"Not like this."

"What? Why?" she was confused.

He had gotten the hotel room so why not make love.

"I thought that's what you wanted."

"I'm not here to have sex with you, Tiara."

His rejections made her want him even more.

"Can you just hold me?"

He wrapped his arms around her waist while she lie against his chest. He'd succeeded at winning her over.

"What you want from me?" he asked her in a deep base voice.

"I don't know." She hunched her shoulders. "I just know I got to be around you. I'm sick when you don't call. Can you tell me what I need to do? To make you want only me?"

He kissed her a few more times on the forehead, before taking her over to a table.

"I'ma be honest with you, your father is in the way of what I'm tryin' to do. I mean, I respect the dude cause he's your pops, but it's time I took care of you now. I already know if I do the things I want, he's gonna be in the way. And with everything goin' on in my life, I don't need that kind of drama."

"I don't understand."

"Tiara, I'm a hustler." He said looking up at her. "I don't feel like lyin' to you no more cause that's not even me. Plus I think you know already. I'm everything your father warned you about and more."

"I know." Her voice low and weak. "And I don't care. I just want to be with you."

She gripped his hand softly and saw something in his eyes. *Is this all a game to him*? She wondered. Something whispered, walk away. But she was in too deep.

"What my father don't know won't hurt."

"Tiara, that ain't good enough for me. It's all or nothin'. I'm not runnin' hidin' from your peeps no more."

Just as he was waiting on her response his cell phone went off.

"Give me a second." He said throwing a finger at her answering the phone. He was silent before he said, "He still there? A'ight, I'ma get wit you lada 'bout that. One."

"I got to take you home, shawty."

With that he put everything he bought for her in the bags. But Tiara couldn't take her gifts home, not right now anyway. The bags would make too much noise.

"Can you keep my stuff for me? Until tomorrow. I don't want my father seeing all of this before I tell him about us."

"See that's the shit I'm talkin' about!" he yelled. "You know what...fuck this shit! I know plenty of bitches who would kill to be in ya shoes right now and here I am wastin' time on you! This thing...between me and you...not workin' no more. Let's go."

Her heart ached hearing those words, and although he was rushing to leave, she didn't want him to go like this. She wrapped her arms around his tensed body and felt his muscles loosen.

"Move..." he pushed weakly. "I can't do this with you. Your mind too young to be with a man like me."

"Cray, I'm sorry! I'll tell him I swear! I'll tell my father about us. Hold me. Don't leave like this." He could feel her young heart beating against his chest. "Please...make love to me."

Silence.

She knew she was a virgin and wasn't ready for a man like him, but she had to have him.

"I can't...." he whispered. "I got to handle somethin' anyway. I ain't 'bout to fuck you and then run out on you like you some fuckin' whore."

"Well stay...and make love to me right." She said seductively.

Her words were bold and with promise and even though she was inexperienced, she was ready.

He lifted her off the floor and took her over to the bed. She stared into his eyes as she undressed herself. He looked at every inch of her body. Tiara didn't mind him staring because she wanted him to see that every inch of her was his and that she was untouched.

"You're beautiful...I never seen a woman look like you before."

"Because I'm not a woman until I'd been with a man. Making love to you will make me one."

He rubbed his rough hand over her stomach, her bare legs, soft perky breasts and lips. She shivered. Reaching down he gently kissed her. Not knowing what to do, her lips pushed into his prematurely. She was trying hard to do the right things and hoped he could tell. Their lips remained connected for the next minute before he looked at her once more.

"You sure about this?"

"Yes. Please make love to me, Cray. I wanna show you that I'm real about you."

Cray stood up, removed his clothes and exposed his tattooed chiseled body. In all of his splendor, what got her attention was his stiff large penis. Cray slowly crawled into bed without putting all of his weight onto her. His hips went fishing for the right spot, and when he found her dampness, Tiara's eyes widened.

"I'll be easy with you, I promise."

All the things her father talked to her about entered her mind but she pushed them out. She trusted Cray and needed to be with him. And the moment he eased inside of her, she tensed up and a tear fell from her eyes.

"Want me to stop?"

"Nooooooo."

The pain was borderline unbearable as he slid in what was left of his thickness. Instead of pumping her like she was a professional, he stayed inside of her for a second, motionless. Still it hurt so badly she wanted to tell him to stop. But how could she? It was she who encouraged him in the first place.

And then he said, "I think I'm fallin' in love with you."

It was all she needed to hear. Slowly his body moved again widening her tight whole.

"Relax, baby....relax." he whispered.

When she obeyed she noticed the pain started to subside and was mixed with pleasure. She smiled when she heard him moan knowing it was all because of her. For five minutes he stroked her slowly looking into her eyes periodically. But she noticed whenever he stared at her, his strokes would stop before starting again. And she wondered, did staring at her bring him closer to ecstasy. While her mind thought about if having sex with him would keep him, she felt his strokes speed up. And his head fall back, and just like that, he pulled out of her, and came all over her stomach.

"Oh shit...I'm soooo sorry."

"Don't be."

She didn't want him thinking that she was so shallow that she'd be worried about how long it last. In his defense, he'd never had a tight virgin pussy in all his life. The only problem for her was that she didn't reach the orgasm she heard so much about from Felecia.

"Stay right there." Cray got up and walked to the bathroom naked. He returned seconds later with a warm washcloth.

She smiled when she felt the warmth from the washcloth against her exposed flesh. Cray, a murderer, and a monster, was gentle as he cleaned up his love juice between her legs and on her belly. .

"Girl, you tryin' to make me fall deep."

"I just want you to stay with me."

And she proved it, she gave him what she cherished the most, her virginity. And unlike a lot of things in life, it could only be given away once.

Before he could respond his phone rang again. He answered and listened to the caller.

"Where you at?"

"We waitin', man."

"Meet me at the drop in Bladensburg in an hour." When he hung up he said, "We have to go Tiara."

Sensing the urgency, they both jumped up to get dressed. She would've loved to have stayed with him after a moment like this, but knew it was not the time or the place. They jumped in his car and headed down the road.

As Tiara looked at him while he drove angrily, she couldn't help but feel as if having sex with him meant nothing. He didn't even address her. Pulling up at the corner of her house, he parked and put his hands on the steering wheel. She wanted him to say something. To tell her he still cared.

"I'ma pick you up here every morning so leave your car. You need a flyer one anyway. We'll talk to your pops together cause he needs to know about us. And he needs to know about me."

She threw her arms around his neck and smiled. As mad as he was, he made it clear that they were official. She got out.

"Bye." She waved excited about their relationship.

He pulled off.

It wasn't until he left that she realized she left her car at the school. All of that quickly left her mind when she opened the door and saw her father waiting.

"When did we get here, Tiara?"

"Get where?"

"To the place in which you start lying to me."

Her head hung low.

"I came to your school to take you out for your birthday and you weren't there. " he said standing up from the couch. "Why the lies?"

"Daddy, I'm so sorry…it's just that…I met somebody."

"Well how come he can't come in here and introduce himself to me like a man? Why he got to steal you away in the middle of the night like you some whore?"

"He didn't do that, daddy. I never came home from school."

"I had plans for your birthday, Tiara. You've never done anything like this."

"I'm sorry, daddy! Please forgive me. I wanted to tell you but I knew you'd be mad. I love him."

"Tiara, you don't know nothin' about love! You too young and naive."

"I do know about love! And we made love!"

He took two steps closer.

"Are you tellin' me that you had sex?"

"Yes! And he bought me nice things too!"

"That's all you care about is materialistic bullshit! You're just like your fuckin' mother."

That hurt.

"I don't mean to be, daddy." She said softly.

"And what about everything I've been trying to teach you? It's about what's in your heart and mind! I thought we agreed, focus on books and your life and worry about boys later. Don't you realize if you don't get an education, you won't be able to care for yourself? Don't you see it's important for you to depend on you and not some thug nigga?"

Tiara hung her head.

"Go to your room."

"Why?"

"For lying to me. And tomorrow come straight home. Don't ask me about the phone cause I'm taking it out of here. Do I make myself clear?"

"But, daddy."

"Do I make myself CLEAR!?!!!"

"Yes…daddy."

"And you're not to see him anymore. Now go!" he pointed toward her room.

Her world was over. How was she going to keep Cray if she couldn't talk or see him? She felt like dying and it was all her father's fault. Suddenly she hated him. It was nothing else for her to do but to run away with Cray. She immediately locked her door, picked up the phone and called him.

"Baby…it's me. My dad found out and he won't let me see you. You were right! I hate him!"

"You okay?"

"No…can you come back and get me? Please."

"I'll have my man Blunt pick you up in front of your spot in five minutes. He drives a silver Durango."

"Thanks, baby. I love you."

"I love you too."

She loved being able to express those words while feeling as if she meant it.

She hung up the phone and busied herself with what to take and decided on nothing. She knew Cray would by her all new things anyway. Luckily for her Kavon wasn't in the living room, so she jetted out the front door. That one move began her new life.

KAVON
SO MUCH LEFT TO BE SAID

Kavon felt like a failure in his car driving up and down the dark roads in the neighborhood looking for Tiara. Having been in Baltimore county for less than a year, already he lost his only daughter to the streets, again. And if he didn't find her, she might be gone forever. All he wanted to do was wrap his arms around her and tell her how sorry he was.

He drove around for fifteen more minutes before remembering Tiara didn't have her car and realized it was probably at her school. He drove there quickly. When he saw her car was still there, he parked far down on the same block, so that if she pulled up, she wouldn't see him first.

Seconds later, a silver Durango blasting music pulled up to the school. Is this the nigga that's fuckin' wit my daughter's head? The moment Kavon exited his car, Tiara hopped out of the Durango and stopped in her tracks when she saw her father's face. The expression on her face showed that she was sorry for leaving the way that she did. But for some reason, her eyes widened in horror. It was as if she'd seen a ghost walking behind Kavon.

Sensing something was wrong, he rushed toward her. All he wanted was to tell her how much he loved and cared for her. And that he wanted them to grow stronger together and in life.

"Daddy no!!!!!" She screamed putting her hands out in front of her. "Behind you!"

When the words exited her lips, Kavon felt a stinging sensation rip through his body and he dropped. What was this feeling? Tiara ran in his direction with Blunt who had gotten out of the truck. Blunt removed the gun from his waist and hurried in Kavon's direction. When Kavon fell, he saw Tiara's look of horror. More bullets followed. The bullets entering his body began to feel like soft nudges instead of pain. Kavon's breath was fading fast. Who had he wronged?

Now on his back, the person who had shot him stood over his bleeding body. And then he saw his face. A familiar face. Except he was much older. It was Lil Shawn. Shy's son.

"That's for my father!" With that he ran off and jumped into a waiting car a few feet ahead.

Blunt fired immediately but the shooter was too quick. He had gotten away, with his mother Candy in the driver's seat.

"Daddy! Oh my GOD, somebody call 911!" she screamed gripping his body.

"Shit!" Blunt yelled putting his gun away to make the call. He didn't sign up for this shit. All he was supposed to do was drop her ass off still he placed the call.

"Daddy! Daddy! Can you hear me. Please!!!!!!"

"Tiara. I never loved anyone as much…as," blood filled his mouth yet he was determined to speak. "as I love you."

Kavon appeared to be reaching for something around his neck but he couldn't hand it to her, and just like that, he was gone away.

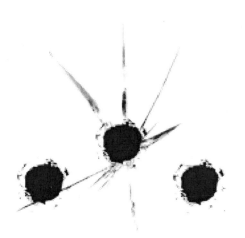

NYZON
BABY MAMMA DRAMA

He heard she had his son on a Sunday morning. Although his first child, he was far from happy. He didn't understand why she couldn't see things as he did. Everything about the pregnancy was fucked up. Nyzon spent fifteen minutes outside of her apartment building before he knocked on the door. It was late and for all he knew, she wouldn't even be up. Once he got enough energy to deal with her bullshit, he knocked on her front door and she opened it wide.

"You got my money?" she asked closing the door slightly after walking into the hallway.

"Yeah....here." he handed her five hundred. "I'll give you more later."

"Ummmmm...I mean, this enough for the baby and all, but where's the money to keep our secret."

He shook his head and gave her three hundred more.

"Better."

"Now can I see my kid?" He said before he stopped himself from drop kicking her ass on the ground.

"No you can't." She folded her arms and leaned up against the wall. "Have you lost your mind?"

"Have I lost my mind? What the fuck is your problem?"

"You are my problem...just given me a little money don't make you no father Nyzon. So if you think it do, get that out ya fuckin' mind."

"Does givin' you more make me one?"

She held out her hand.

"Yous a dumb bitch." He said reaching in his pocket and handing her more money totaling two grand..

"I expect this much in cash every two weeks. If you miss one payment, not only will I tell the family our little secret, I'ma go down to the court house and file for child support. Now the baby's sleep so come back tomorrow." She slammed the door.

This bitch had him vexed. He was sick of her ass! It was starting to be real expensive handling her but he made his shitty ass bed and had to lie in it. The only thing that made him rest easy was since he hooked up with Cray, they made money hand over fist. Everybody he rolled with was paid. Still, Monesha was a force to be reckoned with and it was a matter of time, before they bumped heads.

TIARA
A NEW DADDY

Tiara sat in the empty room of Cray's new house in Owings Mills, Maryland. Outside of a bed, there was no furniture anywhere in it. With the house being over five hundred thousand dollars, you'd think it would be laid out.

Cray knocked on the bedroom door twice before walking in and sitting on the bed. She buried her father that day and barely had enough energy to live. Before her father reentered her life, she always felt somebody out there loved her, and now that person was gone. Forever.

"Hey...I got you some coffee from Dunkin' Donuts." He placed the warm cup in her hands and she held onto it.

She'd been crying so much her skin was dry under her eyes.

"Thank you...I don't know what I'm gonna do, Cray. I loved him so much. He meant everything to me. What I'm gonna do without my daddy?" she looked up at him with puppy dog eyes.

Cray's face became a little distorted. He looked angry but tried to soften it up a little. Still, she noticed.

"Tiara, your father's gone, and I'm sorry, but you have to move on." He said as if he was talking to one of his block niggers. "He wouldn't want you in here crying all day and shit. You got to keep it movin'. You feel me?"

"But I don't know how, Cray. I ain't got nobody out here. He was all I had."

"You got me and I'ma take care of you. If you want, I'll even let you call me daddy."

She couldn't believe what he said. She didn't know that part of him was jealous that she had a father who truly cared for her when his was a no good ass heroin addict. He didn't even know what inspired his anger.

"Can I be alone, Cray? I just want some time to think things through."

"There's nothin' to think about, Tiara. You ain't out here buy yoself and I'ma make sure you takin' care of. I got my folks goin' over to your crib to take care of gettin' that stuff out and everything, so you ain't got to worry about that."

She was silent as she listened.

"So where's yo key?"

She dug in her purse on the bed and handed it to him.

"I love you, baby." Cray rubbed her face. "Do me a favor before I leave, suck my dick."

"What?" she asked her eyes opened wide. "But I just buried my father." She couldn't believe what he was saying.

"You know what, fuck it! If you don't want to do it I got plenty of bitches that would. Maybe I'll move one of them up in here with me and put your ass out."

Tiara's head was throbbing as she tried to get her mind around Cray's insensitivity. Not wanting to be alone, she took him in her mouth and sucked his dick as best as she could. When he was done he watched her swallow, like he'd taught her, and wipe her mouth.

"When I get back we gonna go to the store and get some stuff for this bedroom so you can feel comfortable." He closed his pants. "I'm not about to let you mope around here like your world is over cause it ain't."

She didn't say anything and her silence confirmed their agreement.

He leaned in toward her, lifted her chin and kissed her sloppily on the lips. It felt inappropriate given the situation but she was helpless.

"And remember, I'ma always take care of what's mine. And never bring up his name again in my house. Ever. I'll see you lada. I got some shit to handle."

With that he smiled. Tiara had no idea that he'd taken the key from around Kavon's neck on his deathbed, and was on a mission to find out what it opened. After some diligent searching, he'd discover it belonged to a lockbox inside of the house that held over a half a million dollars. Kavon had plans to give it to her after college so she'd never have to depend on a man. Cray didn't need the money because he was already one of the richest dealers alive, but he wanted her to be dependant on him for the rest of her life. So, he'd never say a word to Tiara. Ever.

NYZON
WEST BALTIMORE
NEW ADDITION TO THE FAM

Nyzon pulled up in a parking spot outside of Cray's old house in West Baltimore. Cray ended up buying the spot to hold meetings with his crew when needed. The moment he parked, he saw Jinx, Blunt and Cray hanging on the corner. With the chains around their necks and expensive cars parked on the curb, they stood out like diamonds in the rough.

"Bout time you got here, nigga!" Cray joked as Nyzon parked his new white Benz, paper tags. "I was just 'bout to break these fools."

"That's right. You was 'bout to break 'em befo I got here." Nyzon said easing out the car removing the cash from his pockets.

Nyzon and Cray had gotten so close it was eerie watching them sometimes. Once rivals, people now referred to them as the new Nino Brown and G-Money. The love of money brought them together.

"Hell I need some new rims." Nyzon said as if he didn't have enough money in his pockets to buy rims for the entire block.

Nyzon embraced Cray, Jinx and Blunt in a one armed manly hug before they all stooped down to play craps. With all the money that covered the sidewalk, nobody dared tried to rob them or interrupt their game. Cray earned respect before he ran Bmore and niggas from miles around knew about his murder game.

"Damn! I ain't been here but for twenty minutes and I already got ya'll niggas for seventy grand." Nyzon bragged. "Let me find out my DC blood givin' me luck!"

"I'm 'bout to silence that ass right quick." Jinx said. "I was just showin' you some Bmore hospitality."

Cray and Blunt laughed as they sipped beer from their cans. They were so into the game that they didn't see two shabby looking kids walking up to them, but Jinx did.

"Fuck ya'll want?" Jinx asked going for his heat.

Everybody stood up and took noticed at the two twelve year old boys.

"Please don't shoot!" one of them said with a red shirt on. "We was just gonna ask if ya'll wanted us to go to the store or somethin' for ya'll."

"What ya'll want some money?" Blunt asked.

"Yeah. We wanted to buy somethin' to eat." The other in the blue shirt said.

Nyzon uneasy about the way they walked up on them felt better when he realized they were just kids trying to make a buck. They had over ninety grand on the ground so giving them some money wasn't a problem.

"I'm good but here." Nyzon said handing them fifty bucks.

"That's all you givin'?" Cray asked giving them three hundred.

"Both of ya'll niggas cheap!" Jinx said giving them a grand a piece.

It was no longer about the kids, it was about flossing. Still their faces lit up after they looked at all the cash they held in their hands.

"When I grow up, I'ma be just like yall." The one in the red shirt said to Nyzon and Cray.

That moment meant more to Cray and Nyzon than anyone realized. When they were their ages they wanted to be like the dealers around their way. Now they were bigger. Larger than life. And they were just getting started.

"Are ya'll a gang or something?"

"Yeah, we're The Kings of 295." Cray said. It was the first time they all heard the name, but it wouldn't be the last.

In a parked car a block down

"There they go." Grimy Mike said to Monty, the dude he was going to have kill Cray."Givin' away money and shit. Punk mothafuckas!"

Ever since they took over, they were making it hard for them to sell on the same blocks they had been for years. They felt Cray's business skills were trash.

"Which one you want me to get?" he asked as he put several bullets in his gun.

"The curly head bitch in the red Braves cap." Grimy said referring to Cray. He wanted him dead so bad he was shaking.

"If you can get all of them that'll be better." J-Swizz said as he sat quietly in the car.

He was the first person cut when The Kings took over. He had to resort to sticking up people just to make a living and was tired of it. He wanted his blocks back.

"A'ight." Monty said getting out the car. "Watch a pro and learn."

They wanted Monty to do the killing because he was extra thin and could fake a crackhead better than anybody they knew. So when he approached the Kings, nobody thought much of it at first.

"Ya'll got anything on you?" Monty asked doing the Crackhead Shuffle.

"Get the fuck away from here!" Blunt yelled.

"I just need a fix." He continued.

"Man, he said give the fuck out of here!" Cray yelled louder.

Nyzon stood up and took notice. There was something about him he didn't like, and then he saw it. The moment Monty turned around to walk the other way, Cray and the rest of them returned their focus to their crap game. And when they did, Monty turned back around and aimed at Cray's head. Nyzon spotting him whipped out his weapon and hit Monty in the chest. The bullet pierced his heart.

"Oh shit!!!" Cray yelled realizing he was almost dead. He was touching his body to see if he'd been shot.

Monty's body dropped as the rest of them went for their heat while looking around to see if anybody else was coming for them. It was the second time Nyzon put a body on his gun. The fact that he killed for Cray proved he was down for him and that whatever beef they had was more than over. And Cray indebted to him.

When the body drop Cray looked at Nyzon. "How you know he wasn't legit?" Cray asked.

"Look at his shoes? They too fresh! Don't know Crackhead where no shoes like that."

They all peeped the new white Air Force Ones and said, "Damn!"

JASON
WEST BALTIMORE
IN TOO DEEP

It was a beautiful day and the sun shined against the water making it look like liquid crystals at the Baltimore Inner Harbor. Jason stood the moment he saw Markise walking toward him.

"What's up man? I missed work to come out here." They both sat on the bench. "So this betta be good."

"Aye, yo, I 'precciate you comin' to," he said giving him dap. "But I ain't have nobody else to talk to about this."

Jason saw Markise eyeing him. Jason wasn't wearing racks of gold chain like he use to five months earlier. He was finally growing up and Markise wasn't use to seeing him like that.

"What's up?" Markise asked seeing him on edge.

"Cray run Bmore. Basically he got wit some DC niggas and we takin' ova. They callin' us The Kings of 295. We got the 295 parkway from Bmore to DC locked down!" he got excited just saying it. "'Kise, I ain't neva seen dough like we gettin' now. We spend money, just to get rid of it. And wit all the cash we stackin', Cray still don't respect me."

"Did you think that would change, Jason? You know how that nigga is. His peeps got him fucked up. Why you think I cut his ass off? When that nigga did that shit over Blunt's crib I was heated for weeks, but I already know he gonna get his in the end."

"You act like you don't love the man no more. We still family."

"Fuck that shit, Jason. He ain't the same. I'm not the same."

Silence.

"So how you play into all this?" Markise continued.

"Well Cray needed to find out where all the major blocks were. Cause with the weight we got from NY, we needed access to D.C. and Bmore just to move it. So since nobody was gonna walk up to us and give us the info, he put me on J-Swizz's bitch."

"The white broad?"

"Yeah."

"Hold up! So ya'll took this nigga's corners?"

Jason nodded.

"Well I know Melody not standin' for that shit. So how much heat he bringin'?"

"You can't bring heat if you dead."

Silence.

"Don't say nothin' else to me about that shit, J. I ain't feelin' this shit already. So what you need from me, dude?"

"I need some advice cause I fucked up. I mean all I was supposed to do was get some info and play her ass close. And 'Kise this bitch told me everything. She even went as far as to write where the blocks were for me in her own handwriting. She beefin' with J-Swizz for some reason, so I guess she ain't give a fuck no more. Everything was going fine until I deviated off the plan."

Markise was listening but you could tell he was fucked up about Jason being involved in all of this. He felt he wasn't strong enough to be involved in the game.

"This nigga's out of his league." Markise interrupted. "And I can't believe you tied up in this shit eitha. So please tell me...how did you fuck up more than you already have?"

"Everything was going fine until the white girl Carolyn comes over one day and catches her co-worker Lisa leaving my house. She flipped! She started slashing my tires, banging out the windows to my car and everything. She started to put sugar in my tank but I ran out there and turned my gun on her ass and she ran off. I wanted to ring this bitch's neck out but I couldn't touch her. We needed her too much."

"Let me guess, she thought ya'll were exclusive?"

"Yeah....Cray's gonna flip when he hear this shit. He already think I can't hold my own and that he can't trust me. And now this bitch been runnin' around tellin' anybody who'll listen what happened. Now we already got the info we needed from her so for real, she's disposable."

"Don't talk like that, Jason. I'm not tryin' to hear that shit from you. Murder not your thang."

"I'm just keepin' it real. If word get back to Cray that I got wit Lisa before he got that block info, he gonna cut me off, yo. I just know it."

"You got to tell him." Markise said straight up. "That nigga is a time bomb waitin' to explode. If you gonna play this game, you got to man up. Don't forget about that shit with Kris when we were kids. That nigga been murderin' mothafuckas since before he was legal."

"I know...I know. That's why I'm coming to you."

"All I can say is that you need to tell him. You don't want somebody else doing it for you. They not going to care about ya'll bein' friends since E-School. They gonna tell him to get in good with him. And if that happens, it's not gonna be a good look for you. Other than that, you're on your own. Cray's more dangerous now than ever before."

"You right."

"I really wish you wouldn't fuck wit this shit, J. This not like you, man."

"Yes it is. What else I'm gone do, 'Kise? I been in these streets all my life. This all I know."

They walked over to the ramp and looked at the water from the harbor. Jason didn't go too close having been afraid of water all his life. Still, Baltimore city was a sexy ass city.

"I feel you. But somethin' has to give, before it's too late." He said giving him a pound. " Well...let me get back to work. Keep me posted."

"Brothers for life?" Jason said extending his hand.

"For life." Markise embraced his hand.

And when he opened it he saw that Jason had handed him a piece of paper.

"If anything ever happens to me, that piece of paper will tell you all you need to know."

"Jason...I don't want nothin' to do with...,"

"Please, Kise. Just keep it. If I have to die, I want to die with people knowing the truth. Keep it, for me."

Markise was silent before saying, "You got it, man. You got it."

THE KINGS OF 295 BALTIMORE
Bring The Pain

Everything Cray said came to pass. From getting more money than anybody ever dreamed of to the rebellion from certain niggas on the blocks. The Kings of 295, both the DC and Bmore families, sat assembled at a table in a private restaurant in Bowie, Maryland. They received great opposition from Grimy Mike and Charms from Bmore. And after the hit on their lives, they all knew they had no intentions of relinquishing blocks.

"So what you want us to do, man?" Jinx asked while the rest of the crew looked on. "The nigga is runnin' around tellin' mothafuckas he can't be touched. And that it's just a matter of time befo he come at us again."

Cray looked at Nyzon for help. But the way they ran the operation was simple. Cray operated the Bmore business, and Nyzon held down D.C. Now trust, if either one of them needed help from the other, they were there no questions asked. These rules were established early on.

"You need help from the DC fam?" Nyzon offered.

"Naw. You know the rules. I got us."

"If you need gun power we got it." Royala offered, being a respected member in the crew. "But you know Bmore betta than we do. So it's your call on how you want to carry it."

Cray looked around the table and thought on the matter.

Finally he said, "We've given them enough options. It's time to take what's ours." Cray responded simply.

"You got a plan?" Jinx asked.

"I always do."

They sat at the table for an hour discussing a plan so vicious, that they were positive they'd be able to claim their blocks within a week.

JINX
WEST BALTIMORE
BOUT IT

Jinx strolled out of his crib, jumped in his ride and parked it one mile from a Wal-Mart. He walked into the parking lot looking for another ride. When he glanced at his watch he saw it was ten minutes to 10:00 p.m. Slowly he scanned the surroundings for his prey.

It took him all of three seconds to find the appropriate victim.

Walking up to him swiftly, he stood behind him pressed his burner against the small of his back and said, "If you move I'll kill you."

"Don't hurt me." He said, his hands shaking in the air as Jinx rummaged through his pockets until he found his wallet and car keys. When he was done, he tucked them firmly into his own pocket.

"Now get on the ground and don't move."

"Yes…yes, sir! Just please don't hurt me. You can take whatever you want."

"Shut the fuck up!" Jinx yelled as he slammed the back door shut and jumped in the driver seat.

"Don't take my car. My…"

"I said keep yo mothafuckin mouth closed!" he responded turning the ignition on.

He was just about to pull off when the old man jumped up, reached through the driver side window and held onto Jinx's neck. Jinx couldn't believe the old man was a fighter. His nails scrapped across his face, peeling the skin off under his fingernails. Usually they surrendered but this situation was different. Jinx was living up to his name already.

The man still had a hold of him until Jinx stole him twice in the face. He hit him so hard his teeth ripped into his flesh. Finally he dropped to the ground and out of view. What Jinx didn't know was that his tie got caught onto the hinge of the truck, while he drug his body alongside the vehicle.

"Stop the truck!" people yelled as he barreled out of the parking lot. He was pulled fifty feet before he finally fell off.

"Shit! Shit! Shit!" he yelled hitting the steering wheel.

He thought about ditching the truck to get another one but he didn't have time. Cray gave specific orders and he had less than twenty minutes to drive back to the city, and follow through.

"Why the fuck did he grab me?! Why didn't he just let me go?!"

He didn't want to hurt anybody unless he had to because Jinx was more spiritual than most people knew. And he often battled with himself based on what he was doing in the streets, versus what he perceived to be right in God's eyes. For him physical violence was a last resort.

He was still thinking about the man when he heard a baby crying in the back seat of the truck. He quickly adjusted the rearview mirror and saw a six-month old *white* baby strapped in a car seat as its arms and legs jerked fiercely.

He had to get rid of the truck! It was hotter than a stack of marked one hundred dollar bills. He knew every cop in the world would be trying to find his black ass and that white baby. He pulled the truck over a few miles from Wal-Mart, jumped out and saw a woman putting on her makeup at a stop light in a black Ford Taurus. Through her open window, he grabbed her by the hair, unlocked the door and through her to the concrete. She fell and rolled into the middle of the street, jumping out of the way minutes before the light turned green.

When he looked through the driver side mirror he saw her hands in the air like,' *What the fuck just happened?'* She still had her makeup brush in her hand and everything. Jinx put the peddle to the metal as he swung in and out of traffic. He had to get away from the scene as soon as possible before the cops started swarming. Things like this happened to him too many times and he knew timing was everything.

He was a few miles out when he saw a black Coach bag in the passenger seat of her car. He dug his hand inside and found a wallet, took out the thirty bucks and flung it to the floor.

When he dug a little deeper, he found a big bulky cell phone. The moment he powered it on he dialed 911. "Yeah...I'm the nigga that just jacked the dude's car at Wal-Mart off Reisterstown road."

"What's your emergency?" the operator asked.

"Bitch, I said I just jacked a car. Now I ditched the car and kid two miles up the road. Send somebody to come get his lil ass."

He through the phone out the window.

After dealing with the bullshit, it took him fifteen minutes to spot his targets off of Franklin Avenue in West Baltimore. He ditched the car, loaded his weapon and got out on foot about seven blocks away. Based on the info he was given from Cray, the stash house was recently re-stocked. If he was lucky, he'd score drugs and cash over $100,000. That would temporarily put them out of business.

Dipping in between two vacant row houses, he saw his target. When he checked his watch he saw it was 10:23. And just like planned, when he looked up the block further past his target, he saw three cars flash their lights once. The Kings of 295 were there and ready to come through if need be.

Based on their plan, and wanting to get in without being spotted, one *sure shot* nigga was plenty. Now he had to rely on his intuition to make things happen.

"Get me a chicken box and a large half and half." James Factory said to one of his hoppers.

"Can I get somethin' too?" the ten year old little boy asked taking the money from him.

"Not until you bring my shit back and I check to make sure everything is right. Now get the fuck out my face." He said checking his surroundings and guarding the front door.

The little boy ran off to get the food and James Factory was left alone to man the outside of the house. The moment he turned to the left and saw a girl with an ass so fat, it put Buffy the Body's to shame, he let his guards down. And when he did, Jinx moved up to him and cracked the back of his head with the barrel of his gun.

Clink!

"This can go easy or quick. Which way you want it?" Jinx kept the heat to his dome.

Blood from the wake up call he just gave him dripped down the back of his neck. Plus he was still salty at the attack on their lives the other night.

"Easy!" he said with an attitude, trying to play tough.

"My man!" Jinx said shoving him to the door as he looked around to be sure no one was coming behind him. "Now I already know the re-up is in there, so tell me how many mothafuckas on duty."

"Two. That's it." He lied.

Clink. Clink. Clink.

"Shit man!" he yelled rubbing his head.

"Shut the fuck up! Now I know for a fact Springman, Grimy Mike and Doles in that mothafucka. So already that's three so why the fuck you lyin'? Now how many on duty?"

James knew right then that the man wasn't playing. Somebody definitely gave him the inside scoop so he couldn't bullshit him anymore.

"Now you wanna keep lyin' to me and hit this concrete, or do you wanna start tellin' me the truth and live?"

"Doles is on the door and Springman guardin' the weight. What about Grimy?"

"He in the back."

"Cool. Let's move." He said pushing him inside.

They walked up six steps before coming up on a thin wooden door. Using James' body, Jinx pushed him in knocking the entire door down. Springman went for his heat and Doles was already aiming in his direction. Caught off guard, Jinx unloaded his weapon hitting Springman in the middle of his fore-head twice.

"What you wanna do man?" he asked Doles as the two of them aimed at one another. "I'm a sure shot."

Doles looked at his man lying on the floor, put his weapon on the table and raised his hands in the air.

"Smart dude." He eyed all the money, weight and dope on the table. "Where's Grimy?"

"He left five minutes ago out back. He ain't here." Doles said.

"Get up!" he said kicking James in the ass. "Bag that shit up for me." He told him spotting a trash bag in the corner.

James crawled on his hands and knees to get the bag.

"Hurry up, man. I'm gettin' nervous, and when I start gettin' nervous I start shakin' and when I start shakin' I start shootin' niggas."

James sped up and threw all the weight and the money in the same bag. When he was done, he handed the bag to Jinx and dropped to the floor again.

"I'm wit the Kings of 295 and these our blocks now. If you got a prob-lem wit it, get use to seein' us. Now spread the word." He said walking out the door backward.

The moment he turned around someone was standing there and on instinct, he fired his weapon.

Thump! Thump! Thump! Thump!

The sound of a body falling down the stairs resonated through the dark hallway.

Although it was difficult to see, some light peaked from out under the front door. Because of it, he was able to see a white chicken box, a Styrofoam cup and a few wings on the steps. He realized it was the kid he saw earlier.

"Fuck!" he yelled angry he shot a child. It was the first time he shot someone not in the game. "Where your car at?!" he turned around yelling at James.

"Out on the curb. It's the black silver Wagon."

"Give me yo keys!"

He threw them to him, and he ran down the steps, scooped up the kid, all the while maintaining his hold on the bag of dope and money in his hand. He saw a few members of his crew exiting their cars and he threw them the money and rushed past them. He'd explain later. He couldn't see the little dude dying on his watch.

The minute he arrived at the hospital and the employees saw the injured child dangling in Jinx's arms, a few hospital personnel members rushed out with a stretcher.

"He's been shot! Take care of him." He said placing him down carefully. "I'm out of here!"

He ran back to the car, and drove five miles before he ditched it and picked up another one.

On the way to Cray's he thought about the boy, the baby and the man. He hoped they were okay but couldn't dwell on it either. This was the game, and the game was made to be played and sometimes the innocent were pawns.

NYZON
BLADENSBURG, MD
WHO ARE YOU ANYWAY

He couldn't run from it anymore. He had to deal with his mother. It had been almost a year and he managed to stay away from her all that time. In the end, he realized he still didn't have the answers to the questions he so desperately desired. He even stayed with Angel sometimes even though he didn't have to because he had more than enough money.

He walked slowly into the IHOP off of Bladensburg road. It was partially crowded and most people seemed to go about their day as if all was normal in their lives. He couldn't deny that seeing her again fucked up the normalcy in his life. He had gotten use to not having her around and for real, all he wanted to do was stay on his grind and get money. But she popped up at the boxing gym saying she'd keep coming back unless he agreed to see her. So he decided to dead the situation once and for all.

He was still looking for her when he heard her soft voice.

"Nyzon. I'm over here." Her voice appeared to echo for moments after.

He turned around slowly and looked at her sitting at a table a few feet from where he stood. The moment she saw his face she smiled.

"Sit down please." She said softly.

He moved into the available seat at her table contemplating walking out without hearing the truth, knowing full well he'd never be able to do it.

"So what's up?" Nyzon asked.

"I miss you, Nyzon and I feel it's time for us to talk."

"So why you just gettin' in contact with me now?"

"Because I needed some time to sort things out. And whenever I called your old cell, you'd never answer my call." Silence. "I thought about popping up at the gym later."

Nyzon adjusted in his seat as if he were trying to get comfortable.

"Now I know what I did was wrong by not reaching out after that," she said touching his hand across the table. He pulled it away. "But I figured you didn't want to see me anyway. I even tried to reach out to Royala and Lazarick and you told them not to get involved. What did you want me to do?"

"I want you to tell me the truth. What I've been asking you to do all along. I mean, after you pulled me out of school when the teacher's tried to get you to sign those papers, I knew something wasn't real with you."

She took a deep breath before answering.

"Can I take your orders now?" The waitress appeared to come from nowhere.

"We not hungry! Come back later!" Nyzon yelled.

He was irritated by her interruption. He wanted to know what the fuck was going on and he wanted to know now. When the waitress took off, he looked back at his mother.

"Go 'head."

"I had just come from having dinner with my boyfriend Justin. We were together for three years before that night. We had our problems and stuff, but we always seemed to get pass them. Justin was the best…I mean…all he talked about was having a family and getting married."

She looked at the ceiling before focusing on Nyzon again.

"He use to say that we'd get married, have our baby and run away so that nobody would find us. He kept talking about moving to Mexico but he wanted to have a child first. So we tried, and tried and tried Nyzon. And every time we didn't succeed, he kept blaming himself for failing me as a man. It devastated him that we couldn't have kids together. He went from having a good job as a foreman for R&R construction company, to losing his job because of drinking everyday."

"I'm still waitin' on the part that involves me and you not being my real mother."

"Nyzon…please work with me. This is hard enough as it is."

He took a deep breath and waited for her to continue.

"After seeing how the pregnancy effected him, I went to the doctors. The doctor ran a couple of tests and found out I could not have children…ever."

Outside of meeting his real family for the first time, those words were the first real confirmation that she was not his mother. Something he'd known his entire life.

She started crying before she even finished because she saw the hurt in Nyzon's eyes.

"I didn't want him feeling pain anymore. I wanted to place the blame on me. Justin was so good to me and he deserved happiness, you know?

"So I met up with him for dinner and told him everything. About the doctor's appointment, about what he said to me….all of it. And he flipped on my Nyzon. Instead of being there for me like I was for him, he got angry! He blamed me for everything and said that without a child, he didn't want me or our relationship. I felt my world had ended.

"I went to a corner store, got some drinks and drank until I couldn't drink anymore. I jumped in my car and started driving. And as if that wasn't bad enough, the rain began to pour down on me. All I wanted was for everything to be washed away. And the next thing I know I ran into a car that began to swerve out of control."

Nyzon shook his head in disgust having known his mother had died in a car accident, and that it was all her fault.

"The moment the car stopped I jumped out to see if everyone was okay. She was thrown out of the window a few feet ahead at the top of the road."

"She being my mother?"

She nodded yes.

"When I checked her pulse she was dead."

Nyzon's breaths got heavy.

"And there was nothing I could do about it. I tried to do CPR on her and nothing worked Nyzon. You would never believe how hard I tried. I was going to get some help until I saw you on the side of the road. And...I...,"

"Took me." He finished her sentence.

"Yes."

"What the fuck is wrong wit you?! Who takes a fuckin' kid off the street after you kill their mother! I had a family! A big family at that and you took them from me."

"You found your family?"

"No! They found me! And I believe my mother...my REAL mother, led me to them!"

She was hurt and it showed.

"I'm happy for you and sad about what I did. But...I thought if I kept you, he'd love me and I'd make you happy since it was my fault she was gone anyway. You see it was all done out of love, Nyzon."

"You're not capable of fuckin' love!"

She sobbed heavily.

"I just wanted us to be a family. I was wrong but by the time I realized it, it was too late. Please forgive me."

"You didn't stop to think that somewhere out there somebody else might miss me? You didn't even care."

"Can you ever forgive me, Nyzon?"

He stood up filled with rage and hate. Gripping his cup in his hands, he lifted it up off the table and through the ice cold water in her face.

"If I ever see you again, I'ma kill you. Stay the fuck away from me!"

The people around them dropped their mouths as he walked out the door.

Nyzon decided to go to Cray's crib to drink and clear his mind. In one aspect he had everything going for him. It wasn't farfetched to say that he and the rest of the crew were self-made millionaires. Already. And than another part of him recognized that his world was falling apart. His mother wasn't his mother. He had a baby by his cousin. And he lived with a woman who he secretly despised. The funny part about it was that through it all, he and Cray were starting to get close.

He was driving down Painters Mills road in Owings Mill when he passed the most beautiful woman he'd ever seen in his life. She wasn't ordinary. He never saw a female with chocolate skin and golden hair. Her hair rested on the black sweater she was wearing and she sported a pair of jeans so form fitting, he thanked God for being so kind.

Parking his white 2006 Benz on the side of the road, he jumped out to get her attention. He wondered why she was walking until he saw she was going toward a community college. The girl was startled when he tapped her shoulder. He could tell she was about to let him have a piece of her mind, until she looked into his eyes. Nyzon was fine. But above all, he reminded her of someone.

"Yes. Can I help you?" she held a book closely to her chest with her arms crossed over it.

"Name?" Nyzon was straight forward.

"Excuse me?"

"I need to know your name so I can know who I'll be spending the rest of my life with."

She giggled. And when she did, he knew he had her.

"My name is….Tiara, I mean, Tishona." She was hesitant. Plus she knew if Cray rolled past the community college and saw her on the side of the road talking to some dude, he'd knock her block off. "But I have to go. I'm sorry."

"You have a man?"

"Yes!" she yelled approaching the college's doors.

"Fuck him!"

She laughed again.

He moved closer and said "You come here everyday?"

She nodded yes.

"I'll be here everyday until I make you mine."

She giggled again.

That woman is made for me. He thought. He just had to get her to believe it.

TIARA
To Deal With A Hustler

Their home was fully furnished. They had everything ballers needed to feel comfortable. Tiara had more clothes, jewelry and cash than she ever imagined in her entire life. She really did go from rags to riches.

Once a peon, now Felecia and Yolanda looked up to her. Tiara was the richest person they knew. Even now while loafing around the house, wearing a burgundy Dior one piece dress with a diamond necklace and five carat earrings, she looked like a superstar. Not to mention she had a brand new white Benz in her four-car garage which she hardly drove.

"Tiara, what difference does it make that the curtains match the couch?" Felecia asked plopping on the large blue sofa in the living room. "You got a nigga who can pay to have somebody design all this shit. Why you fussin' wit it?"

"Because I want to do things nice for him. That's why."

Tiara looked at her and tried to be nice even though she was tired of her coming down on her. She was hating all the time.

"It's my job to take care of our home, Felecia. He's going to be my future husband."

"Felecia, can you ever bite your tongue?" Yolanda asked as she looked at the large book with Tiara as she picked out the right color scheme for Cray's movie room.

"I'm just sayin'. Some shit you should let somebody else do. I wouldn't be worried about it if I were you."

"But you're not me."

"It's like that?"

"It has to be, Felecia. You tryin' to make me that girl you can push around and I'm not her anymore."

When Felecia walked over to where Tiara and Yolanda were sitting at the table, they could smell a fishy odor. As usual she'd caught some infection and failed to get it taken care of. It was so bad that both girls had to close the book and find something else to do just to get away from the situation.

"So T, tell me about the dude you met earlier." Yolanda said flipping on the TV.

Tiara's eyes widened and she couldn't believe she brought up her new friend in front of Felecia. They both knew that if Felecia found out, she'd never be able to hold water. Plus although Cray wasn't home, she didn't want him sneaking up and overhearing their conversation.

"Let's talk about somethin' else."

Felecia cut her eyes at both of them. It pissed her off that they chose to hide things from her.

"So it's like that? Now we hidin' stuff from each other?" Felecia was getting loud and ignorant as usual, and it made Tiara uncomfortable.

"I'm sorry, T." Yolanda whispered knowing this was all her fault.

She felt Tiara was lucky to have someone care for her as much as Cray did, even if he was a drug dealer. She saw how she went from busted Tiara to a queen in less than a year. Yolanda looked up to Tiara because she felt like she finally made it.

"It's nothing really. I was just tellin' Yolanda that I met this dude when I was walkin' to school earlier today."

"Why are you walkin' anyway when you got that Benz out front?" Felecia interrupted.

"Because me and my dad use to walk all the time and when I walk, I think he's still walking with me. It relaxes me."

Felecia rolled her eyes. "Go head."

"That's pretty much it. He rolled up on me and I thought it was funny because we got the same car. He's cute and all, but I'm not gonna see again. Even though he claims he'll be up at my school everyday until he breaks me down."

"Is that all?" Felecia through her hands up in the air and Yolanda and Tiara looked at each other. "It's okay to have a lil dick on the side cause best believe, Cray gonna fuck who he want to."

"I'm not like that." Tiara advised.

"Well you betta be like that." Felecia continued. "Cause if you fuckin' wit a hustler, you best realize and understand, that he's going to do whatever he wants to you. And if you don't believe me, in time you'll see."

THE KINGS OF 295
CLUB ONE, BALTIMORE MD
STRONGER

Cray and Nyzon wanted to make sure the crew stayed tight. They understood the importance of building camaraderie. Because the more you got
along with your partners, the more money flowed. So if they weren't man-
aging their blocks, they took their top men out of town on shopping sprees
or rented private jets to Vegas just because they could.

They were rich, young and dangerous. Now Cray and Nyzon thought it
would be a good idea for the Kings to know the cities that before they united in the name of money, they hated.

"Yo, Cray, I don't know about this man." Royala stood at his side as he
and the rest of the Kings strutted into Club One in Bmore. "I heard about this
club music shit and I ain't feelin' it."

"Give it a chance, yo!" Cray patted her on the back. "I ain't gonna let
nobody feel up yo pretty ass." Jason, Jinx and Vic laughed. "That is unless
you want them to."

"Don't get fucked up in your hometown, dude!" she giggled stepping
inside with the rest of them as the guard escorted them to the VIP section at
the top. "I'll probably pull more bitches than all you niggas put together."

"I don't doubt it," Jinx joked.

"Ny, you straight?" Cray asked as the lights, camera and action overwhelmed him.

He was so drunk off the Hennessy that in his mind he was spinning. Plus
Monesha was threatening to tell Cooks, who was right beside him, about
their baby if he didn't give her more money. Giving her more cash he could
deal with. He had plenty of it to give. What he worried about was the day
when cash would no longer be acceptable. He knew what she really wanted,
was him and he wasn't up for sale.

"That nigga Ny zoned out!" Jinx said pointing at him. "You aigh't man.
I know the B-More vibe may be too much for you to take. DC niggas got to
handle this shit in sessions."

"Naw I'm good. This some wild shit man. I woulda neva thought I'd be
in a Bmore club." He said eyeing a few of the girls.

"You'll live. We got some of the baddest bitches on the east coast in
Bmore." Cray added.

Cooks and Simon didn't waste time mixing in until they heard, "*Beat that bitch wit a bat. Beat that bitch wit a bat! Beat that bitch wit a bat!*" the lyrics to an old Bmore club music classic.

Nyzon, Royala, Cooks and Simon looked at the DJ, like he'd lost his fuckin' mind.

What the fuck is he playin? They thought.

And just when they thought it couldn't get any worse they heard, "*Girl don't waste my time. Cause I wanna fuck tonight!*" Blaring threw the speakers.

When the DC crew looked at their Bmore side of the family, they noticed they were in their element. With drinks in their hands raised in the air, they rocked to the music. It was a good thing they were leaving soon due to the Bmore spots closing early because Ny didn't think he could take much more of it.

"Yeah!!! The mothafuckin' Kings of 295 are in the house!" Jason yelled drawing more attention to them. "Ain't nobody gettin' money like we gettin' money! We the richest niggas alive!" The DC crew, grabbed their weapons on their waists just in case somebody got out of line. "Name one nigga in the room who can fuck wit' us! Just one!" he continued with a drink raised in the air.

"Calm down, yo." Vic yelled tapping him on his shoulder.

"Fuck that! We run the world! We run the city!"

"Jason, relax." Cray told him. "You makin' access noise."

Everybody looked at him for a second and got mad. Lately he had been grandstanding and bragging about their status. He was the hype man for the Kings even if they didn't want it.

"Ya'll a'ight?" Cray laughed directing his attention back at Nyzon and the DC squad. A waiter brought over two bottles of ACE of Spades champagne to the table.

"We cool, but I wanna see what you got to say when we hit up Takoma Station tonight." Cooks laughed.

"Man I can fit in anywhere." Cray responded.

"We'll see about that." Nyzon joked.

Takoma Station
Washington, DC

The moment the crew walked in deep, all eyes were on them. The sound of Congo's mixed with familiar R&B hits filled the small club. Everyone was feeling the *Rare Essence* band that was performing.

In the club for only five seconds, Nyzon and their crew gave dap to everyone they fucked with. They were respected. Their reputations proceeded them and with all of the money they had flooding in, they were superstars in their own right. Surprisingly Jinx, Vic, Jason and Cray bopped their heads to the groove. Nyzon was shocked they fit in so well.

"You feelin' this ain't you?" Royala asked Cray as she spotted Simple, the girl she kicked it with in the middle of the dance floor.

"It's a'ight." Cray said. "But I still like club music."

"Don't fake," Nyzon said. "You all ova this shit!"

"I wanna be all over some pussy," Cray told him. "If you really know your city, point me to the bitch who can suck dick the best."

"I'll do betta than that," he said. "Yo, Konya! Get over here!"

A thick light skin girl with big titties, a phat ass and big lips walked over to them.

"Can you give my man *The Crucial?*"

She smiled and said, "Anything for you, Ny."

And just like that, she took Cray to the back of the club and handled her business. Nyzon laughed having realized that he was now partners with a man that at one time, he couldn't stand. And now that he knew him, he saw they were alike. They both had aspirations and they both had dreams. It no longer mattered what city they hailed from.

As they all spread out around the club, Royala became heated after seeing a dude palming the hell out of Simple's ass. Simple and Royala were friends with benefits but they worked hard at being sure they never went to the same spot as the other at the same time. Royala was also mad because she claimed she wasn't into dudes, but here she was playing herself off like a whore.

Cray had gotten taken care of and had rejoined his friends.

"Good look with that chick." He told Nyzon.

"I knew you'd like that."

"You had her?"

"Naw. I heard she was too much for me. I knew you could handle her though."

Nyzon was really saying that he didn't trust freaks.

"I guess you know me already. But damn, who's that?" Cray asked pointing to this female in a pair of tight ass jeans on the floor.

Nyzon looked.

"She cute but she ain't badder than this broad I saw on the way to your house the other day."

"For real? What she look like?" Cray asked eyeing the female harder. Her camel's foot shown between her legs like she'd done it on purpose.

Nyzon was just about to give him the full details when he spotted Royala staring hard in Simples' direction. He knew off the bat it was time to bounce. Royala was feeling that girl more than she wanted to admit it. And if they didn't leave, she was about to crack the dude's skull.

"A'ight ya'll it's time to roll." He told the crew.

"I'm just feelin' the music." Cray said peeping the shawty he wanted to put in his bed later that night despite having a girl at home.

"Naw let's leave now." He nodded in Royala's direction. When Cray saw where his attention was at he also noticed the evil look in Royala's eye.

"This ain't good is it?" Cray asked.

"Fuck no!"

Nyzon knew she'd been drinking all night and wasn't in her right frame of mind. Cray got everyone together and decided to finish the party at another spot. When everybody was together and ready to leave, they realized they reached Royala minutes too late. She'd already grabbed Simple by her hair and had pulled her to the floor.

"Fuck you doin' up here huh? I thought I told you to stay in the house?"

"Get off me, Royal!! Get off me!" She yelled trying to get away from Royala's grasp.

Nyzon and them tried to pull her off of Simple but she was drunk, pissed and strong.

To make matters worse, Royala accidentally hit a tall light skin brown dude in the chest breaking his platinum chain.

"Aw shit!" Jason yelled. "This nigga 'bout to start trippin'"

"Bitch, what's your fuckin' problem?" he questioned about to slap the fuck out of Royala.

"My man, it was an accident. She ain't mean to do that shit." Nyzon explained.

The entire crew was by his side and Royala was now fully aware of the drama she'd caused.

"Well if she wasn't out here tryin' to act like a nigga, it wouldn't be a problem."

"Aye yo, my man said it was an accident." Cray said ready to pop him if he made a wrong move.

The dude looked at everyone they were with, and decided to step off.

"So ya'll gonna jump me?"

"Naw. We gonna spare your life." Cray told him. "But you gotta bounce now.

"It's cool. We'll meet again."

"We don't doubt it," Nyzon said.

"You got it this time." The man said before walking away.

Everybody looked on and the band made an announcement about not fighting and how violence was the main reason why DC officials were trying to get GO-GO music banned.

"Sorry ya'll." Royala said as they all walked toward the door, Simple at her side.

"Ain't no thing." Cray said. "He was bullshittin' anyway. I been lookin' for a reason to bust my gun in DC and he wasn't tryin' to give it to me. "

Everybody said their goodbyes and walked to their cars. Nyzon and Cray stayed behind and talked about a few details of the business they had before them the next day.

Cray was in his car when he remembered he had a sack of weed in Nyzon's car that he wanted to fire up on the way home. So he shut the door and walked toward Nyzon's car. Nyzon saw him in his rearview mirror so he didn't pull off. But right before he reached Ny's car, Cray's phone rang.

"Speak." Cray said not recognizing the number.

"Crayland Keon *Mothafuckin'* Bailor!" An unfamiliar voice bellowed from the other end of the phone. Cray stopped in his footsteps.

"Yo who the fuck is this?!"

"Don't worry bout who the fuck it is. Let's just say, I got somebody you care about in my custody. And if you don't call off your dogs, and stay away from our blocks, you'll never see them alive again."

Nyzon seeing the look in Cray's eyes from his rearview mirror got out of his car and walked up to him.

Cray's heart raced.

All his boys had left and he wondered who he was talking about. And then he thought about Tiara.

"And who is that?" Cray asked.

"Your pops. And if you want him alive, I suggest you back the fuck off." Silence.

"You there, mothafucka?!" The caller yelled on the phone when he didn't get a response.

"I'm here."

"So what's up?"

"You got the wrong dude, yo."

"Fuck you talkin' about?"

"I ain't got no pops."

When Cray hung up Nyzon said, "Everything straight?"

"Neva been straighter."

In a rundown Baltimore City Row house

Grimy Mike looked at the cellphone as if he didn't hear Cray correctly. Cray's father sat on the middle of the floor tied to a chair, his mouth gagged.

"What he say?" Doles asked with the gun pointed at his father.

"The nigga hung up!"

"What?" James Factory said looking at him crazy.

"He hung up."

Silence.

They all looked at one another.

"Damn, he really don't give a fuck." Doles said.

"Exactly." Grimy confirmed.

"What we gonna do now?" James asked.

"Kill his ass."

With that, they lit his father up like a tree on Christmas day.

KIRK BOWLER
COMMON GROUND

Kirk parked his car and walked down the street with one of his white KYC captains in the D.C. police department. They were in the 7th district off of Southern Avenue. He was showing him one of his most crime ridden areas and his desire to put more patrolmen on the beat.

Normally Kirk wouldn't listen because he busied himself with consulting only with William Jamison. But now since he'd lost yet another mayoral race, and was told by his advisors that making a major impact on crime might win him office, he was willing to listen. He knew one major drug bust could help him a long way.

"This is where I'd really like to have more patrolman stationed. I don't know but it seems like the past year crime has saturated this area."

"So what are you doing now?" Kirk asked wanting answers.

"Well we use the men we have to cruise up and down the blocks, and we've made a few arrests but nothing's sticking. It looks like they have mostly juveniles selling hand to hand and taking the hit. And when we arrest them, they're not saying a word. So we can never find out who's really behind the money."

"If they do that enough they'll run out of folks."

"Like I said they're kids so we can't keep them long. Eventually the system will spit them back out into the streets and they'll be rewarded for not snitching."

"You're saying they're organized?"

"That's what I wanted to talk to you about sir, there's a new crew and they're calling themselves, the Kings of 295. They're much more organized than what we're accustomed to seeing around here. In fact based on the information I have, they have the entire beltway from D.C, to Baltimore locked."

"Who are they?"

"No one knows. Nobody's talking."

Kirk was finally listening. If they were as big as he says they were, this would be the perfect case to break. With him as mayor, he could finally make good on his promise to a few big real estate companies who wanted to see DC clean by moving the niggers out. Since it was obvious they didn't care for their city anyway he figured he'd help them on their way. He'd do this by knocking down the projects and making the cost of living in the same areas impossible to live in.

"I didn't realize how serious this was. What do you need from me?"

"More black undercover officers on patrol. These drug dealers are smart and not for nothing, we stand out like sore thumbs around here. Look around."

When they did everyone was looking at them. Kirk swallowed hard and said, "You got it. But you better get me more info on this crew."

"Thanks chief!"

"Thanks, shit! You got to get this block clean. Then we'll have something to be thankful for."

Royala in her car across the street from them

"Yo Ny, guess who was out here on the beat?"

"Who?"

"The chief of police! That's some funny ass shit, dude! Niggas got ghost when they saw him and some otha white cop."

She was out there making sure her money was right from her runners. 7th District was her area.

Nyzon laughed.

"It don't matter what they do, they can't stop us now."

"You mothafuckin' right about that."

TIARA
OWINGS MILLS
SWEET STRANGER

Tiara walked slowly to the college hoping to see her new friend. It was Thursday and he didn't come yesterday as he promised. She'd gotten use to his presence and he was starting to be the highlight of her day. But most of all, she wondered why she even cared.

"Tiara!" she heard a voice call out to her from a black Hummer. A smile broke across her face instantly. "Can I holla at you for a minute?" she peeped the DC tags and liked the idea of him not living around the way, plus her father was originally from DC.

"Didn't I tell you I have a man?" she tried to play hard to get.

"And didn't you tell me your name was Tishon?"

"How do you know it's not?"

"Cause you answered to Tiara." He smiled at her and the scent of vanilla from his truck rummaged through her nose. "Let me take you to get something to eat."

"No! Anyway I have to go to class."

"Play hookie with me."

"You don't go to school."

"How would you know unless you go to dinner with me."

"You're a bad influence."

She couldn't stop blushing, there was something about him she liked.

"I'll be the best influence in your life. If you let me."

Her heart fluttered. It was the nicest thing anybody had said to her in a long time. Because truth be told, Cray had been an entirely different person since the money started pouring in. He never had time for her anymore, and when he did, he smelled of perfume. Still loyalty and fear of taking care of herself kept them together.

"I got to go...bye stranger."

"I'll be back tomorrow."

"You said that before and didn't come."

Silence.

She realized that her feelings had shown through.

"So you were waiting on me?"

"Bye stranger." She said before disappearing into the building.

The Next Day

"Tiara! Tiara!" Cray yelled from his movie room. "What's up with these weak ass curtains?!! I don't like this bullshit."

When Tiara came running down the stairs, she saw a girl sitting on her couch with her legs folded Indian style, and him taking the curtains down.

"What happened to the black ones I ordered?"

Tiara heard him but couldn't get her eyes off the cute chocolate girl. She was wearing a T-Shirt, which read, DC's finest. She knew they must have had some sort of past because she felt comfortable enough to take her shoes off and plop down on *her* couch. It was the girl he met at Takoma Station.

"I put them in the closet. I wanted it to be brighter in here for you." She said slowly waiting for an introduction. *Is she his cousin?* She thought.

"Well go get em 'cause I want those up instead. This a movie room so it's 'spose to be dark."

She couldn't' move. He was disrespecting her in the worse way.

"Tiara!" he said waking her out of her trance.

"Yes."

"Did you hear me?"

Tiara was hurt and embarrassed. He didn't bother telling her who the woman was. Instead he bossed her around like she was a child.

"Yes. I heard you."

"Good and stop being rude." He said softly, looking at the TV. "Give my friend Dimples a kiss."

"Wh…what?" she stuttered.

"I said give her a kiss, on the lips."

"I'm not going to do that, Cray!" she cried. This was too much for her.

"Do you want me to get up?" he threatened.

She shook her head no.

"Than give her a fuckin' kiss."

Dimples thinking it was funny giggled as she puckered up and Tiara did as she was told. Her stomach turned when their lips touched. She stepped away and wiped her tears.

"And before you go to school, bring me two glasses and the Belvy. Me and my new friend are thirsty."

On the way to school…same day

As promised Nyzon was parked right at the corner waiting for Tiara. She knew he was there before she saw his face because his music was blaring. But today she didn't feel like entertaining anybody. Cray hurt her more than she'd ever been hurt in her life. But she knew if he left her, she would be homeless and alone. She was nowhere near finishing school and couldn't provide for herself. Now she finally understood why her father wanted her to get an education. She finally understood why he wanted her to be self sufficient. How she wished she could hear his voice now.

Not in the mood to talk, Tiara rushed past Nyzon's car to dip inside the building unnoticed. But Nyzon had been waiting on her, so he saw her crying.

"Tiara…what's wrong?" he jumped out of his ride and blocked her way.

"I don't want to talk! Just leave me alone please!"

"I'm not gonna leave you alone." He rested his hands on her shoulders and it comforted her. She felt safe around him. Again, he reminded her of somebody, but who?

"Now what's goin' on?" He continued. "Are you hurt?"

"It's my boyfriend!" she started wiping her face with the back of her hand. "He got some bitch in our house and is totally disrespecting me."

She decided not to tell him about the kiss.

"Did you knock her ass out?"

"No…I didn't want to embarrass him."

"Hold up, a chick is in your house and you didn't want to embarrass *him*?"

"No. He takes care of me and I don't want to seem ungrateful. But he could care less about me. I'm such a fool!"

Nyzon was interested but he wasn't Dr. Phil either. He didn't know what to say because truthfully he'd been dogging his share of girls all his life. So who was he to talk?

"Let me get you something to eat. Or better yet, get some drinks. And we can talk about everything you want."

Tiara's shoulders dropped and she considered going with him. After all, Cray had company so why couldn't she? Why not give him a taste of his own medicine?

And when Nyzon felt he was breaking her down he said, "*Belvy* on the rocks will do the trick. You won't think about his bitch ass for the rest of the night. I promise."

And than she looked at him. Belvy was what he was drinking with another woman, in their home. Her stomach flipped. He had said one thing too many.

"I can't do this." she cried running into school. "I just can't."

After Class

Tiara had been thinking about the stranger all day. His kindness despite how rude she was made her respect him. A lot. She couldn't help but wonder how things would've been if she would've jumped into his Hummer. She wouldn't have to wonder for long.

When she came outside, she heard music and smiled brightly when his truck came into view. She strolled up to it and looked through the passenger side window.

"What are you doing here?" she smiled trying to hide her pleasure.

"I figured I'd speed the next day up till today. So you gonna stop playin' games and roll wit me?"

"I don't know."

"Okay how about this. I'ma ask you three questions. If you answer yes to all of them you have to go with me okay?"

She nodded yes.

"Is the one who hurt you from Baltimore?"

"Yes."

"Are you lonely?"

"Yes."

"Were you thinking about me before I showed up?"

She smiled.

He opened the door.

"Get inside. It's safe in here."

She looked around to be sure nobody saw her. And suddenly not caring anymore, she jumped in. What did she have to lose?

"What's your name?" She fell into the butter leather seats. "Shelton."

THE KINGS OF 295
THE HOUSE STRIP CLUB

The Kings of 295 occupied the entire right side of the Penthouse strip club in DC. They had huge stacks of money on the table and the peeled it off based on the shawty who was doing her thing the best. Management tried everything in their power to get the girls to remain focused on *all* the customers in the club, but it was next to impossible. The Kings were throwing money everywhere. Two strippers had already gotten into a fight trying to get the King's attention.

"So you know we can't find the nigga Charms right?" Cray asked as he smoked a black and mild and watched a stripper with the body of a Goddess work the floor. "We searched high and low for yo and can't find him nowhere. And he still on our blocks."

"This nigga gettin' on my last fuckin' nerves." Nyzon said sipping his Hennessy.

"Exactly. He see we ain't backin' down but yo don't give a fuck. He ready to die for them blocks."

The rest of the crew sat around them as they enjoyed the view. They'd spent so much time together that it was no longer about DC versus Bmore. It was about loyalty and money.

"He may be willing to die but I know he got a weak spot. We all do."

"Not me," Cray offered. "Ain't nothin' wcak about me."

"Let's hope no one will ever prove it."

"I got an idea though. I'ma send a message this time that he won't forget. I might need some fire from the DC fam if things get out of hand but I'ma let you know."

"Cool. So you still havin' that joint for your cousin who's gettin' off lock?"

"Yeah...And I'ma be killin' they asses when I come through the spot."

"Me too. I'ma show you Bmore niggas how DC do it."

"Yeah whateva, man. You just betta not fake. I know you been keepin' time with some broad 'round my way." Cray laughed. "But it's gonna be mad pussy there that night so you got to get up wit her lada."

"Oh I'ma be there. And for real I neva thought about gettin' wit no Bmore chick before now. Shawty fire! The only thing is, she fuckin' wit some nigga and they live together. But if she don't give a fuck, I don't either."

"Aw shit now these DC niggas gonna start migrating' up north tryin' to get at our bitches."

Nyzon laughed.

"Don't get scared nigga. I'ma leave some for you."

"I'm just fuckin' around. Whoever the nigga is must not be takin' care of business if she sniffin' behind yo ass."

"I said the same thing. She don't seem to be worried, so why should I?"

"His loss. A nigga couldn't pull my bitch if he wanted to. She so green she think I'm God." Cray laughed. "That's how you got to treat these females."

Nyzon nodded in agreement. "You right about that. And what he don't know won't hurt him."

Cray laughed before saying, "True dat! Anyway, she ain't as cold as my girl." He threw three hundred dollar bills on the dance floor. "Trust."

"I wouldn't know cause you don't bring your girl out. I been at your crib how many times and I still haven't seen her?"

"I know. She in college and shit so she be busy. But she'll be at the party."

"You mean we finally get to meet the queen of Bmore?" Nyzon joked.

"Finally."

They were just getting into convo when a dude walked quickly in Royala's direction with what looked like a gun in his hand. Nyzon's eyes zoomed toward her and saw that she was so enveloped into the dancers, that she didn't see him coming.

Right before Nyzon could pull out his piece, dude sent a bullet spiraling in Royala's direction. Cray and Nyzon realizing what was going on, went for their heat but they were too late. All accept Jinx. Jinx hit him in the arm once and Cooks popped him in the shoulders. When he fell they walked up on him and fired more bullets into his body.

It was pure pandemonium as bystanders fought to get out of the club, safely. One of the strippers got so scared she fell off the pole and flat on her ass.

Royala's eyes were too sizes too big when she saw her life flash before her eyes. They quickly noticed it was the same dude at the club the other night. The only difference was, he wasn't running his mouth anymore. His mouth and eyes were shut.

The drama, although unnecessary, drew them even closer together.

MONESHA AND GABRIELLA
FEELIN' USED

Gabriella sat in a tub full of cold water crying her eyes out. No matter what she did, she couldn't make Monesha love her. She was dead set on getting back with Nyzon despite their family ties. All she wanted was to make her happy, and take care of her. But Monesha wasn't having it.

When she heard four knocks at the door, she wiped her face with a cold washcloth and said, "Come in."

Monesha came strutting in the bathroom dressed to go out as she busied herself with her makeup in the mirror. She was clueless that Gabriella had spent two hours crying in a tub full of cold water nor did she care.

"Gab, can you do me a favor?"

"What's up?"

"Nyzon coming by to drop some money off and to pick up Ryan."

"And?"

"I want you to get the money for me and get Ryan dressed."

She touched up her blush. Ever since she had the baby, her body filled out so her sex appeal was off the chain.

"And don't let him short change me either. It should be three thousand."

"A'ight."

She looked up at her hoping she'd say something else like, 'And when I get back we'll work on us.' But it never happened.

"Where are you going?"

"Gab, please! We already been through this. Don't try to clock this pussy cause you can't. Now are you gonna do it or not?"

"You know I will."

Figuring Gabriella could be trouble she sat on the edge of the tub and looked down at her.

"Do this for me, and I'll eat your pussy so good tonight, you'll have to call off of work for weeks."

The thought turned her on but she'd said that before and sometimes, she wouldn't have sex with her. And if she did, it didn't feel as sensual as she promised.

She even followed up with a kiss.

"Okay. I will."

Monesha hopped up like her work was done.

" I'm just trying to figure out when you gonna tell Ny the truth."

"Don't worry about what the fuck I tell Ny. Just do what I ask and I'll talk to you later."

When she left out the bathroom door she sat alone with Envy, Hurt, and Pain as her accomplices. They told her things she knew she shouldn't listen to, but what else could she do? Monesha had been playing games with her heart for years. So she left her no other choice than to get mad and get even.

Later

Nyzon sat in the living room waiting for his son to come out. It disgusted him that Monesha had plasma TV's in every room in her apartment courtesy of him. Not to mention all of her furniture was expensive and shipped from out of the country.

He waited five minutes for Gabriella to get Ryan dressed so he could take him. And every time he looked at Gabriella, he felt like knocking her out because he never got over that it was her that set him up. At the same time, had it not been for her, he would've never known his family.

When Nyzon saw Ryan he smiled. He didn't say anything but he was making plans to get him away from Monesha's money hungry ass. He just had to tell Cooks the deal first.

"I thought you wasn't comin'." She handed him the baby. "Monesha said you shoulda been here over an hour ago."

While she was talking, he peeped his gear and noticed he wasn't wearing shit he brought him.

"Where's the clothes I got for him?"

"You got to ask Monesha that shit!"

"I ain't got to ask her nothin'! You the one who got him dressed. Look at this bummy shit ya'll got my son in."

"Nyzon, don't come at me with no shit! All I did was put the clothes on him she set out. If you got a problem take it up wit Monesha."

"Both of ya'll some bum, bitches!"

Nyzon was so angry he forgot his kid was in his arms.

"I'm a bitch?!" Gabriella pointed at herself and through her hands on her hips.

"You heard what the fuck I said, cunt! Ya'll up in here snackin' on each other's pussies and got my kid out here fucked up! I'm sick of this shit!"

"You's a dumb ass, nigga."

"Fuck is you talkin' about?"

"You're so stupid, you don't even know when you're getting played." She laughed and rested on her back foot.

"Played? Fuck you talkin' bout?"

Gabriella smiled a little although she really didn't want to put Monesha out there. She knew the moment she opened her mouth, it would be really over between them. It was obvious after all this time that she still couldn't see past Nyzon.

"Your little boy's cute ain't he?"

"What you trying to say, Gab?"

"I'm just sayin', it's a shame for him to be as cute as he is that he ain't yours."

"What you just say?"

"He ain't yours, Ny!" She let out a sigh. "Monesha been runnin' game on you ever since she found out you liked me. She got pregnant just to trap you, but he ain't even your baby."

Nyzon's nose stung a little as he listened to the coldhearted truth. He looked at the baby in his arms carefully. His eyes. His little nose and even his lips. Nothing about him said he was his son.

"Gabriella, if you're playin' wit me, you're as good as dead. I put that on everything."

"Ny, I'm not playin'. He's not your baby. Look at him! Look at him good! The proof is there."

She went from gangster to crybaby in seconds. Tears streamed down her face as she told it all and Nyzon rubbed the sides of his head to ease the headache.

"There's more Nyzon."

He looked up at her evilly.

"She's not your blood cousin. Your aunt Jackie married her father after Monesha was born. She was gonna tell you until you told her if she wasn't related to you, it still wouldn't make a difference. And that ya'll couldn't be together."

"She's not my cousin?"

"No."

"You lyin'!"

"I'm not! She decided to blackmail you instead. She never knew her mother and that's why your aunt still looks out for her even though she divorced her father."

Nyzon thought about when he was in the kitchen and his aunt said Monesha was *like a daughter* to her. And Monesha said, I am your daughter.

Part of him was relieved they weren't related until he thought about the game she ran on him by pushing a baby on him.

"Well who's the father?" he asked looking at the baby who played with a rattle in his hands.

"Lazarick." She said softly. "Ryan is Lazarick's baby."

MONESHA
ROYAL BITCH

Monesha was walking to her car in a mall parking lot when Nyzon jumped out and grabbed her by the neck pushing her face into a random car.

"Bitch, I should murder your ass right now!"

"What's wrong, Nyzon?" she asked terrified he'd kill her. "What did I do?"

"Fuck that shit! I need to know right now if that baby's mine." His grip was aggressive and firm.

"Yes. He's yours. Why would you ask me that?"

He gripped her neck tighter and pushed her body up against the car harder. If he squeeze a little more, he'd crack her vertebrae.

"I'ma ask you again. Is that kid mine? If I think you're lyin' to me, I'ma kill you. I ain't got shit to lose."

Silence.

"No. He's not yours."

Nyzon's breaths were heavy. At first he didn't want the kid but now that he was here, he wanted him in his life.

"And are you my cousin?"

"No, Nyzon," she sobbed. "No I'm not related to you! I'm sorry I lied. I love you so much that I was willing to do whatever I had to, to keep you."

"Shit!" he yelled hitting the body of the car, inches away from her face with a closed fist. "Fuck you put me through all of this for?"

Monesha rubbed her neck and looked at him with pleading eyes.

"Because you denied me. I loved you, Nyzon and I still do." She walked up to him.

He smacked her in the face so hard her lips bled.

"Stay the fuck away from me."

"Nyzon, please." She rubbed her face. We aren't family now. There's no reason why we can't be together."

"If my aunt didn't have ties to you I'd murder you right now."

Suddenly the pain from her face was wiped away and was replaced with rage.

"You're gonna wish you didn't know me."

"I already do." Nyzon said backing up walking away. "I already do."

TIARA
LOVE HIS SWAG

Tiara had been kicking it with Shelton strong. Everyday he'd stop by her school and they'd talk for hours at a nearby restaurant. She know longer worried about Cray finding out because he spent so much time in D.C. with his squad, that he didn't have time for her anymore.

It was 1:00 in the afternoon and she waited fifteen minutes in the Target parking lot in Maryland for Shelton to pull up. She had a hair appointment at 1:00 but knew they wouldn't get around to her until 7 because they were so unprofessional. So she hadn't planned on showing up at the salon until five. This would give her more time with Shelton.

"Excuse me, can I talk to you for a second?" Nyzon asked pulling up to her.

"No. Sorry." She played along. "I'm waiting on this cute dude I'm feeling from D.C. so you might as well keep it moving."

She giggled trying to contain herself. She loved the games they played. With all the fun they had with one another, they still had not been intimate.

"It's like that? Cause on the real, I know that nigga ain't finer than me."

She looked him over once and said, "You right. I'm rollin' wit you."

Soft laughter filled the car when she hopped inside and kissed him gently on the cheek. She was falling for him, and he was falling for her. The relationship grew strong because they were friends above everything, with nothing to lose.

"My girl," he said.

"I'm so happy to see you. Why you got me thinkin' about you all day everyday?"

"You not alone."

"I hope not. I don't want to be a fool."

"Trust me." He said. "Where you goin' later?" he asked as he whipped out of the parking lot.

"You know I got my hair appointment later but I got some time to kick it with you. There's a party I have to get ready for." She placed her seatbelt on and he looked at the curves of her body. She was the baddest female he'd ever seen in his life.

"A'ight...there's been a slight change of plans."

"And what's that?"

"What I tell you about trustin' me?"

"That no matter what, I always can."

The Airport

Tiara sat nervously in the airport waiting on Shelton. He disappeared for a minute to make a call and she wondered where he'd gone. Minutes later he returned and held her hand. She wondered what his plan was because wherever they were going, she had to be back that night.

"You a'ight?" he asked excited at whatever he had in store.

"I'm fine." Her voice low and worried.

"You trust me right?"

"Yes. I just don't trust myself. I feel reckless with you. Why is that?"

"Let's not worry about the details. Let's just be."

Once she boarded the plane leading to Vegas, she was suddenly excited. For that day she'd act as if her life with Cray didn't exist. Shelton filled something in her heart that she longed for and had been missing ever since her father died. And she wanted to hold on to it for as long as possible.

When they landed they jumped into a beautiful silver stretch Hummer limo leading to the MGM. He'd rented a Sky Loft for one night just to get away. The moment they opened the door she saw beautiful red roses and a large dish of chocolate covered strawberries on the table. The large window was open and the view captivated her. She'd never been out of DC and Bmore in all her life.

"This is beautiful." She looked out the window. Shelton pulled up two chairs for them to sit down to enjoy the view. For a second she stared at him. "Who are you? And where did you come from?"

"I'm just a man, feelin' a woman." She blushed. "Tiara, I don't want you thinkin' I'm bringing you out here just to fuck. I mean if you want to, we can get busy but it's not like that with me."

She laughed.

"I'm really feelin' you." He reassured. "And right now, I got a lot of shit going on in my life, and being with you is the only time I'm not trippin' off of any of it."

"I feel the same, Shelton."

"So let's get somethin' to eat and kick it. No strings attached. You cool wit that?"

"Of course."

They talked for hours about life and their dreams. He asked about her father and when she cried, he held her tight. She wasn't even allowed to mention her father to Cray so off the break, Shelton made her feel comfortable. Cray said talking about Kavon made her weak, but Shelton embraced the memories. Through it all, she never mentioned, Cray's name and Nyzon never asked.

He wanted to know about the man who was responsible in bringing Tiara into the world. And when she talked about her mother, she cried even more. He was disgusted at how she lived in DC, and how her mother turned her back on her. He wanted to talk about his experience with his mother but decided against it. This was her time and he wanted to be there for her.

When it got later, she remembered her hair wasn't done. Cray would definitely know she lied if she walked in the house like that. If he noticed nothing about her, he noticed her hair. He could tell when it had been washed because it had a golden sheen to it and smelled fresh.

"What's wrong?"

"If I don't get my hair done he'll know I lied." She was careful not to mention Cray's name realizing he was well known and she was pretty sure Shelton dealt in drugs too.

"I thought you trusted me?"

"I do but..." just before she could say anything else someone knocked at the door.

When he opened it, a pretty black girl with a golden weave was on the other side. Her name was Tangee. She had a large gold bag in her hands filled with hair supplies. Turns out she was a hairdresser who when she was done whipped Tiara's hair up so good, she had to get her card. Shelton flew her all the way from Baltimore just to hook Tiara up. That was what he was doing when he left her in the airport. With her hair done and the night approaching an end, they left the hotel to get back on the plane.

Shelton was sleep until he felt her staring at him. He opened his eyes slowly to take in her beauty.

"What you lookin' at girl?" he joked.

"Nothing. I finally figured out who you remind me of."

"Who?" he asked ready to hear her answer.

"My father. He was the only man that truly loved and cared about me."

"Well as long as I'm alive, and as long as you let me, I'll always care about you too."

She sat back in her seat and exhaled.

For the first time in her life, she'd come within the presence of real love.

NYZON
SAME GIRL

Nyzon pulled up fifteen minutes early at Cray's crib to grab his dough to jet back out the front door to see Tiara. Devon was just released from prison on a drug charge and Cray was throwing a party so big, it cost him half a million dollars.

The moment Nyzon knocked on the door he laughed after realizing Cray was already drunk.

"What up nigga?" he had a glass of Hennessy in his hands.

"Damn! You startin' already?"

Cray laughed.

"You know how we do! It's nonstop today, man."

"I heard that. But look, I can't stay. You got the cash?"

"Yo, just dropped it off."

Cray opened the door wider and Nyzon walked inside eyeing his crib as usual. Everything was neat and in its place and he could tell his girl kept a clean house.

"My bitch got ya cash downstairs."

"You wild, man. You betta not say that shit loud before she hear your ass."

"And do what?" Cray said breath smelling like the alcohol bottle. "I run this shit. Watch this. Hey, bitch!" he screamed downstairs. "Bring that duffle up here!"

Nyzon laughed so hard he couldn't contain himself.

"Let me sit over here away from your ass in case she come up here swingin'."

Nyzon plopped down on the couch and texted Tiara.

I can't wait to see you. I know you're life is full, but I wanna discuss the next level. For us. I think it's time.

He was still waiting on her response when he saw a beautiful woman with golden hair walking upstairs with her phone in one hand and a duffle bag in the other. The phone in her hand chimed and she smiled after receiving a message. *His* message.

"Here you go, baby?"

She was totally oblivious to another man inside their home or him calling her a bitch. She was used to the disrespect and with Nyzon in her life, she no longer cared.

"Tiara put that shit down. I want you to meet somebody."

She smiled handing the bag to Cray until she saw Nyzon sitting on her sofa. Both of them looked at each other as if the devil had presented himself to them both. Nyzon felt a major blow as he looked at Tiara. How could he be so stupid? A female that bad had to belong to a nigga who could afford her. And in Baltimore city, Cray was it. Had he asked more questions, he would've figured it out.

"Nyzon...you a'ight man?" Cray asked sensing the tension between them. He looked at them both trying to figure out what was up.

"Oh...yeah...uh...when I first saw her, she reminded me of somebody I thought I knew."

Silence.

"So you gonna introduce us or what?" Nyzon said. He stood up and walked over to them.

He was doing his best to ease the thick vibe in the air. And when he looked at Tiara, he saw a single tear fall from her eye. She thought as he did, their romance although new, was already over.

"Oh...yeah, this is my shawty Tiara and this is Nyzon." Cray placed one hand on Tiara's back and the other on Nyzon's shoulder. "This my partner from DC I been tellin' you about."

"Nyzon?" she said as if it were a question more than his name.

But I thought his name was Shelton. She thought.

"Yeah...Nyzon." He shook her hand as if it he hadn't just held it for hours on a plane.

Cray no longer caring about the connection he saw between them, because he was so drunk, dismissed Tiara.

"Aight, get lost. I gotta talk to, Ny."

She couldn't move.

"Bitch, you heard what I said? Get lost."

"Hey...you don't have to talk to her like that, Cray."

Cray laughed.

"Stop trippin' off of these bitches. You gotta keep 'em in check."

Nyzon was seconds from dropping him on the floor. Luckily for him, Tiara hurriedly walked down the stairs.

When she left, Cray rattled off the plans for tonight's events. On and on he talked about the shit he had lined up for his cousin Devon. And how when Devon came home, he'd be set for life.

While Nyzon and Tiara on the other hand, saw their lives falling apart.

THE KINGS OF 295
MARTIN'S WEST, WOODLAWN MARYLAND
THE RELEASE

Martins West was filled to capacity the evening of Devon's release. Cray made sure his money was well spent. There were ice sculptures in the shape of dollar signs and free flowing fountains of Kettle One and Hennessey. And he even sent out free IPod's with video invitations loaded on them a month before the event with all of the latest music.

The party was hot!

To top it all off, Cray saw to it that the women outnumbered the men two to one.

Through all the chatter, Devon's voice could be heard clearly over the music and the sounds of champagne glasses clinking against one another played in the background. Cray had yet to arrive and when everybody kept calling him on his phone, he kept saying he was on his way. The Kings knew he was trying to make an entrance with Tiara on his arm. It would be the first time he'd introduce his trophy girl to everyone else in his crew. Some saw her before he cleaned her up but most didn't.

"So I here ya'll out here doin' big things!" Devon said to Jason while a female especially chosen for him sat on his lap and kissed him on his neck. "They tellin' me ya'll youngins got so much money, ya'll can't even spend it."

"You heard right, man. Cray got up wit them DC niggas and we ain't looked back since."

"I heard about that shit." He sipped his vodka before kissing the chocolate female in his lap then pouring the liquor in her mouth from his. "I don't know about some of ya'll decisions though."

"Why you say that?"

"I'ma cut to the chase cause that's how I do. I'm not down with yall trustin' DC niggas and shit?"

"Why?"

"Cause history shows that they can't be trusted."

"Nyzon cool. He got Cray's back."

Devon laughed.

"You still a kid." He said shaking his head.

Jason was offended but kept his comments to himself. Besides, he respected Devon.

"Look, I'm back home and a lot of shit gonna change. For real if we runnin' shit the way they say we do, ain't no need to deal wit DC blood no more. Let's keep it in the family. The more money, the more betta."

"I feel you." Jason said nodding in agreement. "The thing is, Nyzon got the connect info so it ain't that easy."

"Cray let that shit ride like that?"

"He trusts him. We trust him."

Just when Devon was getting ready to pick Jason's bitch ass for some more information, Cray walked through the door with Tiara on his arm. She wore this stunning form fitting red dress by Valentino and all mouths dropped. It would be the first time some people saw her but her beauty would be engraved in their minds forever. There wasn't a female in the room who could touch her.

Cray came through the door wearing a pair of Red Monkey jeans, a red shirt and some fresh red Air Force ones. He was also sporting a brand new platinum diamond chain he had made which read, The King of 295.

Shortly afterwards, Nyzon came through with Angel on his arm looking as luscious and as phat as ever, in a short pink one piece dress. But as bad as she was, the moment Nyzon saw Tiara, the two stared at each other as if they were all alone. For that moment, Angel didn't exist. It was like falling in love all over again. How could they get through the party without talking to one another?

Nyzon's dark blue pen stripe suit made him look edible. And the five carat diamond ring in his left ear shined like the star he was. The Kings were doing it balla style! Nyzon mingled a little allowing Cray the time to kick it with his cousin.

"Is that my cousin ova that mothafucka?" Cray yelled walking up to Devon.

They embraced each other in a manly hug as the females flocked hoping to get their attentions. Cray had hired a video team to follow him around like paparazzi so he seemed larger than life. Before Devon could answer his cousin, they posed for a picture.

"Who else can look as fresh as me?!" Devon responded as they took their seats and Devon eyed Tiara.

"Baby, this is my favorite cousin." Cray said. "The one I was telling you about."

Tiara shook his hand softly. And he shook his head three times in disbelief. Her exotic appeal got his dick hard.

"Hi, it's a pleasure to meet you." She said. "I've heard so much about you."

Devon licked his lips before saying, "My man, I see you've done better for yourself than I thought. Where did you find her? They don't make 'em like this no more."

"You thought I was play pippin'?" Cray asked. "Only the baddest bitches for the baddest nigga."

They both laughed but Tiara felt humiliated.

"Baby, let me find my friends."

When she stood up, he smacked her in the ass. She was so embarrassed her face turned red. And, the moment she stood up, two sexy twins came and sat on his lap. It was like they were waiting in the darkness like most snakes do.

"Don't go too far. I might need to show you off to a few more niggas. And we gonna have to get that tattoo on your arm that says, Cray's bitch, we talked about. 'Cause I know niggas gonna be gawking'. Remember who you belong to aight?" he said as one of the women kissed him in the mouth.

"I know who I belong to," she smiled thinking of Nyzon.

Knowing Cray was in his element, she walked off to find Felecia and Yolanda who were around the other Kings.

When she left Cray and Devon got situated and got right down to business.

"So I'm hearing you puttin' in work wit DC dudes?" Devon asked downing more liquor. "What...ain't no loyal Bmore niggas 'round no more?"

"It ain't even like that. Da nigga had access to a connect wit the best shit around. We can step on his product five times and still put out a banger."

"Well I'm out now so you betta put it down to main man that I'm gonna be hands on wit the family business. Seein' as though I put funds in the original package too."

Cray didn't want to tell him that his measly fifty thousand couldn't even cover one percent of the dough they spent. It was the money he stole from Tiara that Kavon hid in his apartment that helped with his portion of the weight. Tiara had no idea that the key around her neck belonged to a safe deposit box full of cash, and he'd never tell her.

"Plus I gotta watch my cousin's back."

"No doubt." Cray responded as he spotted Nyzon and Angel walking in his direction. He wanted to have the conversation Devon was trying to have at another time. "Speakin' of DC cats, this my nigga, Ny."

Nyzon walked up to Cray with his winning smile.

What's up, nigga?! You wasn't lyin'. You went all out!"

"Fuck you think I was playin'?" Cray joked.

Devon studied them and could tell they had a genuine respect for one another and that bothered him.

"Angel, go get us somethin' to drink," he told her.

He didn't bother introducing her because she wasn't relevant.

"Ny, this my cousin, Devon."

Ny shook Devon's hand and felt instant tension.

"My cousin tellin' me you cool peoples. So if you are, you can understand me when I say I'ma have his back, so if you down wit him, I got yours too."

Nyzon looked at Jason, Cray and Devon and laughed.

"Main man, I see where you comin' from because my family got me too, but I'm good on the back watchin' tip. I ain't locked up." Devon was shocked that Nyzon wasn't going for his shit. And the three of them looked at one another. "On another note, I'm glad to see you home, young. Cray been talkin' bout you since I've known him. That's real talk. But this is a celebration! Lada, for this business talk shit! You home, nigga! Let's make it a party."

"Oh...yeah. We'll rap lada," Devon responded.

"Indeed," Nyzon said before walking away.

"I told you he's cool," Cray said. "I ain't use to fuck wit' him but he's aight."

"We'll see about that. We'll see."

NYZON
MARTIN'S WEST
THERE'S NO DENYIN'

Nyzon kept Tiara in his peripheral vision as she walked around the ball-room.

She was a queen and stood out like a one hundred dollar bill on a black marble floor. Everyone couldn't get over how beautiful she was, and eventually Angel picked up on his stares.

"Nyzon, I'm leaving." She grabbed her purse and stood up from the table they sat at.

"Not this bullshit again." He shook his head. "Sit the fuck down and stop trippin."

"Look how you talk to me. You don't have any respect for me and for us."

"Now what's wrong? You makin' a fuckin' scene."

"I'm makin' a scene? You been eyeing' Cray's girl all night and you sasy I'm makin' a scene? Plus I see her keep lookin' over here. If you want her so bad go get her, but don't use me as an excuse."

"It's not even like that." He stood up. "Sit down and stop trippin'."

"I'm serious. When you ready to be for real about me, you got the key to my heart *and* the key to my house. Use them." With that she stood up. "And don't worry, I'll catch a cab home."

She passed Tiara who looked at Nyzon with concern. Angel was halfway out the door when she decided to say something in Tiara's ear. "I don't know what's goin' on between ya'll, but he's feelin' you too. But be careful, he breaks hearts on a regular. Good luck." She continued as she strolled out the door.

Tiara smiled lightly as she turned around to see Nyzon staring in her direction. She looked around the party, spotted Cray with two girls on each arm and mouthed, "Meet me outside."

It was done.

Out Back

Tiara stood with her back faced the back door when Nyzon came out. It screeched a little alerting her that he was there.

He didn't approach her right away. Instead he spent a few seconds admiring her physique under the night sky and wondered who wouldn't want to be with her all the time. He thought Cray had lost his fucking mind by not wifing her immediately. He never wanted a woman more than he wanted her, and he knew she was the woman for him. *I know this woman's made for me.* He thought again.

"Damn you look good." He said behind her.

"And you look good too, Nyzon." her back still toward him. "Or is it Shelton?"

"I'm sorry. And you're not gonna believe me, but Shelton is my birth name. So I didn't lie to you. And the real story is too long to tell you right now. I just wanted you to know, that this shit is killin' me. I can't see you wit that nigga."

"It's hard for me too." She finally turned toward him and he could tell she had been crying. "Nyzon, I don't know what this is between us, but I hated seeing you with that girl. Do you love her?"

"Fuck that bitch!" Nyzon wanted her to know off the back that Angel was not a problem.

"Good...cause I can't *not* talk to you. I can't *not* see you. You're the only thing in my life that's consistent. And...I'm not ready to let you go." Her eyes looked at the ground before meeting his again. "So what do we do?"

"You follow my lead. And be with me tonight."

"But what about Cray? He may look for me."

Nyzon could've been a grimy ass nigga and told her he knew Cray had already arranged to fuck the twins he was running around with but instead he said, "Do you trust me?"

She smiled and said, "You don't have to ask."

What they didn't know was that Jason was on the side of the building, fucking Felecia and overhearing everything.

At The Hyatt Hotel, Baltimore Inner Harbor

The music played softly in the hotel room. And this would be the first time they made love. Tiara relatively experienced in the bedroom, took two steps back from Nyzon, unzipped her dress and allowed it to fall to the floor. She was completely nude. Her sexy and perfect body caused Nyzon an immediate hard on. Afterwards she unfastened his pants, removed his shirt, and looked at his rock hard chest and fit body. His dick stood at full attention.

Their lips met as their bare skin touched. For ten minutes they stood on the floor and danced quietly to the music, holding each other closely. When Nyzon couldn't take it anymore, he lifted her up and put her softly in the bed. For a second, they held each other and looked into each other's eyes.

"You're made for me." They said at the same time. "I feel like my world was rocked when you came into my life." He said.

She laughed.

"What's funny?" He asked.

"My father told me that would happen once I met the right one. I feel the same."

It was eerie, but real, that Nyzon Peate and Tiara Cartier had fallen in love. He eased into her as his eyes remained open the entire time. Her wetness told him she was feeling him.

"Damn, Tiara…why do you feel so good?"

"Cause my body is happy to see you. To be with you."

"That nigga's a fool." He said.

"I'm glad that he is. Because if he wasn't, I would've never met you."

"You're right, baby."

"Make love to me. Make love to me slow, Nyzon. Please."

With those encouraging words she whined her hips onto him.

Nothing was rush.

Everything was right.

They made love ten times that night, back to back. For the first time, she reached and orgasm and she had Nyzon to thank. And in the morning she went home, like nothing happened.

And Cray didn't even know she was gone.

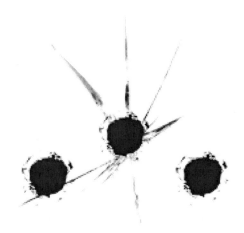

CRAYLAND
WEST BALTIMORE
POPPIN'

Cray, Jinx, Vic and Jason were in Mondawmin mall flossing. Each of them had over ten thousand dollars on them a piece as they hit the stores.

"Cray...let me holla at you for a sec." Jinx said.

"What's up?" he asked as they walked away from the Bmore crew while they walked into a store.

"Yo Jason is gettin' reckless wit his mouth game. He stay tellin' mothafuckas what blocks we got. How we gettin' our money and all this otha bullshit. Yo be braggin' like shit, Cray. So if niggas wanted to, no doubt they could hit our heads. He dangerous, man."

Cray was quiet because he also noticed he had a mouth-piece on him. And the only reason he didn't deal with it earlier was that he was hoping it would go away. And Jason was his man, and he couldn't push off on him like he normally would somebody else.

"Oh...and I heard when you put him on Swizz's broad, he started fuckin' wit her home girl and almost fucked everything up. The chick was runnin' around tellin' everybody that he was a bum nigga. It almost fucked us up."

Now *that* he didn't know. Something was going to have to give. Cray just needed time to think.

"I'm on it. Thanks for lettin' me know."

"No doubt," he said giving him a pound. "I been tryin' to tell you all day, but Jason be on you like a leech."

Cray grinned, still fucked up about what was said.

They walked slowly back into the store and tried to pretend as if nothing happened. But Cray was going to pull Jason up before shit got out of control.

"Yo...give me six boxes of them timbs in all colors...size 13." Cray told the sales person in Foot Action as he pulled out his cash and flung a grand on the counter. "And throw in a couple of the plain white-t's, size double X."

There were a bunch of females inside of the store hoping to be seen by Cray and his crew. Although they would've settled for either one of them, they really wanted Cray because he had money, power and respect.

"Ya, ass buyin' up everything." Jason said as he brought ten pairs of sneakers to the counter his self. "Aye, let me get that New York Yankees fitted size 7 and a quarter."

Jinx and Vic had four bags full of clothes from Changes and grabbed a few timbs for themselves too. By the time they left Foot Action, the manager had to place an order just to restock her store.

"Yo...I hope ya asses don't fake on me tomorrow night." Jason said as they walked down the mall. "Cause club Choices gonna be off da chain!"

"I ain't fuckin' wit' no club Choices." Vic told him. "I'm goin' to New York."

"Well I'm wit it." Jinx said trying to handle his bags.

"Good. But I think that bitch Nesha gonna be there. I don't feel like dealin' wit her dumb ass." Jason said. "She always runnin' her mouth tellin' niggas we fuckin'."

Jinx and Cray looked at each other. This was the best example of the pot calling the kettle black that they'd ever seen.

"She run her mouth, huh?" Cray said sarcastically. "Maybe you should put somethin' in it."

"Like my dick?" Jason laughed.

"Like your gun. That'll stop the shit for good."

All of the men stopped walking and looked at Cray trying to determine if he was serious.

Cray laughed making them think he wasn't.

"Anyway, nigga, the other day you were hollerin' about her givin' you the crucial ass head job! Now you actin' like you don't know the skeezer." Vic laughed.

"Make up ya mind, yo," Jinx chimed in.

"Fuck that, bitch." Cray added walking to the doors leading to the parking lot.

"I just fuck her. She got some good pussy."

"My man said she got that shit. You betta get checked." Vic said. "Or that lil mothafucka gonna fall off" he joked.

"What shit?" Jason asked walking toward Cray's car. "She got the AIDS?"

Whooooom. Crash. Whooooom. Whoooom.

"What the fuck?!" Jason yelled hitting the ground.

"Awwwww shit!" Vic screamed holding his arm, blood spurting from all angles to the concrete. "I been shot."

Whooooom. Crash! Whoooom. Crash!

Bullets continued to fly, smashing the cars around them. People were running and screaming everywhere.

"Somebody shootin'." Jinx yelled as they hid behind a white Suburban.

"No shit, nigga!" Cray said grabbing his heat from his pants.

When Jinx looked around the truck, he saw Doles, the nigga he robbed a few months earlier.

"Fuck!" Jinx screamed. "That's the nigga Doles. How the fuck they knew we were here?" He asked although he already suspected Jason.

Now Cray was enraged. If this was because of Jason he was through with his ass. But first he had to get them out of it.

"Ya'll got ya'll lighters on you?" Cray asked.

"Yeah." Jason and Vic said.

"A'ight...we gotta hit his ass or else he gonna keep coming." He said looking at them and then at Vic. "You gone be a'ight man. We gonna get you out of here."

With Jason, Vic and Jinx looking at him for direction, Cray knew he had to step up. If he didn't get them out of this, he'd never be able to save face. He had to think.

If this nigga got away, he and his crew might as well leave the city because everyone would be coming for their heads. He knew Jinx was a good shot, but the way this nigga was busting off, he'd never get a good view. He had to be the one and he was crazy enough to do it.

To pump himself up he thought about every foul thing that happened to him in his life. And when he was filled with enough anger, hate and greed, he stood up gun in hand, and fired bullets as he walked toward Doles.

"Cray, get down man!" Jason yelled as he saw him facing oncoming bullets.

Whoooom! Whooom! Pop! Pop! Pop!

Cray walked up on Doles firing and hit him right in the arm he was busting off with. Doles tried to pick up his weapon but Cray fired again, hittin him in the shoulder. Cray was maniacal as he approached him. When he was close enough, he saw his body fall on a silver Altima leaving a bloody trail as he leaned on it and slid to the ground. A mother and her child sat nearby watching the entire thing.

"D...Don't k...kill me, man." Doles stuttered when Cray walked up on him and held his chest. "Please."

"I like when my bitches beg." Cray said standing over him barrel pointing in his face. With that he hit him in the chest again.

Pop!

When his eyes were closed he tucked his weapon in the back of his shirt and saw a woman and her child watching the entire thing.

"Am I gonna have problems from you?" he asked looking at her quizzically.

She shook her head no, holding her child closely.

"Don't hurt us...please."

"Give me your wallet." He demanded.

She did and he removed the driver's license and tucked it in his pocket throwing the wallet back in her lap.

"Just in case." He said walking away.

He got three feet ahead of her and figured it was best to take care of loose ends.

She was no longer a woman.

She was a witness.

So he turned back around, pulled out his gun and shot her square in the head leaving her kid alive, screaming.

Cray proved then that he was even more vicious than he realized. But it wasn't the first time he murdered somebody, and it most certainly wouldn't be the last.

CRAY
MY BROTHER'S KEEPER

It was nighttime when Cray sat at a community pool with Jason tied to a chair. Devon, Jinx and Vic stood by his side. This meeting was so secret they didn't even alert Nyzon and the DC crew.

"Cray, please! You have to listen to me! It wasn't like that!"

"It wasn't like what, nigga?"

"It wasn't me who told somebody where we were. You know I'd never do that."

His face was wet from crying and that alone enraged Cray. Nobody would vouch to keep his punk ass alive after such an awful display of manhood.

"It's nothin' else to talk about, man. You fucked up. Had it not been for my own quick thinkin' one of us coulda been killed at the mall. You runnin' around town tellin' niggas how we get our money, and where we be it and you askin' me to spare your life? Why shouldn't I kill yo ass, J?"

What the members didn't know was that Cray wanted him to say something, just one thing to convince him to spare his life. He was the one dude Cray knew would bend over backwards for him, but he had female tendencies, and Cray hated that about him. He let the money rule his thought process and that was a bad trait to have in the drug game.

"'Cause you know me."

"You ain't said nothin' yet, nigga."

The men cocked their weapons.

"Okay...Okay. Uh...I know somethin' that you want to know."

"Start talkin'." Cray responded.

"I know somethin' bout Nyzon and Tiara." He cried. "They ain't all the way real wit you man."

"Fuck this nigga talkin' bout? Put it too his ass Cray." Jinx interrupted.

"Man I'm givin' you a chance to tell me why I should spare your life and you rappin' to me about Ny and Tiara? You betta come wit somethin' else man."

"It's true. I saw them."

"Cray, don't listen to this shit. Scared niggas have no heart," Jinx replied.

Cray looked at his cousin Devon and he shrugged his shoulders. Because even if it were true, would it be enough to save his life? It could be a reason to kill him considering he waited until his death bed to let him know. Cray decided then that he didn't believe him.

"You got one more chance to convince me."

Jason was silent before saying, "You should let me live because I love you. And we been boys since we were kids. Don't nobody got secrets like us, man. Don't do this. I made a mistake but it won't happen again. Please."

His response did tug at Cray's sensitive side a little, but it was also *too* soft to be taken seriously especially in front of the men.

"Not good enough." He told him coldly. "Break his arms and legs and throw him in the pool."

"You gonna drown me?! Just shoot me, Cray. I'm scared of the water! Please. You know that."

His pleas were hard for Cray to hear.

"Break his legs and throw him inside!"

"Cray, please! Let me have a better death than this. Give me a soldier's death, man!"

Devon smiled when the orders were given. It did his heart good to know his cousin was a beast in these streets.

Not wasting time, Jinx grabbed Jason's right arm while Vic stood over him with the gun to his dome. Devon stood over top of him and cracked his left arm by stomping on it with his boot.

Crack.

"Awwwww shit!" Jason screamed.

Left arm.

Crack.

When Devon was done he cracked both of his legs and Jason continued to scream in pain.

Once all his limbs were broken, they put him on the poolside. Cray walked over to him and stared down at him. It hurt him to do this, but he had to. Jason needed to be the example of what would happen, if he was crossed.

"Since you wanna be a jelly fish, wit no back bone, swim like one." Cray said. "Throw his ass in."

With that they threw him in, and watched him fight for his life until he drowned.

BLUNT
WEST BMORE
MASTER PLAN

Blunt had a mission and it was simple. He had to send a strong message to Charm courtesy of the Kings. Despite their threats, Charm was still running around town telling people he couldn't be touched. So he had to show him that he could.

Placing a ski mask over his face, he walked to a cute little brick house in a residential community in Baltimore county. With his identity concealed, he walked to the back of a house, and knelt down next to a window leading to the basement. The lights were out. It was just what he wanted. When he was sure no one was watching, he removed the screen from the window, took a stone off their lawn and smashed the glass. He waited several minutes to be sure no one was coming or that an alarm didn't sound.

With the coast clear, he pushed his slender frame through the window until he landed on a couch. Then he paused...looked around, and stepped off the couch. Slowly he crept up the steps leading from the basement. When the basement door opened, he moved into the living room cautiously. He hoped Charm's wife was there so he could kidnap her as planned. Walking further inside, he still hadn't spotted her. The lights were dim and the television was on but still know signs of her.

But when he bent another hallway, and looked to the left, she was right before him. To be thick she looked sexy in her yellow fitted pajama pants and tight yellow t-shirt. If she acted right, maybe he'd fuck her before they left.

"AAAAAAAAAAAAAAAAAAAAAHHHH!!!!" she screamed running the opposite way.

"I see I'm in for a long night," he said out loud.

He could tell the moment he looked into her eyes that she would be up for a fight.

He ran up behind her, caught her and knocked her to the wooden floor pressing his body against hers. She was strong and ready to fight.

"I'ma bout to kick ya ass! You came in the wrong bitch's house!" she told him.

"You betta calm down for I murder your fuckin' ass!"

She ignored him and moved vigorously until she was finally able to turn around and look him in the eyes. Face up, she managed to free a hand and she used it to steal the fuck out of his face.

He hit her back like she was a man.

"Is that all you got nigga?" she asked laughing, licking the blood from the corner of her mouth.

She hit him again, this time cracking the cartilage in his nose.

"Ahhhhhhh!!!" he was pissed.

"I'm done playin' wit your ass."

He cocked his arm back and hit her so hard, the bottom tooth flew out his mouth.

"I see you aint' talkin' shit now."

Instead of crying, she laughed harder.

"You must be tryin' to make me mad." She continued as she tussled with him.

He tried to reach for his gun in his belt and when he did, she smacked him in his right eye, got away and ran toward a closed door. He knew she was going for a weapon and figured if he didn't catch her, he'd find out what kind it was. There was no way in he could kidnap her now, he had to kill her.

Luckily he caught her right before she turned the knob. Grabbing her by the throat he squeezed tightly from behind her. Her arms swung widely as she tried her hardest to breathe. When she was weak enough, he watched her eyes close and only then did he release her. She fell to the floor. The kidnap plan didn't go well. And without a stronger message, Charm would remain on their blocks.

He was on his way out the door to consult with Cray when he heard, "Whannnn….Whannnnnnn….Whannnnn."

She was going for her baby. He realized then that the baby would be easier to transport and less confrontational. He stepped over her crazy ass, and opened the bedroom door. In the middle of the room he saw a white crib with gold hearts embedded around it. It was a girl. Removing her from the crib, he turned around and was preparing to leave when *she* was standing before him.

I knew I shoulda shot this bitch when I had the chance too! He thought.

Whop!

Charm's wife stole Blunt in his face with the baby in his arms.

He knew right then that there was no way he was getting through that front door with her alive. He could see immediately why Charm made her his wife. She was gangster in every sense of the word.

With the baby in his arms and his gun in the other, he fired. She dropped the moment the bullet pierced her throat.

"I bet you won't get up now." He said picking his self up.

Placing the baby back in the crib, he wrote a message on a nearby Post-It pad and pinned it to the baby's jumper.

It read, *'Stay off our blocks, or your kid could be next. P.S., you've been touched.'*

THE KINGS OF 295
CANCUN MEXICO
AMIGOS

"I'm tellin' you, yo, them niggas was shook!" Cray said as he sat by the poolside, on a lounge chair with Tiara on his lap.

With fake passports in their possession, they bought out suites for all of the lieutenants, and fifty of their best block captains from DC & Baltimore at the Fiesta American Grand Coral Beach. Champagne bottles dressed the outside of the pool and they filled up all of the seats at the wet bar. T.I's "What You Know", boomed from the stereo system. And the warm weather was comforting under the night sky.

"Blunt put the murder game down!" Cray continued. "Niggas in B-more shook and Charm moved out of town! Can't find his ass no where. They know we ain't fuckin' around. We run this mothafuckin' game. Ain't that right, Ny!"

"Yeah. That's right." He responded. Nyzon was out of it. Tiara had his head fucked up.

"That nigga's bitch was crazy!" Blunt said as he downed ACE champagne right from the bottle. "I had to give it to her though. She was more thorough than a lotta niggas I know. I had to kill her fuckin' ass!"

"If she was as thorough as you said she was, I coulda gave her ass some work." Cray laughed palming Tiara's breasts. There were over sixty people out there and he was treating her like a freak.

"I bet they got the message though." Royala added lying on the pool bed with her girl Simple. "No doubt they'll step the fuck off now."

"That was a good look by grabbin' yo's kid." Cray continued. "That shit was genius!"

As everybody talked about business openly, since they were the only ones in the private pool, Nyzon eyed Tiara. His stomach churned watching another man's hands all over her.

I'm sorry. She said with her eyes.

"Hey Ny! Come get in the water man." Royala said seeing his look. "Nyzon hadn't told her about them yet, but if anybody could read him, she could.

She knew about their secret romance at Devon's party. She felt their passion when they were together and hoped that it was all in her mind. It wasn't.

"Naw...I'm good." Ny said looking at Tiara. He felt like cracking Cray in his head with a bottle full of champagne.

"You a'ight, man?" Cray asked catching the uncomfortable glance.

Everybody looked in Nyzon's direction. Cooks, Simon and Blunt turned around from where they sat at the bar.

"Yeah...I got to get somethin' real quick though. I'ma be back." He said as Tiara watched him with puppy dog eyes.

She didn't want to be sitting on Cray's lap anymore than Nyzon wanted her to. But Nyzon was making it known to her that he couldn't do the secret lover thing much longer. Something had to give. He had to give her up. She wasn't his girl and he'd have to deal with the fact.

The Kings resumed their conversation as Nyzon walked toward the beach. The night sky on the blue water appeared to go on forever as he stared at it. How did he get himself into this situation? Once a hater of love, now he wanted nothing more than to be with her all the time. He would've given everything up for Tiara and that scared him.

"Nyzon." Her voice caused him to shake and sounded as beautiful as the ocean's waves. She had complete control of his soul.

"Man, I'm not feelin' this nigga puttin' his hands on you." Nyzon said seriously turning around. He walked up to her. "I was five seconds from turning my gun on this dude. But that's my man and you his girl and this shit is fucked up. I wish I neva met you!"

"Don't' say that."

"It's fuckin' true! This not a game, Tiara!" He yelled not knowing who to be angry with, himself or her.

"I know." She said softly. "I wish things could be different."

"We can't do this no more. We can't."

"Don't say that, Nyzon. You're the only reason I'm able to be with him."

"What are you talking about?"

"If I didn't have you I wouldn't be strong enough to deal. And I know he'd come looking for me if I ran away."

"Something gonna have to give, baby."

"I know, Nyzon. I love you so much." She kissed him. The yellow bathing suit she wore showed her sexy body and all he wanted to do was make love. "Say you won't leave me."

"I can't say that," he said in between heavy breaths as their lips touched.

"Please, Nyzon. Tell me you won't leave me." She kissed him softly on the neck.

"Fuck are you doin' to me?" he said pushing away from her. "Together, me and that nigga worth millions! I don't even know if this shit is worth it. Being with you means war."

She walked up to him and grabbed his hand placing it on her perky breasts.

"Am *I* worth it?"

Silence.

"I hope you are. 'Cause I'm in too deep."

"You don't know how hard I been tryin' to get away from him!"

"How did you?" he asked looking toward the pool only to see the Kings loud talking and doing cannonballs in the water.

"Yolanda asked him to play Marco Polo with her and Felecia and he went for it."

"She know about us?"

"No. I'm afraid to tell anybody."

"Good." He said kissing her again as they walked further out of view. "I got to think things through, but I know I can't stand you not being in my life."

"And I can't stand not being in it."

When they walked far enough away, they made love on the beach with the beautiful Cancun sky as their witness. There love was one that would last, at least they hoped.

TIARA
OWINGS MILLS, MD
I PUT A SPELL ON YOU CAUSE YOU ARE MINE

Tiara stood in the kitchen singing as she cleaned the dishes by hand since that's the way Cray preferred them to be done. The dishwasher hadn't been used since they moved in. As the water ran over her skin she thought about the way Nyzon licked her entire body in Mexico on the beach. She smiled and stopped washing dishes. Rinsing her hands off, she lifted her skirt and reached between her legs. Biting her bottom lip softly, she shrilled with pleasure as she fingered her wet mound. The water had been running for a minute and was just about to spill out onto the floor.

"You aight?"

Chills ran through her body when she turned around and saw Cray standing in the kitchen.

She pulled her skirt down and faced him. Thinking he could see her unfaithfulness, she got nervous and ignored the water spilling everywhere. He walked up to her and looked into her eyes. When he reached up, she flinched thinking he was about to hit her. Instead, he reached around her and turned the water off.

"Fuck you so happy for?" He stepped away and opened the fridge, drank orange juice out of the container and stared her down.

Tiara tried to wipe the thoughts of Nyzon out of her mind but as long as she thought about Ny it was difficult to think straight.

"No reason...just happy to be alive." She grabbed the mop and began to clean the floor.

"I never got a chance to ask you if you was feelin' Cancun."

"It was nice." Another smile popped up and Cray saw it.

"Oh yeah? What you like about it most?"

"The people. They're nice."

Something was up with Tiara and it bothered him. She hadn't been this happy since her father was alive. Brief thoughts of what Jason said entered his mind. Was something going on with his right hand man and his woman afterall? He pushed that thought out of his mind after realizing wasn't another nigga alive like him. Tiara loved him because he was in control. And in his mind, he hadn't changed a bit. Still, he wanted to be sure.

"Look...Tiara, I been fuckin' up cause I ain't been treatin' you right."

"That's not true." She lied. "You treat me good, baby.

"Tiara, you know that ain't true, but I'ma change. No more disrespect-ing' you wit bringin' bitches in our house or any of that shit. I been lettin' this dough get to my head and I'm wrong. I'ma start bein' home more and doin' right by you."

Tiara was stunned. If he was at home more, that meant she'd have to see Nyzon less. And she needed him.

And if that wasn't enough, he hit her with, "I love you, Tiara." He had-n't said those words in forever. "You are the best thing that has ever happened to me. Don't ever leave me. You the best thing about me."

Her head dropped.

"I…I'm happy."

"Stop lyin', baby. I was supposed to take care of you when your father died, and I didn't. Let me do right by you. Let me treat you how you're sup-posed to be treated. Your father raised a woman who deserves to be respect-ed. You not out here like some of these bitches who be sleepin' around smut-tin' themselves out."

Her stomach churned.

"You're wifey material all the way and I'm sorry for not realizing it." He placed both hands on the sides of her face and kissed her lips softly. The same lips that had been wrapped around Nyzon's dick earlier that day.

What was she doing?

Cray was right. Her father didn't raise her to be a whore. And sharing her body with Cray and Nyzon at the same time was doing just that. She wasn't even trying to make it work with the man who took her in when her father died. She owed him her life.

Cray wrapped his arms around her and she fell into his chest. Perhaps if she had been a better woman, Cray would've never stepped out on her. She needed to end things with Nyzon and she knew it would be hard. Little did she know that Cray smiled as she cried, realizing she was under his spell. Once again.

CRAY AND NYZON
295 PARKWAY
THE THICK

Cray was driving a new black 07' Maserati Quattroporte as he and Nyzon cruised down the road on the way to DC. There was a lot going on with the cops and for some reason, they were targeting all of their shops.

"The cops been fuckin' wit us hard, dude." Nyzon said smoking a blunt. "I think Kirk Bowler's bitch ass tryin' to become mayor by sacrificing' us."

"I know. So what's the plan?"

"The main problem is the re-up and not havin' nothin' on our folks when they raid and start locking' niggas up. And some of these block niggas singin' like birds when they get caught. So I'm bringin' this dog trainer in from Kansas to come out and..."

"A dug trainer?" Cray said cutting him off as he passed a tractor trailer. "We got problems wit the cops and you bringin' in dug trainers?"

"First off its *dog* not *dug*." He joked. "Secondly, this nigga can train a dog so good, they can understand commands based on hand signals. With them dogs we can attach the re-up around their necks with these pouches Crackhead Tina gonna make. When somebody want somethin', we'll have a dog not too far away ready. The thing is, the dogs will break the moment the cops come through and nobody will get caught with nothin' on em. I'm tellin' you Cray, the shit is genius. We'll just have one person near the stash to restock the dogs. And you ain't catchin' no dog. Trust me."

"So how you get the dug back? And what if somebody tries to take the re-up from around their necks?"

Nyzon laughed. "Did I forget to mention these dogs are killas? If somebody tries to take our product the dogs don't recognize, it's a wrap."

Cray liked it. In fact, he loved the idea.

"It may work. But you could kill the dug."

"And we'll get another one."

"I see. I see. Has it flaws but it's good."

"You B-more niggas hate to give a nigga credit."

"I'm said it may work."

"Yeah aight, nigga. It *will* work," he joked. "So what's up wit Charm? Heard anything from him yet?"

"Yeah. We got most of our blocks back but Blunt told me he heard a few of them was puttin' out product on one of our corners. Charm may be behind it. They not movin serious weight so I'm not trippin' right now. I'll get at em lada."

"It should be sooner than lada. We don't want this shit gettin' out of hand. Let one nigga take advantage, we might as well go out of business."

"I got this," Cray assured him.

"I hear you. But look, I hear we got bounties on our heads. Can we deal wit the heat?"

"No doubt. We know who it is and that situation will be dealt with in a few days."

Nyzon peeped his chain that said *The King of 295* and hated it.

"Nice chain." Ny said mugging it a little. "You forgot the "S" though?"

Cray laughed.

Nyzon didn't.

There hadn't been heat between them since they squashed the drama. Only a woman could make a man hold his tongue where he wanted to speak his mind. But Nyzon knew that what he felt for Tiara wasn't the only reason there bond had been strained. Ever since Devon got out, he'd been filling Cray's head up with shit. Telling him DC niggas wasn't needed.

"Yeah. When I picked it up, I found out he left the S off. Ain't that somethin'?"

"Yeah. But for all the dough you dropped, you'd think a nigga would spell it right."

"You can't pay know body to do shit right nowadays." he said picking up the one hundred thousand dollar medallion. "It ain't nothin'." He continued driving. "So what's up wit shawty you use to check from around my way?"

"Aw...I ain't fuckin' wit it no more."

"That's good. Cause I been thinkin' bout that for some reason."

"Word?"

"Yeah. You betta be careful cause she may have a nigga."

Nyzon looked at him and wondered if he knew.

"Why you say that?"

"Cause Bmore girls get down differently than DC ones. I wouldn't want no bullshit poppin' off you can't handle."

"I can handle anything that comes my way." Nyzon looked him in his eyes and they both felt the message.

"You sure? That nigga's heat might be too much."

"Doubt it. He's probably a bitch."

Cray laughed.

Nyzon didn't.

"That's cool." Cray said smoothly.

"And what's good wit Jason? I ain't seen the nigga in a minute. Why he wasn't in Cancun?"

"I don't know where he is." Cray adjusted in his seat. "Maybe he buried himself."

Nyzon knew then that he killed him. What fucked him up was not that he killed him because everyone knew he was loose with his lip game. What had Nyzon angry was the fact that he didn't tell him. Right then he knew the Kings were not as strong as they used to be and with the love he had for Tiara, he doubt they ever would.

KIRK BOWLER
A Vacant Alley In DC

It was midnight when Todd Jamison called Kirk and his father and told them to meet him at a vacant alley in DC. They'd met there before to discuss other matters that could only be done in private. Neither Kirk or William wanted to deal with him because lately Todd's behavior had become out of control. When they saw his car pull up they waited impatiently.

"What is your son doing now?" Kirk prayed no one saw him. "Trying to ruin my career?"

"Your guess is just as good as mine." William said. "This boy is out of control."

When Todd got out he tugged at Carolyn and J-Swizz who were gagged in the car. Everybody was confused but especially Carolyn and J-Swizz who were sleep in an apartment they'd rented when Todd kidnapped them. All this time William thought Carolyn was living by herself and here she stood before him, his only daughter, with a nigger.

"Todd, what the fuck is going on?!" Kirk yelled.

Todd was high as usual. "I want to prove that I'm still useful to the KYC."

"And this is helping?" William asked removing the gag from Carolyn's mouth and untying her arms. She rubbed her wrists and helped J-Swizz out of his restraints.

"I should kick your fucking ass!" J-Swizz yelled running toward Todd. When he waved his gun everyone backed up.

"Calm down, son." William said softly. "We don't want this kind of heat."

"Trust me, dad! You'll be happy after you find out who he is," he yelled waving the gun wildly. "He's involved in the case you're working on, Kirk. He has information about the operation and everything. And all this time, Carolyn has been fucking him! At one point she was even pregnant by him."

"What are you sayin'?" William asked. "Carolyn, is this true?"

"Dad, can we talk about this later?"

William looked at Kirk than at his daughter. He was repulsed.

For Carolyn, it was the first time it was confirmed where her pregnancy test had gone.

Todd had no idea that J-Swizz had been cut off from Melody's operation the day Melody was killed. All he wanted was for his father to accept him.

"Todd, you've gone too far!" William said angrily. "You two get in my car." He pointed to a black Lincoln Navigator. He never thought he'd see the day when a nigger would be in his ride.

Kirk disgusted at everything just walked off and jumped back into his cruiser.

"But, Dad!" Todd called out as both of them jumped into their cars and pulled off. "I love you! Why won't you accept me? Why?!"

They both left him in the alley, alone with his feelings and emotions. With nothing else to do, he took his gun out his pocket, placed it in his mouth, and pulled the trigger.

NYZON
SHAWTY GOT ME STRUNG

Nyzon was laying on Angel's bed on his back fucked up. After two weeks he still couldn't get in touch with Tiara. Wearing a black pair of basketball shorts and no shirt, he stared at the TV although he didn't know what was on.

"What's on your mind?" Angel asked taking her index finger and rubbing it through the grooves in his chest.

"Nothin." He said grabbing her hand and pushing it off. For some reason her touch irritated him.

Since he'd been staying there, she wanted three things all of the time. Sex, Money and a Relationship. Sex and money he could give but a relationship was out of the question.

"Nyzon...you come and go when you want to and I neva say nothing to you. But you still treat me like shit. You must got her on your mind again." She remembered the connection between him and Tiara at Devon's release party.

"You want me to leave?" he threatened with his eyes. He didn't have time for her shit.

"You know I don't want you to go. But I need some attention, Ny."

"Well you betta take it how it is."

"You use to like when I was around you." She reminded him, hinting to the time he was a kid. "Remember?"

"You mean do I remember when you were a pedophile?" he laughed trying to hurt her feelings.

"Nyzon! I wasn't a pedophile. I...I," she couldn't think of the proper words.

"You were fuckin' a kid. They call that a pedophile."

"I cared about you, Nyzon."

"Yeah...and you let me know right away what kind of female you were."

"Fuck that supposed to mean, Nyzon?"

"Angel, please! I got a lot of shit on my mind. Okay?" He said jumping up off the bed and looking at his self in the mirror.

"Alright, Nyzon." She sat on the edge of the bed looking at her hands as she spoke to him. "But I wish you would let me in. I could be so good for you if you'd just give me a chance."

He laughed to himself. Angel had no idea that the only reason he allowed her back in his life was to exact revenge. He was fucked up for months when she did him the way that she did.

"Yeah well I'm done wit givin' people chances."

"Can I do anything to make you feel good right now?" she asked walking over to him wrapping her arms around his body. "I don't care what you do to me, Nyzon. I just want to be that bitch you need. Beat me. Fuck me. Do anything you want to me, just try to love me."

"Is that right?"

"Yes. What do you want me to do?"

"I'm sure you could think of somethin'." He said licking his sexy thick lips.

He was treating her like a whore, but it was the only way he could control what he was feeling. Here he was worried about Tiara, a bitch that wasn't his, when he should've had his mind on his money. Still the question loomed...where was Tiara?

"I'm feelin' you, Nyzon." Angel said waking him out his thoughts.

"You gonna keep talkin' or get to work?" he removed himself from his shorts, already to a partial hard.

Angel got on her knees and sucked his dick like she needed to survive. She moaned so much you would've thought he was eating her pussy. It was a shame how good she handled business. Every lick, suck and kiss made his body shiver. He placed his hands on the sides of her head and pumped into her mouth. The look on her face told him she loved it, but she could not have more than he did.

"Don't stop." He told her looking down at her. "Am I the only nigga you want?"

"Yes." She whispered making her dick sucks wetter.

"Tell me how much you want me." He demanded.

"I would do anything for you, Ny. I can't see not being with you."

"Don't stop sucking." He told her.

And she didn't. And when he came, he fucked her...proper like. The best part about it was, he had got his revenge, because he wasn't even trippin' off this bitch. She couldn't hold a candle to his true love, Tiara.

Later That Night

Hours after giving Angel the crucial dick, Tiara called. He crept out of bed to talk to her.

"Where the fuck have you been?" he asked eager to hear why she'd been dodging him. He was so worried he made plans to pop up over Cray's house just to confront her.

"We have to talk, Nyzon. Can you meet me tomorrow?"

"Fuck that shit, Tiara! I been worried about you for weeks. Tell me what's up now."

"This is hard for me." She sounded like she was crying. "Real hard, Nyzon."

"Did that mothafucka touch you? Did he put his hands on you? I'll murder his bitch ass if he did."

"No...no!" she was quick to get that notion out of his mind. "It's the exact opposite. Shelton....Cray asked me to marry him."

Nyzon felt faint. This girl was his world but the man inside him would not allow him to beg like every cell in his body wanted too.

"What you tell him?" his heart raced as he waited for the answer.

"Yes." She sobbed. "I told him yes."

"Tiara, don't do this bullshit. Don't you see this dude is fuckin' wit you? He probably knows what's going on between us and he tryin' to wrap your mind all up."

"I'm sorry, Nyzon."

"Don't fuckin' do this! You deserve a real nigga. I'm that nigga, baby. I'm that nigga you need. Let me be that for you."

"I can't."

"Why you wanna fuck my head up like this? You my fuckin' life. Why you want me to murder that nigga?"

"Please. Don't hurt him."

"I will if you marry him, Tiara."

"Don't say that!"

"I'm serious! All he doin' is fuckin' wit' you!"

"He's not!"

"You betta give me a good reason why I shouldn't."

"You shouldn't because I love him."

Nyzon fell back into the wall for support.

"You...what?"

"I...I...love him. Goodbye, Nyzon."

When she hung up he started boxing the air wildly. He brought himself to a sweat from moving around so quickly. He didn't get it how a woman could stand by and let a dude dog them out, and carry somebody who gave a fuck. And then Crazy thoughts like telling Cray what happened between them entered his mind. And than he remembered, it was all about the dollar and Tiara complicated things anyway. As far as he was concerned if she wanted to be with a nigga that didn't respect her, she could suck his dick! Now all he had to do was convince himself that, that was how he really felt.

At Royala's Crib

Nyzon went to Royala's to get away. But who did he see the moment he hit the door? Lazarick's hoe ass. Things were going from piss to shit quick.

"Fuck this bum ass nigga doin' here?" he asked pushing his way past him and into the door.

"Nigga, this my sister's house. Fuck you talkin' about?"

"Hold up yall! Don't do this bullshit in my crib!" Royala had her arms stretched out between Nyzon and Lazarick. "Now hear me out. Laz, you was wrong as shit for fucking Monesha and not puttin' it to Ny. I told you that the moment I found out."

"I ain't think he would give a fuck." He said raising his arms in the air. "I thought they were cousins." Lazarick was copping a plea.

"That's some bullshit!" Ny yelled. "You were still supposed to tell me nigga! We were boys. And just so you know, that bitch stay hittin' me up to this day." Nyzon could tell Lazarick didn't know about her calls because his face was tight. She told him she wasn't tripping off Nyzon anymore.

"No she ain't."

Nyzon laughed. "You know what, fuck it! You stuck wit her ass now, I ain't even trippin' off that shit no more. I got otha shit on my mind."

Really Nyzon started to think about the situation in its entirety. He was mad at Lazarick for fucking Monesha and not telling him, yet he fucked Tiara behind Cray's back. He was participating in the worse hypocrisy.

"I'm sorry, man. I shoulda told you."

"Fuck that. You do owe me some dough for all that cake I kicked out on her ass and your kid." Nyzon laughed.

"Good luck on tryin' to get it back, man." Lazarick chuckled. "I ain't one of the Kings."

"Be lucky you not."

With that they shook hands and put the shit behind them. Where it belonged.

TIARA
MAKIN' IT WORK

Tiara rushed home from school early to get ready for Cray's and her night together. She was doing her best to make it work, despite the fact that Nyzon consumed her thoughts. When she opened the door to her home and jetted upstairs she heard heavy panting.

"Damn your pussy wet as shit!" Cray's voice called.

Was she hearing things correctly? Was she losing her mind? Slowly she opened the door to her bedroom and saw the white sheets moving up and down. The muscles in Cray's back flexed with each thrust. And suddenly she heard the rain pounding against their home. All it did was symbolize the pain in her heart.

"Cray? What's going on?" She walked further into the room and stopped. A force wouldn't allow her to go any further.

He jumped up from the bed snatching the sheets off the woman's body to cover his own. What she saw forced her to question if God really existed. Because if he did, she couldn't understand why he would cause her to hurt so much. In her bed, lay Yolanda, her dearest and closest friend. She'd expect Felecia to do some bullshit like that but not Yolanda. Still, she couldn't help but remember all the times Yolanda told her she was lucky to have Cray. She even remembered how she kept jumping on him in the pool in Cancun. She'd been obsessing over him for years.

"Oh shit, babe! What you doin' here?"

"I live here, Cray! I fuckin' live here!" Tiara never got loud with him before. "How could you do this to me?" she sobbed. "You said you wanted to marry me!"

"I'm sorry Tiara!" Yolanda said covering her sweat soaked body.

"Bitch shut up!" she yelled pointing at her. "If I thought you were worth it," she said looking at Yolanda. "I'd scratch your fuckin' eyes out."

She stumbled backwards, and the wall caught her limp body. She was done. No longer did she care about living a lie. Some how she got enough energy to leave. And it felt like a force was carrying her out of the house and her spirit told her it was her father. She heard Cray's voice trailing behind her as she jumped in her Benz. Fuck him! He could have the house, the money and Yolanda. All she wanted was Nyzon. She didn't care what it took but she needed to convince him to take her back because there was no place she'd rather be.

At Nyzon's Crib

Tiara parked in front of Nyzon's house and walked toward the door after seeing his car out front. The rain poured heavily on her body drenching her totally. If he rejected her, she didn't know what else she'd do. All she wanted was for him to hear her out. But before she could knock, she heard the alarm on his car disarm and the door open. He stopped when he saw her in the rain...hair sticking to her face.

"Nyzon...I'm sorry. I'm sooooo sorry, baby. I made a mistake and I need you in my life right now."

"Fuck you mean you need me, T? You playin' games wit me, makin' me think we were down like that then you cut me off without even tellin' me why? Fuck out my face." He walked around her and toward his car.

"Nyzon, please! I was such a fuckin' fool! I know it now and I'm willin' to ride with you no matter where we go. Don't do this to me! Don't do this to us!"

"Do this to us? You did this shit! I was ready to take a bullet for you! And you made me realize you ain't worth it."

He stopped and she ran up to him, dropped to her knees and wrapped her arms around his legs. The rain soaking them both didn't stop the emotions from running heavy. All he wanted to do was lift her up and tell her everything was okay. But the games. The hurt. He wasn't willing to deal with it. In his book, it wasn't worth it anymore.

"Nyzon...what's going on?" Angel asked witnessing the entire thing as she stood behind them, umbrella in hand.

"Nothing...go to the car." He told her as she walked passed them both, without a rebuttal. She knew Nyzon would rip into her if she didn't obey him.

Tiara stood up and kept her eyes on Angel until she got into the car and closed the door.

"Nyzon, I know you don't love her. She's not the woman for you. It's me. It's been me all along. Let's start our family. She can't love you like me. She can't make you call out her name like you call out mine when we make love. Your body needs me and mines needs you."

"It don't matter cause it's over, Tiara." He was saying all of this without looking into her eyes.

"I was afraid, baby." She continued ignoring his comment. "Afraid to let you love me. I thought Cray was what I deserved because he was there for me when my father died. But I was wrong. So wrong. I deserve better. I deserve a man with the honor my father had. But if you leave me, I'll die." She was crying heavily.

"You shoulda thought about that before you chose. I'm out of here."

Nyzon walked to his Benz and pulled off. Tiara held her stomach as she cried so hard that it felt as if she'd been doing sit ups. Her life was officially over and she needed God himself to come down and give her direction. The headlights going completely out of view symbolized the end. She dropped to her knees and prayed for an answer.

"God, do You want me to die? Do You want me to kill myself? Because if that man leaves me, I don't want to be here. I don't want to live!"

And then she saw him, running back toward her as if he'd forgotten something. He'd sent Angel on her way, without him and his ride. Just the sight of him eased the ache in Tiara's heart.

Standing before her, Nyzon reached down and extended his hand. She rose. Wiping the wet hair from her face he said, "If you're down wit me then be down wit' me. Don't fuck wit my head, Tiara. It's all or nothin'."

"I am down with you, Nyzon, and I don't care what happens."

"All hell is getting' ready to break lose if we stay together." He said calmly. "Are you ready?"

"I'll go through the fire with you."

"Good." He said seriously. "Cause that's what you gonna have to do."

With that, they engaged in a heavy kiss, and she gave her heart to him, and he vowed his life to her.

NYZON
CALM BEFORE THE STORM

Nyzon and Tiara had been staying at his aunt Jackie's for two weeks. All he told his aunt was that he was in love with her, and that they had to get away. Pouring the love she had for her sister onto Nyzon, she willingly allowed them too.

Cray still didn't know that Tiara had run off with Nyzon but everyone saw the visible effects of Cray missing her on his face, not to mention business was suffering greatly in Bmore. He didn't shower and he became meaner than ever before. And as if matters couldn't get any worse, the DC cops had made it known that anybody who was willing to give them solid information about the Kings of 295 would be rewarded....greatly. All Nyzon wanted to do was stack his chips and leave the state. And after talking to his boxing coach, he knew exactly where he'd go.

"What's wrong?" Nyzon asked after hearing Tiara sniffling next to him as they lay in the bed together.

"Did you have a good relationship with your mother?"

Nyzon moved uncomfortably never fully telling her about his past.

"Not really."

"I...I never understood why my mother didn't love me."

"How you know she didn't?"

"It never felt like it. It felt like she hated me for some reason."

"You said she was on drugs baby. If that's the case, you never got a chance to know your real mother. That shit gets your mind fucked up."

"I'd really like to see her before we leave. I got to know why she did me the way that she did. But I don't know where she is."

Tiara was going through a mental breakdown worrying about everything. Just like her mother, when the heat was on, she lost all reason. And she wanted loose ends tied before they left.

"I'll find out where she lives. DC too small to hide. I'll take you to her before we roll. I promise."

"I love you Nyzon."

"I love you more."

CRAY
MY MAN, A HUNDRED GRAND

Three weeks had passed and still no word on Tiara's whereabouts. Cray was at his wits ends. He wasn't handling business, he didn't bathe and he drunk Hennessey like it was water. He was sitting in his living room with Devon, Jinx and Blunt when his phone rang. An insignificant female he picked up earlier sat by his side as he pressed the button to the speakerphone.

"Who's this?"

"Somebody who knows where Tiara is going next."

"What's your name?"

"Monesha."

They all looked at one anther.

"How you know her?"

"I don't know her but I *do* know Nyzon. And she's with him."

"With Nyzon?" he asked looking at the phone like it was a science project. "Fuck you mean she wit Nyzon?" He'd just seen Nyzon yesterday and he acted as if all was good. I guess it was, he was fucking his girl.

"I overheard Lazarick talking to Royala about it and me and him together. I think there over my stepmom Jackie's house. They're planning to run away together."

"You heard all this shit?"

"Yes."

Cray wanted to dismember Nyzon for embarrassing him. And to think, he'd killed his best friend right before he tried to put him on to Nyzon's deceit. If Jason knew, he wondered who else did. The alcohol made him believe everyone was in on it.

"Ya'll knew about this shit?" he questioned his boys.

"Why you gotta ask me some bullshit like that?" Devon asked. "I told you not to trust them DC niggas."

Cray cracked his knuckles and for no reason, hit the female with him in the face so hard, her jaw automatically readjusted itself and she passed out cold.

He rubbed his knuckles carless about whom he just hurt. He was beyond furious. He had this nigga in his house and here he was fucking his girl. His boys shook their heads in disgust after hearing the news and witnessing the victim on the floor. The same nigga who saved his life wanted his wife. The Kings of 295 were no more after this shit.

"You betta not be fuckin' wit me." Cray told her. "Cause I'm the wrong dude."

She paused sensing his evil. "Uh...uh...I'm not lyin! I heard about you." She assured him.

"What do you want?"

"I got the address and all I'm askin' for is some money and for you to leave my aunt Jackie out of it."

"Stop lyin'. This ain't about money. What is this about?"

"I got my reasons."

"What's the address?"

She gave it to him.

"You're not going to bother my aunt right?"

"I'ma pay ya ass," he said ignoring her question. "but let me know if they go somewhere else. I gotta find this nigga like yesterday."

"I will. But what about my aunt..."

He hung up. When he got off the phone he looked at his boys angrily.

"I want this mothafucka found and brought to me! And if anybody get in the way, murder them too!"

"I told you not to trust them DC niggas." Devon said not helping the matter one bit.

"It don't even matter no more. Bring his bitch ass to me, I don't care if you have to launch a thousand bullets to find him."

"What about the connect info?" Blunt asked.

"If you keep Tiara alive, he'll tell us everything we need to know." Devon reminded him.

"Cool, and when we're done," Cray said sipping the last of his drink. "I want them both buried!"

NYZON
TIARA OF DC

Cooks and Simon couldn't believe their eyes. Tiara although beautiful was forbidden and standing in the Jackie's kitchen. All were relieved that Jackie wasn't home.

"You remember Tiara right?" Nyzon asked as he held her hand.

Royala already knowing the deal dropped her head.

"Tiara of Bmore?" Cooks asked hoping she had a twin out there somewhere. In his heart he knew the obvious, she was Cray's girl.

"No...Tiara of DC." Nyzon said calmly.

"What you doin', man?! This niggas gonna flip when he find out you wit her. You know he been searching' high and low for this bitch."

"You family and I love you. But don't disrespect her again." Nyzon told her.

"Well what you want me to say?! You're about to start a war over this....girl," he said exchanging his original words for less harsh ones.

"It's too late now," Royala added. "We got to deal with the situation as it is."

"And what about The Kings?" Simon asked. "What about the money?"

Tiara held her head down feeling as if all the violence that was to come, was all her fault.

"Tiara, go to the guestroom." Nyzon advised. She walked away sadly.

"That's what I wanted to talk to ya'll about. The cops have been comin' around the blocks more anyway. Ya'll know that. I don't know what's going on, but I think somebody tipped them off. I got enough dough saved up for all of us to be a'ight, but we have to get out now before things get out of hand. This shit ain't got nothin' to do with Tiara. It was war anyway."

"But look how you doin' it, man?" Simon insisted. "You broke bread wit that man. You ain't got no business bein' wit' his girl."

"It may have been his girl but she's gonna be my wife. And we in it too deep to turn back now."

The kitchen was silent.

"Fuck, Nyzon! I can't believe this shit." Simon said shaking her head. "This nigga gonna kill you man! You have to let her go."

"I can't." Nyzon said slowly. "Cause if I could, I would've done it by now."

Just when he started to explain, bullets rang through Jackie's house crashing the windows. Based on the angles, they could tell it was more than one gun. They hit the floor reaching for their pieces when they remembered that Jackie didn't allow guns in her house so they were all outside in Cook's car.

"What's going on?" Tiara screamed running toward them from the back room.

"Get down, baby!" Nyzon called out pulling her to the cold porcelain floor.

With no weapons to defend themselves, they were defenseless.

"Move toward the basement!" Simon advised. "The backyard has a high fence so they can't get in or see us. We can jump in Cook's car."

"Cooks, your car still runnin' right?" Simon asked. Cooks didn't answer. When they looked at him he was hunched over on his knees in the corner. "Cooks your car still runnin' right?"

When Simon moved him, his body slumped backward and onto the floor. He'd been shot in the chest and blood was pouring everywhere.

"Oh no!" Nyzon yelled going toward him. "Get up, Cooks. We gotta go, man! We gotta leave!"

More bullets loomed over their heads and shortened the time for grieving. Nyzon was still tugging at him when Royala pulled his arms. Simon was right beside him speechless. His brother had just been murdered and Tiara sat by the sidelines crying. He looked at her once wandering if her death would put him at ease.

"This not her fault, Simon." Royala said reading her mind. "This not her fault. We gotta go."

"Cooks! Come on!" Nyzon continued in shock and not knowing how to deal with the situation.

"We got to bounce, Ny! Come on Simon we got to move!" Royala yelled. She was in charge.

Bullets still ripped through the house as they ran toward the basement. It was obvious they were trying to kill everybody inside, innocent or not.

"My brother!" Simon yelled swinging into the air. "My fuckin' brother is dead!"

"I'm sorry, man. This is all my fault. I fucked up. I shoulda neva came here." Nyzon yelled.

"Lada for that shit, we got to get out of here." Simon grew stronger in the minute.

Out the back door they dipped and into Cooks awaiting car. All of their weapons were tucked inside on the floor. Cray, Blunt, Devon and Jinx saw the car rushing from the back knocking Jackie's wooden fence down. Cray's car pursued them in a high speed chase shooting bullets out the window. They wanted blood.

In Cray's car

"I want that nigga's heart!" Cray reloaded his weapon as Devon drove.

"But what about the connect info?" Devon reminded him. "If we kill him it's a wrap. We can forget about findin' out we been dealin' wit'."

"He's right," Jinx added. "We need him alive."

"Shit!" Cray yelled remembering. If he told them to shoot him anyway, it would be obvious that the only thing he cared about was getting revenge on Nyzon for stealing Tiara from him.

He knew they couldn't understand. He was the one who molded her pussy. He was the one who fucked with her young mind until it was just right. He was the one who made her a queen by forcing her to be *willing, wanting* and *able*. And at the end of the day, he didn't know what he had until it was gone. Still he had to regroup.

Coming to his senses he said, "Slow down Jinx. Let's let them think he got away." Cray said softly. "I'll catch up wit his ass later."

No sooner than he said that, he saw a saw a Maryland tag he thought he'd seen earlier. But with everything going on, he thought he lost his mind. *I'm just trippin'.*

In Cook's Car

"Looks like we lost him." Royala said as Simon continued to speed off down the road.

"Yeah…for now." Nyzon said knowing he'd never give up until he had them. "For now."

MONESHA HEART
SOUTHEAST D.C
SUCKER*S*

"That feels so good baby." Monesha moaned as she lie face up on the couch while Lazarick sucked her toes. "Make it real wet." She loved when he put extra spit on them and twirled his tongue around her toes. It turned her on.

She was wearing a pink mini t-shirt and her thong panties. Lazarick had always been wanting Monesha since middle school and now that Nyzon made it clear that he wasn't entertaining her, despite her, she settled for a flunkie ass nigga.

"Like this, baby?" he asked putting four of her toes in his mouth at a time.

She was just about to play with her pussy when she heard a slight knock at the front door of the apartment they shared together. Lazarick jumped up to open it without seeing who was behind the door first. They ordered some pizza and thought it was there.

When he opened the door, Cray unleashed four bullets into his body. Once he dropped to the floor, Cray, Devon, Blunt and Jinx moved behind him and inside the apartment.

"Awwwwwwwwwwwwwwwwwwwwwwwww!" Monesha screamed.

Cray walked up to her and wrapped his hand around her throat silencing her.

"Shut the fuck up!" he warned. He had the eyes of a killer. "Now you got my cash so tell me where I can find Nyzon."

When he released her, she rubbed her throat and said, "I told you where he was when you gave me the money. That's all I know."

"Yeah well he ain't there no more."

"But I don't..."

Before she could finish her sentence, he shoved the barrel of his gun inside her pussy and jabbed upward. The heat from him just shooting Lazarick burned her skin.

"I promise." She cried harder, shaking her head from left to right, careful not to move too much for fear of the gun going off. "I don't know where he is. Please don't kill me. I wouldn't lie to you. I know you don't play that shit."

Cray not up for the games cocked his gun back.

"Okay...Okay...I might have something else."

"Start talkin'."

"A few days ago I think Nyzon called Lazarick to find Tiara's mother."

"Tiara's mother?" he said. He had forgot she was even alive.

"Yeah. He said he seemed upset. He didn't tell him why."

"Go head."

"I think...I think the number may be in his cell phone. Lazarick stored it in there for Nyzon when he got it from work. Maybe he's going there." Lazarick worked for Verizon, the telephone company, so he was able to get any information he needed. "His phone is in his pocket."

"Get it." He told Blunt.

Blunt rummaged through the men's jeans on the floor releasing a cell phone. Cray sat impatiently.

"You see it?"

"I don't know what I'm looking for." He said scanning through the numbers.

"I think her name is Tara."

When Blunt saw the name he nodded that he had it.

"See...I told you." She said hoping he'd leave her alone. "I wouldn't fuck wit you."

"Yeah you really came through. Good lookin' out."

She smiled. "So...so you gonna let me go now?"

"Yeah. After you hold something for me."

He fired inside of her, killing her instantly.

"Damn, man!" Blunt said. "Fuck you do that for?"

"No witnesses. You know the rule."

Blunt and Jinx thought he was going too far. He was crossing the line between business and vengeance and they didn't like it one bit.

"Now lets go get this nigga." Cray said wiping the bloody barrel of the gun on Monesha's shirt. "I'm tired of fuckin' wit this dude."

NYZON
TIARA'S MOM'S APARTMENT IN DC
APPLE OF HIS EYES

Tara's apartment was small and cozy but lonely. She'd been clean for a year but still looked unhappy. Nyzon believed she needed to see Tiara just as much as Tiara needed to see her. It was amazing how much they looked alike and before now, he never thought another woman existed whose beauty could challenge hers. He was wrong.

When Nyzon glanced at the coffee table, he saw a framed picture of a man who looked familiar to him. Where had he seen him before?

"Who is that?" He asked Tara.

She lifted the picture and gazed at it as if it was the first time she'd seen t. She smiled and said, "It's Kavon, Tiara's father."

Tiara looked at the picture also and a single tear fell down her face. Nyzon softly kissed it away and held her closely.

"He still loves you." Nyzon reassured her. "And trust me he got your back." Tara looked at their display of affection and knew it was genuine. "I've seen him somewhere before."

Tiara looked up at him slightly confused. Neither she nor he knew he was the man Nyzon encountered when he went to the safety deposit box a while back. And because he'd come in contact with so many in his lifetime, he left the matter alone.

Tiara's eyes suddenly searched her mother's apartment. It was as if she was looking for something.

"I'm sorry, Tiara. I don't have any pictures of you here."

Tiara's head dropped.

"It was too painful. After all, I am the reason we don't have a relationship. I failed you."

"Is it something I did?" Tiara asked. "Was I bad as a child?"

Hearing her pain caused Nyzon's heart to ache and he was hoping her mother accepted her failure fully, thereby freeing his girl from years of pain.

"It was me. All me."

"But Why? I want to understand what I did to you to make you hate me." Tiara said looking at her mother, with tears in her eyes. "Why would you put me through so much? All I wanted to do was make you happy."

"I was strung out. It took me a year to come to terms with what I did to you. But I'm willing to work on our relationship if you give me a chance. Will you?"

Tiara looked at Nyzon and he said, "I'll support whatever you want but only if you do it for yourself."

He wanted her to know without saying, that whether she accepted or denied her invitation for a relationship, he didn't care. He just wanted her happy.

"Yes mamma." She hugged her. "Yes I will."

Nyzon remained quiet as the two talked for hours. His mind was on the drama that lay before them. Tara told Tiara stuff about her father she never knew, including the fact that he was a drug dealer and that his best friend raped her while she was pregnant. Tara went on to say how much Nyzon reminded her of Kavon. And because Tiara had been saying that for the longest, he believed her.

"I'm gonna make you guys something to eat." She pulled herself away from them after checking her watch. "I'll be right back." She walked into the kitchen and disappeared.

"I love you for finding my mom for me." Tiara said kissing his lips softly. "And I can't wait to spend eternity with you."

That reminded Nyzon why it was as important for him to find Tara. He wanted to ask her for her blessings to propose to Tiara. In fact, it was the only reason he was there and not trying to retaliate against Cray for killing his cousin. They had to get out of town. Of course he still had plans to repay him but he realized now was not the time. He had to get Tiara away safe.

"Anything for you, babe." He placed his hand on her knee. "Just as long as you're happy. Let me talk to your mother for a minute. Alone. I have to ask her something."

"Okay." She smiled.

With the ring tucked in his pocket, he walked toward the kitchen. He was nervous but knew there was no other woman for him.

But the moment he walked into the kitchen he heard, "Yeah…they're here."

He stopped in his footsteps.

"I'll keep them busy, just bring my money."

Nyzon couldn't believe his ears. How could a mother be so devious that she'd put her only child in danger? When she turned around and saw him standing there, the phone dropped out of her hands.

"If Tiara wasn't in there I'd put a bullet in your face right now."

She smiled.

"Do you really think I care? I died the moment she took Kavon from me." He knew then she was a selfish ass bitch. "That little whore stole everything from me the moment I pushed her out of my bloody pussy."

"You think your daughter took your husband away from you? You're fuckin' sick!" he said as he grabbed her face and squeezed it in his hands. Her entire face turned red. "Stay the fuck away from her!" he turned around and yelled, "Tiara!"

Tara's eyes widened wondering if he was going to confront her right there. When Tiara came in the kitchen smiling, he hugged at her waist.

"What's wrong, baby?"

"We gotta go. Your moms havin' company and we got to keep movin'."

"But I'm not ready."

"Tiara!" Nyzon said firmly. "We gotta go and we gotta go now!"

Nyzon never talked to her so firmly so she knew he was serious. Plus with everything going on, Nyzon was right. It was selfish of her to ask him to stay longer when he'd just lost his cousin.

She grabbed her things and said, "Bye, mama." She hugged her tightly. "I'll be in contact."

Not if I can help it. Nyzon thought. He called Royala while she talked to her mother and within five minutes she was there.

The moment they left and jumped in Royala's silver Escalade Nyzon asked, "Where's Simon?"

"He ain't comin'." She said softly opening the door. "He's messed up about Cooks."

Nyzon understood as he slid in the backseat and Tiara sat in the front. The door wasn't all the way closed before bullets rang out crashing into the back window of Royala's new ride. They ducked inside and the bullets exited out the front window shattering it terribly.

Royala raised her foot and kicked the front window out. Her driving skills couldn't be fucked with and she managed to pull off before anybody was hurt.

Nyzon's mind raced. The love of his life and his best friend were in that car and he had to make a decision. He couldn't risk something happening to them. He had to settle things for once and for all. It was already his fault that Cooks was dead, he would've died if Tiara and Royala were hurt too.

"Royal, pull over and let me deal with this shit, man." He said loudly spotting a closed Honda dealership up the street.

"Naw dog I got you! I'ma bout to shake these niggas off our trail." She looked at him from the rearview mirror while dodging the danger that followed.

"Royal! I'm serious!" He said looking back at her. "Let me out."

Royala was still driving hurriedly when she realized he wasn't playing. "Stop at the car lot up the street on the left."

"Ny, now is not the time to play hero."

"I'm serious! Just take care of Tiara for me."

"Baby, what are you doing?" Tiara asked turning around to look at him. "He'll kill you."

Nyzon was silent. Besides, she was right.

Royala dipped into the car lot far enough ahead of Cray for them to get away.

"Dog, what are you doin?" Royala asked.

"Later for that shit. Right now I'm about to ask the woman I love to marry me."

Tiara looked at him lovingly but with a frightened face.

"Baby, I didn't know what love was before I met you." He said as he grabbed her hand and caressed it softly. Royala kept a look out. "I couldn't even imagine it. Now I can't see my life without you in it. You're fuckin' everything to me. All the shit I ever did both good and bad was for this moment."

"Nyzon, please....don't," she was interrupted.

"Let me finish. Now I planned on asking you to marry me under better circumstances, but I need the strength of your love right now to get me through this shit. So I'm askin', will you be my wife?"

He opened the ring box and exposed the six-carat diamond ring.

"Yes! I will! Yes I will!"

She through her arms around his neck and he gripped her as best he could from the back seat.

Royala wiped a single tear from her face too.

"Hold up, I know that ain't my dog up there cryin'."

"Nigga. fuck you!" she joked. "But you gotta go, Ny. They comin'."

"I'll be back, Tiara. Wait for me."

When he opened the door, Tiara tried to jump out. "Hold her Royal! Don't let her get out!"

Her legs dangled from the car door as Royala grabbed the back of her shirt and her hair to keep her inside.

"I'm comin' back Ny!" Royala promised putting the car back into gear.

"Just go! Get her away and safe! I love you, Tiara!"

Right before Tiara jumped out, Royala pulled off leaving Nyzon standing. When he saw the passenger door closed, he exhaled. They were safe and he was thankful. He hopped on the roof of a new Honda Accord, took his shirt off and waited for Cray.

CRAYLAND BAILOR
FACE OFF

They dipped in and out of traffic until they saw what looked like Nyzon sitting on a car in the parking lot of a Honda dealership.

"Yo am I trippin' or is that, that nigga right there?" Cray asked spotting him standing on top of the car.

The car whipped into the lot so quickly, they almost bumped the car Nyzon was standing on. He hopped off the car, dusted off the back of his pants and stood up. He waited patiently for the four men to approach him.

"You gotta be on somethin'." Cray said with crazed eyes. "Or you must be ready to die."

They surrounded him but Nyzon *wasn't* scared, he was just *alone*.

"I'm out here 'cause I'm not a bitch." Devon stood behind him Cray. "You are."

"I'm a bitch?" Cray said pointing to himself. "You steal my girl and I'm a bitch?"

"I aint' steal shit! You can't steal what doesn't belong to you." Nyzon responded as the two men stepped closer to each other.

"You's a funny nigga, huh? You DC niggas always think you funny. Ya'll ain't nothin' but a bunch of clowns."

"If you a real man, you'd put the gun down and fight me straight up." Cray and his boys laughed.

"Yo, Cray why we wastin' time?" Devon asked. "Put him in the trunk and lets run this fool until he gives us the connect info." He looked nervously behind him afterward.

"Is that all you want?" Nyzon laughed looking at Devon than Cray. "You ain't got to take me no where for that shit. If this nigga can whip me straight up, I'll write the information down and call him for you right now." Nyzon offered Cray up in front of his boys and if he didn't take the bait, he would no doubt look like a bitch.

"Take the offer, Cray. That's what we need, man," Devon advised.

"What about Tiara? Where is she?"

"I'd lay down my life before I tell you where she's at. Take the connect, or take my life."

Devon was growing irritated with his lovesick cousin.

"Let me find out you scared to fight me wit the hands." Nyzon continued realizing he was scared. Nyzon was crushing his rep big time.

"A'ight…you got that." Cray took off his shirt. The lot was desolate so nobody was around for miles. It was the perfect place to stage a war.

Nyzon swung the first punch and missed. Cray laughed and the moment he did, Nyzon knocked the smirk off his face and a tooth down his throat. Before he could get himself together, Nyzon him with a left so hard, Cray's nose instantly spouted blood.

"And you got skin like a bitch." Nyzon laughed watching Cray wiping his mouth.

"I'ma see how much shit you talkin' when I put you on yo back Golden Gloves."

Cray swung two times and missed but the third one landed right on Nyzon's chin. And before he knew it, Cray gut punched him. The air was violently released from his body. But Nyzon being the trooper that he was nailed a left, and than a right. The fight was good until Nyzon stole him so hard Cray's knees buckled before he fell to the ground.

"Get up, Cray!" Devon yelled as Jinx and Blunt stood on watching.

Cray's men had mixed feelings about the whole fight because they hated that business was over because of a woman. Blow after blow was thrown and they could see Cray tiring. He was no match for Nyzon's fighting skills. Nyzon knowing his life was over anyway because there was no way they'd let him walk away alive, beat him even more. He had nothing to lose. He was fighting to be remembered. He knew that after he punished Cray properly, that he'd always remember him. He wanted his name to live on.

"Sh…shoot em!" Cray cried out while Nyzon straddled him and pounded him over and over again. "Shoot him."

Devon with all the shit he talked wasn't ready to put in work since he just got out of jail. Instead he looked to Jinx and Blunt to pull the trigger but they couldn't. Nyzon use to be their man and they still fucked with him. They had respect for him. Plus they knew Cray was out of control. If he got away, he'd fuck shit up worse than he already did.

"Wh…what are you waitin' on?" Cray questioned.

Cray with his eyes barely opened looked up at his cousin for help. Nyzon was punishing him unmercifully. The life was being taken from his body.

"Give me yo heat!" Devon told Jinx.

Jinx reluctantly handed him his weapon. Devon was just about to fire when he felt a stinging sensation through his back. Seconds later, he dropped down to the grown and fell on his face. Everybody ducked and hid behind cars. They wondered where the bullet came from until Royala appeared from behind one of the cars. She'd parked her truck a half of mile up and ran to Nyzon on foot. She couldn't leave him alone. Not on her watch anyway.

"Don't make me shoot all of yall." She said calmly. "Keep your hands where I can see em." She said to Jinx and Blunt. She fucked with them both but wouldn't hesitate killing them if forced. She walked toward Nyzon still aimed at Jinx and Blunt. "Get up, Ny! Let's go."

Ny rose off of Cray's half weak body.

"Damn...you really came back!" he said running by her side.

"I told you I would." She winked, still aimed as they walked backward.

They were so busy with the chivalries that they didn't see Cray moving toward the gun that Devon dropped on the ground near him. With the gun in his hands, and still on the ground, he aimed at Royala and Nyzon.

"Don't move. I'm warning you." Cray said half out of breath.

They turned around to face him.

He cocked the hammer and was about to pull the trigger until a bullet ripped through his arm. The gun fell and another bullet hit his chest. Cray's head fell against the concrete. Everyone turned around to see Markise standing there. Royala and Nyzon didn't know who he was, but they were glad he came through when he did.

"That was for Jason." Markise said as he dipped off, and back into a car that had been following Cray the entire time. It was the car Cray spotted hours ago. His suspicions were correct.

Everyone looked on in disbelief as Cray, the most dangerous nigga in Baltimore, lie dead on the concrete. And just like that, the Kings of 295 were no more.

KRISTINA'S DINER
PRESENT DAY

Beliza's mouth was agape after hearing the story. She thought it was one of the most violent, yet romantic things she'd ever heard in her life.

"So let me guess, you're Nyzon." She smiled knowing the answer.

"No...I'm not." He said on his third piece of pie.

"Wait a minute. You can't be Cray because he's dead. Right?" she asked as she moved in her seat. Remembering the story of his violence had her frightened.

"No. I told you he was killed." He winked.

"Than who are you?" she breathed heavily with excitement.

Right before he could answer a beautiful pregnant white woman walked into the restaurant. She smiled when she spotted the stranger Beliza had been talking to for the last hour.

"Sorry, honey!" she said kissing him on the cheek. "I was held up for hours in a traffic jam. The weather is getting worse out there."

"Wait! You're...you're J-Swizz?" Beliza said excitedly.

"Yes. And this is my wife Carolyn."

Beliza immediately recognized her from TV. She knew her as Carolyn Daye so she didn't put one and one together when she heard the story. "I know you from TV."

Carolyn smiled, "That was probably me although TV makes me look five sizes bigger." She laughed.

After William let Carolyn and J-Swizz go when Todd kidnapped them, J-Swizz never said a word about anything he knew about the drug operation. He wanted to be part of the solution but not that way. Especially after learning from Carolyn the truth about her racist father. J-Swizz hated his life and made some serious changes, and Carolyn loving him, did also. She cleaned her act up and decided to run for councilwoman of DC. She won. She was known around DC as being brutally honest about racism and the real problems plaguing the city. She wanted things changed and she was causing enough ruckus to get things done.

She had plans to run for mayor, and people were pretty sure she'd win. J-Swizz on the other hand helped run the Take Back the Streets campaign with Modell and Cray's mother who was totally clean and active in her city.

After she buried Cray, her only child, she dedicated her life to the war on drugs.

"But...I don't get it. How did you know so much?" Beliza responded thinking about the story again.

"You're not telling the story again are you?" Carolyn asked as she took the seat next to him and ate from his pie.

He winked. "You know I am."

Carolyn laughed. "Well go ahead. Finish up so we can hit the road."

"Well, Beliza, a year later, after seeing Carolyn on TV, she received a package in the mail containing a journal. The person sending it said they wanted her to have the story chronicling her life and the things she'd gone through. The woman felt Carolyn was brave for comin' out and she wanted to do the same. She felt someone could benefit from her story. And she asked that she share her story, but keep her identity. Always."

"Was the package from Tiara?"

"We can't say." Carolyn smiled.

"But it has to be!" she said as they collected themselves to leave. "Are Nyzon and Tiara okay?"

"That's all we can say for now."

Beliza exhaled. The story moved and inspired her.

"Give me a second." She held her finger up. Afterwards she pulled her cellphone out of her purse and dialed a number. "Daddy it's me, Beliza." Silence. "I just wanted to tell you that I know you care about me and I love you for that. But I have to do what's best for me, and what's best for me is Trent." Silence. J-Swizz and Carolyn looked down at her. Instead of being upset, her eyes brightened. "Thanks for listening, daddy and I know you're not totally happy about my decision, but I won't let you down. Goodbye." She ended the call and put her phone in her purse.

"Thank you." Beliza continued looking at J-Swizz. "You saved my life."

"No problem, shawty. Good luck on your future."

"And good luck with yours," Beliza said.

With that J-Swizz and Carolyn walked out the door.

EPILOGUE

Everyone was cheering in their native language as Nyzon, who now went by Shelton raised his boxing gloves in the air. He'd won yet another fight. His coach back home had international connections and was able to get him the match in Africa after learning about his legal woes.

With the money Nyzon saved and won from fighting, they bought a beautiful home on the water in Africa. But as beautiful as their home was, it was Tiara's six-month pregnancy that made him proud. For the first time in their lives, both of them found happiness.

Kirk Bowler in conjunction with the FEDS continued their work to take down the Kings of 295, not realizing they were done. Someone sent an anonymous piece of paper listing the major stash houses as well as a few key player names. That paper was the document Jason gave Markise at the Baltimore Harbor before he was murdered. In the end the only people Kirk could arrest was Charm, Grimy Mike and a few block niggas. Needless to say no one would be jumping at making him mayor, especially since Carolyn Daye was running.

Jinx took his cash and moved to LA to become an ordained minister. While Blunt was shot in a Laundromat a few months after Cray was found dead. He roams Baltimore alone.

William Jamison continued to have his racists views but realized times were changing. If he wanted to get his message across, he'd have to do it underground. So he held his meetings in private. The KYC although small, are as big as ever.

After the boxing match Tiara and Nyzon went home to celebrate. Their home was filled with new friends who wished them well. The music boomed symbolizing there was much to celebrate. But with all of the excitement, Tiara forgot about her life back home. She needed to share the great news with someone she promised she'd always keep in contact with.

She picked up her golden handset and said, "Momma...it's me." She watched Nyzon out of her huge bay window entertaining some friends by the water.

Silence.

"Tiara?" she repeated surprised that she'd called. Nyzon not wanting to hurt his pregnant wife failed to tell her of her mother's betrayal. "Where are you?"

"In Africa, mamma! I'm in Africa!"

Cartel Publications Order Form
www.thecartelpublications.com
Inmates ONLY get novels for $10.00 per book!

Titles		Fee
Shyt List	_____	$15.00
Shyt List 2	_____	$15.00
Pitbulls In A Skirt	_____	$15.00
Pitbulls In A Skirt 2	_____	$15.00
Victoria's Secret	_____	$15.00
Poison	_____	$15.00
Poison 2	_____	$15.00
Hell Razor Honeys	_____	$15.00
Hell Razor Honeys 2	_____	$15.00
A Hustler's Son 2	_____	$15.00
Black And Ugly As Ever	_____	$15.00
Year of The Crack Mom	_____	$15.00
The Face That Launched A Thousand Bullets	_____	$15.00
The Unusual Suspects	_____	$15.00
Miss Wayne & The Queens of DC	_____	$15.00

Please allow 5-7 business days for delivery. The Cartel is not responsible for prison orders rejected.

(CARTEL CAFÉ AND BOOKS STORE REQUESTS)

Inmates we are now accepting order requests for ANY PAPERBACK BOOK you want outside of the Cartel Titles. Books will be shipped directly from our bookstore. If it's in print, we can get it! We are NOT responsible for books out of print. For Special Order Requests, Please send $15.00 and the name of book below. To prevent refund if 1st special request novel is out of print, please include 2nd requested novel in case the other is unavailable. SORRY, NO STAMPS ACCEPTED WITH SPECIAL ORDERS!

Please add $4.00 per book for shipping and handling. NO PERSONAL CHECKS ACCEPTED!

The Cartel Publications * P.O. Box 486 * Owings Mills * MD * 21117

Name: _____

Address: _____

_____

Contact#/Email: _____

THE CARTEL COLLECTION

The Cartel Collection
Established in January 2008
· We're growing stronger by the month!!!

www.thecartelpublications.com

I've never felt more sexier than the way I do now. Strength comes with focusing on your dreams defying all those who stand in your way. I adore the love affair I have with my readers. And I owe the NEW swag in my hips to you.

T. Styles
President & CEO,
The Cartel Publications

CPSIA information can be obtained at www.ICGtesting.com
Printed in the USA
LVOW07s1507291113

363227LV00002B/301/P